COPYRIGHT

CONTENTS

1. Chapter 1   3

2. Chapter 2   12

3. Chapter 3   20

4. Chapter 4   27

5. Chapter 5   39

6. Chapter 6   50

7. Chapter 7   59

8. Chapter 8   72

9. Chapter 9   78

10. Chapter 10   86

11. Chapter 11   99

12. Chapter 12   111

13. Chapter 13   123

14. Chapter 14   136

15. Chapter 15   145

16. Chapter 16   153

17. Chapter 17   168

18. Chapter 18   176

19. Chapter 19   192

20. Chapter 20   208

21. Chapter 21   216

22. Chapter 22   230

23. Chapter 23   239

24. Chapter 24   248

25. Chapter 25   259

26. Chapter 26   267

27. Chapter 27   274

28. Chapter 28   281

29. Chapter 29   289

30. Chapter 30   303

31. Chapter 31   313

32. Epilogue   318

To everyone who thinks they're not worthy, not loved—a tool to be used.
You're loved and will always be.

CONTENT WARNINGS

This book is a dark science fantasy story. Please take care while reading. It is not intended for anyone under the age of 18. For a more in-depth list of content warnings, read on. Please stay safe! FIRST SNOW includes but is not limited to: Ableism, Alcohol & drugs, Blood, Child abuse, Confinement, Cursing, Daggers, Degrading use of pronouns, Emotional abuse, Forced Marriage & Pregnancy, Graphic Death, Guns, Needles, Medical Procedures (non-consensual), Sexual Abuse, Suicidal thoughts, Suicide, Torture, Vomiting.

If you have any questions or anything to add, please feel free to email Jake at jake.vanguard.author@gmail.com

CHAPTER 1

Zanoah had dreaded this moment, but it still came without any warning.

Cuffs bit into Zanoah's wrists, despite standing stock-still next to his brother, Shaan, who was doubled over on the ground. Zanoah took in the sweat matting his short hair, slicking his skin, slipping past the tape over his mouth, which covered the sound of his panting. The urge to get closer to his brother to further examine him for any wounds was overshadowed by the guards flanking them, ready to pull them apart at a moment's notice.

The room they'd been brought to had always brought up an awkward feeling in Zanoah, no matter how light and perfect it was supposed to look for any visitor. It was perfectly tidy, sterile even. In the center of the room was an enormous light gray desk, only a few small monitors filling it. Along the walls, several similarly gray filing cabinets were bolted into place, no decorations or splashes of color to be seen anywhere.

The only accents were two dark green armchairs in a different corner of the room, barely visible from Zanoah's position. The room felt suffocating, and he was glad there rarely was a reason to visit it at all.

It resulted in him trying to evade said room as much as possible, much to its inhabitant's delight. High Chancellor Cato Antias was no friend of visitors, at least not when it was a foreign visitor like Zanoah.

The High Chancellor was throned on his impressive chair, legs crossed, staring at the brothers. His face was devoid of any emotion, like every other time Zanoah had seen the man, and he doubted that would change tonight. Neither did the High Chancellor look like it was three in the morning and he'd been disturbed from sleep. No, instead Antias was clad in his regular white dress shirt and tight black pants. His dark, straightened hair was combed back, revealing his signature earring dangling from his left ear—a green stone framed by silver, catching every spark of light and reflecting it.

Next to him stood a young man, one Zanoah knew very well by now, having been married to him for several years. He wasn't dressed as perfectly as Antias but still wore regular gray pants and a casual yet tight dark shirt, his red, shoulder length hair a tad tousled. Zanoah's eyes fixed on his green ones, realizing he felt no real surprise, just uncertainty at what was to come.

Zanoah's muscles tensed, realizing his husband had betrayed him—no, not just him; his brother as well. He'd sold them out to the High Chancellor. Though Zanoah should've seen this coming, it still hurt, knowing Julyen had played him the same way Zanoah had played him all these years. This was exactly the reason Shaan hadn't let him get close to anyone, why Zanoah hadn't wanted to get close to anyone. It only ended in hurt.

He couldn't suppress the shiver surging through his body, feeling cold from the inside as well as the outside. After all, he was only clad in his underwear, having been dragged out of his bed in the middle of the night and not allowed to put on any clothes, take his wristband, or ask what this was even all about. Now it made sense why Julyen hadn't protested at all. He'd known this would happen, probably even opened the door for the guards. It also explained why he had been dressed already, ready to jump into the flaicar.

Zanoah had just wanted to sleep, enjoy one night where he didn't have to work. He'd been exhausted from training with Shaan, from his nights at work, and had just wanted to curl up in bed to recharge and relax. And now he suspected he'd never have a good night's sleep ever again.

A muffled moan from his left broke Zanoah from his thoughts, his attention shifting to his brother. So far, he hadn't realized Shaan was fully dressed, seemingly ready to venture into the city. Next to him lay his backpack, carelessly dropped there, the zipper halfway opened. What the fuck had Shaan been up to? Why were they here? Worry flooded him as he realized Shaan had his face turned away from him, covered in shadows, but his breath and low moan filled the silence of the otherwise silent room. What had they done to his brother?

"Looks like you're confused about why you're here," Antias said. His voice was cool, and goosebumps covered Zanoah's skin. "I don't intend to have a long meeting. Your brother doesn't have much time, anyway." The look on his face just deepened Zanoah's fear. "Shaan Vargas tried to assassinate me at 1:45am this morning. The intended weapon was poison—very potent but apparently not tested yet. Credit to his skill to reach my rooms, but he didn't realize I was awake and able to fend him off, using his own weapon against him."

Panicked, Zanoah's head snapped to his brother. Poisoned? Surely there had to be an antidote, especially with their level of medicine and technology. But considering Shaan had tried to assassinate the High Chancellor, Zanoah doubted they would spend any resources on finding an antidote. If this was even true, he wouldn't put it past Cato Antias to lie about the assassination attempt to justify killing his brother, who'd been a thorn in his side for quite some time now.

Shaan had always warned something like this would happen, to be careful and be prepared. Now here they were, unprepared and confused, leaving Zanoah unsure what to think about all this.

"Since Mr. Vargas brought no antidote," Antias continued, "there's no way to heal him. The only thing we could do was give him more time and ease his pain." Then he leaned forward a little in his chair. "But it's not the only thing he did."

Antias gestured for a guard to bring him the backpack, revealing an object from within. Zanoah had seen it before, but Shaan hadn't told him what it was. A small rectangular black box sat in Antias' palm. Inside of the box was an external disk, capable of storing quite a lot of information. Without any explanation, Antias connected it to his workstation, and the screen immediately flashed up, demanding a password.

Julyen pulled something familiar from the bag slung across his shoulders: Zanoah's diary, the one he'd stored in his personal safe, which was only available to him through a retina scan and, in dire life or death situations, to Julyen. Right now, Zanoah only wondered why he'd even been so dumb as to write anything down. Shaan had always warned him not to, but he hadn't listened.

Antias smiled grimly as he looked through the book. "Thought so. Brothers work together, right?"

Antias typed in the password written down in Zanoah's diary, unlocking the files. So far, Zanoah hadn't seen them yet. Shaan had only asked him to keep the password safe, leaving his little brother in the dark on what it was even for. If he had known it was for such a device, he wouldn't have written it down. He wondered why Shaan had even trusted him with this password, since he rarely let him in on his plans and secrets at all.

For a moment, he wondered if Shaan had planned all this in case of failure so he could drag Zanoah down with him. No, he shouldn't think like that about his brother, his family. It wasn't right. Shaan wouldn't do this to him...would he?

There was a lot of information. Zanoah glimpsed classified files, pictures and diagrams he couldn't understand. Antias didn't look surprised at all, seemingly only scrolling through them to confirm his suspicions. When he'd seen enough, he finally got up from his chair and stopped in front of the kneeling Vargas brother, looking down on him.

"Attempted murder of the High Chancellor and stealing classified data," Antias said. "If you weren't dying, it might be a death sentence, anyway. If you were lucky, maybe cryo prison for the next hundred years."

Neither would be fun alternatives, but at least Shaan would have a chance at life, even if it would've been a hundred years later. This way, he would just die, painfully and without any achievements. Zanoah knew his goal had been to gather more information about the secret experiments Antias was doing and put an end to them, to find something to overthrow this whole government and get revenge for their parents' deaths.

Shaan had only told him people were getting hurt during these experiments and that they were perverted, transgressing human evolution and ethics. Of course, Zanoah wanted to help, but Shaan had always kept him in the dark. Besides hiding the password, the only thing his brother had ever asked of him was to keep his eyes and ears open, to stay close to Julyen and, therefore, also the High Chancellor. Zanoah had never really understood exactly what position his husband held in the government, just that he was some sort of assistant to Antias.

Suddenly, Antias rounded on him. "As for you…"

Antias came closer, stopping in front of him. They were almost the same height, Zanoah just a tad taller. Uncertainty and fear clouded his eyes while his gaze flickered from Antias to Julyen and around the room, unable to focus on one person.

"What do you think?" Antias turned halfway toward Julyen, who was still standing next to the desk, observing everything quietly.

"He's never done any harm of his own accord," Julyen finally said. "His brother roped him into this."

Julyen had never liked Shaan very much, for whatever reason, so of course he would lay all the blame at his feet. But after all the backstabbing tonight, it surprised Zanoah to hear Julyen speak in favor of him, even if he was his husband. He was even more surprised when Antias seemed to think about what he'd said. Zanoah couldn't recall a time when he'd seen him take another person's words into consideration.

After a moment, Antias nodded. "Banishment, then." He sneered at Zanoah. "See it as a fresh start. You won't be able to come back to the city, but you will be able to create a new life for yourself. We're not monsters. It's for the best."

Not monsters, my ass. They were leaving his brother to die right in front of them. Zanoah wished his restraints weren't so tight. He would've loved to punch Antias in the face, make him realize how fucked up he actually was. In a fair fight, Antias would have problems keeping up with him. Zanoah was taller and more skilled. His brother had pushed him to train every day, sparring with him regularly. *"Being prepared,"* Shaan had called it.

While Antias walked back to his desk, searching for something, Zanoah's gaze turned toward his brother once again. He seemed even more in pain than before, his chest barely moving anymore. Poison. Who would've thought Shaan would someday die of poison? Zanoah had always bet on a wound received in combat. But poison? Never. Shaan wasn't one to go out quietly.

He hadn't even realized Antias had found what he'd been searching for and was heading back toward him, a crooked, black dagger in his hand. What was that for? Zanoah didn't even want to know, but he was sure he was about to find out.

"Get down," Antias ordered.

When Zanoah didn't move, Antias only sighed and nodded toward his guards. One of them kicked Zanoah's knee from behind, forcing him to the floor, pushing him down, and making sure he wouldn't be able to get up again.

What was Antias planning to do? Why was he holding this dagger? Panic built in Zanoah's chest, as did a certainty that whatever the High Chancellor was planning would be painful.

"Hold his head still."

While the guards followed the order, grabbing his long hair and keeping him still so he was forced to look up at Antias, Zanoah tried to struggle free. But he knew it was futile. There was no way he'd be able to escape his shackles and the guards, not when he didn't even know where he would go if he managed to escape. Without Shaan, he was all alone.

"It won't hurt for long," Antias informed him, pulling away some of the tape over his mouth to expose his cheek. "The blade's sharp and will cut easily. It will heal, but the scar will stay."

The dagger came closer, and Zanoah braced for the inevitable pain. His heart was racing, his body instinctively trying to escape before it was too late. His struggles were in vain as hands pushed him down and held him still for Antias' dagger.

The sharp blade found its target about half an inch beneath his left eye, slowly and precisely cutting down, until it reached the crook of his jaw. Pain flooded Zanoah's face, and he could feel blood running from his wound, hot and burning, down his neck and dropping onto his chest.

Just for a moment, he stared at Antias, his jaw clenched, trying to bite back a cry. After all, he was used to enduring pain, but that didn't mean it didn't still hurt every single time. He certainly wouldn't give this asshole the satisfaction of a reaction. But there was no glee in Antias' cyan blue eyes, only duty. Zanoah watched him stand up and wipe down the blade on a dark piece of cloth before he turned toward Shaan again.

Antias sighed, sounding almost disappointed. He crouched down next to Shaan, ripping the tape from his mouth, then grabbing his chin and urging him to look up, just for a moment, before he let the older brother go again.

"Any last words from you?" Antias asked. "Anything to say to your brother?"

Shaan turned his head toward Zanoah, gritting his teeth. His skin was ashen, almost gray, and his eyes looked lifeless and clouded over already, not the same dark brown as Zanoah's anymore. The poison was working through his body, wasting it away. He knew Shaan was dying and nothing could stop it. And now the last sight he'd see would be his bleeding baby brother, marked but at least still alive.

Would Shaan be glad he survived? For a moment, Zanoah doubted it. No, Shaan would give everything to trade places. He knew as much. No matter how loyal and bound Zanoah was to his brother, Shaan had made it clear what he thought of him, how he felt about him: A nuisance and tool, someone Shaan had invested in only for Zanoah to become useful at some point. But Zanoah hadn't cared, had always clung to Shaan, doing whatever he wanted, just to not be alone, to receive some appreciation. And now, his one anchor in life was fading away.

"You know your duty," Shaan whispered, almost inaudibly. They were his last words to his brother, the last thing anyone would ever hear him say.

Zanoah just stared at him, unsure what to think of this. He couldn't quite process that he was witnessing his brother's final moments, his last order.

"I'll be merciful and give him a quick, painless death," Antias promised, getting up to stand behind Shaan.

The dying man didn't even struggle when Antias pushed his head to the front, exposing his neck. When the dagger met the soft spot right underneath Shaan's skull, Zanoah couldn't help but scream against the tape over his mouth, pushing against the guards still holding him down. The cut on his own cheek was no longer important, but the image of his brother's now lifeless body slumping to the ground burned itself into his brain.

Nothing mattered to him anymore: not Antias pulling out the dagger or nodding toward a guard. Zanoah barely registered any of it. His body was numb, and he didn't care what happened to him now.

Shaan... He was actually... dead. Gone from this world. Zanoah wished they could've swapped places, that he'd been allowed to die instead of Shaan. He was of no use, anyway. Shaan had been much cleverer than him. Zanoah knew his brother wouldn't have mourned him, only been annoyed to lose a tool, but Zanoah didn't care. How could he live without Shaan? Did it even matter? There was no use for him anymore.

When his neck was poked by a syringe, Zanoah didn't even twitch. His eyes were fixed on Shaan, no matter what happened around him. Not even the darkness and slumber that came over him changed any of that.

For the first time in his life, he was utterly and completely lost.

CHAPTER 2

Waking up felt like Zanoah had been hit in the head with a brick. He was nauseous and had no idea where the fuck he was. When he took a deep breath, Zanoah realized the air was different than he was used to. It smelled...fresher? The smell brought back memories of his childhood, before his parents had been killed. They'd lived outside the city in a small hut on their own, trying to survive while keeping the ever-growing plants out of their house.

Slowly, Zanoah opened his eyes, feeling soft ground underneath his fingers. Moss and grass made for a good undergrowth to lie on, soft on his bare back. Pushing himself up, he winced, his hand rushing to his throbbing cheek and skimming the surface of the adhesive dressing there.

Shit, now he remembered what happened.

Antias had killed Shaan and marked Zanoah for banishment. What Zanoah didn't quite understand was why his wound had been cared for. He thought he'd be callously thrown out to fend for himself. It was already a surprise he'd survived the journey out of the city, and he didn't quite know how it was possible. And now he had another worry: what did he do now? Would he even find other people, or could he survive on his own?

From what he'd learned in his history lessons, for the last few centuries, plants had mutated and formed dangerous new varieties, able to grow fast and kill an adult man, if angered. During the last three decades, they had become increasingly hostile and aggressive toward humans.

A memory of when Shaan was a teen came to mind. Zanoah remembered his brother wielding a machete, hacking at the vines creeping toward him, cursing in all sorts of colorful languages. Zanoah had watched from the safe interior of their house, not understanding why nature meant them any harm. He still didn't understand.

It had been an almost daily occurrence for his brother and parents to fight the plants, so Zan knew the dangers very well. But it was also the reason he wasn't sure other people had been able to survive outside the city at all—or if *he* would.

As he slowly got up, cool moss seeping between his toes, his gaze wandered toward the city. The gray towers were barely visible in the distance, hidden behind a raging storm that stretched over several miles of desert surrounding the city.

A dome of energy encompassed the whole city as well, keeping it clear of wind and sand. A fitting way to make sure no one would ever enter—or leave. These unnaturally constructed security measures had been explained by the government as protecting the city from nature's mutations, but Zanoah was sure it wasn't just that. Tadena was isolated, and if there were more cities, there hadn't been any contact for several decades at least. It stood to reason the barrier was also a measure to keep it that way.

Standing here, on the edge of the jungle, he realized the ring of desert around Tadena had grown even more during the last twenty years. Maybe this was the reason they'd survived the journey into the city at all, back when Shaan brought them here after their parents had been killed. Zanoah had never seen anyone else enter the city's protective dome. Neither did he remember their journey into the city, just seeing the sandstorm and suddenly being on a bed in the medic center.

How had he even gotten out here? Frowning, he looked around, searching for a clue and maybe something—*anything*—to help him. Several feet away, crashed against a tree, lay a capsule, barely big enough to fit one person inside. Slowly, he came closer, observing the badly damaged vessel.

It didn't seem the crash had caused most of the damage, but the storms. The hull was eroded already, and the front half was broken. When it crashed, he must've been catapulted from the vessel. Maybe there was still something inside he could use.

Zanoah leaned closer, inspecting the inside of the craft without touching anything. A *backpack*. If he was to survive on his own, he would need rations, clothes, whatever contents this bag held for him. He could already see boots knotted to it. Having his feet protected while wandering through the jungle would be a good idea.

As soon as he touched the vessel, it started moving. Slowly but steadily, it was pulled further into the jungle. Confused, Zanoah watched for a moment before he saw more and more vines covering the craft. Taking his chance, he yanked the backpack out before the vines started crushing the hull, reducing the vessel to a ball of metal and polymer. No way back then.

Hopefully, the vines—or whatever the fuck was going on with this jungle—wouldn't see him as a threat.

First, he opened the backpack, checking out the contents: some clothes. He wouldn't need them for warmth, since it was as hot out here as it was in Tadena, just more humid. But they would hopefully protect him at least a little from thorns digging into his skin.

The tight black pants and muscle shirt were for sure from his own wardrobe. Did this mean Julyen had packed this bag? One thing Zanoah had certainly learned was that his husband wasn't the person he'd thought him to be. Or maybe he was exactly that. Loyal to his High Chancellor, following his orders without a second thought, even if it meant betraying and exiling his own husband.

The thought left a bitter taste in his mouth because Zanoah had done the same thing these last years. Deceiving and playing a game, following someone's orders. He wasn't any better than Julyen.

He shoved the thought into a corner of his mind and grabbed the clothes to put them on. Skin-tight, like everything Tadenans owned. It was pretty much impossible to find clothes to Zan's liking—comfortably wide and hiding more than they showed. No, Tadenans liked showing off the shapes of their bodies for everyone to gawk at, and tight clothing was their best option since full nudity wasn't appreciated in public. The muscle shirt also displayed the sleeve tattoo on his left upper arm—not that anyone would care in the jungle, but it was a constant reminder of Shaan.

At least these clothes were quite light and breathable, perfect for the hot climate. Apparently, Julyen had even thrown in some hair ties so he could gather all his hair in a thick ponytail. Although maybe a bun would be better, considering he'd be wandering through thick jungle. The bun probably looked quite messy, but considering the amount of hair he had to tame, Zanoah considered it a success.

When he checked out the contents of his backpack, he found several protein bars, probably enough for two weeks, maybe a little more if he stretched them, and a water purifier. Hopefully, he would find some water, otherwise he'd just die of thirst.

After one last glance toward Tadena, Zanoah slung the backpack over his shoulders and started his journey into the jungle.

So far, he'd walked several days now, resting in clearings during the night. He had yet to see any animals but had found a stream, which he was following now. Maybe he would find something at the end of it. At least it provided a steady supply of fresh water and a guideline, so he wouldn't get lost that easily.

Thankfully, it seemed even the plants didn't care much for him. After he'd seen the vines crushing his vessel so easily, he was wary and quite careful not to upset the plants around him. He wished he knew what would upset them or not, but so far no vines were reaching for him, as he'd feared at first, nor was the jungle blocking his way.

It would be helpful to even know where the fuck he was supposed to go. Shaan never gave him a backup plan if anything happened to him. Either this was an eventuality he'd never planned for or he hadn't cared to.

All his life, Zanoah had only done what Shaan had told him to do. There had never been much consideration of what *he* wanted to do. Now he had to survive on his own, but why? What was his goal? Find other people and connect, maybe find someone to help him avenge his brother. It was the right thing to do, wasn't it? That's what he was supposed to do: care for his family.

After all, he had to fulfill his brother's goal to avenge their parents and find out more about these experiments the High Chancellor was doing behind closed doors. He wasn't sure what to do with this information, but he knew he had to find out, even if just to please his dead brother's memory.

Zanoah wasn't sure what to do now because he'd always been given a goal. Figuring out what survival meant on his own terms was a daunting task. He never had ambitions, had only followed orders, and it was so much easier to just cling to these instructions and take Shaan's thinking and striving as his own, rather than figure out what he wanted out of life. He just wished it hadn't led him here.

It wasn't all bad, he had to admit. Though it was hard adjusting to a new environment, it was much calmer and more relaxing than the buzzing streets of Tadena. He'd grown up near here; maybe this is where he really belonged.

His rations would only last for two more days. Maybe he could stretch them some more, but he was already exhausted and sore, walking every day without a destination in mind. Sometimes he felt like he was being watched, but he could never spot another being.

Yesterday, he washed himself, but without washing his clothes, it wouldn't make much of a difference. He was still smelly and dirty. He was glad Shaan had always pushed him so hard, gave him constant, rigorous training, so he was able to endure the journey now. He would've given up much earlier if it wasn't for that.

The bandage on his cheek had come off by now, and he'd washed the wound. It seemed to have healed quite nicely despite his dire situation. Still, he hoped he wouldn't get an infection. He was still in a jungle without any way to disinfect the wound after all.

Rations ran out two days ago. No matter how much Zanoah had stretched them, at some point he'd had to eat the last piece. His stomach was aching and everything around him looked so edible. He knew some plants could be eaten, but this jungle had changed too much during the last twenty years. It wasn't like when Shaan had gotten them food on their journey to Tadena. He wasn't sure if he could even remember or recognize the right plants anymore. He would probably poison himself, but would it be worse than slowly starving to death?

At least the stream was still there, and he could follow it. Having a direction to travel and fresh water to drink comforted him a little. Day by day, the stream had gotten broader, becoming a river, so maybe he would actually find something at the end of it. A lake or an ocean? Or maybe nothing at all. Except for the stream, which Zanoah followed blindly, as blindly as he'd followed Shaan's guidance, his orders, no matter where it led him.

With every step he took, a noise in the distance became clearer. It sounded like... rushing water? Louder than the river, it grew into a roar as he stumbled to the cliffside. Carefully, he shuffled to the edge, realizing where the noise was coming from. The river was rushing down into a cave underneath it, disappearing into the stone. He couldn't say how deep it went, but judging by the fact that he couldn't see the bottom, he'd say deep enough to jump into without risking injuries. But it would most likely be suicide because he couldn't spot a way out of the water. Any attempt would probably lead to him drowning in the darkness.

Frustration flooded through him him. After following this damn river for so long, he'd lost his guideline and his fresh water. Where should he go now? Looking around, everything still appeared the same: trees and vines and bushes close to each other, nothing that stood out in any direction. There was no way he wouldn't get lost if he just wandered around without something to guide him.

He heard a branch breaking behind him and spun around. Maybe he was about to see the first animal he'd encountered so far? Or even other people? For a moment he only saw black—not eating for several days was taking its toll now—and fumbled to find a steadier grip again. His head spun as he took another step back, suddenly feeling his stomach drop as the ground gave out from under him, and he hurtled down past the rushing waterfall and toward the cave below.

Just for a second, he could see a person leaning over the cliff, exactly where he had stood just a moment before. The only thing he could make out was black hair and piercing white eyes. *Who...?*

But he couldn't think about it more because he was still plummeting. It wasn't a pleasant fall; his body collided with the rock several times, no matter how much he tried to curl up to shield himself. When he finally landed in water, his whole body hurt, and the walls around him were spinning.

"The fuck are you?!"

Where did that voice come from? Zanoah didn't know, and he was too occupied with trying not to drown and keeping his exhausted, aching body afloat. A moment that felt like an eternity later, he heard a splash close by and was grabbed by hands, which dragged him out of the water.

When he was safely splayed out on land, he coughed and sputtered, his lungs and throat burning. Had he really found people? Or had it been a hallucination? Right now, he was too tired, and his exhausted body decided to just shut down, drifting into unconsciousness.

CHAPTER 3

When had his life become waking up in strange places with his body hurting?

At least Zanoah didn't wake up in the middle of the jungle this time. But where exactly was he? The last thing he remembered was falling down a waterfall into a cave. That at least explained how sore his body was. Someone had grabbed him from the water, rescued him from drowning. Right. Slowly, the memories came back.

Very carefully, he tried to sit up and realized he was on some kind of bed inside a cave. Goosebumps covered his arms, which were unused to such temperatures and dampness. He was shivering, the cool air sinking into his skin, so different from the long weeks he'd spent trekking through the heat of the jungle.

"Finally, he's awake. Thought you'd be a goner."

Abruptly, Zanoah turned his head toward the voice coming from his right—the same voice he'd heard when he crashed into the water. So this guy had saved him? Zanoah studied him silently, taking in the black locs, dark skin, and brown eyes. Whoever this guy was, he was seemingly several years younger than him.

"Damn, are you always so quiet?" the stranger asked. "Hoped you'd be more fun. You look like fun."

A cheeky grin appeared on the stranger's full lips as he obviously checked out Zanoah's body. Uneasiness settled in once Zanoah realized he was naked except for his underwear. His fingers gripped the thin blanket more to cover his body, shielding him from the stranger. He'd never been comfortable with people seeing him almost naked, but especially not when he was in such a vulnerable state and didn't know the person staring at him.

"Where are my clothes?" Zanoah wanted to know.

"Well, we had to cut your shirt off to get you out of it. How did you even fit in it? And your pants are somewhere...over there, I think." The guy pointed toward some kind of natural shelf, more an indentation in the stone, where some clothes were stacked. "Y'know, we have other entrances than the waterfall. Some that won't give you bruises and broken arms."

Frowning, Zanoah tried to piece everything together. The bruises made sense; his body was screaming. But what was this about a broken arm? Pain radiated from his right arm, and when he looked down, he saw bandages wrapped around the wooden splints keeping it in place. Shit, now he was even more useless than before. But maybe he didn't have to travel anymore. He'd found people here, after all.

"Got a name? I'm Vance, by the way." When Zanoah didn't say anything, Vance sighed and leaned back on his bed, still watching him. "Talk to me. Jeez, you're so boring."

"I'm sorry," Zanoah mumbled. He really wasn't used to asking questions or talking to people casually. "My name's Zanoah. Where...where am I?" He wasn't sure if it was alright to ask, but he had to know.

"Zanoah...Zanoah...Zanoah. What a weird name," Vance concluded before sitting straight up again. "Where are you? So, you didn't look for us on purpose? Huh. Kelcie was wrong then."

Vance was obviously surprised by this news, but why exactly? Zanoah had accidentally tumbled into their home because he was weakened and starved, a fact his stomach reminded him of by growling loudly now.

Vance laughed. "Hungry? Well, you gotta meet Kelcie anyway. Get up and put on some clothes. If you want to. I like the view more this way."

Once again, Vance grinned at him, making it clear what he thought before he got up and grabbed some clothes from the little shelf-like hole in the cave wall. He dropped a washed out gray-green shirt and black pants into Zanoah's lap. Without hesitation, he put on the pants quite easily, even with his broken arm, but the shirt was proving a bit more complicated. At least it wasn't as tight as his normal clothes; ty was looser, like Vance's clothes were. Otherwise, he wouldn't have been able to squeeze his bandaged arm through the hole.

"Let's go," Vance said. "No need for shoes—unless you can't walk on stone? No idea where you're from, anyway."

For a moment, Zanoah considered the options but opted for putting on his boots, which had been lying next to his bed. They were still a bit wet, but he decided to just ignore that. If he had to run, they were better than nothing. Vance seemed nice so far, but Zanoah didn't know where he was and who these people were, and he wanted to be ready in case they couldn't be trusted.

Vance jerked his head toward the exit. "Ready? But don't fall over again, yeah? I won't catch you this time."

Now Vance was just teasing him, but Zanoah remained silent. He'd learned not to speak back if he was being teased, especially not when he didn't know the people he was talking to. Whenever he'd tried to protect himself from teasing, Shaan had called his reactions too harsh and rough, but Zanoah was just doing what made sense to him. He'd only said what he'd been thinking, but his thoughts were never appreciated. So he'd learned to keep them to himself, to drown them out and only do what was asked of him.

Instead of responding, he focused on taking in his surroundings. The room he'd woken up in contained several beds made of wood beams close to the floor and some of these carved out shelves. Otherwise, it was bare. The "door" was just an opening covered by a gray-brown curtain, which Vance shoved to the side to let them through.

Several lamps on the wall glowed, but Zanoah couldn't quite see how they were powered. It looked like inside was real fire. They surely weren't fueled by electricity like in Tadena. It reminded him more of his childhood, where they'd used dried plant fibers and resin to light their torches and hearths.

Zanoah guessed the lamps in here were fueled by a similar material. It was enough light to illuminate the narrow and winding corridor in front of them. To the left were more rooms, covered by more curtains, while the corridor turned out of sight on the right.

Vance went toward the turn, probably expecting Zanoah to follow him, so he did. What other choice did he have? There was no natural light anywhere to be seen, and the damp air hinted that they were under the earth, so it would be hard to find an exit on his own. Especially when he saw several corridors branching off behind the turn. Vance confidently strode in one direction, and Zanoah followed him, curiously looking around. His muscles were still tense from nerves. For all he knew, Vance could be leading him to a dungeon.

After several more turns, they arrived in an empty room that was much bigger than where he'd slept. Small rugs were spread across the floor, and in one corner, there was some kind of primitive fireplace. A big pot held up by chains was bolted into the ceiling, keeping it hanging over the fireplace, and whatever was in it was still simmering.

So this is how they cook? he marveled. It was very different from what he was used to in Tadena but, on the other hand, so similar to what his childhood kitchen had looked like. His parents hadn't had electricity, either, so they'd cooked with fire. Above the fireplace were also some holes in the ceiling, presumably so smoke wouldn't choke the people in here.

Vance gestured toward the carpets. "Sit, I'll get you some food."

Zanoah sat close to a wall so he could see the whole room, which he realized was a combination kitchen and dining hall. Everything felt surreal, like he'd been thrown back into his childhood and…it wasn't a good feeling. It brought back the dreadful feelings he'd had in his own home, even as a child, and a shiver ran up his spine. His parents had always treated him differently than his nine-year-old brother: screaming at him for every little mistake, the occasional slap across the face, or just straight-out ignoring him for days. Zanoah had gotten used to it all, while his brother had been coddled and praised.

"Here. Eat and drink," Vance said.

Vance shoved a carved wooden bowl into his hand, filled with steaming food that looked like stew made of whatever they found in the jungle. He could still see some mushrooms and lots of greens, but otherwise, the contents were a mystery. It certainly smelled amazing, especially to an aching stomach like his.

"I'll look for Kelcie," the younger man continued. "She'll explain some more, and you can ask her all the questions you might have. I'll be back soon."

Carefully, Zanoah grabbed the big wooden spoon sticking out of the bowl and tried one bite. It tasted really good, a salty flavor mixed with the spongy consistency of mushrooms and herbs he didn't know the names of. Without thinking twice, Zanoah emptied the whole bowl within a few minutes, savoring the heat filling his empty stomach, warming him up from the inside after wandering around the cold cave. It wasn't easy to eat with just one hand, but he managed.

He set the bowl down next to him and grabbed the big cup of water, emptying that as well. Now he certainly felt better and immediately a bit stronger. His head felt clearer as well, but he was still uncertain and nervous.

Hopefully, his arm would heal fast. He carefully touched the bandages, and immediately, pain rushed through his arm and up to his shoulder. Shit, this really didn't feel good at all.

"Better not touch your bandage," someone said. "The herbs to ease the pain will have stopped working by now."

Startled, Zanoah looked toward the woman entering the room. She had a strong aura, her head held high, and looked like a leader. Her voice was clear and didn't leave any room for discussion. She reminded him of Shaan, and he guessed this had to be Kelcie. Zanoah judged her to be around her mid-40s, maybe even older. After all, he had no idea if people aged the same way here as they did in Tadena. But she had some wrinkles around her eyes, and her hair was mostly gray with some lingering dark brown streaks. It was something you barely saw in Tadena, since most people colored their hair once it went gray.

Zanoah didn't get a chance to respond because she squatted down in front of him and grabbed his chin. "So, you fell into our water reservoir, and Vance had to save you, huh?" She tilted his head a little, so she had a better look at his cheek. "Where did you get this from? Judging by the healing process, I'd say it happened roughly four or five weeks ago?"

"I've been exiled from Tadena," Zanoah answered truthfully, not sure if she even knew about the city. It was a long march from this cave.

She released her grip, a sparkle in her dark brown eyes now. She looked him up and down, seemingly lost in thought. "What was your name again?"

"It's Zanoah," he obediently answered.

"And your last name?" she impatiently demanded.

"Toomer."

"Certainly not your birth name. What is it, boy?"

For a moment, Zanoah frowned, not sure exactly how she knew or why she cared so much about his last name. "No, it's my husband's last name. My birth name is Vargas."

The glitter in the woman's eyes grew, as did a smile on her lips. "Welcome home. You'll find we'll be able to take much better care of you than anyone in Tadena, ever could. You're with family here. I'm your Aunt, Kelcie. Your father's sister."

Confused, Zanoah looked up at her, not quite registering what she'd said. Aunt? He didn't know his father had a sister. No, that wasn't right. He'd mentioned her once, but she lived far away and couldn't make the journey to see them. His dad thought she had already died, taken by the jungle. Now Kelcie was here, right in front of him and very much alive.

CHAPTER 4

Being around these people, whom Zanoah had gotten to know a bit better by now, was still weird. Most were friendly, smiling at him when he passed by, but also not really approachable. No one sat near him during meal times nor had they struck up conversations. Except for Vance. He was always around and teased him all day long, making comments Zan tried to ignore.

Kelcie also talked to him a lot. She wanted to know what happened to Shaan and the rest of the family. Zanoah told her everything, glad to hear that she also hated the High Chancellor for killing not just Shaan but her brother and sister-in-law as well. Shaan had never elaborated on how their parents died, only focused on getting revenge. But Kelcie could fill in the missing information, how the High Chancellor had brought a small troop to the jungle to exact revenge. Shaan was right. The High Chancellor and his minions *had* killed his parents all these years ago—for some petty generations old family feud. Or so Kelcie explained.

What didn't make sense to Zanoah was the timing. It never had. If he calculated correctly—though he was only guessing High Chancellor Antias' age to be around the mid-thirties—he would've been in his teens back when Zanoah's and Shaan's parents were killed. Certainly not yet High Chancellor, even if Zanoah guessed his age wrong. It had always bothered him, but Shaan had brushed off his concerns and pointed out it didn't matter who had been High Chancellor at the time. They were all the same, only using people to their advantage.

Zanoah had believed him, still did, especially after seeing what Antias had done to his brother. Did it really matter who'd held the title of High Chancellor when his parents were killed? They were all gruesome, deciding the fates of human lives as if they were merely pieces on a board, only interesting as long as they were useful. Kelcie held a similar belief, which only strengthened Zanoah's conviction that his brother's crusade was righteous.

But even Kelcie had grown distant since he first arrived. So, it was either talk to Vance or no one at all. And Zanoah didn't like the idea of sitting alone forever.

"Where are you from anyway?" Zanoah curiously asked Vance while they were cleaning the dishes after breakfast.

Every person in the community did chores on a ten-day-rotation. So far, Zanoah had been asked to accompany Vance, to get to know all the tasks, since there wasn't much he could do on his own with just one arm to use.

Vance just shrugged and put away the bowls, stacking them in a corner. "Oh, I'm from nowhere. I was born here. My mum died years ago too."

"I'm sorry. So you've never seen a city?"

Now Vance looked at him, tilting his head a little. "No, and I don't need to. City people are greedy and arrogant. Only thing is, it gets lonely here. But whatever." Vance pushed his locs back and his trademark cocky smirk appeared on his lips. "Let's go bathing. Well, and untangle that mess on your head."

Zanoah knew his hair was quite a mess lately. He couldn't brush it very easily with one hand, not at this length, and the moist air didn't really help either. He kept his hair in a bun most times, so it wouldn't become too entangled and knotted. Instead, it slowly became matted. Caring for it had already been hard back in Tadena, even with having access to shampoo and conditioner, but around here he had neither of those.

Zanoah just nodded and followed Vance toward what passed for bathrooms around here. They weren't that different from the reservoir he'd fallen into, except there was a water flow, so any waste and dirty water would be swept away immediately. The light was dimmed here as well. He had learned the lamps used a certain tree's resin to burn and had to be refilled roughly every ten days or so. Therefore, rooms that didn't need much light, like the bathrooms, only had a few lamps.

While Zanoah still struggled with getting out of his clothes, Vance was much faster and had already undressed, put his clothes away, and grabbed two towels as well as a wide-tooth wooden comb before Zanoah had finished taking off his pants.

"Need a helping hand?" Vance offered, grinning while he watched him struggle with his underwear.

Zanoah just looked at him for a moment, tightly pressing his lips together in discomfort, before breaking his gaze again. He still disliked being in the bathroom with Vance like this. It embarrassed him, especially since he knew Vance wanted more of him than he was prepared to give, but he really could use the help.

"Alright, alright," Vance conceded. "When does this stuff come off your arm, anyway?"

"Cerdwyn said five more days, and then she'll open it up."

Hopefully, his arm was healed by then. It already felt fine. The itching underneath the bandages annoyed him, but he wasn't in pain anymore. Having the wood around his arm really made moving it much more difficult, and Zan just wanted it gone.

After Vance helped him undress, Zan headed toward the basin. The idea behind it was quite good. On either side of it were holes, connecting it to the water flow and making sure fresh water was always streaming in, transporting the dirty one out of the cave. The basin was handmade and not very big, just enough for one person, two if they squeezed together.

Zan slowly dipped into the water. It was cool, as usual, and moved around him comfortingly. Water had always had a calming effect on him, and he felt his muscles relaxing. A sigh escaped him, and for a moment,

Zan closed his eyes to enjoy the fresh stream washing away all the sweat and dirt.

"You should really wash your hair too," Vance suggested, watching him intently, too close for his own comfort. He was almost pressed against Zan in the water.

Zanoah could barely see his face in this light, but he considered it for a moment. Sighing, he nodded and got out of the water to lie down on his back on the edge of the basin, untangling his hair from the hair tie and drenching it in the water. It was much easier like this because Vance could help him wash it. Zanoah really cursed his broken arm.

A few moments later, he could feel Vance's hands in his hair, scrubbing it and probably tangling it even more than it had been before, but at least it was clean now. He also felt the comb being dragged through his hair, gliding through the mess much more easily while it was still submerged in water.

"Say, what do your tattoos mean?" Vance asked, and Zan noticed the younger man was staring at his right hand. "I've never seen such inking."

Right, his tattoos. Zan had pushed the thought of them far away, always a reminder of his life and commitments. He pursed his lips and glanced at his left upper arm, where a wild mix of swirls and hidden symbols even Zan himself didn't understand were inked into his skin.

"My brother decided on the design and made me get the tattoo." He lifted his right hand, so Vance could see the small inked band around his fourth finger. "This is a marriage band." He had no intention of talking more about it, explain why and to whom he was still married.

"Huh, you're married? Well, you're free now." Vance grinned at him, and a wave of discomfort flooded Zan. He wondered what Vance thought of marriage, if it was even common in the caves—apparently, at least, Vance had heard of it.

When Vance was finally finished, Zan sat up again and grabbed the towel. Drying himself was complicated, but at least he was able to do it himself. He would rather walk around still wet than let anyone help him with that.

"Sit. I'll do your hair."

Vance was still naked, but Zanoah had already put on his underwear, sitting down on his towel, so he wouldn't be on the bare stone floor. It wasn't much to shield his body, but it was the only thing he had right now. His hands clenched into fists when he felt Vance settling down behind him, grabbing his hair and untangling the remaining mess strand by strand.

"Why do you even have such long hair? It's so impractical," Vance complained but still cared for it.

Slowly, his hand wandered from Zan's hair to his shoulder and farther—over his chest. Zanoah's muscles stiffened up immediately. So far, he'd never had a sexual encounter of his own free will. He'd only been with his husband to help Shaan get closer to his goal, and there'd never been another person he'd gotten close to because he liked them. He wasn't sure what Vance was doing here, but he could feel him leaning closer, his bare chest touching Zan's back, his lips close to Zanoah's ear.

"It gets really lonely in here," Vance said. "Don't you wanna fuck me? You're real pretty." Vance's hand was still wandering. Now it was running over his stomach, clearly with one destination in mind.

For a long moment, Zan was frozen in place, neither his body nor his brain working anymore. Where others felt joy and arousal, Zan only felt nausea and panic. "Please...don't. I...I can't."

Knowing Vance wouldn't like it but not caring about that right now, Zanoah jumped up and grabbed his clothes, hastily putting them on without really thinking about his bandage. He didn't quite realize it became loose and fell off his arm, revealing his bare skin, still a bit purple-yellowish but otherwise looking healed.

Without even taking a look at Vance, he fled the bathroom, heading through the maze of corridors. By now, he mostly knew where to go and what would be at the end of certain paths. There were only a few Vance hadn't shown him yet.

Apparently, he'd found one of those right now. Sunlight blinded him as he stumbled into a clearing right in front of the cave. For a moment, he looked around, but there was no one in sight. Right now, he just wanted to have a little quiet time for himself, to get away from all this. To get away from Vance.

He headed toward a fallen log, half hidden behind some trees in the shadow, where he sat down and took a deep breath. What was happening here? Sighing, he covered his face behind his hands, trying to get a grip—to calm down.

Never in his life had he felt sexual attraction to anyone. Yes, he'd slept with Julyen, but it had been a duty to keep him happy—to keep up the facade of a happy marriage—rather than out of love or even lust. Zanoah had never actually wanted to sleep with him—or any person. Shaan had always called him a weirdo for it. But was he? Was it really so odd not to want that with someone?

Zan didn't know. But as he closed his eyes and sighed, he wished he could explain how he felt inside.

4 years prior

"Get a grip, bro," Shaan said. "Fuck someone. Enjoy life."

Shaan grinned at him and downed his drink: Palm Velour, black and glittering, a high percentage alcohol with a hint of citrus. It was way too bitter for Zanoah, who didn't quite like drinking alcohol at all. But Shaan loved it and was his best customer. Well, he never paid, of course, but he was the one Zanoah served most.

Zan had started working as a barkeeper at Galaxya five years ago, two days after his eighteenth birthday. Shaan had urged him to get a job at a place where he would meet people, gather intel, and make contacts. And where Shaan could get his drinks for free, of course.

He'd learned not to say too much when Shaan made comments like that, just smiled, swiping the empty glass from his brother's hand and making him a new drink. Not much to it, really, since Palm Velour got delivered in bottles, ready to serve, and Zan didn't have to mix it. He just poured the black liquid into Shaan's glass, filling it up again.

"See him?" Shaan pointed toward a young man with red hair and lots of freckles on his face just entering the bar, looking a little lost. "That's an Open Mind graduate. He's supposedly close to Antias—and celebrating his twenty-first birthday today. Get him drunk. Find out if he's actually close to Antias. If he is, I want you to get close to him. Flirt with him. Got that?"

This was typical for Shaan, giving him orders and not caring if he wanted to do it or not. It was only about their mission. The older he got, the more straightforward Shaan's orders turned.

"You know I'm bad at flirting," Zan reminded him. "You sure that's a good idea?"

Maybe he could still turn this around, try to show Shaan what a bad idea this was. A bit more alcohol might change his mind, so he almost shoved the filled glass of Palm Velour into Shaan's hand.

"I know you're bad," Shaan said, taking a sip. "Time to learn. You know how to be subtle, you know how to keep secrets, you know how to mix good drinks, and you know how to fuck. So use whatever you have and get me some information."

Of course, there was no way to sway Shaan. Once he had set his mind on something, there was no changing it. Shaan had trained him the last two decades for tasks like this. He wouldn't budge.

The older brother just chugged his drink and got up. "See ya tomorrow. Have a fun night."

Shaan grinned at him—his mean big brother grin. It reminded Zanoah that he was the slower, dumber, and quieter brother. Shaan had always been the one with a plan, no matter how much he drank his brain away.

His gaze followed Shaan until he left the bar. It was a quiet night, not too many people around, and his colleague was finally back from her smoke break.

"I'll be back in a moment," Zanoah informed her and headed toward his "victim," who was now sitting a little awkwardly in a booth at the corner. Zanoah put on his best customer-service smile, trying to make it even sweeter and nicer. He had to give this his best shot in order to keep Shaan happy and content. "Hi, there. Sorry about this, but I have to card you."

"Oh, yeah, sure." The guest turned his wristband and let him scan it.

"Alright, perfect. Oh, happy birthday! Are you waiting for someone, or do you want to come to the bar? There's still space there, and you'll get a free drink for your birthday," Zanoah offered, smiling and making sure not to be too pushy but still give good reasons for this guy to come closer to him.

"I'm actually waiting for someone, but he's late," the guy said. "If he doesn't show, I'll come check out the bar." Then he smiled sheepishly. "Can I get a drink, actually? I'm new to alcohol, so can you just make me something nice? Something fresh, maybe?"

At least this guy wasn't ugly, nor did he seem unfriendly. He was actually cute, with curious green eyes in a young face, barely through his teens, and mellow, pink lips. And despite being a graduate of Open Mind, the city's military academy, he didn't sound too arrogant. Zanoah would be able to deal with him, one way or the other.

He wondered if Shaan's intel really was correct since he doubted such a young guy would be close to the High Chancellor. Maybe he was an assistant of some kind? He had to trust his brother to have his intel right here.

"Of course, I'll be back soon."

Zanoah headed toward the bar and started making their trademark drink, the Galaxya Stardust. It involved lots of citrus, mint, and gin. Fresh and fruity for his redhead. He was almost finished when a person sat down in front of the bar. Looking up, his eyes immediately met green ones.

"My date canceled," the young man said. "I'm all yours now. Looks good!"

It seemed Zan would be able to find out more after all. With a smile on his lips, he put down the glass of purple-glittery-swirling liquid in front of his guest. "How lucky for me. Enjoy your drink. What's your name again?"

"Thank you so much!" The redhead closed his lips around the straw and tried a big gulp. "Oh, this tastes great. You're good. And my name's Julyen."

"Why are you outside?"

Kelcie's voice roused Zanoah from his thoughts. Maybe it was for the better. The past should stay in the past and had nothing to do with his current situation. Dwelling on memories of his brother and husband wouldn't help him here.

"Sorry, I didn't really notice where I was going," Zan said. "Vance didn't show me the exit yet, but I found it by accident."

It was true, Vance really hadn't shown him the exit or several other places inside the cave. In particular, there was one barricaded door behind the common room that Zanoah was curious about, but he'd decided not to press the matter. Being impatient and demanding never helped him. He could wait.

"Lucky for you, the jungle doesn't see you as a threat yet," Kelcie said. "Now get inside before it decides otherwise and swallows you whole."

For the first time, she really seemed annoyed at him, and it made Zanoah follow her command instinctively. He got up and was heading closer to the entrance when he heard a rustling behind him. But instead of him, the vines started creeping toward Kelcie, who just held up her hand in a "stop" motion. As soon as she did, the vines stopped, swirling around a little but ultimately retracting into the green jungle behind the clearing.

What the…?

Zanoah was fascinated and intrigued, staring at the retreating vines in stunned silence. What happened just then? He'd never seen plants being commanded like this, especially ones that were on the verge of harming a person. Strange things were going on in this cave with these people. Otherwise, they wouldn't be able to survive in the middle of this jungle, not as leisurely as they did.

Before he could ask, though, Kelcie said, "Another time. You see now, staying outside will get you killed."

She gestured toward the entrance and barricaded it behind them once they were inside. It hadn't been barricaded before when he'd stormed out here. Had she already been outside at that point? Or was she trying to imprison him here? He wasn't sure how much he could trust Kelcie, but she was his aunt. He should always trust in family and follow their lead. Both his parents as well as Shaan had taught him so.

"Your bandage is gone," she noted. "Cerdwyn took it off already?"

"No, it got loose and fell off before…I went outside."

A little white lie. Not even a lie, really. It *had* fallen off. But he didn't want to talk about his encounter with Vance at all. No matter how much he was used to getting used by now, he never wanted to sleep with someone just to make them happy ever again. It made him feel disgusted with himself.

And it felt even worse now that, no matter how much Vance had teased him all the time, Zan had considered Vance a possible friend—the first one he ever had. But he should know better by now. He didn't deserve any friends.

"Good for you," Kelcie said. "Get it checked, and if you're ready, you'll train with Vance. Judging by your physical state, you were, and hopefully still are, well-trained. Show Vance how it's done. He needs to learn how to defend himself, how to bring an opponent down."

So much for keeping his distance from Vance. It honestly wasn't really feasible anyway. During the day, they worked together, and during the night, they shared a sleeping room, the same one he'd woken up in after Vance had rescued him.

"I will do so," Zanoah dutifully agreed, staring at the ground.

"Good. Keep him occupied. He's more trouble if he's bored."

For a moment, Zanoah considered telling her what Vance had asked of him, but he decided against it. In the end, Kelcie might tell him to keep Vance happy in *every way*, and that would be an order he couldn't ignore.

In the end, he just nodded and slipped away, heading toward the kitchen, where Cerdwyn could be found most of the time. She not only cared for any injuries and other physical problems, she also cooked most of the meals.

"Cerdwyn? Are you here?" he asked into the room.

Often, she was hidden away in a corner he couldn't see, but he could hear her. She was older, in her 70s, and rather small, especially compared to him, who had to duck in parts of the corridors to avoid hitting his head.

"Boy?" she called out to him. "Come here and help me for a moment."

So many people here didn't bother with names at all, especially when talking to younger people. At first, it needled him, especially given he was a grown adult. In the end, though, he found he didn't really care. It was just another odd thing about living in this place.

He came closer, looking for the old woman, and finally found her behind a shelf, likely searching for another herb or spoon. "Will you stir the stew?" she asked. "It'll burn otherwise."

Of course, he obliged and took the few steps toward the fireplace and pot, stirring the stew with the big wooden spoon sticking out of it. It wasn't easy to feed fifteen people every day, but she always managed to keep everyone happy and healthy.

"I wanted to ask you to look at my arm," he said. "The bandage came off accidentally, but it looks fine. No pain anymore, either."

His gaze wandered toward the shelf, where Cerdwyn finally reemerged with some dried herbs in her hands. "Looks like you can use your arm, too. Why listen to me at all if you know better? Youths these days," she grumbled and pinched several small leaves from her bundle, throwing them into the stew.

Only now, Zanoah realized he was actually stirring with his right arm—and without any problems as well. He really thought it would take longer for a broken arm to heal, especially without good medicine or a real cast to stabilize the bones while they mended. And yet, it felt and worked fine.

"I didn't realize I was using that arm," he admitted. "Kelcie wants to know when I can train again."

Now Cerdwyn just shrugged and shoved him to the side and stirred the pot herself. "Even if I told you to wait longer, you wouldn't listen. Do whatever you want to, but don't complain to me if your arm's hurting again."

Do what he wanted to do? He almost scoffed. More like do what Kelcie wanted him to do. He would ask Vance later when they should start training. Hopefully, they could just forget what'd happened between them. Zanoah really didn't want to think about it anymore.

CHAPTER 5

Talking calmly to Vance would be a problem. As soon as the younger man saw Zan, he crossed his arms and furrowed his brows, making clear he had no intention of just forgiving and forgetting. Why were social interactions so complicated? Why was it always Zan who had to adjust and fulfill everyone's wishes and needs?

"Vance, I..." He wasn't even sure what to say. He didn't want to apologize; it hadn't felt wrong to tell Vance to stop. "Kelcie wants us to train together," he finally said. It was only the truth.

Vance didn't seem to like that, judging by his even darker expression. Slowly, he came closer and, even though Vance was smaller than him, Zan retreated until he felt cool stone behind his back. Vance stopped right in front of him, their bodies almost touching, a feeling Zanoah detested since it usually resulted in shouting or hits. One way or the other, it always hurt.

"If she wants this, so be it," Vance said through clenched teeth. "But don't think I'll forget you left me sitting there. You're just as arrogant and selfish as all these city people Mom told me about. I don't even want to fuck with you anymore. You're disgusting."

Those last words were almost hissed at him, but Zan said nothing to defend himself. How could he when he'd never learned how to do so? Instead, he just took the words and Vance's shoving him against the wall once before he left.

So much for having a potential friend. When you didn't comply and do what they wanted, you apparently weren't worth being a friend. Nothing new there, either. He'd just hoped it would be different here with different people than in the city.

But it was all the same.

Training with Vance was much different from training with Shaan, mainly because Zanoah had to be the one giving commands and making sure Vance actually learned a thing or two. He was anxious, knees trembling and skin damp from cold sweat, and he was quite unsure of what he was actually doing here. Trying to mimic what Shaan had done with him might be the best idea.

So far, they'd only tested which skill level Vance was on.

"You can go harder, don't worry about that," Zanoah said, motivating his training partner to put more power into his throws. He wanted to know what he had to work with so he could make sure he wasn't over- or underworking Vance.

So far it seemed Vance really just went with his raw young power, swinging at him while Zanoah blocked his punches. He'd decided hand-to-hand combat would be a good start for training, since he really didn't want to give Vance a weapon he couldn't control. And given where they lived, it was the most likely type of attack Vance would face out here.

He could feel Vance's fists pounding his defenses, but they couldn't penetrate at all since they weren't aimed at weak points. Vance was just using up all his strength, aiming for Zan's chest, not realizing he had to change where his fists landed if he wanted to break through. Nothing good would come of this in a real fight. He had to learn to control himself and his emotions.

Zanoah knew too well from his own experience how bad a fight could end, especially when your backup just didn't give a fuck and let you fight for yourself. His brother had done that the few times Zan struggled, and though it made him a better fighter, it also left him feeling betrayed.

"Stop." Zan held his hands up. "Alright, your strength is good, but you have to learn where to aim. We'll try it the other way. You defend, and I'll attack. I'll show you some tricks."

Vance didn't even say a word to him, just glared for a moment before nodding and going into a defensive posture. More or less, at least. It looked a little like a mocking copy of Zan's own stance.

"Elbows higher, feet more apart," Zanoah corrected while readying himself to attack.

His punches were light and probably wouldn't even leave marks, but they hit almost every single time. When one landed, Zanoah corrected Vance's posture and gave him tips on how to block his punches better. They really were starting from scratch here.

Slowly, it got better and fewer of his punches actually hit, successfully blocked by Vance. Zanoah was honestly rather happy about it. So far, he'd never trained anyone. Shaan had been a strict teacher, mercilessly punching him and not giving a damn if he was exhausted or tired. No, Shaan had just gone all-in every time, leaving bruises over bruises on his body during their training. If today's session was any indication, Zan could teach someone in his own way, without Shaan's draconian standards.

Just for a moment, his concentration wasn't on point, but it was enough to change the strength of his punch, which hit Vance's stomach. He huffed and stared at him with resentment before retaliating and attacking him rapidly this time, without any regard for safety or hitting the right points, just payback in his mind.

Zanoah barely had time to raise his arms and get back into defending, but he managed to block Vance's attacks. At least he could feel an improvement—Vance actually aimed for better points. But his strength had become wilder, rawer, the punches harder and more furious. Zanoah couldn't block one of them, and it hit him right in the chest, sending him flying backward several feet and ripping the air from his lungs.

This was more strength than he'd anticipated. Even Shaan hadn't been able to push him off his feet like this, and Vance was smaller than him and much less trained. Confused, he looked up toward Vance, who stood there, his fists balled up, heavily panting, sweating profusely.

"We'll continue tomorrow," Zan decided. "Rest and take a bath."

"Don't you fucking dare tell me what to do!" Vance snapped. "I'm doing this because Kelcie told me to, but aside from that, fuck off."

Vance glared at him before leaving the common room, almost ripping the curtain from its fixture. Zanoah sighed and slowly got up from the ground. Where had Vance gotten all this strength from? Just spite? It felt different from before, and so far, Zanoah had never felt a punch that hard. Maybe it was nothing, just emotions fueling Vance's urge to retaliate. There was still tension between them, lots of it.

Zanoah really was bad with people, and he'd once again angered the only friend he ever could've had. He wasn't even sure if he was mad at Vance or himself. Should he have just given in? Slept with Vance to keep him happy? To finally not be alone anymore? But the thought alone made Zan nauseous. He'd rather deal with yet another person hating him than the unbearable itch under his skin after forcing his body to perform sexual favors.

It hadn't even been his idea to train. He was just following Kelcie's orders, too. She was his aunt and this cave's leader. Disobedience would end in more hurt. Whichever path Zan chose, all of them led to despair, and he'd given up hope of bettering his situation.

"What are you doing?"

The voice came from the entrance, and Zanoah looked over at the person standing there for just a second before he sighed silently. The other people of this little community, except the ones younger than him, didn't quite trust him. Understandably, since he'd traveled through the jungle, a journey they couldn't imagine anyone doing without help.

This woman, Frey, had been suspicious of him from the beginning. She was one of the earliest occupants of this cave and, as far as Zanoah had heard, was around the same age as Kelcie. The two of them had been acquaintances for ages.

"I've just been training with Vance," he offered as an explanation for being here.

Frey just huffed and went over to her spinning wheel and sorted through freshly dried hemp. It was one of the plants that grew in abundance near the cave and made for great fabric.

Though everyone had to pitch in, in the time he'd been here, he hadn't done much. Mostly he had tried to occupy himself by doing chores and learning basic things, like spinning and carving. So far, he had only been allowed to watch since he couldn't do much with just one arm, but he would hopefully be able to be more active now. If the others let him use their tools.

He thought about asking Frey to show him, but she was giving him a dirty look. He would ask her for another practice round some other time. Right now, Zanoah wanted to be alone for a moment, which wasn't easy to do in these caves., There was always someone around, and he couldn't just go outside, as Kelcie had demonstrated to him.

So he headed toward the water reservoir—the room the waterfall ended in. Hearing the water rushing down had a calming effect on Zanoah, no matter if he'd been hurt by falling down said waterfall. Another good thing about this room was it rarely had visitors. It was also one of the few rooms with daylight, the only other one being the kitchen.

It was a wonder, he realized now, that anyone had been in this room when he fell into it. Vance really had been at the right place to rescue him.

Zanoah sat down close to the water. In Tadena, water was rather rare, though there had been improvements to reduce water waste everywhere.

Showers were extremely short, and water was collected to be used for flushing the toilet later. Often, they didn't even use water to get clean but a sonic shower, to save more precious water.

There was no rain in Tadena, ever. The city was encased by desert and raging storms, and no cloud could get as far. Even if it could, the dome, the barrier to protect the city from the storm, wouldn't let rain or sand or wind enter. So water was drawn from underground by digging deep into the earth. Zanoah only knew about these digging sites because Julyen had let it slip once, telling him they were hidden inside buildings, so the people wouldn't know and worry or attack in a rebellion to get more water for themselves.

Compared to Tadena, the jungle had an abundance of water and plants. It felt like paradise, especially if one was used to such a neon city. Maybe it would've been different if he'd been born in Tadena and never known the jungle. It was dangerous, of course it was, but Tadena was too intense for him—all the sounds, the smells, the bright lights. It was too much for Zanoah's senses, overwhelming him on a regular basis. He was always glad when he had the apartment to himself, when he could just sit in a dark corner and recharge, try and calm his mind and his shivering hands. How he had wished to become number to all of it, to just not care, not hear all these voices and noises. But his mind hadn't given him such release.

Zanoah had always felt wrong in Tadena, never at home. Though, to be fair, he'd always felt wrong in general, everywhere, even as a child.

21 years prior
　"Have you left your things lying around again?!"

Zanoah bit his lip and scurried toward the angry voice, grabbing his freshly washed and folded clothes. He'd forgotten to bring them into his room, the one he shared with his big brother, and put them away.

"One more time and I'll send you into the jungle!" the angry voice warned.

"I'm sorry, Daddy. It won't happen again," young Zanoah apologized and promised, rushing toward his room and stuffing his clothes into the closet.

Mainly they were old clothes passed down from Shaan, more holes than fabric, but it didn't really matter out here. No one was here except their little family, anyway.

"What'd you do this time?" Shaan asked in his usual, mildly disinterested voice. Mostly he didn't care what his six-year-old brother did, as long as he didn't annoy him.

"Left my clothes in the common room," Zanoah explained shyly.

"Gotta learn at some point, idiot."

Shaan just shrugged and went back to scribbling in his notebook. Zanoah was so curious about what Shaan wrote in there; he wished he could read and write, too. But he'd never dared to ask his brother to read it to him. He knew better than to anger or annoy him.

Instead, he headed toward the back door and snuck outside. So far, the jungle had never been mean to him, and he didn't quite understand why his family was always so afraid to go deeper into the woods. They said stuff about how they had used the plants and therefore angered the jungle, but Zanoah had never done stuff like that. At least, not that he could remember.

Right now, he just wanted to head toward the small pool close to their house. A waterfall transported fresh water from the mountains down here, where they got their drinking water and baths every few days.

Whenever he wanted quiet, away from his family, Zanoah headed here. The sound of water crashing into the pool always calmed him, drowned out the angry voices and all the mean things they said.

Carefully, he balanced on big rocks around the pool, feeling the cool wet stone under his bare feet. He didn't care about the dangers of falling into the water and drowning or hitting his head on a rock. Would his family even miss him if he didn't come back? Would they realize he was missing at all? Zan doubted it. He was in their way all the time, being pushed aside, even if he wanted to help. They called him a nuisance, whatever that meant, and annoying, unwanted. He understood these words.

Distracted for a moment, he miscalculated a step and slipped down a rock, hitting the cool water close to the waterfall. He was pressed down under the water, unable to surface again. He could swim but not like this.

Panic settled into his small body, and he fought, moving his legs and arms desperately, trying to stay afloat and hold on to whatever his little hands could grab.

He lost all sense of time as he struggled, his head bobbing underwater more and more often, the fight inside him dimming. Right when he couldn't keep his head up anymore, he felt a strong grip around his waist and chest, pulling him from the water and gently placing him safely on a stone next to the pool.

Coughing, Zanoah looked around and his eyes grew wide when he saw vines retracting into the jungle. Plants had saved him?! That couldn't be.

His family had always said the jungle was mean and wanted to hurt them all the time. He must have imagined it! Something else must've happened. Maybe he had grabbed a vine by accident and pulled himself out of the water. Yes, that must've been it.

Certainly, nature wouldn't save a useless child like him from drowning.

The next few days were filled with training Vance and learning about many of the things Zanoah had only seen demonstrated to him so far. The people in the cave taught him more, showed him how things worked in practice. Even Frey decided to show him part of her skills and guide his hands as he learned to spin.

It was a good feeling, finally being able to help and contribute to the community, but Zanoah still had a nagging feeling in his head. It didn't feel quite right around here, and he didn't really belong either.

He still wanted to avenge his family. No matter how much Shaan had pushed him, how badly they all had treated him—his family had still made sure he grew up and had enough food and shelter. Shaan had trained him, gotten him a job, and Zan was still convinced it had to mean *something*.

But it didn't seem like Kelcie or anyone else would leave this cave, not farther than a few hundred feet into the jungle. Certainly not several weeks through the jungle to Tadena.

And no matter how at peace he felt with nature around him, Zanoah felt empty—unfulfilled. He was missing a kind of guideline, someone who pushed him to his limits, like Shaan had always done. Sure, Kelcie gave orders here and there, but she wasn't as rigorous, nor did she have an ulterior motive in mind. Not like Shaan.

He wasn't used to living on his own, making decisions of his own free will, and he was glad for any guidance and every single order Kelcie offered. Sadly, it wasn't too much except to keep training Vance and learn how best to help the community. That offered little reprieve from how he felt. All the rage and hate for Tadena and, mainly, the High Chancellor was still burning inside of him, not being fueled by Shaan anymore, but still simmering, unable to fade entirely.

Training with Vance helped him a bit. He could push toward his physical boundaries and exhaust himself. Vance was a strong opponent and a fast learner, but for some reason, his punches seemed weaker the last few days. It was like his strength was declining. While Zanoah was worried about this, he didn't dare ask Vance what was wrong because the two of them were barely talking, and when they did, Vance's manner was cold. Nothing of their early friendly exchanges remained.

Training today was especially hard because Zan had to contain his own strength so he wouldn't hurt Vance, who seemed distracted the whole time. In a real fight, that would get him killed or at least badly beaten up.

Since Vance had told him to fuck off several times when he asked him to concentrate, Zanoah didn't even try to ask or correct him anymore. Instead, he grew more and more frustrated by their training, and at one point, Vance didn't hold up his defense anymore, taking the full blow of Zanoah's hit and falling down on his ass.

Surprised, Zan stared at Vance. He hadn't expected this and immediately apologized, holding back an "I told you so." Instead, he offered Vance a hand to help him back up. But the younger man just glared at him, panting heavily by now and covered in sweat.

"Vance, Zanoah. How's training going?" Kelcie walked into the room and eyed them, probably wondering what had happened—why Zanoah was barely sweating while Vance's shirt was soaked.

"It's going…slower the last few days," Zanoah answered honestly. He didn't want to cast Vance in a negative light, but it was the truth, and he didn't know why things had changed.

Kelcie seemed to know and just nodded, switching her focus toward Vance, who had gotten up on his own now. "Get cleaned up. It's Protection Day, anyway."

While Zanoah had no idea what this was supposed to mean, it seemed to lighten Vance's mood a lot. His expression relaxed, and he nodded, leaving the room immediately. For a moment, Zanoah contemplated if he should ask what "Protection Day" meant, but he didn't have to because Kelcie gave him a small smile.

"Sit." She gestured toward one of the sofas close to the wall, which was made of wooden beams with cushions and pillows filled with dried leaves. "I'll explain what's going to happen. It'll be your first Protection Day, so you should know."

Zanoah sat down next to her, curious. He was always eager to learn but too anxious to ask. His parents and Shaan had always scolded him for unsolicited questions, called him dumb and annoying for having to ask.

"We had to make sure you would stay with us and could understand our way of living before telling you about the rituals of Protection Day. It's how we get the power to control the jungle, at least partly. Enough to protect us from it harming us, hence the name. Otherwise, we couldn't survive out here. The jungle would've killed us a long time ago."

This explained why Kelcie had been able to tell those vines to leave her alone and why she hadn't wanted him to be outside. Because he didn't have said protection yet. It sounded weird, but weird didn't have to mean not true. Even if it wasn't and was all just a weird religion or whatever, he certainly wouldn't say so and would instead play along.

"And...where do you get this protection from?" Zanoah wondered.

For a long moment, she looked at him, and Zanoah could almost hear her considering if she really should tell him or not—if he was trustworthy or not. She had to protect her little community.

"Come with me."

CHAPTER 6

Zanoah rose and followed Kelcie toward one corner of the living room, where she pushed open a wooden door covered by a carpet. It was the only real door he'd seen in this cave system so far, so what lay behind it had to be important.

Kelcie grabbed a miniature torch next to the door and lit it by holding it close to the flame of a lamp in the common room. Only then did they enter the corridor behind the door. As Kelcie navigated the long, dark path ahead, she lit the lamps along the walls. This passage seemed narrower than anywhere else in the caves, making it much harder to pass through.

Finally, they arrived in another bigger cave, illuminated only by their torch. Slowly, the room filled with more light with every lamp Kelcie lit. By now, he could see carpets on the floor, all lined up to point into one corner.

It took a moment for his eyes to adjust to the light, then he could see what was in the corner. Or, rather, the center wall of the room: a person, hanging from the ceiling, bound by golden chains around their wrists. They weren't moving at all, and Zan wondered if they were dead.

What the...? This is what they'd been hiding? A prisoner?!

"Don't you worry," Kelcie said. "It's not dead. It just decided to ignore us. Do you know what it is?"

Kelcie stood beside him, looking at him expectantly. He shook his head, confused. What it was? Wasn't it a person? Slowly, he stepped closer, feeling drawn toward whoever—or whatever—this was.

"You can feel it, huh?" Kelcie said. "It's a deity. The deity of nature, to be precise. Every 50 days we pray to it and fill it with energy, then take this energy to protect us from the vile jungle outside. Nature wants to hurt us, but we won't let it."

Zanoah didn't know what to say. Everything about this felt so inherently wrong. Nature wasn't evil, no matter what he'd been told all these years. It had never hurt him, never even tried to. But no matter what he thought or felt, he wouldn't—no, couldn't—object. He knew he would face too many consequences if he did, and he had no idea how to speak his mind at all. Every time he'd done so in the past, he'd been punished for it—thrown out of the house or beaten up by his family. They'd taught him to just shut up and not ask any silly questions, a lesson he still listened to now. If he doubted Kelcie, he surely would be thrown out of the cave to fend for himself again as well.

"I...How..?" His voice was coarse, and he felt nauseous but tried to hide it.

"When all are gathered here, we'll pray to it," she explained. "Then everyone gets their turn to take energy. You'll be last today. After all, you're new. Just copy what the others do during prayer. You'll know what to do."

Kelcie patted his shoulder and looked at the deity again. Zanoah hadn't been able to take his eyes off of them at all. His gaze was fixed on this morbid silhouette.

"I'll gather the others," she said. "Stay here."

He barely noticed her leaving, but it appeared the deity did. When Kelcie's steps grew quieter, they moved, looking up and directly at him. Blue-green eyes met his own, and it felt like they were looking straight into his soul. Zanoah couldn't help but take one, two, three steps forward. Now he was so close, he only had to stretch out his arm to touch this deity.

He was also able to get a better look at them. Their body was covered in moss, not fresh and green but dried up and brown, revealing more skin than it was hiding. Their blonde hair was partly in dreads, the rest limp and covering their shoulders. A golden thread was stitched through their lips, sewing their mouth shut. It seemed to be the same material the chains were made of, as it had the same everlasting shine to it.

The only part of them that really resembled a deity was the crown on their head. It was an intricate design of vines and ivy, which also had seen better times, twining around a band of thorns. Some of them had embedded themselves in the deity's pale skin, almost like the crown was fused to their head.

Zanoah's eyes met the deity's again, holding their gaze, and slowly, he understood what he had to do. He didn't know why yet, but he felt it was right. And he knew the deity of nature's name.

Their name was...

"Caean."

Zanoah didn't know how long he stood there, staring at Caean. Eventually, he realized their eyes were slowly wandering over his body as well, stopping at the scar on his cheek for a moment.

What was happening here? Why did he feel such a connection to this deity? He'd never believed in something like this before, though he'd heard stories about deities—old gods with immense power. Being confronted with it now, he thought he'd be terrified, but he was oddly okay with it. Even more, he actually felt at peace and like he had found a missing piece of himself.

A missing purpose in life.

Slowly, he stretched out his right hand, wanting to touch Caean's hair, their cheek, every single inch of them. He'd completely forgotten where they were. An invisible connection pulled him toward Caean, as if they were meant to be together, two sides of the same coin. Different and yet connected.

He was sure he could trust Caean, and Caean would help him become who he was supposed to be. They were a missing piece of his soul and the reason he was alive. Zan couldn't place where this feeling was coming from, couldn't grasp it, but he didn't care either.

Only when Caean's attention shifted toward the corridor did Zanoah take a few steps back. No one should know about this, not now. It would only cause the people here to distrust him. He didn't really understand what was happening yet anyway, and until he had figured it out, he certainly wouldn't tell Kelcie or the others about this.

Just moments later, Kelcie, Vance, and the others entered the room, spreading out the room and kneeling down on the carpets, which were aligned so their deity was right in front of them, perfectly displayed.

It was disgusting.

No one should be held captive and used like this, no matter who or what they were. But he couldn't do anything about it, not yet, no matter how much he wanted to. Anger welled up hot inside him, and he felt sick to his stomach, gritting his teeth.

"Are you ready?"

Kelcie looked at him, and Zanoah nodded. He was ready, not for this ceremony, but for whatever would come afterward in his life. He just had to figure it out.

He took his place among the others, knelt down, and followed the ceremony with growing disgust. They mumbled, almost chanted, lines he followed.

Oh, deity of nature, let us give you thanks for the beauty of creation.

Thank you for the rich jungle we are privileged to have and the beautiful plants that sustain us.

The plants they regularly fought and used for their own use. How hypocritical. Shouldn't they respect the plants more if they cared for their deity so much?

Thank you for the blessing of harmony in nature,

and may the earth continue to thrive under your loving presence.

Harmony in nature? There surely wasn't any harmony in nature anymore. Plants weren't supposed to attack other lifeforms, Zan knew as much. No, all of this was wrong. This whole "prayer" felt wrong.

A deity wasn't supposed to be chained up in a damp cave either. They should be with their jungle, their home. It angered Zanoah, and he had to tap into his lifelong training to keep his anger down.

Grant us the wisdom and power to care for the flora as you care for it,

nurture it so it can sustain us and our children, keep us safe from ruin.

These people really disrespected the deity of nature by a lot. This so-called prayer was wholly focused on themselves and less on actual love for their deity. His body felt hot by now, consumed by an anger he didn't know he could harbor.

The whole ceremony was blunt. The pathetic prayer was repeated three times together, and Zanoah just mumbled along, trying to fit in and keep the cave people happy with him, no matter how sick and outraged he was.

Although he didn't know what was going on, he could feel energy radiating from Caean. The moss covering them was growing and expanding, now more of a sickly yellow than brown. Their energy felt warm and fresh at the same time, like swimming in a small pool after the sun had passed its highest point.

After their pathetic excuse for a prayer ended, Kelcie got up and closed the few steps toward Caean, placing her hand on their chest. Although Zanoah couldn't see what she was doing, he felt Caean's force slightly dwindling. Next up was Vance, then the younger people who mostly went outside gathering.

With every person, Caean's energy grew smaller, less detectable, until it was Zanoah's turn. The other's hadn't hesitated at all; every single person just went straight for it and took the force they thought belonged to them. But Zan didn't want that, and he wondered if this would even work. And if it didn't, would the others suspect him of something, some wrongdoing?

Gently, he placed his hand on Caean's chest, right over the point where their heart must be. During this whole process, Caean hadn't moved at all or even acknowledged what was happening, but their skin was cool and a little clammy, like cold sweat. Did deities sweat? They for sure could shudder slightly, like Caean did now.

But nothing else happened. There was no energy exchange. Zanoah didn't want to take any energy after all.

"What's going on?" Kelcie demanded, stepping closer.

"I...don't know. It's not working."

Zanoah had learned how to play dumb all his life. No matter what happened, it was always easier to do that than to admit he'd knowingly done something wrong.

"Let me have the rest," Vance said. "This idiot's not ready."

In that moment, Zanoah realized how much of an asshole Vance actually was. He wasn't much different from his own brother, really, who had only used him to get what he wanted. Just like the people in this cave, Shaan had taken what he wanted without a thought for others.

Zanoah's gaze wandered to Kelcie, who considered the request for a moment before nodding. Vance pushed Zan to the side and took his place, draining more energy from Caean. Vance didn't seem to notice, but Zan saw they winced ever so slightly, and the urge to rip Vance away from the deity grew inside him.

"That's enough, Vance," Kelcie warned. "You'll kill it." Kelcie grabbed Vance's shoulder and pulled him back

At least they wanted to keep Caean alive, though it was so they could use them more, again and again.

Unsurprisingly, Vance wasn't too happy about being reprimanded and turned toward Zan, chin high so their height difference wouldn't be too obvious. "You're a coward, can't even take power to protect yourself and your community. You only do what you're told but deny me. You're so pathetic."

Before he could react, Vance hit him right in the stomach, exactly where Zanoah had shown him to, right where it would hurt most. He couldn't help but sink down to his knees, holding his stomach, trying to breathe through the pain. At least now he knew where Vance's enhanced strength came from. Didn't make it less painful, though.

He didn't even care when Vance stormed off; it was a relief to be away from him.

Kelcie stood over him. "He's not wrong. If you can't do it next time..." She stared down at Zan, and he forced himself to look at her. "Turn off the lights when you can stand again, would you?" Then she smiled at him, a small, mean smile, before leaving the cave as well.

Fuck them! At least now Zanoah knew what he could expect from these people—nothing at all. He'd be better off on his own. After taking a deep breath and deciding to ignore the pain for now, his gaze shifted toward Caean, immediately meeting these teal eyes, framed by long light lashes, again.

Slowly, he got up and came closer, bridging the distance between them. Very gently, he touched Caean's cheek, maintaining their eye contact. He could drown in these eyes and would be content if this was the last thing he saw in his life.

"I promise you I'll get you out of here," he told them. "You don't deserve a life like this—being used by these...idiots."

Caean tilted their head slightly, and Zanoah could almost hear them thinking. Only now, he realized the moss was already drying up again, their force spent—no, stolen almost completely.

How he wished he could speak to Caean, hear what they had to say. He wanted to hear their story, just listen to them talk. Never had he felt this way. Of course, he'd liked people despite never pursuing any kind of relationship, but this...it was different. It was a bond between them. He just wanted to be with Caean.

Caean leaned forward, letting their crown slide into Zanoah's hands. He'd expected the thorns to sting, but their tips were blunt. But...why? Why had he been given this? Confused, he looked at Caean, who just stared back, now seeming naked without their crown. But they just nodded toward the entrance.

"I...should take the crown and leave?" A small nod. "What should I do with it?" He wasn't sure and didn't want to assume anything. Caean nodded toward his head, and Zan frowned. "I...Should I put on the crown?" Another nod. "Now?" Caean answered with a shake of their head this time. "When I'm alone?" Caean's nod confirmed his thoughts. "Thank you. For trusting me with this."

He could only imagine how important giving up their crown must be for Caean. Zanoah held it in his hand while dousing all the lamps, one by one, shrouding the cave in darkness again.

Standing at the entrance, he took another gaze back at Caean, whose eyes followed him wherever he went.

"I'll be back," Zanoah softly promised before leaving the cave and turning off the lamps on his way down the corridor as well.

Before he reached the common room, he pushed the crown underneath his shirt, deciding to walk with a little stoop, pretending to still be hurt.

He could hear laughing and talking coming from the common room and it got louder when he entered, silently, closing the door behind him. He just crept through the room, hoping they wouldn't care about him. It seemed he wasn't so wrong. He got through the room without any incident and relaxed a little more when he was back in the corridor,

Where could he put on the crown? Right, the reservoir. He would be alone and undisturbed there, especially at this time, he was sure of that. He just hoped no one would cross his path, since he had to walk through the whole cave system to get to the water reservoir. But everyone was celebrating after the ritual, and he met no one along the way. When he finally arrived, he sat down in his corner and thought hard about everything he'd just experienced.

What the fuck happened today? He'd met a deity—no, the deity of nature. It was crazy, but it also explained so much. It was no longer surprising that the jungle was sentient and violent, when its deity was in chains. He wondered how long they'd kept Caean captive, how many years they'd been draining the deity's lifeforce.

Carefully, he revealed the crown, tracing a leaf with his fingertips. Then he took a slow, deep breath, lifted it over his head, and prepared to put it on.

CHAPTER 7

The moment he placed the crown on his head, Zanoah understood why Caean hadn't wanted him to do so back in the chapel. It was overwhelming. His surroundings vanished completely. Instead, he could feel a presence, full of energy that was somehow familiar and comforting.

"You're here."

Where was that voice coming from? Confused, but in no way scared, Zanoah looked around. Or did he? He couldn't quite say since his perception was so different in here. It was much more intimate, like there were no boundaries between Caean's and his mind at all, like they had become one.

"I know, it's so much right now," Caean said. "It will get easier; you'll get used to the feeling, better able to navigate it." Caean's voice was so soft and gentle, like wind in the leaves, leaving Zan more relaxed than he had been the whole day—no, the whole time he had been on the run. "Look at me. Not outside but in here."

Slowly, Zanoah turned his attention toward Caean's presence and could see them—could feel them. He'd only glimpsed a small part of Caean's true form back in the cave. Here, in their minds, he could see them more clearly. Caean's presence was glowing, sparkling golden and green, surrounded by warmth and more plants, vines and ivy. They looked so much healthier and full of life.

Despite all the green life blooming around them, they were also surrounded by a black mist, an oddness Zan felt didn't belong here, and he immediately wondered where it came from.

"You're beautiful," Zanoah whispered, barely registering what or how he said it.

He was still figuring out how their connection through this crown worked and what he was dealing with right now. It was much different from anything he'd experienced in Tadena. They'd had ways to connect minds as well, but it was artificial and left a bitter taste in his mouth. This...it was the most natural thing in the world.

Caean only smiled, and Zanoah blinked a bit confused, but their aura dimmed, making it easier on his eyes, less overwhelming. Their body was even covered by human clothes now, although only a white blouse and dark brown pants, both of which looked comfortable.

"That's easier for you, at least for now."

Caean tilted their head a little and looked at him. Zanoah could sense them thinking, but he couldn't look into their thoughts. It was a weird feeling, but not an unpleasant one. More like there was still a barrier between them that wasn't supposed to be there, one that stopped their connection, their bond, from becoming whole.

Still, he felt strangely comforted by Caean's presence, more than he ever had with his family, a family he still wasn't sure what to think about, especially after learning what Kelcie was up to.

"Zanoah, do you want to know what actually happened to your parents? I don't know your memories, but I know those of everyone who's drawn energy from me," Caean explained.

"Didn't the Tadenan military kill them?" Zan asked. "That's what I'd always been told."

"No, they didn't. Let me show you."

Caean offered their hand, and after a moment of hesitation, Zanoah took it. Immediately he felt a spark and like he was inside someone else's head.

Finally, she'd found a solution, a way to control this damn jungle so they could live free and without fear. She just wished her brother was here to celebrate all this. In all honesty, she didn't quite get why he'd left her at all.

But she knew where he lived with his little self-made family, at the foot of the mountain ridge, north-east of her own new home. Wandering through the jungle was so much easier with all this force coursing through her body, and it didn't take long until she arrived. Normally, the trip took several weeks, but this time, she was there in less than one.

She was so excited to finally see her brother again, to knock at his door. What a pathetic excuse for a door, anyway. This whole house was just pathetic and looked like it would be blown away any second. Some of the windows were covered by broken slats, and the roof surely leaked.

Finally, the door opened, and she saw her brother again, with the same dark brown eyes and curly hair he always had. Broadly grinning, she slung her arms around him, holding him close.

"I missed you so much!" she exclaimed.

"What are you doing here?" her brother demanded. "I told you I never wanted to see you again."

She was shoved back and held at a distance by his strong arms, and she teasingly pouted at him. He'd always been like this, playing around and making weird jokes.

"But I've found a way! See." With a little gesture of her hand, she and drew on the energy inside of her, willed a vine to come closer. She grinned as it grew up her leg. It felt so good to have such control.

"I don't care!" he said. "I have a family. A son. A wife."

"But you're mine! I promised I'd find a way, and I did! You promised you'd come back to me if I did!"

Now she was pushing him a bit, willing the vines to grow up his legs, holding him in place. She wouldn't leave her beloved brother with another woman, hiding in this rotten shack.

"Stop it, Kelcie," he pleaded. "I won't go with you. I'll never love you, not the way you want me to. It's wrong, always has been."

"Are you telling me I'm sick? I don't care! You will *come with me!"*

The vines grew thicker and stronger around his body, strong enough to carry him with her. He would learn to love her! Turning away from the shack, she took a few steps before feeling a sharp pain in her side. Confused, she looked at the person who'd stabbed her—a woman. Was this his bitch of a wife?

"What the—" She glared at the woman.

"You will not *take my husband away!"*

Kelcie lost control. The energy inside her was new, barely contained, and too much for her to actually handle by herself. It exploded from her, vines getting their own ideas and slinging around the bodies of her brother and his wife, squeezing, not stopping, even when they weren't breathing anymore.

Kelcie could only watch in horror, unable to control nature anymore. The blade in her side was still stuck there, the pain forgotten.

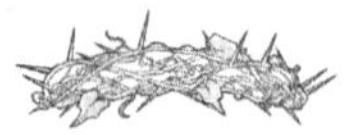

For a long time, Zanoah was silent.

This was a lot different than he'd expected.

He didn't mourn his parents, never really had. They'd treated him like garbage. His father had even told his sister he only had one son. But it was still weird seeing them die like this. How had Shaan gotten the idea that they were killed by the Tadenan military?

Right now, Zan wished he could ask his brother, but it just wasn't possible. This vision did explain a lot, though, like the fact that Cato Antias would've been too young to even be High Chancellor back then. It explained why she didn't leave the cave, why she appeared to have no partner.

"She killed them because she loved her brother too much," Zanoah concluded, no emotion in his voice at all.

Before today, he could barely remember what his father looked like, so seeing him in Kelcie's memories was a bit of a shock. Zan looked so much like his father that it was no surprise she recognized him.

"Yes. She captured me some years before but couldn't figure out how to use my force. When she did, she ran straight to him." Caean's presence came closer, warm and comforting. "How do you feel?"

"Not so bad, actually. My parents hated me. I didn't grieve their death. I was only ever helping Shaan with his vendetta because it gave me a purpose. It's good to know what actually happened, though."

It was reassuring to find out that the Tadenan military hadn't been involved at all. This was just a family feud gone wrong. He felt kind of sorry for playing with Julyen's heart for so long, for hating the High Chancellor and wishing him dead. But Antias had still killed his brother. And there was still the secret experiments, of which Zanoah had seen actual proof.

He wondered what had pushed Shaan to believe Tadena had killed their parents. Had he only searched for an antagonist to blame? Had he even known about Tadena before arriving there? Or had he merely decided the High Chancellor had to be responsible for their parents' mysterious deaths, fueling his rage and urge to avenge them?

Zanoah wasn't sure what to believe anymore. Despite not mourning for his family, for his brother, anymore, shouldn't he feel responsible? Shouldn't he do what Shaan had set out to? Kill the person who'd murdered his parents? He might be the only one who knew these secrets, and he could make Kelcie pay for what she'd done. But Zan didn't want to take yet another futile path of revenge, as his brother had. He wasn't Shaan, and for once in his life, he wanted to find a way forward by himself.

Even if it meant following Caean's guidance. They were different and depended on his help, and Zan would do everything in his might to set them free. The idea of serving them was pleasant, and Zan looked forward to it.

He sighed and tried pushing these thoughts to the side for now. More important things were in front of him, and one was most important of all in the moment..

"How do we get you out of here?"

Zan slipped out almost every night to talk to Caean. He'd hidden the crown in a small gap in the wall of the reservoir room, where no one would look. It wasn't visible either, wrapped in cloth, hidden in the shadows.

He'd become addicted to their nightly conversations, to the feeling of their presence in his mind, and he wanted to be with them all the time.

Everything was different with Caean, and for once in his life, Zan could talk openly.

"You're so different," Caean said, eyeing him curiously.

"Me? Why?"

Zan was confused. He'd never been called different before. Well, he had—a weirdo, outsider, useless, kind of *different*. But from Caean's mouth, it sounded like a compliment and not an insult.

"I already told you, I can sift through memories if people either take my energy, like they do on Protection Day, or once a connection through the crown is formed. But not with you. I can't access your memories freely."

Was this a good thing or a bad thing? Zan squirmed and was unsure what to think of it exactly. He was glad Caean wouldn't freely search through his mind; it reassured him that he could keep some of his secrets. But he also wondered if it annoyed Caean.

"You're making me curious," they stated, smiling at him now.

Relief rushed through Zan. So, it *wasn't* a bad thing.

"But you can still feel my thoughts, right?" It was hard to grasp the concept, but Zan had an idea of what Caean was thinking and feeling, and he guessed it was the same for them.

"Yes, and they're quite interesting."

Heat rushed to Zan's face and didn't get any better with Caean's smirk. "We...we should figure out how to free you," he sputtered, and Caean's smirk slowly ebbed away.

"It won't be easy," Caean said. "The chains holding me are made from Luskite, as is the thread. They restrain my true nature, my energy, and I'm barely able to feel the jungle around us." They sighed and closed their eyes for a moment. "There's a key you have to find first. It unlocks the chains."

Zan nodded but wasn't sure where to start. Kelcie must have hidden the key in a place she thought was safe, somewhere no one would stumble upon it accidentally.

"Any idea where it might be?" he wondered, ready to venture through caves to find it.

"Not yet. I thought about it a lot but gave up hope of ever being free again a long time ago. I'll try to remember any details before we meet again tomorrow."

Caean smiled at him, and their presence came closer. Zanoah couldn't explain their connection. Being together in their minds was similar to the simulations in Tadena, where people might immerse themselves in fantasies tailored to them, augmented realities where they could touch and feel artificial memories. This was different from that, not artificial at all. Being with Caean was the most natural thing to ever happen to Zan.

"What is Luskite exactly?" Zan asked.

Caean halted in front of him, tilting their head a little, their long hair following the movement of their head. "It's an ancient material, forged to hold deities. It renders me unable to use any of my abilities and burns my skin instead. The knowledge of how to forge it has been long forgotten, and Kelcie hides how she found the chains."

They sighed, and a sad smile covered their lips. Inside the two of their minds, those lips weren't stitched close, and Caean appeared free—how they were supposed to be.

Zanoah knew one thing: "I will free you. I...just don't know how yet."

He'd never made any plans on his own, had never figured out how to fulfill missions without specific instructions, and despite his drive to free Caean, he was overwhelmed by how to start.

"It's okay. Come here."

Caean offered their hand, and without hesitation, Zan took it. The deity's fingers felt warm in his own, their skin soft.

"First, you'll have to find the key," they said. "I hope I can give you an idea where it might be tomorrow. Since the day you entered the caves, the entrance has been guarded. They might hide it from you, but they can't deceive me. You will have to fight your—*our*—way out."

Zan swallowed, anxiety rising in him again. Suddenly, his hands felt numb. He was used to fighting, but not like this. Kelcie was still family, and no matter what she'd done, Zan dreaded having to stand up to her.

A soft squeeze of his hand urged him to look up again, only to meet Caean's gentle smile and their caring teal eyes. "I know it's hard; I understand. But Kelcie isn't your friend. You're not her pawn, okay?"

Slowly, Zanoah nodded, although the dread inside him still lingered.

"It's best if we use the next Protection Day. Ask to go first this time, to make sure you can get my energy. I'll provide enough for you to win any fight."

But wasn't it a bad idea to free Caean when everyone was gathered? Wasn't it easier to just take them and run away in the middle of the night? Zan didn't dare offer this option. Never to speak his mind was still ingrained into him, and even Caean couldn't change that, not within few days.

Caean pulled him closer and pressed his hand against their chest, their heartbeat steady against Zan's palm. "Trust me. You'll scare them enough that they won't try to follow us. You're strong, Zanoah, much stronger than you think."

He felt Caean's fingertips on his cheek, brushing against it, and they gently urged him to look up, holding his gaze. Slowly, a crooked smile crept on Zan's lips, a bad mirror of Caean's own smile.

"I don't want to hurt anyone," he whispered. It didn't matter that they'd hurt him. Zanoah didn't like to inflict pain, and he'd rather just snatch Caean up and run as fast as he could.

"Sadly, it won't stop people from hurting you. It's time you fight back."

The prospect of that made his stomach sink, but Zan had already decided to free Caean, to follow their guidance, no matter what. The deity's fingertips wandered to the nape of his neck, pulling him closer until Zan's forehead leaned against their shoulder. The pressure was reassuring, reminding him he wasn't alone anymore.

"Things will be better once we're both free," Caean promised.

Zan had to trust in their words, their wisdom.

Training with Vance was bad now. He still did it, but most times Vance just beat him up, having fun doing so. Kelcie didn't seem to care at all, so neither did Zanoah.

He wondered what would happen if he just left. Would they search for him? Would they even stop him? Would the jungle still be friendly toward him? Zan didn't know. He couldn't leave yet, not without Caean. Their freedom was more important than his own discomfort.

He realized his body was healing much faster than a human should heal, but he had no idea why. He just leaned into that and took Vance's punches. He was always so full of anger, and Zanoah wondered why.

It was one of the questions he asked Caean during their nightly talks.

"His mother came from Srale. It's a city west of here, behind the mountain ridge. She was heavily pregnant when she arrived here, but she told no one who Vance's father was. I guess I'm the only one who knows. She was raped outside the city but decided to keep the child. It wasn't Vance's fault, after all. She really was a gentle woman." Caean sighed. "The first few years, she took part in the rituals, but she never took much of my energy, just enough that no one would be suspicious. At one point, she couldn't anymore. She was exiled soon after. You know what being exiled from here means?"

Zanoah shook his head.

"It means Kelcie does pretty much what she did to your parents. She says the corpses fertilize the jungle."

Caean's voice was bitter talking about this. Zanoah could understand. After all, Kelcie talked shit about nature, which would already make them resent her. But killing people?. Nature wasn't cruel like this; it never was.

"How old was Vance?" Zan asked. "How did he deal with it?"

"It's hard to keep track of years here, but I'd say he was around seven or eight. He got angry so fast. Took more and more energy over the years. He learned to do so from birth and, next to Kelcie, he's the most convinced that everyone has to do so to survive."

In a twisted way, Zanoah could understand that logic. Vance really didn't have anyone or anything left. His mother was dead, sacrificed because she didn't want to use another life form's energy anymore. He was convinced he could only survive by taking as much energy as possible, by being strong and proving himself. It wasn't surprising that Vance hated him for denying him "love" and for being weak—or at least what he *thought* was weak.

"I feel sorry for him," Zanoah concluded, opening his mind up a little more to Caean, so they could understand his thoughts more.

"I get that. He never learned differently. He's not dumb, but he's fueled by emotions and his conviction that he won't survive without my energy. He hates himself and thinks he was too weak to protect his mother."

That surprised him. He hadn't really considered that Vance hated himself. He always seemed so strong and confident. But maybe that was exactly the problem. Dealing with such a great loss at such a young age would do terrible things to anyone's mind.

"Why does the jungle attack them but never hurt me?" Zanoah wondered.

Caean frowned, thinking about it. "I'm not sure, actually. It attacks the cave community because they use it, rip out plants, log trees and so on. But it's grown more hostile over the years since I was captured. It's not normal for plants to behave like this. They should cooperate with humans, help each other."

"How long ago were you captured?" Zanoah softly wondered and hoped he wouldn't poke any wounds.

"I'm guessing I've been around here about 30 human years. When Kelcie captured me, she was around Vance's age."

Then it really was possible it had been roughly thirty years. From what his parents told him, Zanoah knew nature started changing around then. And history classes in Tadena taught him that the ring of desert around the city had expanded rapidly over the last three decades.

"Have you found the key yet?" Caean interrupted his thoughts.

Right, the key. Without that, Zan wouldn't be able to open the chains holding Caean. So far, they hadn't had an idea where it could be, and Zan hadn't come across it.

"Not yet," he admitted. "I've searched everywhere, but I've got no idea where Kelcie hid it."

He sighed and really wondered where it could be. She had to hide it somewhere no one could easily get to it. So he doubted it'd be in one of the sleeping or common rooms. So then where...

"I've got an idea," Caean said. "She hid things all over the caves, but they were always wrapped in cloth. The only one she never visited again is in water. Behind a stone. Guess she wanted to hide it from the others and didn't need it again?"

In water, huh? There weren't many possibilities, either the bathrooms or here.

"I'm at the water reservoir. Not sure how deep it is, and there's a current, but she could've hidden it here. I'm hiding the crown in here as well."

"I'm sure I'll recognize the spot when I see it. Let's try something. Open your eyes but keep your mind concentrated on me."

Zanoah did and saw the pool in front of him again.

"You still hear me?"

"Yeah, I do," Zanoah answered, wincing a little when he heard his voice echoing off the walls.

"Keep your voice inside. I'll hear you if you talk in your head. I can see what you see and guide you. Are you a good swimmer?"

Now Zanoah smiled a little crookedly. He'd almost drowned in this pool, and he guessed it wasn't easy to navigate when it was dark like this. Last time, at least a little sunlight had shone down here. Now the water looked almost pitch black.

"I can swim, but I'm not sure if I'll be able to see anything down there."

It took a moment before an answer came. *"We have to try. Or do you think you'll have a chance tomorrow without someone surprising you?"*

What a good question. It was much more likely he'd get surprised in here during the day, and he wasn't sure if he wanted to risk getting caught. Especially with the crown on his head. He might be able to explain why he'd taken a dive in the reservoir but not why he was wearing the deity's crown.

"Maybe. I can try but not with the crown. If I'm seen, I can't explain that."

"Then I'll give you the image of where she hid the key." A second later, Zanoah could see a corner underwater, marked by a long tear in the wall, almost like a cross. He would find it. *"When you go down there, don't drown. Would be a waste."*

For a moment, Zan wondered if Caean was teasing him, or if they were actually concerned they'd be on their own again if he drowned. Sometimes, Zan still couldn't read them. Zanoah just sighed and hoped he wouldn't drown. And he certainly hoped he wouldn't get caught, either.

After a few hours of sleep, he got up before everyone else and immediately headed to the water reservoir, taking off his clothes and diving into the refreshing cool water.

The current really was stronger than he remembered, and it pulled him to one side. He had to fight to keep up, trying to find what Caean had shown him. Finally, after several dives down, he saw a scratch resembling a cross in one corner.

Carefully, he wiggled his fingers inside the crack until they touched fabric. He slowly pulled it out, keeping it firmly in his hand while he surfaced and got out of the water. He peeked out of the room, but no one was there, so he opened the little package. Inside was a key, Luskite like the chains. *Did it!*

Before anyone would suspect him, he put the key, still in its fabric, next to the crown and put on his clothes again. He would free Caean. It was just a matter of time now.

CHAPTER 8

The time for the next Protection Day had come. Finally. Zanoah had waited for it, patiently plotting with Caean. He'd returned the crown the night before, so no one would realize it had been missing at all. He'd also packed his bag, ready to leave this cave with Caean. Their food wouldn't last long, but Caean had taught him which plants in the jungle were edible, so they would be able to survive. Luckily enough, he'd found a water purifier as well, hidden on a storage shelf.

He felt way too calm right now, especially considering he was about to betray everyone here, leaving them without protection from the jungle. Though maybe the jungle wouldn't try to attack them anymore. Caean had suggested that might be the case, that nature would calm down when they were free.

It had been hard playing his role the last weeks, but Zanoah managed it, keeping the cave people in the dark. They'd made it clear they didn't like that he'd lacked the will to take energy last time, but he'd assured them he wouldn't be as weak next time. And he wouldn't be, not with Caean on his side.

"Kelcie, can I prepare the room for later?" Zanoah asked, finding her in the hallway.

"Of course. I've seen how excited you are. It's time to reward you." Then she leaned in, her tone dripping with a warning. "And I really hope your willpower is stronger this time."

Zanoah knew what awaited him if he failed to take any energy today, the same fate as Vance's mother: sacrificed to the jungle.

Zanoah smiled brightly, tapping into his mental training, playing his role. "Thank you so much."

Before heading toward the chapel cave, Zanoah wandered close by the entrance. It was raining today, heavily. Hopefully, the weather wouldn't influence their escape too much and the caves wouldn't flood either. Although he'd heard and seen rainfall several times by now, it was still fascinating to him. In Tadena, there was no rain at all. It was the same weather, every day, all year long. Out here it was so different, and he enjoyed the sound of rain a lot, at least what he could hear of it in here, muffled by the thick walls of the cave.

He took a deep breath, strengthening himself, smelling the fresh air outside, before heading toward the common room, opening the door, and grabbing the torch. Last night, he'd only carried the torch but hadn't lit any lamps, unlike today. No, today he prepared the room for the others, illuminating the room so they could find their way here.

Finally, he arrived in the chapel and lit all the lamps, putting the torch in its stand. Only then he did he acknowledge Caean, who was watching him. Zanoah could feel their gaze upon him and came close, not stopping for a moment.

"We'll get out of here today," he softly whispered a promise.

The key for Caean's chains was in his pocket, ready to be used. When Zan had unwrapped it from its fabric, he'd felt a soft pain, a burning sensation, in his fingertips, emanating from the material. So far, he wasn't sure why, but he hoped it wouldn't hinder him using the key later.

How much he wished they could communicate right now, but it was too dangerous to use the crown. It would expose all they had done. No matter how hard it was, Zanoah sat down on a carpet and just watched Caean silently. Hopefully, the others would hurry.

Caean was watching him as well, and he felt a bond he never had with anyone before, not like with his brother or Julyen. It was like he and Caean belonged together. He didn't even mind being used to free Caean; he was happy to follow their wishes and do as they pleased. His gut told him it was right to help them escape, but another little voice asked him if he might try to keep them chained to himself as well. Where did this voice come from? Zanoah didn't want to acknowledge it and was glad he heard other voices coming from the corridor. It was a welcome distraction.

One gaze at Caean revealed their eyes were closed again, disconnected from this world, like they didn't hear or feel what was happening around them. By now, Zanoah knew Caean could feel and hear everything around them but often tapped out when it got too much. It didn't matter to them what happened since it was the same every time, no surprises in these ceremonies.

Finally, the whole community was gathered in the chapel, and Zanoah remembered he had another favor to ask of Kelcie.

"May I go first this time? I'm sure it'll work out then, and I won't take much, I promise."

Sounding as naive and trustworthy as possible, Zan looked at Kelcie with pleading eyes. He had to get to Caean first, otherwise their force wouldn't be enough to escape, especially if any of the others already had their energy inside them.

This time, it took a lot longer for Kelcie to answer, but finally, she nodded.

"Just this once," she conceded.

Zanoah nodded. Just this once indeed…

Kelcie raised her arms. "Let's begin."

While everyone got in position and started reciting their prayer, Zanoah just mumbled along, gathering his courage.

Finally, it was time.

He got up and walked toward Caean, feeling their force radiating like a green-golden glow from them. The moss had grown thicker, but it was still a sickly yellow-ish and patchy pattern. These people didn't really trust in their deity, and it was obvious by looking at them, seeing the pathetic excuse of their prayer's impact.

"I'll trust in your power, your wisdom and your kindness, to protect and free us," Zanoah whispered.

Immediately, he could see the moss growing thicker, losing its yellow color and turning green, covering more of Caean's body. In the same moment, the crown fell into his hands. It felt only natural when he put the crown on his head, the thorns merging with his own hair and skin, keeping the crown in its place. His right hand found its way onto Caean's chest, and as soon as they touched, the feeling of pure energy was overwhelming.

It was as if they had become one. There was nothing to compare this feeling to, not even their nightly planning sessions. Caean hadn't been nearly as energized as they were now. And they were giving all this force to Zanoah, willingly.

He could hear gasps and shouts behind him, but right now, he didn't care. He knew they wouldn't be a match for him by now. When he turned, he could see Kelcie running toward him, screaming "traitor!" It was all a bit hazy. His and Caean's minds tangled; their senses mixed. And it felt good.

When he turned toward the gathered crowd, ready to fight, his senses flared up. Too much! His hearing was enhanced, and the torches' light was too bright in his eyes. Zan stumbled over his own feet, too connected with Caean's mind and still trying to figure out how to deal with this new force inside him. He almost fell to the ground but righted himself. No, he couldn't fuck this up now. He had to get Caean out, had to force his body and mind to comply with his mission.

Two deep breaths realigned his senses, and his gaze landed on the first person storming toward him, blocking her punches mechanically. Without a second thought, Zanoah used his newfound strength, combining it with his fighting skills to incapacitate half of the room, every single person who tried to come for him, except...Vance.

"Now you think you're better than us, huh?" Vance spat. "You're still a coward and a naïve idiot. I won't let you get away with this!"

The young man looked furious, but Zanoah didn't care. He did feel a bit sorry for Vance, but nothing would change how he felt about freeing Caean. And it didn't change the fact that Vance had no chance against him.

Zan blocked the hits Vance tried to land, rather glad Vance's stolen energy was almost exhausted. It wasn't hard to fight Vance. Zan's momentary inhuman strength outmatched Vance's rage-fueled mortal punches. They barely hurt Zanoah. A real fight was much different from training, and Vance had no practice in those.

Now Zan understood how it felt to have such energy, to have no real control over it. With barely a thought, he threw Vance against a wall, and the younger man slumped down onto the floor, coughing and staring at him with hatred in his eyes.

For a moment, Zanoah looked at him but decided he better get out of here, fast. So he grabbed the key and headed back to Caean, ignoring the burning sensation in his fingertips. Caean wasn't alright, he could feel that. Their connection seemed to be getting weaker. There was still energy inside him, but there was no new supply coming in, and he'd used quite a lot during his fight, not being used to the feeling, spending it wastefully.

They had to hurry and get out of here. As soon as Zanoah touched the Luskite chain, his hand burned like he'd touched hot metal. Caean had warned him there might be a slight discomfort, since he harbored Caean's force, but this was more than slight discomfort. It hurt a lot and singed the inside of his palm, like the key had done. But Zanoah didn't care about the pain now. He had to manage holding Caean and unlocking the second chain because Caean was seemingly unconscious now. Shit, something had gone very wrong here.

"If you try to follow us, I'll make sure you regret it," Zanoah warned the cave people. They looked scared, and they better be. He would protect Caean with his life.

For now, he had to get them through the narrow corridor, which wasn't easy at all. In the end, he had to sling Caean over his shoulder and carry them like this, up to the entrance, where he'd stashed his backpack in a dark corner.

He was worried about Caean since it seemed their force was almost gone again, far more than he'd seen the last Protection Day. The moss was almost dead, barely covering their pale skin, and he still couldn't feel Caean's presence, despite wearing the crown.

"Please, don't be dead. Come back to me. I need you. I can't lose you, too."

Zanoah only whispered these words, begging Caean, hoping it would have an effect, but it didn't seem so. Maybe Caean just needed nature around them? It was worth a try. So Zanoah put on the backpack and lifted Caean in his arms, holding them close to his chest, while hurrying outside into the rain.

Back to freedom.

CHAPTER 9

Where should he go?

Returning to Tadena wasn't an option. Maybe he should try the other direction. He'd gone west when he left Tadena. Caean's energy gave him a much better sense of orientation, and he could understand where he was much clearer.

Continuing west was probably the best option for now. Something had to be there, somewhere. After all, the people in the cave had to come from somewhere. They hadn't all been born in the cave. Caean had shown him a few cities from other people's memories. Srale, where Vance's mother was from, was the closest city. But he still had to cross a mountain chain to get there.

From the memories Caean had shown him, he'd seen the cave people leaving their homes for several reasons—escaping an abusive partner or dodging an arrest warrant. He saw them struggling to get to the cave. How they'd been able to cross the mountains Caean had mentioned was still a mystery to him. Some had lost their companions in the jungle as well, unable to deal with the enraged vines using their exhaustion to sneak up on them.

Zan could only hope the jungle was still friendly toward him, like it had been all his life, especially now considering he was carrying the deity of nature in his arms.

The jungle around them was quiet, as it always was. There was no sound other than the rain falling on leaves, soaking the earth, and branches grunting when they rubbed against each other. Caean still hadn't woken up, despite them already walking for hours. They looked worse than in the cave, no energy left inside them, and the moss covering their body had dried up further, revealing more and more sickly pale skin.

Zan worried he'd done something wrong, taken too much energy, but there was no time to stop or think for long. They had to get as far away from the cave as possible before anyone found them.

They had only had one small break so Zan could rest, drink some water, and eat something. It was getting dark by now, and they had to find a place to stay for the night, hoping no one had followed them.

It got harder to find a way through the jungle, to see clearly through the darkening green. So far, the jungle had made way for them, and sometimes Zan had heard rustling behind him. When he turned around, the path they'd taken had vanished, grown over by lush green.

He couldn't just lay Caean down on the ground; he had to find an elevated place, so his companion wouldn't be in the mud. But maybe... He had another idea.

Stopping next to a big tree surrounded by smaller bushes and plants, Zanoah tapped into the force still inside him, asking the nature around him to shelter them and help them keep out of the rain. He didn't force his will on them, merely asked. A feeling inside told him that's how you got the jungle to cooperate best.

It only took a moment before he felt movement beside him, vines forming steps upward, where he could also see them forming a net over his head, big enough for two people. Hopefully, it was also strong enough to hold two people, but Zanoah had to trust the jungle to keep them safe. Otherwise, he'd stay awake the whole night or try sleeping on a big branch, similar to what he'd done on his first trip when it rained.

Carefully, he shifted Caean's weight from his arms to his shoulder, holding them there so he could grab the steps with one hand. He had no intention of falling down the tree, breaking his leg or other bones. One broken arm had been enough.

It wasn't easy to climb upward, but finally, he reached the net and draped Caean on it so they could rest comfortably for the night. By now, the moss was completely gone, crumbling to the ground, and their skin was almost gray.

"Caean, I'm so sorry I did this to you. I shouldn't have tried to rescue you, not if it meant..."

Zanoah didn't want to say aloud what he feared. Caean had given up too much energy and couldn't recover from that. Or the chains had had another effect they didn't know about. How should he know? He was just a coward who'd grown up learning only what his brother taught him.

Dread and fear welled up in him, and the urge to run far away to evade any consequences grew with every heavy breath he took.

"Nature rescued me once. I can't let you die now," he whispered, not even daring to touch Caean at all. Instead, he took off the crown with trembling hands and put it back on Caean's head. At least it stayed there, thorns embedding themselves into Caean's skin, so that was still working. It wouldn't if Caean was dead, right?

His eyes wandered toward Caean's lips, which were still sewn shut. Hopefully, he could hear words coming from those lips soon. Hopefully, Caean would wake up at all. Without the crown, Zanoah didn't have much of a connection to the deity anymore, but he hoped it would help Caean regain their strength.

All the rain pouring down on them had soaked his clothes and also the backpack containing clothes for Caean, if they wanted any. Zanoah wouldn't dare put them on a sleeping deity by himself, not if he didn't know if they wanted it or not. No matter how much they had talked in the last weeks, how close he felt to Caean, they were still a deity and Zanoah merely a human—one who'd never been worthy of much.

The adrenaline of their escape had faded, and now panic took its place. Where should they go? Would Caean even stay with him? Why should they? After all, a deity surely had better things to do than stay around a human. Maybe Caean wouldn't even care about him at all when they woke up. That's what he was used to in his life, people pretending to care for him, at least enough to give him food and shelter, but in the end not giving a fuck about him at all.

All logic was thrown overboard, and Zan just wanted to run; he didn't care where. He just wanted to protect himself from being hurt again. Caean surely would be okay without him now that they were back with their jungle, with nature, and he didn't know how to help them, anyway. He'd become useless to them once they were free.

His breath quickened, and his heartbeat raced, hammering against his chest. His hands were trembling.

Zanoah couldn't bear yet another person leaving him, telling him they didn't really care, and he was a burden. He couldn't bear the thought of Caean pushing him away. He wasn't even sure if the connection between them was real anymore. Had Caean manipulated him to get him to free them?

The moment the thought emerged in his mind, dread filled him. At the same time, hate at himself boiled up. Caean wasn't like other people, and there was no way their connection could be faked. Or could it..?

Why should he be special? He was just a scared idiot who wanted to run away to avoid another rejection.

All these years, he'd suppressed a lot of his childhood and teenage memories. A few of them were slowly coming back, like his mother looking at him annoyed and angered all the time, telling him to get out of the way and to make himself useful. And he'd also tamped down a lot of what he'd felt in the last several years. Though he could pretend it hurt that Julyen was barely home because of work, he'd actually been relieved. It helped him ignore the fact that he was deceiving his husband. All of that and more played on his mind as he listened to the rain falling around him.

While climbing back down the tree, he realized his hands were reddened where he'd touched the Luskite chains. The rain cooled them down nicely, so there was no pain, but he still saw evidence of the metal touching him. Evidence of their escape.

Caean would be okay. They had to be, even without him.

Zanoah didn't know how long he'd been wandering through the jungle, but he was slow. Even slower than before, when he was carrying Caean in his arms. An invisible resistance was keeping him from going any faster. The jungle had grown thicker in front of him, and he almost had to fight his way through it.

He didn't care that the jungle was seemingly turning on him for leaving Caean. He embraced the thought. At last, he'd be one with the plants. He'd fulfilled his mission, freed Caean. What happened to him now wasn't important anymore.

It must have been hours since he'd left Caean, as the sun was slowly rising again. Only a little sunlight got through the thick green above him, but what filtered down illuminated some of the path in front of him.

At one especially thick bush that he tried getting through, he felt a soft touch and a slither entangling his ankle. It was cool and familiar. Looking down, he realized it was a vine holding him in place.

"Get off me. I've got to get...somewhere."

He had no real destination, but he wanted to go, just keep walking and get away from here, out of this jungle. No matter how good he felt here, he wanted to run away from Caean, from the possibility of them sending him away. He didn't want to give them the chance to break him down.

The vine didn't budge and instead tightened its grip slightly.

"I don't want to hurt you," he warned, "but I will."

Zanoah took off his backpack and searched for the stone knife he'd stowed in there to cut through the Luskite thread stitched through Caean's lips. Before he could use the knife, though, a small object fell to his feet: a crown. No, not *a* crown, Caean's crown. Zanoah froze and just stared at it. How did it get there and why? He'd left it secure with Caean, up in the trees. But only Caean could take it off their own head...

Slowly, Zanoah picked it up and held it in his hand, staring at the crown for a long moment. No matter what, he wouldn't find out what was going on without putting it on his head. So he did.

Immediately, the overwhelming feeling of connection and familiarity was flooding him. It was stronger than when he'd left Caean by themself. Their presence was a fluttering glow of gold and green, surrounding him in his mind.

"Zanoah!" they exclaimed. *"I've found you. Please, come back!"*

Caean's voice was still weak, but at least they were awake again. It was good to know they weren't dead, but Zanoah still didn't move, despite the vine retracting from his ankle.

"Are you sure you need me?" he asked. *"I got you out, and now you can heal. You won't have a use for me anymore."*

Zanoah sounded harsher than he'd intended to, but he didn't want to get hurt again, especially not by Caean, whom he'd started to like so much.

"Zanoah, I'm still weakened, and I may need you, but I mostly want you by my side. I don't intend to use you."

The fact that Caean couldn't freely access his memories meant they couldn't know he'd been used all his life and had only said that to calm him. Or they were lying. Whatever the case may be, Zanoah couldn't deny the connection he felt to Caean. He would be dumb to throw this away now that he was feeling real longing for the first time. Wasn't it better to not be alone, even if it meant getting orders again? He wouldn't be completely lost around Caean.

"Okay, I'll come back. Are you still in the trees?"

Zanoah was already heading back in that direction. The rain had stopped, too, so hopefully his clothes and hair would dry soon.

"Yes, I'll wait here," Caean told him before dozing off again.

So, they weren't quite strong again yet and barely awake. They'd had just enough energy to send the jungle to stop him and bring him the crown.

The thought sent a warm feeling through his body. Caean's first thought after waking up had been him, finding him. Would they think like that if they didn't care about Zanoah at all? If they only wanted to use him? It was so hard for Zanoah to figure it out since he had never known real care in his life.

The way back was much faster, and he hadn't even gotten far away. The jungle really had slowed him down good, and soon, he arrived at the trees. Caean was still up in the net of vines, but they were moving a little now.

Although they didn't say a word, Zanoah felt their presence waking up. Vines embraced Caean, slowly lowering them down on the ground. It was quite fascinating to watch, and it looked like the most natural thing in the world.

When the vines retracted, Caean held onto the tree to steady themself. Carefully, Zanoah came closer, stopping in front of them.

"Do you want clothes? I can also try to cut the thread and see if you can talk," he suggested, not relying on their inner voices right now.

Caean just nodded, and Zanoah put down the backpack, grabbing the clothes he'd packed for Caean: a plain tan shirt and dark pants. Since Caean couldn't quite stand on their own, Zanoah helped them get into the clothes. Only now did he realize Caean had scars on their wrists, exactly the width of the Luskite chains. *So many years of pain*, he thought sadly. He wondered if Caean still felt the pain or if they'd just gone numb at one point, but he didn't dare ask such a question.

Instead, he grabbed the knife from his backpack, hesitating for a moment. Knives close to the face brought back unpleasant memories from his own experiences, but this was different. It was to help Caean. One hand carefully held their chin, while the other grabbed the knife. Slowly, cautiously, Zanoah started cutting the thread on one side, working his way through the golden material, until every single strand was loose, and he could pull out the strings, leaving nothing but small holes. A few of them started bleeding slightly, but they should heal fast.

"You okay?" he softly asked Caean, letting go of their chin and watching them. He could only imagine how painful but also freeing it must be to finally be rid of that damn thread.

Caean was overwhelmed, touching their lips with their fingertips, a movement they hadn't been able to do in decades. They opened their mouth, but no sound came from their lips. Caean frowned and tried again, but again, no word, not even a single sound.

"It doesn't work. Maybe I'm still too weak."

No matter how calm Caean sounded, Zanoah could feel their frustration, and he fully understood it. In theory, they should be able to use their voice. He had to find a way to help Caean regain their strength.

At least they were awake again, although they almost looked like a regular human now that they were clad in human clothes and not wearing the crown. Dark rings under their eyes made them look exhausted, and their hair was still wet, the loose strands tangled up.

Still, Zanoah thought they looked absolutely marvelous, and a smile crept onto his lips.

CHAPTER 10

*"W**e didn't really plan where to go after escaping the caves,"* Zan said. *"Where do you want to go? I'll get you there."*

And then they would see what would happen, if they would stay together or part ways when they arrived at Caean's destination. Although Zanoah hoped they'd stay together, he tried pushing that down, not wanting to get hurt once more.

Caean tilted their head a little and looked up into the thick canopy of leaves overhead. The sky was barely visible through it. Zanoah missed it, just watching the stars at night. He'd loved doing so as a child. Back at their little hut, close to the mountains, the jungle hadn't grown up to the rocks, and he'd found some nice spots to see the night sky. But when they moved to Tadena, it became almost impossible to see the sky. The whole city was covered by the dome, and it always distorted the view outside the city.

"You need human interaction," Caean said. *"The closest city should be Srale, at least from what I know."*

Zanoah frowned. He needed human interaction? So far, human interaction had overwhelmed him and gotten him nowhere except into lousy situations, unable to really live, merely surviving on the orders of others. Srale would probably be no different than Tadena, which had been no different from where he'd grown up. No matter how much he craved love, he never got affection, not even when he did what he was supposed to. And saying things like that had only made things worse. Human interaction overwhelmed him regularly, since he rarely caught cues of how he should behave. Whatever he said was wrong and so he had decided to just shut up instead. No matter how much he had craved some love from time to time, he had learned he didn't get affection, not even when he did a good job.

So, he decided not to speak his mind and to just say yes, like he was used to doing.

"Then we should go there," he agreed, already grabbing the backpack again.

His gaze fell upon Caean, who seemed very unstable on their feet. When they stumbled a couple steps forward, Zanoah barely caught them from tripping over.

"I'll carry you. Here, take the backpack and get on my back."

He put the backpack on Caean's back and presented his own back to them, hoping they understood what he wanted. He saw Caean struggling for a moment, pressing their lips together in displeasure, and their frustration seeped into his own mind. Finally, two arms wrapped themselves around his neck, and a weight settled on his back. It was much easier to carry Caean like this than it had been the day before in his arms.

They walked silently for quite some time, and the mood felt weird. An unspoken thing stood between them, but Zanoah wasn't sure what exactly. They had never talked about what they would do after getting out of the cave. In hindsight, that had been a big mistake. They should've talked about it, planned for it, or at least decided if they were going to part ways or not. Right now felt like a bad time to ask, especially since Caean had dozed off on his back. The whole ordeal really had taken a lot of their strength.

After several hours, Zanoah decided it was time for a break. He heard flowing water nearby and headed in that direction, finding a small stream where he could fill the water purifier. He decided there was no reason to wake up Caean and gently put them down, leaning them against the trunk of a tree.

He was hungry by now and grabbed one of the yellow fruits he'd packed, peeling it carefully. Back in the cave, he'd learned which plants gave good energy and would keep him fed for some time. Caean had refreshed his memories as well. Fresh water was also helpful, and he drank two bottles before filling it up again.

In the back of his head, he felt Caean waking up and glanced in their direction. They looked much more vulnerable than a deity should look, at least in his mind. Wasn't a deity supposed to be a being to fear or, at least, respect? Right now, Caean looked more like they'd been dragged through the jungle for days, which was basically the truth.

"After we've arrived in Srale and I've gathered more strength, you'll be free to go. I hadn't expected to take so long to recover."

Once again, Zanoah frowned before turning his gaze away again. So, Caean wanted to part ways with him, too, only use him until they were strong enough to carry on on their own. Although Zan wasn't surprised, it still hurt to be pushed away once again. This was the reason he'd wanted to run away in the first place, to shield himself from this pain.

Despite the crown and their mental bond, Zan didn't understand Caean's reasoning. First, they said he needed human interaction, something he dreaded so much, and now he was free to go? Even with their connection? They sounded almost as confused and unsure as him. Zan just wanted to be with Caean; didn't they understand that?

"What do you want with me?" he whispered, staring at the leaf-covered jungle floor, so quietly that Caean might not have heard it at all.

After a long moment, he heard a mental sigh and felt a barrier crumbling, one he hadn't known existed between their minds. Inside his head, Caean offered him their hand, smiling at him, and when Zan hesitantly accepted the offer, he slid right into the deity's soul.

After crossing the mental distance between them, only a few imaginary steps, he felt Caean open up to him entirely, offering him everything. He felt so many things, emotions that didn't belong to him: fear, embarrassment, guilt, longing, love, insecurity. They weren't so different from his own ones. A bridge had been built between them and he could understand so much more of Caean's thoughts and emotions despite not knowing where exactly they originated from.

Zanoah didn't want to break into their memories and fears without consent, so Caean would have to tell them where these emotions came from themself. He could also feel the same had happened to Caean, that they could perceive his emotions, understand how they were related to them but not where they originated from.

"I don't want to be alone anymore. Please stay with me," the deity whispered, barely audible.

Zan knew how it felt to be alone, he knew the feeling too well. "I'll stay with you," he promised, gently taking Caean's face between his hands and leaning their foreheads against one another.

It was a vow to stay with Caean, no matter what happened. He knew in his heart that Caean would do the same. All the fear he'd felt before vanished. He knew Caean wouldn't use him up and toss him aside. And neither would he.

An even stronger bond had formed between them, invisible and still fragile, but undeniably existent.

Caean's hand grabbed his own, gently tracing the healing burn marks on his palms, so similar to Caean's own wounds around their wrists. This, too, was a vow, a silent promise to heal together and not leave him alone.

They didn't talk much on their journey, mostly because Zanoah still had to concentrate on the way so he wouldn't trip over some vines or roots and cause them both to fall. They were slowly heading west, hopefully getting closer to Srale.

Every day, every night, they were close to each other, staying together. Caean was still sleeping a lot, but when they were awake, they seemed more focused, more *here*.

"Why is it there's no moss covering you anymore?" Zanoah wondered at some point.

When he'd come back to Caean after gathering some water, there hadn't been any moss left on their body, and the clothes had come in quite handy.

"If I'm in a bad situation, it's my last resort cover, so to speak. I knew you had clothes with you, so I didn't bother with it out here. It feels natural to not be covered. I wouldn't mind being nude either, but I feel you're not used to it."

He could get behind that. Although the clothes were a little stained by now, some green here, some brown dirt speckles there, and a yellow sweat stain forming underneath the armpits. There wasn't really much he could do about it, not if they didn't want to stay in one place for at least a day so he could wash their clothes and let them dry.

It was interesting that Caean had thought about him when deciding on clothes, to make him feel more at ease and less anxious. For Zanoah, naked people around him meant he would be confronted with an intimacy he wasn't comfortable with.

"So, you're good with me seeing you naked but not others?"

"Of course. I trust you, but I didn't trust those people back in the cave. I'm glad they had at least a little bit of decency and didn't try...other things besides taking my energy."

Zanoah didn't have to ask what Caean was talking about because he knew. It was a good thing neither Vance nor any of the others had tried to force themselves on Caean, not in a sexual way, at least. Apparently, they still had some manners.

"I understand that. I've never been interested in sex, but..."

Zanoah sighed and struggled with his words. He'd never told anyone about his experiences so far. No one had cared anyway. Being with Caean was different. They listened and didn't judge him. Zanoah trusted them and felt like he could talk to them about his experiences, despite the shame he felt even thinking about them.

"My brother, Shaan, believed that I needed to know how sex worked in order to be useful, to get him information. On my eighteenth birthday, he hired two playmates to take my virginity and gave them more money the longer they kept me...occupied."

They'd slipped him several aphrodisiacs since his body hadn't really reacted to their advances. It was hard for him to get going. He just didn't care for sex. The worst thing had been Shaan grinning happily and telling him he'd finally become a man when Zan had finally been allowed to leave the room, sore and exhausted, humiliated by what had happened.

Even after all these years, nausea clouded his brain when he thought about that very long night. It had taken him hours to feel better, and he used up too much hot water to wash away the feeling. But it never really went away, not completely.

"Your brother was an asshole. No one should be forced to do stuff like that. Ever."

He could feel Caean's indignation, their disbelief about what his own brother had forced him to do, and their relief that he was free now.

A sad little smile crept onto Zanoah's lips. For so long, he'd allowed too many people to step on him, use him for any shit they needed him for. Maybe it was time to figure out what he actually wanted, besides freeing Caean.

"He coaxed me into a relationship—no, a marriage. It was pretty loveless. In fact, I think Julyen was always in love with his boss."

Zan wasn't even sad about it, about his failed relationship with Julyen. No, he was just tired of it all, resignation having settled in a long time ago. His gaze wandered toward the small tattoo on his right ring finger, reminding him of his marriage every single day.

He hadn't seen Julyen much, working mostly at night when Julyen was asleep. By the time he got home, his husband was already at work. They were both rarely in the same place at the same time, only in the late evening hours or on free days. Zan had been glad about it.

He'd had a lot of time to think about their relationship since his banishment, and Zanoah figured they'd both been playing each other since the beginning. He wasn't sure why Julyen had done it. Maybe to help his lover, to impress him, maybe because it had been an order. Zan didn't care. But he now knew something else, something that made him even angrier at this brother.

Shaan had known about Julyen's relationship with the High Chancellor.

Shaan was drinking again, the same as always, his fourth Palm Velour by now. Despite Zan's recent marriage to Julyen Toomer, he was still working the same job, tending the same bar he'd been at for years now.

"What?" Shaan snorted. "You haven't fucked Antias' bitch in months? It's time again, little bro. Keep your husband happy. Remind him who's actually his husband."

Zan had accidentally let slip that their sex life wasn't the best and that Julyen was working late a lot. Zanoah didn't mind. It meant he wasn't forced to pretend to be a happy couple all the time. Instead, he had more time alone to sit in their tiny apartment, staring at the wall since he had no hobbies. Never had. He just enjoyed the silence; it helped him decompress after work.

"I know how hard it is to get hard for you," Shaan said. "Take this."

Shaan gave him a small bottle, inside of which was a swirling, glowing red liquid. He knew what it was, and it brought bad memories back, memories that haunted him whenever he was forced to sleep with Julyen.

"With such a boring husband," Shaan scoffed, "no wonder he's working late all the time."

Without another word, Zanoah grabbed the bottle from Shaan and shoved it into his pocket. To keep Julyen—no, Shaan—happy, he had to do this. Just to keep this charade up.

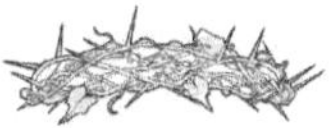

"Zanoah, what happened to your brother?"

Caean's voice in his head was soft, worried even. Why were they worried? No one had ever been worried about him, not like this, not as earnestly as Caean was.

Through their fragile bond, they could feel Zan's emotions, a complicated mixture of grief over his loss and relief at not having to comply and play Shaan's game anymore. Zanoah decided not to tell Caean but instead show them his memories of the night he'd been exiled. Of Shaan dying in front of him.

Caean was quiet for a long time, thinking about what to say. Zan got flashes of what they were feeling, could sense them offering condolences. Then there was anger and, finally, relief.

It wasn't easy to deal with his own emotions, let alone Caean's as well, but Zan was more at ease now about Shaan's death. He was free of him, and no matter how much he hated Cato Antias, at this moment, he also felt grateful to him.

"I'm sorry to say this," Caean said, *"but your brother deserved it. Exactly this death. If what I've seen is just one of the things he did to you, this was a fitting end."*

Hearing it so bluntly had quite some effect.

To have another person telling him that it was okay to feel good about Shaan's death and not mourn him, like a good brother should, made him relax. He'd been ashamed to feel glad about his passing, but it was okay. It was right. Shaan had never actually cared about him or his feelings, just used him to get information to carry out his revenge.

"I know." Zan nodded decisively. "He deserved it."

And what was more, Zan finally admitted something else: he deserved to be free after all these years. It strengthened his confidence and lifted a burden he'd carried around for so long.

That night, they slept high in some vines again, like most of the nights before. It was safest since they couldn't be sure if they were being followed or if there were other people in the jungle. Although Caean should be able to feel it through their connection to the jungle and plants, they didn't want to risk it, not when Caean was still weakened.

The nights before, Zanoah had always kept his distance, slept with a little space between them. Tonight, he felt closer to Caean, even more drawn toward the deity than he had before, like their connection had deepened. So when they lied down on the net of vines, he shuffled a little closer and carefully put an arm around Caean.

Despite being pretty sure that Caean would be okay with it, Zan was still nervous and ready to withdraw at any moment. He felt the spike of surprise in Caean's mind but also their smile as they put their hand on Zanoah's arm, holding him in place. For the first time, Zanoah felt appreciated and wanted. With a warm feeling in his chest, he nuzzled his face in the crook of Caean's neck and closed his eyes, enjoying the warmth of Caean's body so close to his own. Good thing the jungle was cooler than Tadena, especially at night.

He fell asleep rather fast, and so did Caean, but their minds were still connected through the crown Zan wore.

He saw a tall man standing in front of Caean, shrouded in black mist, towering over them. The man had pale skin, almost white, similar to his silver hair. Only his eyes were black, and they were focused on Caean in front of him. Despite the mist partially covering him, Zanoah could make out enough details, like how leanly muscular he was and the little smirk on his lips when he grabbed Caean by their throat, pulling them closer. Zan felt longing mixed with fear radiating from Caean, and the stranger's grip tightened, pulling them closer to him, like they were his property. He heard a little sigh escaping their lips before they met their counterpart, holding onto the stranger's shoulders.

Only now, Zanoah realized he had slipped into Caean's dream and could perceive their emotions. He wondered who this person was. It seemed Caean felt a lot for him, judging by their dream.

With a jolt, he woke up, like he'd been shoved out of Caean's mind, and the door had been slammed shut behind him. Confused, he looked at Caean, whose eyes met his, knowing he had seen their dream.

"Who was that?" Zanoah wondered, regretting his question only a moment later. He had talked about his secrets, and it was only fair that Caean did the same. But Zan couldn't help but think that he didn't deserve to know other people's innermost thoughts.

He felt the deity struggling, wondering if they really should allow him so deep into their memories. In the end, Caean relaxed and let down the walls they had hastily build up.

"You saw Basilios. He is... was the deity of power. And my lover." Caean stopped for a moment, hesitating once again. *"We were together many centuries, happy and bound together by a sacred bond. Until he went mad.*

He started trying to gain more and more power and used humans for his goals. It led to war between many deities and humans as well.

"In the end, the remaining deities forged a pact to slumber and leave this world to humans. I'm not sure if you know how all this works, but many of us can hide deep in the earth, in our most pure and elemental form, slumbering for centuries. That's what myself and many others did. Some others found hideouts, caves or other nooks in this world, undisturbed by humans. We went into a state of trance, hidden where no human could reach.

"It had been the only way to bring peace. Basilios was banished by humans and deities before we retreated, bound by the same chains you already know, forgotten by now. Few humans remember us at all."

Zan had never heard about such a big war, and he wondered if Tadena had even been around back then since Caean mentioned it had been centuries ago. Had other cities survived? Did most people remember deities at all?

It was a crazy story, and some things still confused Zanoah, but he would ask his questions later. Right now, he wondered more about Caean and also this other deity, Basilios.

"Why did you re-emerge? And why did you dream of Basilios now?"

They were very straightforward questions, which Zan normally would never ask, but he wanted to know. If Caean didn't want to answer, they certainly could say so.

"I felt a change, a tug on the bond between Basilios and me, and came out of my trance," they explained. *"Kelcie found me in the jungle, weakened and confused. She took me in, and at first, she was nice, caring for me. Then she learned what I am. I still don't know how she found these chains, but she figured out how to use them on me."*

He could feel Caean's sadness, being betrayed by a person they had considered an ally, maybe even a friend. In the end, Kelcie had only wanted to use them, a feeling Zanoah was all too familiar with.

"Basilios..." Caean sighed. *"I'm not sure. He tried to coax me into bearing his...our child. Something that's been forbidden between deities since time immemorial. Children of deities are too strong and their powers too unpredictable. Even bearing children with humans isn't allowed."*

The look Caean now gave him was one Zanoah couldn't quite interpret. Like they were searching, but for what?

"Basilios and I are still connected through our bond. I should barely feel him, since he's still bound, but...he feels much closer and stronger now. Every step we take toward Srale, I can feel him more."

This was information Zanoah really didn't want to have. Or, rather, it was something he didn't want to be true. So, this deity of power was out there again? Considering Basilios' past, that wasn't exactly a good thing, especially if he hadn't changed and wanted power and war once again.

"What should we do then?" he asked. *"If he's still like you described, do you think he might try the same things again? How did he even escape his chains?"*

He remembered taking them off of Caean very well, although the burns had almost healed by now. Caean's scars on their wrists, however, were still quite visible.

"We can't win against him, not alone," they said. *"Even if I wanted to kill him, I can't. The bond prevents us from doing so. What we can do is to find out where he is and what he's planning, then try to find humans who are strong enough to fight him, like they did last time. We should also figure out how he escaped his chains, so he can't do the same trick again when I put them back on him."*

Caean didn't have to talk about causalities; Zan could feel how worried Caean was. Clearly, if war came again, there would be a great many losses. But was there another way? Zanoah didn't have many ideas—after all, he'd just learned about all of this—but he still wondered.

In the end, he decided to trust Caean and their judgment of what was right.

"Then let's head to Srale and see if we can get information there," he said.

Srale had been their destination, anyway. They just now had a goal for when they got there.

A more dangerous path lay ahead of them, and Zan shivered. Was he ready for what they would find? Were either of them?

CHAPTER 11

How far had they walked already? How long until they finally arrived in Srale? Zanoah had lost all sense of time and wasn't even sure where exactly they were anymore. He knew they were still heading west, but otherwise he was lost in this jungle, which looked the same in every direction. Caean could only judge the path forward from their past experiences, which were many centuries away. During this time, the jungle had changed a lot.

"How does your connection with the jungle work, anyway?" Zan asked. *"You don't really control it, right?"*

Since they were just walking, Zanoah could ask all the curious questions he had about being a deity, what it involved, as well as questions about Caean and their past—as much as Caean was willing to reveal, of course. So far, they hadn't denied him any answers and always tried to satisfy his curiosity. They were awake more often now and could keep up the conversation more easily.

"I don't control it, no," Caean confirmed. *"Most people who know about me, like Kelcie, think I control nature, bend it to my will, but that's not true at all. We're more like...symbionts, two sides of the same coin. We belong together and love each other, but there's no force at all. We take care of each other, and when we're together, we're both at our peak.*

"But we can also keep each other in check," they continued. *"I haven't been around, and that's the reason plants in this jungle evolved into something darker, more malicious. It only got worse when I was captured and used."*

There was a small pause, and Zanoah could feel Caean's hurt. His own anger at Kelcie's and her people's arrogance—the injustice of it all—was heating up again. It took a moment for Caean to relax, but eventually they took a deep breath and loosened their clenched fingers.

"It's okay now," they said. *"I can help the jungle heal and stop it from hurting people deliberately, now that I'm free again. Hopefully, animals will come back as well. They fled when the jungle became too aggressive and saw them as intruders. They need each other to flourish."*

It was a lot for Zanoah to process, but it was interesting as well. He hadn't thought about how all this worked so far. He wondered if it was similar for other deities, like Basilios. How would this symbiosis work for him and power? Zanoah couldn't really imagine it yet.

He did remember one thing, and it was a memory that still confused him to this day.

"When I was a child," he began, *"back when my parents were alive, I almost drowned in a lake. I thought I hallucinated, but...vines grabbed me from the water and saved me. And when I was exiled from Tadena, the jungle never attacked me. How's that possible? Does it have some kind of consciousness and prefer some people over others for no reason?"*

It felt silly to say out loud. He knew he wasn't special. He'd been told that all his life. Still, he'd never been hurt by nature. On the contrary, it had saved him, more than once. Looking back on his childhood now, he'd never been afraid to play in the jungle, the same place his parents and brother feared and fought when they deemed it necessary. Zanoah, on the other hand, had only been afraid to disappoint his family, resulting in him giving up on himself and handing others the power over his life.

"Nature has some consciousness of its own," Caean said. *"I guess it felt the same thing I feel within you. A connection to me, to us. I still don't know where it comes from."*

For a moment, Zan frowned and stared into the jungle, admiring the shades of green and brown and some colorful splashes where flowers grew.

It was beautiful, even after spending day after day walking through this thick jungle. What connection did he have with a deity? He was no different from other people, except for his poor social skills and shy demeanor. Nothing worthy of having a connection to a deity at all.

"I really don't get all this." He sighed. A headache crept up, pulsing under his skull, and he wished he could rub his temple to banish it. Still, his hands stayed tight on Caean's legs, keeping them up on his back.

"Let's take a break. Over there."

Caean pointed toward a space close to a small stream, not too steep or muddy, so he'd be able to get some fresh water from there. Hopefully, it would help with his headache.

By now, their clothes were rather dirty as well, and Zanoah didn't want to think about how they must smell. Several days, maybe weeks, of sweat, mud, and plant fibers coated them. He really should wash their clothes in the next lake or bigger water stream they found. This one was just too shallow to do so.

Carefully, he let Caean down so they could sit close to a tree. That's what they had done every other time they stopped, so confusion rose when Caean grabbed his wrist and didn't sit down.

"Let me get the water," they said. *"Sit, rest a bit. You're exhausted."*

Those sparkling blue-green eyes met his, and he couldn't help but smile a little. He wasn't used to being cared for, not without some service or other being expected in return. Hearing Caean's voice in his head, so soft and gentle, full of honest worry, reminded him that Caean actually meant what they said. It was hard to hide any emotions during their conversations, and by now, he'd learned to trust Caean.

It still felt weird to sit down and watch Caean grab the water purifier from their backpack. That had been his job all this time, to care for himself and Caean as well, making sure they were on the right track, rested and fed.

His gaze clung to Caean's every step as they walked toward the small slope. Sliding down to the water, they held the bottle in the stream. Water filled it up after rushing through the filter on top, giving them clean water to drink.

"You know I can feel you watching me?" Caean said.

Zanoah blushed immediately and turned down his head. He reminded himself how unwelcome his attention had to be. He had only had one relationship, and it hadn't been out of love. Love was a strange concept to him, a feeling Zanoah didn't know from his own experiences at all, and he'd never felt attraction either. Of course, he was able to tell if a person was conventionally pretty, but there were no other thoughts behind such sentiments.

Staring at the earthy floor, he didn't hear Caean's silent approach. Only when their feet appeared in his line of sight did he realize they were already back. He didn't look up, though; he was way too ashamed and also worried.

When he felt Caean's hand on his cheek, nudging him to look up a bit, he resisted for a moment, before he gave up and let Caean direct him. The deity was crouched down in front of him, their gaze worried but still so soft. Zanoah could drown in these eyes, forget the world and everything around him.

"I was only teasing you, Zanoah. What's going on in your head?"

Such a direct question made him even more uncomfortable and insecure, but he knew Caean wanted to know, deserved to know. Still, Zanoah couldn't keep up the eye contact, and instead, his gaze flickered around, until it focused on a tree behind Caean.

"I don't want you to think I expect something, anything, *from you,"* he said. *"Physically or emotionally."*

Zanoah deliberately chose to use the voice in his head. It was easier to convey feelings like this, and he hoped Caean understood what he was trying to say.

"But I don't mind," Caean replied. *"We've been so close the last days. I know you care about me. And I care about you. I'm not saying we should*

jump right onto these feelings or on each other, but why fight it? I've already promised you that I won't leave you. It's okay to care for someone like this."

Surprised and overwhelmed, Zanoah had to look at Caean after these words. His eyes immediately found theirs, which were full of love and honesty. A smile was forming on Caean's lips. The small scars around their lips were still visible but slowly fading by now, a reminder of their imprisonment.

"But what about him?" Zan asked. *"Basilios?"*

All these worries, the self-doubt and the conviction that he only deserved to be a second—or, better, *last*—priority were anchored deep inside Zanoah's mind. He'd never learned any differently, and being confronted by Caean's words and feelings now was overwhelming for him. He had to figure out how to deal with it and how to accept it.

"Basilios and I may still be connected, but it's not out of love anymore," Caean assured him. *"I stopped loving him a long time ago."*

Slowly but surely, Zanoah relaxed, and a smile curved on his lips as well. His anxiety lifted, maybe not completely, but a big part of it was gone. There were still things he didn't know, especially about feelings and relationships, but it was okay. He could learn. He could tell that Caean would be patient.

Especially when he felt a soft kiss being planted on his cheek, intimate but not intruding into his personal space. It was perfect.

After their break, Caean decided to start walking on their own so Zanoah could regain some of his own strength. When he tried to protest, they reminded him they had to start learning to walk again, something they hadn't done in a very, very long time. Every step Caean took became surer, although they still held onto Zanoah from time to time to steady themself.

His worried gaze was often upon Caean, despite their efforts to reassure him they were okay. Zanoah couldn't help it. He cared for Caean and wanted them to be alright.

Their speed wasn't much different from before, when Zanoah was carrying Caean, but the whole feeling was different. It was less eerie and more cheerful, despite the fact they were heading toward Srale, where Basilios might be waiting for them. Caean had mentioned they were being pulled toward the city, that it felt like it was coming through the bond between them and Basilios. But it wasn't just Caean anymore; Zanoah also felt a tug toward Srale.

He didn't quite know where it came from, but it worried him.

They spent their days walking and their nights sleeping high up in vines, cuddling together and enjoying each other's presence. Both of them were gaining more and more strength and, although the sun didn't shine directly down on the forest floor, Caean's skin seemed to have darkened a little. It was less pale and had a healthier tone, slowly turning from an almost lifeless porcelain to a more beige color. It suited them much more, and Caean looked a lot more alive now.

After every break, they switched up who took the lead. The two of them both felt the same pull, and the jungle opened up for them regardless of who was out in front, so they'd been able to traverse it without much difficulty.

Their only problem was a lack of fresh water. The stream had disappeared, and they hadn't found a new source of water in the last day. It wasn't much of a problem for Caean, but Zanoah needed water soon, otherwise he would be in serious trouble. Thankfully, so far, he hadn't perceived any changes in his vision nor balance, not like he had in the past after a too long training session with Shaan. Something was different.

"There's something up ahead," Caean informed him before he could think about that too much.

Though it took a few minutes for Zan to see what Caean had sensed, soon, it became clear to both of them, and it relieved Zanoah so much. At least for the moment. It was a clearing. The trees around here were smaller and further apart from each other, and they were able to see beyond the jungle's canopy. In the distance, mountains towered high above them. And in between where they stood and the mountains began was a big lake, stretching several hundred feet to all sides.

The water looked so clear and fresh, blue-green like Caean's eyes. There were still no signs of civilization around them, which made Zanoah feel more relaxed. They could rest up here undisturbed before they thought about how to get over these mountains. They both knew Srale was right behind this rocky obstacle, could feel the pull getting stronger.

"How do you feel about taking a bath?" Zanoah asked.

He smiled at Caean and crept closer to the lake, inspecting its shore. There were stones all around, perfect to lay their clothes out to dry. He heard Caean's steps following him and had to shield his eyes from the sun reflecting on the still water. He realized they were fully experiencing the sun shining down on them for the first time in months, unfiltered through the trees. It was much warmer than back in the jungle, where the canopy had provided shade.

Caean just stood in the sun, their eyes closed, face lifted toward the sky, a smile spreading across their lips. They were soaking in the sun, clearly savoring every single ray of sunlight they could catch.

Their reaction made Zanoah smile as well, and while Caean enjoyed their little sunbath, he headed toward a flat stone to put down the backpack and take out the water bottle. First things first. It felt so good to drink some of this cool, fresh water. It looked so clear and pure, he probably could drink it without filtering it before. Which was exactly what Caean did. They carefully crouched down and cupped their hands, gathering some water and drinking it from their hands.

"I would like a bath," they finally agreed and nonchalantly took off their shirt, then their pants, wading deep into the water and swimming around a little, diving down for a moment.

Still standing on the shore, his bottle in hand, Zanoah couldn't keep his eyes off Caean. They were so elegant in their movements but still natural. There was nothing weird or forced about them at all.

After he emptied his bottle and drank some of the clear lake water without filtering it beforehand, Zanoah started undressing as well. The sun on his skin prickled and warmed him up immediately. It was so good to feel this again, without the lingering and oppressive heat he'd been used to in Tadena.

Fully undressed, he followed Caean, swimming around a little, getting closer to them. Despite his accident in his youth, he loved water and swimming, especially in lakes like this one. There hadn't been a chance in Tadena, and Zanoah intended to take full advantage of this opportunity. The cool water was welcoming him, surrounding his body and loosening up all the dirt that had collected on his skin and in his hair.

For a moment, he dived into the water, wondering if he could see some interesting things down there. But while there were long green plants, moving in sync with his own movements, there wasn't much else, mostly just rocks.

After he surfaced again, he loosened up the bun his hair had been in for way too long. It was probably quite matted and tangled by now, but at least he could wash it here. Zanoah tried to comb it with his fingers, but the knots were too dense. Hopefully not as dense as Caean's dreads, since he doubted he'd be able to untangle that mess.

"Let's wash our clothes and then I'll help you with your hair," Caean suggested, and Zanoah could already see them swimming back to shore, looking so much cleaner themself, their hair completely wet.

Zanoah followed them and grabbed their clothes, soaking them in the lake. From time to time, his gaze flickered toward Caean, who did the same, scrubbing their clothes and cleaning them as best as they could without any chemicals to really make them spotless again. The little tears and holes from bushes and trees also wouldn't just disappear; they couldn't mend those without a needle.

But they managed to get most of the dirt, and hopefully the smell, out, then laid their clothes on some rocks to dry. After that, Caean came closer and inspected his hair.

"Can you wet it again?" they asked. *"It'll hurt, but we'll get this tidied up."*

Zanoah regretted not having swiped a comb from the cave back when he packed his bag, since it would be much easier to deal with his hair now. He was sorry Caean would have to deal with this mess. Well, they didn't *have* to, but maybe Caean felt obligated to do so? They weren't the first one to try and care for his hair. Vance had done the same thing, back in the cave, and that had ended in a disaster.

"You don't have to," Zan blurted out. *"I'm sorry. I should have cut it shorter. Just... cut it off."*

Caean just shook their head and sat down on a stone, pointing in front of them. Zanoah understood and sat down in front of their feet, his hair dripping wet. Just a moment later, he felt Caean's hands parting a smaller section of his hair.

"Do you want your hair short, or do you just don't want to be a burden? Which you aren't," they assured him.

The question wasn't intrusive or demanding. It was just curious.

"I'm not sure," he admitted. *"I only let it grow because Shaan started complaining I should cut it. He was never a fan of long hair. Too impractical. It was my only rebellion against him."*

Zanoah shrugged and watched the water, which was barely moving since there was no wind. He felt the sun shining down on them, drying their clothes and bodies, warming them up after their little bath. It was almost too hot without a breeze to keep them cool.

"You don't have to rebel anymore," Caean said. *"You can do whatever you want, not anyone else. If you want to cut it short, that's okay. If you want to keep it long, that's okay, too."*

Caean really was so good for his soul. They knew how to help him find himself, how to deal with his insecurities and struggles, which came up often. It was hard for him to relax and trust someone so much. But Caean's words made Zanoah smile, despite the little twinges whenever Caean entangled another knot.

"There's a knife in the backpack," Zan said. *"Can you cut it shorter? Like, maybe shoulder-length?"*

It was a spontaneous decision, but it felt right. Even if he decided differently in the future, it was hair. It would grow again. Right now, it was easier to care for and hopefully wouldn't tangle as much as before.

"Of course."

As Caean got up and reached for the backpack, Zanoah turned his head a little and watched them, once again admiring how silently they could walk. Their hair was untangled by now, at least the loose strands, and their skin was clean as well. It had an almost golden glow to it now, and he wondered if that was the sun on their skin or just something that happened naturally.

"It's not the sharpest, but I'll try to make it look even," Caean informed him, sitting down behind him again before carefully chopping off the first part.

Dark, wavy hair strands fell to the ground, and Zanoah felt relieved, like a burden had been lifted from him. There was so much about Shaan that he'd been carrying around with him. Even his long hair no longer felt like a rebellion but, instead, had become a symbol of Shaan's power over him.

The only other visible part still connecting him to his brother was the sleeve tattoo on his arm, which he'd gotten to always have his brother with him. But that hadn't been his idea, either. Shaan had just decided the design for him and dragged him to a studio to get the tattoo.

Right now, Zanoah tried to only focus on feeling happy to have shorter hair. His head already felt lighter.

"I'll untangle the rest, but it'll be much faster now," Caean said, then kept working on his hair until it was completely untangled. *"Better now, huh?"*

Caean leaned closer, gently wrapping their arms around him, their chest leaning against his back, skin to skin, so close and intimate. For a moment, Zanoah tensed up because the situation was bringing back very unpleasant memories about Vance. They'd been in almost the same position when Vance tried to make him do things he didn't want to even think about. But Caean only hugged him softly, kissed his cheek, then let him go again.

Zanoah relaxed, feeling like he should apologize. He didn't want to react this way to Caean touching him. It felt so much different—so much better—than it ever had with anyone else. But he knew it would take a while to get used to this, to fully trust the deity hugging him. Wanting nothing more than to get to that point, he allowed himself to enjoy being held and hoped that the bad memories would fade the more he gave in to what he felt for Caean.

"I think our clothes should be dry by now. Let's get ready and find a way through there." Caean nodded toward the mountains, towering up high behind the lake.

Zan looked at them with trepidation. Back in his childhood, the mountains had been much smaller, hadn't they? Maybe he was imagining things, or maybe it was because they were at a different location. Zan wasn't sure, but they still filled him with dread.

From where they were sitting, he could spot something white on top of the mountains. Snow? He had never seen snow, only read about it in fictional stories, where seasons were a thing and snow a normal occurrence in winter. Seeing his first snow was so different, much less spectacular than he'd imagined. Maybe, when they climbed up the mountain, he could see it up-close, and it would be more awe-inspiring.

He didn't no how long climbing over the mountain would take and, unfortunately for him, he also had no idea how it would be.

CHAPTER 12

Before they headed around the lake to the mountains, Zanoah and Caean gathered some more fruits, with Caean pointing out the ones that would keep fresh the longest. They wanted to make sure Zanoah wouldn't starve, that he could keep up his strength. It was a good thing only one of them needed to consume food and water, but Zan reminded Caean that they'd to take care not to overexert themself, either.

They packed the bag as full as possible with fruits and filled the water bottle to the brim, hoping they either were able to find another source of water in the mountains or it would be enough for their crossing. Zanoah had no idea how long it might take, and Caean couldn't say either, since they'd never crossed the mountain this way. According to them, the whole mountain range hadn't been nearly as tall all those centuries ago when Caean had still been actively roaming this world.

The first day wasn't too bad. The path was rocky and the trek exhausting, and they had to concentrate on where they put their feet so loose stones wouldn't slide away, causing them to stumble, but still, they made progress. The environment was so different from the jungle. It reminded Zanoah more of the caves, except the mountains didn't have such an oppressive feeling. Instead, they felt like freedom, despite the way getting harder the higher they climbed.

When they took a break and he looked down, Zanoah had no idea how far they had gotten already. He could see the whole lake from here and, behind it, the jungle stretching seemingly endlessly into the distance. It was a beautiful carpet of different shades of green, sometimes mixed with a little brown or some yellow. Zanoah already missed being in the jungle. It had felt good and right, especially with Caean by his side. But it wasn't their destination.

When the sun slowly set, he and Caean settled into a nook of the mountain, protected from wind, which was much harsher up here than it had been down in the jungle. It was a good thing he'd put his now shortened hair up in a ponytail, so it wouldn't hang in his face whenever a strong gust of wind was blowing on them.

He sat down on the cool stone, watching the sunset. How long had it been since he'd actually seen a decent sunset? Certainly never one with such a view. The sun was slowly disappearing behind the jungle's lush green, tinting the sky in orange and deep red shades.

Caean silently sat beside him, watching until the sun disappeared completely and only darkness prevailed. Even then, Zan could still see shapes illuminated by the twin moons' light, stars sparkling in the dark canvas the sky had become.

It was beautiful.

A sense of freedom and hope flushed through his mind and body, and a small smile rested on his face. The world had so much more to give than he knew. And feeling Caean's fingers on his own, warmth emanating from them, only reminded him he wasn't alone anymore.

"We should sleep," Caean said softly, and although Zan wanted to watch the peaceful night sky more, losing himself in this sight, he obliged and turned toward the nook.

When he lay down on the stony floor, he already knew the next days wouldn't be easy. Still, he tried finding a comfortable position, stuffing their bag under his head so Caean could use him as a pillow.

Only moments later, he felt their warm body pressing against his, an arm around his middle and Caean's head on his shoulder. Zanoah smiled, and his hand found its way into the blonde hair immediately, keeping Caean close. It felt right to be so close together, and Zanoah enjoyed every second, despite their long journey, despite the hard floor.

They hadn't talked much today, since they'd been focused mostly on not falling down the mountain, but they didn't have to talk. It was fine to just feel each other, to be together. In their minds, they were connected anyway, with Zanoah wearing the crown like it belonged to him by now.

And although he wanted to talk to Caean, wanted to hear their voice some more before he slept, he fell asleep almost immediately.

"Wake up, Zanoah! Someone's here! Wake up."

After what felt like only moments since he'd fallen asleep, he heard Caean's voice in his mind, forcing him to wake up. It took him a moment to realize what was going on, where they were, and why Caean had woken him up.

They were already sitting up, kneeling, ready to jump on the intruder. Only now, Zanoah saw a person crouching close to the edge, staring at them, only a few feet away. How had they been so silent? He and Caean had made quite some noise while climbing up, so why hadn't the stranger? And where had they even come from?

Zanoah scrambled to get on his knees as well, grabbing the knife strapped to his backpack.

"Don't bother," the stranger said. "I'm not here to hurt you, idiot."

No matter what the person claimed, Zanoah preferred to be prepared and held the knife in his hand, ready to defend himself and Caean.

"Who are you, and where did you come from?" Zanoah demanded in a shaky tone. He could defend himself, even without the knife, but dealing with people and asserting himself verbally? That was something he wasn't used to at all.

He tried figuring out more details of the person, but the only thing he could make out were their eyes—they almost glowed in the moons' light, silvery-white and piercing. He remembered these eyes.

"I've seen you before!" Zan exclaimed, getting agitated. "You were watching me when I fell down into the cave. Or did you push me?"

The eyes unnerved him, but they weren't the only thing that made him wary. They'd been the only thing he could make out about this strange person back then, but now, being so close, he could feel *something* was off about this person.

"Yeah, I've been there," the stranger admitted. "But I didn't push you. That's on you. Was only watching you. Wanted to see if the jungle snatched you up, too. But it didn't. And now you're here with them" The person gestured toward Caean and sighed. "No idea *how* I know your name, but you're Caean, aren't you?"

Zanoah furrowed his brow. How did this person know Caean's name? *"You know him?"* he asked Caean inside his mind, hoping they had more information, but they just shook their head slightly. Damn.

"Who are you?" the stranger asked.

"I'm Zanoah. How do you know Caean's name? Why were you watching me? And why are you here now?"

So many questions he needed answered. There was no way he'd trust yet another person, especially not after they'd watched him fall down a damn waterfall without helping him and were now lurking around them on a mountain. Zanoah wanted to protect not only himself but Caean as well.

The stranger shrugged. "Look, it's a long story, and I'm not sure I understand anything myself. I live around here and sometimes walk around the jungle to see what's up there. I always dodged the cave people because they felt...*weird*. Not sure why I got that impression, but yeah, just weird. Sometimes I'd go look around the area, but I never wanted to go inside. Not with these crazy people. But then I saw you, and you were weird, too, but, like, a different weird.

"Then you fell down there, and I thought, well, you're dead, anyway. But you're not, so that's cool. When I saw you climb up here, I thought I'd investigate some. Find out why you seem familiar, why *they* seem familiar." The stranger looked like they were trying to place something, then shook their head. "Shit, I've got no idea, okay? It gets lonely around here, and people generally don't like me, but you two feel different."

Zanoah relaxed—but only a little. It felt like he was telling the truth, since Zanoah had a similar feeling, like he knew this guy. It wasn't like he'd met him already; it was in more of a spiritual way, like they were connected somehow. It was different from the connection he shared with Caean, and it was quite "weird". That he could agree on.

"Oh, and my name's Ferox."

"What do you make of him?" Zanoah asked Caean while keeping his attention on Ferox.

"He seems genuine," they said. *"I've got a similar feeling toward him like I have to you. It's weaker, but the connection is there. I haven't figured out where it comes from yet. Still, we should be vigilant and get to know him more. He might be able to help us."*

Zanoah trusted Caean's judgment, of course, but he also felt a small sting hearing that Ferox and Caean had a similar connection. He had no intention of being the second choice once again, and yet, it seemed he was destined for it all his life.

"You're...not human. You're a deity, aren't you?"

Ferox's voice cut his thoughts short, and Zanoah watched him now. Slowly, his eyes adjusted to the dark, allowing him to make out more of Ferox. He had dark hair, maybe brown or black, cut short on the sides and a bit longer on top. His expression was more curious than anything else. If Zanoah had to guess, he'd say Ferox must be around his age. He was wearing gray clothes—or, at least, Zan thought they might be gray, since they blended in with the mountain.

"Yes, Caean's a deity," Zan said. "How did you know?"

"Same as everything else. Feeling and guessing." Ferox smiled for a moment before getting up and stretching. "Sun's going to be up soon. You wanna come down and take the easy way through the mountain? We can talk some more then. Or do you prefer climbing up and freezing to death?"

Zanoah didn't even second guess that it would get quite cold on top of the mountain. He'd seen the snow, and he couldn't deny that nighttime here had already been much cooler than it was in the jungle. It had been a good idea to cuddle close, warming each other.

Zan's eyebrows shot up. "Are you suggesting there's a way *through* the mountain?"

"Yup!" Ferox grinned. "But it's hidden. Well, people don't care for what's on the other side of the mountain, anyway."

Ferox shrugged, sounding so lighthearted, like he was already best friends with them. What a weird guy. If there really was a tunnel underneath the mountain, it surely would be much easier to get to the other side. And if Ferox was lying to them, well, they would only lose two days. It was worth a try.

"Let's try it. If he's lying, we can toss him in the lake," Caean jokingly suggested. *"But be vigilant."*

Caean didn't have to tell him twice. He would be.

Zanoah smiled a bit and nodded.

As soon as the sun rose, Caean, Ferox, and Zanoah started their climb down. It wasn't much faster than the way up, and they had to concentrate the same, since they didn't want to tumble down the mountain. Still, Zanoah realized Ferox was much more light-footed than him and Caean, showing them the easiest way down.

Now, with the sun's light out, Zanoah could see him better, make out more details. His clothes were actually a dark gray and of a tighter fit than the ones they wore in the caves but still not as skin-tight as Tadenan fashion. His black hair was short but also completely straight and light, like it floated around his head. Compared to Caean, his skin was darker, more similar to Zan's own one, though it glowed in the sunshine. It was interesting to see new people, especially in real sunlight, not like in the caves, where it had always been half-dark.

Despite Ferox's slimmer build, he had great control over his body and footwork, finding the right spaces to place his feet without struggling at all. It was much harder for Zanoah, who had never climbed so much in his life. He might know physical combat, but climbing was a whole other story.

"You really aren't talkative, huh?" Ferox said. "Thought I'd finally get someone to talk to, but damn, you're so silent, both of you. Haven't heard *you* speak at all."

Ferox nodded toward Caean, who just shrugged, before continuing on their way down the mountain. Hopefully, Ferox really knew another way, otherwise this was a big waste of time and strength.

"Unlike you," Zan said, "we have to concentrate on getting down this mountain alive. We're not used to climbing. Also, Caean can't speak at the moment."

It was still a mystery to him how this worked. So far, they hadn't figured out how to break this curse, as Zanoah thought called it. They guessed Caean's inability to communicate without the crown came from the Luskite-infused thread, but how it worked, they didn't know at all.

"Ooooh, right! Forgot about that," Ferox said, turning to watch them make their way to him from a jut further down. "Yeah, yeah, we'll talk more when we're down."

Zan considered the odd person as he half-slid down the path. Something about Ferox made Zanoah feel drawn to him, but on the other hand, that same feeling made him nervous. Where did this come from, this feeling of being so connected to each other? First Caean, now Ferox. Zan was just a regular, boring human who didn't know much about life at all and wasn't special in any way. So why was all this weird stuff happening to him?

"You can understand them, though, right?" Ferox asked.

Zanoah frowned for a moment. He'd never told their new companion he could communicate with Caean despite them being mute at the moment. Ferox seemed to know or understand it, though he might have just guessed it, since Zan and Caean were pretty much in sync by now.

"Yes, we can talk," Zan admitted. "It's...difficult to explain."

"Cool, you can tell me all when we're down! It's not that far." Ferox jumped down the ledge and caught himself on another one, making Zan worry he was going to break his neck.

He also wasn't sure that he *wanted* to tell Ferox about the crown. Given that the man leading them down the mountain already knew and grasped that Caean was a deity, Zan was sure that he'd be able to understand how their method of communication worked. But he wasn't quite ready to trust Ferox yet. He'd need to learn more about him before he started revealing everything he knew.

"He doesn't seem too bad," Caean said. *"He's chaotic and has a lot of energy, but he's given me nothing to worry about—yet. Let's see what he'll tell us later."*

Zanoah's gaze caught Caean, who didn't look at him but concentrated on keeping their footing and finding the best way down. They were right. So far Ferox hadn't done anything to them, and he seemed okay. *But then, so had Vance,* Zan reminded himself. *And look what happened there.*

When they finally arrived at the bottom of the mountain, Ferox was already waiting for them. He had been a lot faster, and Zanoah had seen him walk toward the lake, resting close to the water on a stone.

"Before we go inside the mountain," Ferox said, "we better drink some water. It's important because dying of thirst is apparently not the nicest death. Not that I'd know how dying feels, but I've been almost starving once, and that wasn't nice. And another time I lost my water while running from guards, so, yeah, that sucked as well."

Ferox was quite talkative, much different from Zanoah and Caean, who were both quieter, even shy. Maybe it wasn't the worst to have someone around who made them talk. Although he wondered what Ferox was talking about exactly. Guards? So he'd been in a city with guards? Zanoah decided to ask him later, when they were settled down. It was already dusk.

He watched Ferox and Caean both getting closer to the water, just dipping their hands into it and drinking from them. Slowly, he came closer, too, and cupped his hands, catching some water and drinking it raw. It still tasted different from the filtered water in his bottle. Cooler and fresher. He took another big gulp before filling up his bottle so he could carry some around.

Ferox filled up an oddly shaped flask. From what Zan remembered from biology classes back in Tadena, it looked a little like a liver made from a rough but flexible material he couldn't identify.

"The tunnel's there," Ferox said, pointing. "My home is, too. Well, kinda. *One* of my homes. I travel a lot. Lucky thing I was around this area when you were here." For a moment, he stopped and frowned. "Well, maybe not so lucky. I felt...*something* here. Something other than them." He nodded toward Caean.

"Zanoah, let's follow him."

Fingers grazed his own as Caean passed him, smiling for a moment, then followed Ferox in a different direction, moving along the foot of the mountains. The touch and voice broke him from his thoughts, and Zanoah followed the deity, keeping close to them. Whatever happened, he would protect Caean with all he had. There was no way he'd let them get hurt again.

He wasn't sure how long they walked for, but finally, they reached their destination. Ferox searched for something in the dark, emerging with a lamp. Inside of it was a candle, which Ferox lighted up with a strange object in his hand. It was small and rectangular, and a small flame emerged on top after Zan heard a little click-sound.

"What's that?" he asked curiously.

"This? Oh, it's a lighter I got in Kheldron," Ferox explained. "They've got such cool stuff there. You ever been to Kheldron?"

Slowly, Zanoah shook his head. He could only guess what Kheldron was, another city somewhere, but he'd never heard of it. The only ones he knew of were Tadena and Srale, and that last one he only knew from Caean's stories.

"Kheldron was only a small village when I went into slumber," Caean said. *"It was north of Srale, closer to the sea. I wonder what it's like these days. Maybe we'll visit it in the future."*

Zanoah very much hoped so. He wanted to see more of the world, see other villages and cities by Caean's side. But first, they had to deal with Basilios. That was their top priority. Everything else, if they survived all this, would come next.

"We have to go through the tunnel. It'll take an hour or so." Ferox looked lost in thought for a second. "Maybe more, if you're not used to the path. And I only have one lamp, sorry. But you can take it. I know the path already, and I see better than you in the dark. Just follow me, 'kay?"

Zanoah only nodded and grabbed the lamp, holding it in front of him. Now they *really* had to hope Ferox wasn't out to betray them. The tunnel in front of them was pitch black. Without the lamp, he would essentially be blind.

"Keep close to me," he told Caean, taking their hand in his own. Just a second later, he felt Caean grabbing him firmly, reassuring him they would stay close.

"I won't be much of help in here," Caean said nervously. *"There's no plants, only rock and stone and darkness."*

Zanoah had already assumed this would be the case. This whole mountain was only rocks and snow. Being inside this tunnel wasn't too different from the caves, except at some places, the caves had holes to let daylight in. Also, there had been more lamps than just one for three people.

Zanoah moved carefully, one step after the other, making sure not to stumble over loose rocks. Caean's hand in his own gave him some reassurance, especially when he barely could make out Ferox's back anymore, his gray clothes melting into the gray of the tunnel. At some parts, he had to duck, being taller than Ferox and Caean, and at other parts, he had to squeeze through sideways, waiting for Caean every time.

All sense of time and place got lost down here, and when they finally emerged, he couldn't say if they'd been down there just twenty minutes or several hours. Zanoah was relieved when he finally breathed fresh air again. He could feel Caean relax as well, breathing deeply in and out for a moment. This had been a tiring journey, but their hands were still clasped together; nothing had been able to break their connection.

"Finally!" Ferox exclaimed. "Gimme the lamp. Don't want you burning down my home!"

Ferox snatched the lamp from his hand and walked toward a small house, more a hut, next to the mountain. It was too dark to make out any details. Zanoah could only guess they were close to a forest, since trees were towering over them. They looked much thinner than the ones in the jungle, and they were standing further apart as well. He'd have to wait to check it out tomorrow, when he'd be able to see more in the sunlight.

For now, he and Caean followed Ferox toward the hut-house, which wasn't much bigger than six or seven feet square. It was big enough for one person, but for three? It would be so crowded.

"Uhm...you can sleep there." Ferox gestured toward a makeshift bed, probably made from straw and some other materials Zan didn't recognize. "I'll take the floor."

The bed felt surprisingly soft when Zan sat down, but he was still uneasy.

"I don't trust him enough to sleep. I'll keep watch, you rest," he told Caean, who had sat down next to him.

They both watched Ferox curling up in the corner furthest away from them—which wasn't very far since the hut was so small.

"No, I'll take the first watch and wake you later," Caean insisted. *"Sleep, Zanoah. You need some rest."*

For a moment, he hesitated before he sighed and silently agreed. Caean wasn't wrong; he really needed some rest, especially after their long day climbing and crouching through the tunnel.

He lay down and made himself as comfortable as possible, his back to the wall and his head on Caean's lap. The deity leaned against the wall, the knife in their hand, while the other hand was in Zanoah's hair, gently caressing him. Even if Zanoah tried, there was no way he could resist sleep now. He was too comfortable and felt too safe knowing Caean was next to him, watching over him.

CHAPTER 13

The night passed by in a moment, without any dreams or worries. Zanoah was glad for all the rest he could get, and having Caean so close made him feel safe and cared for, despite a stranger being close by. He never thought this could ever happen to him, sleeping deeply and undisturbed just because he felt loved and not alone.

Fingers caressing his cheek slowly woke him up, and he whined a little, hiding his face in Caean's lap, trying to escape the sun shining into the hut. It took him a moment to really awaken and realize where they were.

"You didn't wake me!" he realized with a start. *"You were supposed to get some sleep, too!"*

Then he looked up and saw Caean's beautiful smile. How could he ever be mad at them when their smile was like sunshine to him?

"You needed all the rest you could get," Caean replied. *"I'm fine. I've had a lot of rest lately. Our host is outside. He wanted to get some food and check the area."*

Zanoah sighed and slowly sat up, inspecting the hut. Now, in the morning light, he could make out more details. There wasn't much to it; the makeshift mattress, on which they still sat, took up most of the space. Otherwise, the hut was mostly empty, not like a home at all. He remembered the hut from his childhood, which had been much fuller, stuffed with dried fruits in the kitchen, carved toys in his brother's room, and weapons to defend against the jungle. Here, he could see none of that.

Instead, he saw movement in the corner of his eye, close to the window, which was only a hole in the wall that had been covered during the night with a board now propped underneath the window. Slowly, he heard some unknown noises coming from outside, high-pitched and irregular, sounds like nothing he'd heard so far.

"What's that?" he asked. *"What's Ferox doing?"*

He could feel Caean's gaze on him, could feel their emotions, the wonder and sadness. Why sadness?

"You don't know animals," Caean said. *"I almost forgot about that. Tadena has no animals at all. What you're hearing are birds. Little flying things that live in trees and bushes. Come! Let's get up, and I'll show you."*

Animals, right. He know there were animals on the other side of the mountain, but he never expected to find some here. Either plants here were less aggressive and tolerated animals, or the animals were stronger than the plants and had forced their way in here. He didn't quite understand the food chain yet.

There was still so much for him to learn. He wanted to know more, understand this strange world, so he got up and put his boots back on. Just for a moment, he took off the crown to comb through his hair with his fingers, trying to untangle it a little and put it back into a ponytail. As he put the crown back on his head, he smiled at how easy it was to wear it now. The first nights had been quite uncomfortable, but Zanoah slowly learned how to sleep with it on his head, and these days he barely noticed it was there.

He followed the deity outside, peering around him. His rough assessment last night had been correct; they were in a different forest, one in which the trees were much farther apart. There were no vines, either, but there were some smaller bushes, and the ground was littered with fallen leaves. It was a beautiful blend of green, brown and yellow, with Ferox emerging as a contrast in his gray clothes.

"Oh, hey, good morning sleepyhead!" Ferox called out. "Glad you're *finally* awake. Got us some mushrooms for breakfast. Not as fancy as your jungle fruits, but it'll do."

Ferox was carrying a little basket with him, filled with several brownish shapes. Probably the mushrooms he'd mentioned. They looked different from the ones Zan knew from the jungle.

While Ferox walked toward the hut, Zanoah took another look at the forest. There, he could see some small creatures flitting between the trees, high in the treetops. They had wings and were making noises—*"chirping,"* Caean whispered to him—undisturbed by their presence. It was fascinating, and Zanoah marveled at them. How sad that he'd gone his whole life before now having never seen something so wonderful.

Despite the beauty of the forest and animals, there was something more concerning on Zan's mind: the pull toward the west. Srale wasn't far away, and part of him wanted to go there immediately, while another part of him screamed for him to run far, far away. Still, he had to find out more about this land—and about Ferox. Breakfast didn't sound too bad either.

When he turned to join Ferox, he saw Caean standing there, staring toward Srale. Except they looked scared and worried, frozen in place.

"Hey, it's okay," he told them soothingly. *"Nothing's going to hurt you."*

Gently, he touched Caean's shoulder, trying to get their attention. Caean flinched away for a moment before they looked at him, their expression easing a little.

"I'm not so sure about that, but there's no way around this either." There was resignation in Caean's voice, like they'd already given up on a happy ending for themself. *"Let's ask Ferox if he knows more about what's going on in this town."*

Without giving Zanoah another chance to touch them, Caean joined Ferox and sat down next to the small campfire he'd started. Seeing Caean like this, so scared and sad, renewed Zanoah's solemn vow to protect them, to stand between them and whatever—or *whoever*—awaited them in Srale.

For now, he joined the others around the campfire, where Ferox was filling up a small pot with water. After he set it on the fire, he cut the mushrooms into smaller pieces and threw them into the heating water.

"You promised to tell me how you can communicate," he reminded Zan, "so I wanna know now!"

Right, Ferox had asked them the day before, and they hadn't answered.

"It's the crown," Zan explained. "While I'm wearing Caean's crown, we're connected in our minds. I can hear their words, their thoughts, and they can hear mine. If we want to, we can also share memories or feelings."

But right now, he only felt a wall on Caean's side of their connection. They were shielding their feelings and thoughts, offering only their words and nothing else.

Ferox grinned. "That's cool! So, you're speaking for them, huh? How do I know you're telling me exactly what they're saying and not just lying?"

It was a valid point. He *could* just lie and say what he wanted Caean to say, but he'd never thought to do that before.

"If I lied," Zan said, "Caean would give some signals. It's not like they can't make themself known. They just can't speak currently."

"Huh, must be annoying, though." As Ferox stirred the pot, he said, "You know some sign language? I picked up a little in Raco. They're really chill about disabilities."

Zanoah frowned. In Tadena, disabilities were nothing to be "chill" about. Almost no one was born with one, since genetic engineering was very common, and most flaws were erased even before birth. If a person became disabled during their life, there were ways to fix them. So it was quite an insult to hear Ferox call Caean disabled.

Before he could speak his mind, though, he saw Caean smile. Their fingers formed a sign, their thumb and index finger touching each other for a moment.

"Wait, you actually know this stuff?" Zanoah wondered, now quite confused. There was much he didn't know about Caean yet.

"Yes, my best friend Nereia, the deity of seas, is deaf and taught me a lot. I'm not sure if it's still the same, but it's good to be able to communicate more."

Although Zanoah could understand where Caean was coming from, he felt slightly jealous. The last weeks, he'd been the only one able to communicate with Caean, and now Ferox came along and found a way to do so. Once again, he was afraid of being replaced, especially since Caean was also shielding their feelings from him as well.

"That's cool!" Ferox beamed. "Then we can talk a little. I'm better at reading than signing anyway, so it's good I don't have to sign. Uhm, so, how long were you in those caves, Caean?"

Tact was apparently nothing Ferox possessed.

Still, Caean decided to answer since they signed a three and something else. Zanoah could only guess it meant thirty? Maybe he should learn as well, so he could understand what Caean was talking about with others. He also should find some way to break this damn curse, or whatever kept Caean from being able to speak. It would make things easier for them to be able to communicate freely. But it would also change the special connection between them.

"Thirty years?! Damn, I'm sorry. Must have sucked." Ferox shook his head. "Those people are crazy. I've only seen them around the last eight years or so. Didn't realize they'd been around that long." He chattered on as he cooked breakfast. "Never been to the other side of the mountain before. There's so much to explore around here, though I really don't like Srale at all. You sure you wanna go there? Stuff there feels...weird. There's also some sorta cult or something. They call themselves the 'Church of Bas' or some bullshit like this. Weird people. Never seen the leader, though, only some of his followers."

Zanoah's heart raced. The Eye of Bas could only mean one thing. Caean, of course, knew better what Basilios might be up to, but Zanoah could still put the pieces together and understand it was a big problem. Basilios was growing a cult and, if he succeeded and had enough followers, he could do a lot of damage, especially if they really believed in him and gifted him enough energy.

"We have to go there and stop him," Caean said. *"He can't get even more powerful than he surely already is."*

Zanoah could feel Caean's worries, their fear, and he understood it completely. Basilios was the deity of power. If he got even more of it, he could become unstoppable.

"How far is it to Srale?" Zan asked. "We have to get there as fast as possible."

Ferox raised his eyebrows suspiciously. "You don't wanna join this shit, right? If you do, I won't tell you where it is."

"Of course, we don't want to join this maniac," Zan scoffed. "We want to stop him! Before he was banished and sealed hundreds of years ago, he basically destroyed civilization!"

"Cool, 'cause, y'know, we're similar, and I know you feel the same as I do." Ferox leaned in and whispered, "Srale—or him, maybe, no idea—*wants* us to go there. I haven't been there in years because I was worried I might not be strong enough to resist the pull anymore. You shouldn't just throw yourself in there."

Maybe Ferox wasn't wrong, but still, they had to stop Basilios. Zan could only hope he was strong enough to resist whatever weird temptations were waiting for him.

"And what if he's already too strong? You'll just die there, and no one will know," Ferox added.

"He won't kill me," Caean insisted. *"He'd capture me and keep me as his toy. The force inside you two should make both of you strong enough to resist his temptations. I can loan you some energy, so you're even stronger. We have to find out how powerful he is and how many followers he has. And we need to gather allies. You mentioned Tadena is experimenting with enhanced humans. We could go there for help."*

Zanoah thought about all this for a very long moment. There were so many things that could go wrong. What if Basilios actually caught Caean? He didn't want them to be imprisoned. Not again, never again. But they were also right—if they didn't do anything, Basilios might just destroy everything.

He roughly relayed Caean's thoughts to Ferox, leaving out the capturing and keeping Caean as a toy part. Ferox didn't need to know about that right now.

"You want me to go with you?" Ferox shuddered. "Shit, you're crazy, both of you." He stared down into the pot, looking lost in thought. Finally, he said, "But you know what, why not? It's not like I have much to do, anyway. I always wanted to fuck this damn city up."

Alright, so Ferox definitely had some underlying issues with Srale. That was something they could deal with later, if they survived entering the city at all. For a moment, Zan wondered why Ferox had agreed to come with them so willingly, despite the dangers they faced. What all was this strange man hiding? Then he shook those thoughts away, realizing it didn't matter. They needed someone on their side who could show them around.

"Okay, so we'll head to Srale today after we eat," Zan said. "We'll try to find out how much influence and power Basilios has and, if it seems possible, stop him. If he's too powerful, we'll leave and head to Tadena and hope they listen to me. I doubt it, after I've been exiled, but it's worth a try."

He could see how skeptical Ferox looked, and he couldn't blame him. Their plan was crazy, and he knew it. They would probably just die if Basilios found out they were in the city. But they had to try. If they didn't, a bloody, violent history would repeat itself.

After they finished breakfast and cleaned up, it was time to get ready for their voyage to Srale. Ferox had informed them it would take several days to reach the city, so they'd have to camp outside for a few nights. It was nothing Caean and Zanoah weren't used to by now, although the forest here was different.

Zanoah watched Ferox gathering some belongings in the cabin, hiding knives inside the pockets of his clothes, ready to draw one in each hand if need be. Unlike Zanoah, he was used to walking into different cities and dealing with people, being ready for any kind of trouble. Ferox didn't tell them so outright, but every movement was determined and skilled, hinting at him being both comfortable with the trip and used to always being on edge.

"When we arrive, Caean should stay outside the city," Ferox said with his back to him, still rummaging through his backpack. "We're much less noticeable without them."

"What if Basilios still finds us?"

They'd only known each other for a short time, but Zanoah still didn't want Ferox to get hurt, especially since he had no real reason to accompany them into Srale or help them at all. He could've just let them die on their climb up the mountain.

"Eh, don't worry. Doubt he's after vagabonds like us. No idea how all this deity stuff works, but if he can sense Caean, it'll be a lot more dangerous for them." Finally, Ferox turned toward him, his white eyes piercing him. "Whatever's in this city will be a struggle to get away from, for all of us, but mostly for Caean. I've got no idea what connection they have with this Basilios dude, but if they're sure they'll get captured instead of killed, then, I don't know. Maybe they were past lovers or something?"

Ferox didn't really seem to expect an answer and Zanoah wouldn't give him one either. It wasn't his place to talk about Caean's past.

"Whatever. We'll get in there, snoop around, and see what happens." Ferox shrugged and swung his backpack into place, giving all the signals he was ready to leave, head toward Srale. "We just have to hope for the best."

"I won't let anyone hurt Caean, not again," Zanoah promised, unsure if he was saying it more to Ferox or to himself. Through their bond, he felt Caean hurting already, just thinking about meeting Basilios again.

His gaze wandered toward the deity, who was kneeling farther out in the forest. They weren't close enough to hear what Ferox and Zan were talking about, but they were still within line of sight. Their head was bowed toward the ground, one hand pressed flat against the ground.

"Good luck with that," Ferox mumbled, gently pushing him out the door so he could close it behind them.

For a moment, Zanoah considered going into Caean's head to try and find out what they were thinking about, but he knew it was wrong. No matter how close they'd gotten since they first met, Caean deserved some privacy. Which was the reason why Zanoah slowly walked over to Caean and carefully placed his hand on their shoulder.

He knew Caean could feel him getting closer, could read his every move and thought if they wanted to, so it wasn't surprising that they didn't startle. Instead, Caean took a deep breath and looked up at him, holding his gaze. Despite the connection flowing between them and some of their emotions grazing Zanoah's mind, he couldn't pick up on any words or thoughts. That wall Caean had built was still up.

"It's okay, Caean. Let's get going." *I won't pry, but I'm here for you.* A silent promise, sent through their mental link.

The corners of Caean's mouth lifted for a moment, forming a small smile, before they nodded.

"We still have some days to work on our plan," they reminded Zanoah, no sign of insecurity or hesitation in their voice.

"We do, and we'll find out what's going on."

It had become such a habit to communicate with Caean like this, without using his actual voice. Mental communication was much more intimate, and it was harder to hide one's feelings, making it a lot truer and more honest. Right now, it excluded Ferox, which wasn't his plan at all.

"We're ready to get going," he told Ferox.

Caean got up, not caring about the dirt stains on their knees, brown on gray fabric. It was just a little thing, but Zanoah liked this about Caean. Nature was made to coexist with, to gain strength from. It wasn't a force out to kill them, like he'd been taught all his life.

And now, with Caean free, nature could heal. Maybe someday things would go back to the way they used to be, back before humans lived in fear of the jungle, before animals fled from the forest, before storms ravaged the desert outside Tadena. But first, they had to make it through whatever awaited them in Srale.

Zanoah had never seen a forest like this. The trees were taller and further apart than they'd been in the jungle, shooting straight into the sky. Their crowns touched sometimes but still left gaps for sunlight to shine through. As it hit the ground, it left little halos around the brown earth, which was covered with colorful leaves. Zanoah admired their hues—bright green over yellow and crumpled brown—as well as the rich, verdant moss that grew on trees and over rocks. Zanoah would have loved to touch it all, inspect every single plant and enjoy being in this forest.

If only they had time.

Because they couldn't stop and indulge in these little joys, he had to be content with Ferox and Caean explaining about the different plants and how this ecosystem worked. The deeper they wandered into the forest, the more animals and noises Zanoah could hear. Birds were singing, insects buzzed close to them, and it all mixed with the trees creaking in the gentle wind, creating a beautiful symphony.

He'd even seen a group of deer, animals with four legs, brown fur, and big black eyes. One had a big construct on its head—Ferox had called it "antlers." The creatures must've been looking out for predators, or maybe they were afraid of humans, because once they smelled Zan and his companions, they bolted.

Despite Caean being the deity of nature, animals reacted differently to them than plants did, which confused Zan. Weren't they part of nature as well? Although Caean had explained some things about being a deity and how all this worked, the explanations had always been sort of shallow and superficial, probably because Zanoah couldn't understand all of it, even if he tried. It was hard enough trying to understand their mental like, though he'd gotten to a point where he could accept it without thinking too much about how it worked. He figured if he thought about it too much, he probably wouldn't be able to enjoy it anymore.

"This forest is different from the jungle," Zan said through their link. *"It's much...tamer?"*

Zanoah wasn't sure that was the right word, but he hoped Caean would understand what he meant. None of the plants were helping them like they had in the jungle, parting for them and making their way easier, providing them with dry and secure places to sleep. This forest just...existed.

"I haven't asked it to work with us yet," Caean explained. *"There's no need. The jungle was different. It was angry and lonely after I had been chained in its heart. We had to communicate more to calm it down and make sure it knows I'm alive and well. It's not easy to explain. It feels very natural for me, like breathing is to you."*

Silently, they kept walking, following Ferox, trusting him to show them the way to Srale. The closer they came, the weirder the feeling in Zanoah's chest got. It was an aching longing, a pull through an invisible thread, mixed with fear and resentment toward whatever awaited them in this city. He knew he should be trying to figure out what this feeling was, where it was coming from, maybe he to fight it, but he didn't even know where to start.

So Zanoah decided to distract himself, look around some more.

He'd often done this in difficult situations. Whenever his father scolded him for fucking up, Zanoah would distract himself from the shouting and the beatings. To clear his mind, he would run to his waterfall, just sit there for hours on end and watch the trees, listen to the leaves rustling in the wind. The water behind him would splash and gurgle, drowning out the voices in his head still screaming at him, calling him a burden and unworthy.

Right now, he felt similar, afraid to face whatever was waiting for them, wanting to run far away. To distract and calm himself, he kept glancing around, taking in every detail of this strange forest. High up in some trees, he could see small wooden structures, like little baskets made out of twigs.

"What's this?" he asked, pointing up at where a bird was landing in one of them.

"Hm?" Ferox stopped in front of him, looking up as well. "Oh, that's a bird's nest! They gather small sticks and dry moss and leaves and all this stuff to build a nest. That's where they put their eggs after they've mated. Pretty secure up there. Though sometimes squirrels and bigger birds snatch away nestlings. That's hard to watch, but that's how it is."

Ferox shrugged and continued on his way, trusting Caean and Zanoah would follow.

As Zanoah hurried behind him with Caean in tow, he asked, "What exactly are eggs?"

This time, Ferox didn't stop, just looked at him over his shoulder. Immediately, Zanoah felt like he'd asked something really dumb.

But Ferox just smiled at him. "Right! I forgot you probably didn't know. So, y'know how humans reproduce, right? Sex and all that stuff. You push a baby out, and oh, hey, there's a whole new human being."

Zanoah decided not to answer since this discussion could go sideways very fast. He had no intention of having another one of these conversations. The first one with Shaan had been bad enough. He just hummed in agreement. Tadena wasn't really known for natural pregnancies and births, but he knew how it worked. Theoretically.

"Okay, so, birds are different. Instead of growing their offspring inside their body, they lay an egg, or several, which have been fertilized beforehand. Then they sit on the eggs, keeping them warm, until they hatch. After that, it's similar to most other species. Parents feed the baby birds until they're able to fend for themselves." Before Zan could say anything, Ferox exclaimed, "Oh, deer are like humans, by the way! They have pregnancies and births, too. They're shorter than human pregnancies, though."

Zanoah was thankful for Ferox's explanations, for helping him to navigate the world on this side of the mountains better. Despite his initial distrust of the odd man, talking to Ferox was refreshing, especially since he was so excited to share what he knew. And was so...human. Zan really liked Caean, but they had an otherworldly, inhuman aura around them. Having Ferox around made it easier to travel with a deity because he kept Zan grounded.

Zanoah was still bursting with questions, but when he looked over at Caean, they all drained from his mind. The wall between the two of them felt like it was only getting stronger, and Caean's face had become an unreadable mask. Zan wanted to reach out to them, touch them, tell them everything would be okay, but he didn't.

Because, in all honestly, he really didn't know if things *would* be okay.

As the trio walked in silence, Zan hoped that whatever was waiting for them in Srale wasn't nearly as bad as he suspected it was.

CHAPTER 14

"How do you know Srale so well?" Zan wondered, careful not to trip over some unearthed roots.

"Oh, I was born there! I lived in Srale in my childhood. Until my mother and step-father drove me out." Ferox's voice was still lighthearted, but Zanoah could hear a hint of bitterness. "I accidentally carved up their precious baby girl, my younger sister, when we were playing. I've always been called a monster and loved playing with knives."

Ferox pulled one of his knives from his belt, touching the blade with his fingertips. Zan followed him, frowning, a deep worry growing in his chest. Why was Ferox telling him this? And being so straightforward about it, too. They'd barely known each other for a few days, and despite their connection, Zanoah didn't quite understand why Ferox was so open about his past. Zan wasn't sure what to think of him anymore. He was used to the fun, quirky, talkative man he'd first met. This was a side of Ferox he hadn't seen yet—and it scared him a little. He didn't want to get stabbed in the back, quite literally, seeing how much Ferox cherished his knives.

"I didn't mean to," Ferox continued, "but they didn't believe me. They banished me, and I've been a vagabond ever since. Life's easier like this, when you don't have to conform to social norms."

The blade disappeared again, well-hidden underneath Ferox's shirt, where Zan could barely spot a small bulge, a sheath to store the knife.

"How old were you?" Zan asked carefully.

"Twelve. I learned how to survive in the forest pretty fast. Even learned how to tend to wounds. Would've bled out otherwise. You've seen the scars. They made sure I understood never to come back."

By now, Ferox's voice was dripping with hate and resentment for his life and his parents. Zanoah had seen the scars on Ferox's back when they rested to clean up. He'd wondered where they'd come from, but now he knew. Ferox really wasn't much different from him—forcefully driven out of his home and scarred.

"I'm sorry," Zan mumbled, unsure what else to say or if he could trust Ferox's side of the story at all.

"Whatever. One day, I'll burn this fucking town down. It's rotten from the inside."

"Why did you tell me?" Zan wondered.

Ferox looked back at him over his shoulder, a grin on his lips. "'Cause I don't care what people think of me. Thought you'd understand me, though—we're similar. Unwanted fuck ups."

He wasn't wrong about that. Despite wondering if Ferox would betray them, Zanoah pushed that thought away. They had a connection, could relate to each other's traumas, even if Zan hadn't told Ferox about it. He was still their best ally, and Zanoah decided to trust him—for now.

According to Ferox, they still had to walk two days before they reached Srale. Zanoah wasn't sure if he preferred getting there faster or if he should just enjoy every moment in the forest. It had become hard to communicate with Caean through that wall inside their head. Instead, they started communicating with their hands more, if at all.

Their anxiety made Zanoah more nervous as well, especially since he didn't know how he could help Caean. All his life, Zan had never been good at dealing with other people, had always kept away, or been kept away by Shaan, and had no real understanding of genuine worries and struggles or how to be there for someone. Now, he wished he knew how all this worked, so he could be there for Caean, reassure them and just make it easier for them.

He'd also realized Caean could probably still hear and feel everything going on in his own head since Zanoah hadn't learned how to shield his mind. And he didn't even want to learn how to either. He was fine having Caean in his head, being so connected. It felt right.

At least Ferox distracted him a little, explaining a lot about the forest. Zan learned which mushrooms were edible, how to build a nice fire, and how to keep out of the rain that had started pouring down some hours ago.

It was getting dark now, and the three of them were resting under a small, improvised hut that Ferox built with his help. Caean was lying down with their back turned to them and hopefully sleeping. They looked so tired these last few days, in a different way than back in the jungle, when they'd still been recovering from being imprisoned for so long. This was something else, something deeper and darker.

"Zan, can we talk? Like, in private?"

Ferox interrupted his thoughts and made him realize he'd been staring at Caean's back. No matter how few emotional connections he'd had with other people in his life so far, it was different with Caean. He cared for this one.

"Let them rest and come with me, yeah?" Ferox pressed.

He was already getting up, but Zanoah hesitated for just a moment before gently pulling the crown from his head and placing it next to Caean, to keep it safe with them. He'd gotten the hint about "talking in private"—without Caean knowing what they were saying. Although he wasn't even sure if Caean was listening at all these last days. They were completely drawn into themself, only following Ferox and him instinctively, moving their body without any thought at all.

He had no idea where Ferox was heading, but it felt like their new companion knew exactly where he was going, only looking back once to make sure Zanoah was still there, keeping up with his pace. That familiar anxiety was creeping through Zan, and he tried not to think about whether he was about to get stabbed.

Finally, Ferox stopped and started climbing up a tree with wooden slats bolted to the trunk. Why was this here in the middle of the forest? It made no sense. Zanoah frowned, staring up at the oddity before following Ferox up, trying not to think about how far he'd fall if he slipped on the wet wood. Ferox had much more practice with all this and soon vanished between the treetops. How high was this thing?

Gritting his teeth, Zanoah carefully climbed, finally reaching the top, where a small platform and Ferox's outstretched hand awaited him, helping him up. At least the rain was slowly abating, now only small drops here and there.

"From here, you can see up to Srale," Ferox told him. "It's not far anymore."

Ferox gestured out in the distance. Despite the dark of night setting in, Zanoah saw what he was talking about. There was light in the distance, not much but enough to gather that there had to be some kind of bigger settlement there. So, this was Srale, then.

"Why did you want to show me this alone?" Zan asked.

Ferox wouldn't look at him. "Listen, I've only seen this Basilios guy once when I went back there. I didn't tell you 'cause he freaks me out. Back then, he already had some people following him, some teens and some older guys. They looked like fighters or something. We have to be real careful around there. From what I've heard, he's controlling the whole city now, and the people got more aggressive toward outsiders."

While that was useful information, they already knew it wouldn't be easy to slip into the city and find out what Basilios had planned. And it was no surprise he had total control over it. He was the deity of power, after all.

But Ferox still wouldn't look at him. "There's...something else." He swallowed hard. "When I saw him, back then, I...I felt drawn toward him. I now know he's a deity, and maybe that's the reason, but if you and me really are so similar, it might happen to you, too. You have to be prepared for this, yeah? He's got this...this magnetism. Like a promise to make you feel better about yourself, stronger and more important than you ever were before. But there's also something sinister about him. He had this smile..."

For a moment, Ferox stopped, leaning onto the wooden railing of the platform. Zan could feel unease radiating off of him.

"Not a happy smile. It's one I've only seen on wealthy, high-class people who treat others like shit. People who always had it their way and know they have full control. People who will murder to get what they want. "People who think they're better than us. I hate them." Ferox vehemently spit out these words.

Carefully, Zanoah stepped beside Ferox, gazing toward the dim lights of Srale. There was still so much forest between them and the city. "Caean told me Basilios went mad centuries ago, craving power and using humans to achieve his goal. It ended in a big war, and all the other deities left the world in humans' hands after the war. He was stopped once before. He can be stopped again."

"Zan, there's something else I haven't told you. Why I wanted to talk to you alone, without Caean listening." Ferox's deep sigh told him whatever he was about to say, Zan wasn't going to like it. "Rumors travel, and when I was in Kheldron, I heard some merchants talking about the crazy ruler of Srale searching for his mate. There's a bounty on their head, and if anyone can bring them to Bas, he'll make sure to reward them generously. Even if we can get into Srale, I don't think it's a good idea to bring Caean inside the city. If Basilios' followers recognize them, they'll be captured, and I'm pretty sure Basilios won't let them go. That's why I suggested we keep them out of the city."

Suddenly, Zanoah felt cold, much colder than the rain and wind had made him feel before. Dread numbed his fingers and legs, and he barely felt his hands grabbing onto the railing. No way he would let Basilios get to Caean—never again. They'd already been imprisoned for so many years. He couldn't allow that to happen again.

"Caean told me they can't kill Basilios," Zan said numbly. "And I'm pretty sure they're still weakened. If Basilios gets to them…"

He couldn't even put into words what he felt. He wanted to protect Caean, no matter what, and if that meant keeping them far away from the city, he would do that. He'd never cared for anyone so much, and he didn't want to lose them.

"It's up to you if you want to tell them or not," Ferox said. "But I thought you should know. I'll help you protect them, but I doubt we'll have much of a chance against Basilios and his followers."

Slowly, Zanoah nodded, loosening the grip around the railing, trying to get some feeling back into his fingers. A hand gripped his shoulder, and he looked up, seeing Ferox's white eyes right in front of him.

"You're not alone, Zan. I'm right by your side, okay?"

A sudden rush of gratitude and relief flushed his mind and heart, coaxing a small but genuine smile onto his lips. He'd never had anyone to rely on, not like this, someone who cared about what he wanted and how he felt, not just using him to achieve their own goals.

"Thanks, Ferox. I'm glad you found us," he whispered.

Ferox smiled back. "Same, bro. Now, let's get down from here and back to your buddy. Don't want them to get worried about us, hm?"

Zanoah nodded and carefully followed Ferox down the tree-ladder, trying not to look down too much. But when he heard a curse and snap from underneath him, he forced himself to, seeing Ferox dangling in the air, only one hand still holding onto the wooden slat. The one underneath his feet had broken, and his hand was slowly sliding closer to the edge.

"Hold on, I'll get you!" Zan cried.

Carefully but as fast as possible, Zanoah climbed down and put his foot next to Ferox's hand, trying to bend down to get a grip on his arm to pull him back up. Then he heard another crack, right under his foot this time. Shit!

Before they could react, they were already falling, scraping against the rough bark next to them, until a sudden yank stopped their fall. It took Zanoah a moment to realize they weren't plunging to their deaths anymore but dangling in the air, held up by two thin sprouts wrapped around his ankle and Ferox's wrist.

Since he was already hanging upside down, it was easy to spot Caean standing close-by, watching them, while they were slowly lowered down. At least until they were about six feet above the ground, where he fell again, crashing onto the wet earth, Ferox tumbling down in a similar manner next to him. The sprouts hadn't been able to hold their weight for long—just long enough.

Carefully, he sat up and looked at Caean, who came closer, one eyebrow raised, as if they were asking what the fuck they were doing here.

Zan scrambled for an explanation. "Sorry, I...we...uhm, Ferox wanted to show me something."

"Yeah, and that damn wood is rotten by now." Ferox shook his fist at the tree, as if scolding it. "Sorry, Zan. Guess that's the last time we go up there. Maybe, someday, if it's repaired..."

Ferox shrugged and got up, stretching a little before brushing moist dirt and leaves off his clothes. Then he rubbed his reddened wrist and reset his dislocated shoulder with a low whine. Zan checked himself for injuries. He didn't think anything was broken, but his ankle was definitely hurting.

"I'll get back and leave you to it," Ferox said. "Guess you'll find the way back?"

Caean just nodded, waiting for Ferox to go. Zanoah watched him from where he was still sitting on the ground. Now, this was quite awkward. He wasn't sure if he should tell Caean what he'd just learned, but wouldn't it be unfair to keep this information from them? Especially since it was *about* them.

He sighed, still debating if he should tell Caean or not, when a hand appeared in front of his face. It was Caean, offering to help him up. Zanoah accepted the help, holding tightly to Caean's hand, not letting it go even after he was on his feet again. But his gaze still wandered around, too nervous to focus on Caean's face—at least until he felt a soft hand on his cheek, gently forcing him to look into the deity's teal eyes. Despite no words between them, he could understand what Caean was thinking. It made him smile a little.

"Ferox wanted to tell me some things about Srale...and Basilios. It's mostly about...you."

He was nervous about Caean's reaction, but it appeared they had expected something like this. Instead of panicking, they signed him "tell me," one of the easy signs that Zanoah had learned by now.

Slowly, he nodded, still holding Caean's hand, comforted by the deity's grip. It helped keep him calm while he relayed everything he'd just learned to Caean. When he finished, he searched Caean's face for any reaction, and for once, he could actually see some emotion there. Their eyes were wider and their skin paler, a clear sign of worry and anxiety, Zanoah realized as much.

Zan didn't know what to say and was quite surprised when Caean took the crown from their head and put it back on top of Zanoah's dark curls, instantly opening up their mind again. It was only now that Zanoah realized how weird it had felt to not be connected to Caean for a time, being all alone in his head again. He'd missed it more than he could possibly describe.

"I'm afraid," Caean admitted, their voice shaky, eyes now closed. *"But I won't let that stop me from finding out the truth and stopping Basilios again if I have to. I acted too late the last time; I won't repeat the same mistake. I don't want Ferox and you getting yourselves into danger, but I know it's the only way to find out more. So, I'll stay outside the city. But you take the crown and promise me you'll be careful, okay?"*

Zanoah could only nod in agreement, happy he was finally hearing Caean's voice again, this time with genuine emotions.

"I'm sorry I shut you out like that," they said, *"but it's...it's so much. Being so close to Bas again opens old wounds, ones I never wanted to think about ever again."*

Zanoah wrapped his free arm around Caean, pulling them closer to himself, holding them and just being there, like he'd hoped he could be. If someone understood not wanting to think about old wounds, it was him.

"It's alright. I understand. I won't ever pressure you to talk about things you don't want to talk about. I'll be here though, whenever you need me," he promised, feeling a wave of appreciation and affection coming from Caean. It was so good to feel their presence again, fully and without any barriers between them.

"Thank you, Zan. Let's get back to Ferox. You need to rest some more after your little climbing adventure."

The soft amusement in Caean's voice made him chuckle a little. Despite the bad news he'd told Caean, it was alright. They would be alright.

Even while walking back to their camp, his ankle still hurting a little, their hands didn't let go of each other and it felt good to have this physical connection as well, feeling each other's warmth, their presences slowly swirling around in the back of each other's heads.

CHAPTER 15

Regardless of how worried Zan and his companions were, the next couple days after their talk were more relaxed, even if it meant they were getting closer to Srale and, therefore, Basilios. Caean had let Zan inside their head and heart again, easing some of his fears. Having this by now familiar presence in his mind had become a calming and reassuring security he needed, almost as if he depended on it.

"You'll take the crown and make sure you don't get caught," Caean reminded him. *"Just check out the city, find out if Basilios has anything bigger planned, alright? I'll watch you and keep hidden."*

It would be so hard to leave Caean alone at the edge of the city, well-hidden in some trees. But at least they could almost become one with the forest, so no one would stumble upon them by accident.

The crown was now hidden underneath a gray cloth wrapped around Zan's head, so he wouldn't stand out too much. And they were somewhat prepared, as well. In addition to odd gadgets Zan had never seen before, Ferox had some other interesting things in his backpack, among them several knives, for which Zan was glad.

Caean's face was pinched with anxiety, but Zan reassured them, "We'll be careful, I promise."

A small, nervous smile spread over Zanoah's lips. It was the first time he'd actually be doing something so dangerous. Well, the second. The first time had been freeing Caean, an act he didn't regret for an instant. Other than that, he couldn't think of anything. After so many years working in

Shaan's shadow, he no longer saw his job as his brother's spy as dangerous anymore. It'd just been his life.

Warmth embraced him as Caean's arms pulled him closer into a hug. Despite them cuddling at night and holding hands from time to time, they hadn't come closer than that. Zanoah was kind of glad about it. He'd such bad experiences with physical contact, especially more intimate kinds. And he had no longing to get more intimate with Caean, either, despite his affection for them.

This hug was different, and Zanoah didn't want to let go. He wanted to stay with Caean, run far away from this city and keep them safe and at his side. He squeezed Caean close, comforted by their body heat, their scent of earth and leaves, their dreads brushing his cheek. It was perfect.

"I'll take care of him," Ferox promised, reminding him they had to go. The day had just started—the sun was still rising, in fact—and they should use every hour.

Slowly, they pulled away from their hug, no matter how much Zan wished to keep it up. Caean signed "thank you" to Ferox and smiled at him before giving Zanoah another look. He would come back to his deity; he would make sure of this. And he would make sure Caean was safe from his former lover as well.

For now, he and Ferox headed toward the town as he heard the slight rustling of Caean climbing up the tree, helped by some sprouts here and there. They would be alright. They had to be.

"You think we're clean enough for the city?" Zanoah wondered, pulling at his formerly white shirt, which was now gray-brown. They'd washed themselves and their clothes the evening before, but it was impossible to get all the earth and leaf stains out of the fabric.

"Nah, but Srale isn't a high-class society. Many people work in the fields and with animals, so they wear similar clothes. The style is even similar. You got yours from that cave, right? I bet someone there was from Srale and knew how to make clothes."

Zanoah tilted his head a little, thinking about it. Right, Vance and his mother were from Srale. It was possible he was wearing clothes she'd made for herself.

"As long as we'll go unnoticed, we might not have any issues checking out what the Church of Bas is doing here."

"Yeah." Ferox nodded and dodged a puddle in their way. They'd found a small path leading into the woods, one that someone had lined on both sides with logs. Signs of human activity. "And if we're lucky, we'll find some fresh clothes and some food. I got a little money, but it's not much."

It took them about another hour or so to reach the outskirts of Srale. Fields stretched around the city, with all sorts of different plants growing there. Ferox explained what everything was as they passed the fields—beets, cabbages, carrots, peas, and some others he immediately forgot again. There was so much he couldn't retain it all.

"There's so many animals," Zan marveled, seeing a big herd of...whatever animal this was in a big enclosure.

"Yeah, those are cows," Ferox said. "They're used for milk, and some are killed for meat."

What?! He had to have understood this wrong. "Wait, they...what?"

"They're killed." Ferox shrugged. "Most people eat meat, and meat comes from animals. I know there's no animals in the jungle, but didn't you have meat in your city?"

Zan felt shocked and nauseated. As Ferox stared at him in confusion, he stared back in horror. "Of *course* not! Most food is made artificially. Some fruits and vegetables are grown in a green-tower but we don't slaughter innocent animals! That's disgusting!"

For once, Zan couldn't hold back and just said what he thought. It was so wrong, and he couldn't wrap his head around how casually Ferox had said it, how normal it was for him, and apparently these people, to kill and eat animals.

"Zan, focus!" Caean said. *"I know you're not used to this, but please calm down. We'll talk about it later, okay?"*

Caean was in his head with such a force that Zanoah stopped dead in his tracks, clenching his fists. Of course, Caean was right; they had to focus, and he shouldn't make a scene. He'd been trained better than this, to not let his feelings get the better of him or distract him. Shaan had beaten it into him, but as soon as he'd let some feelings into his heart, he'd immediately forgotten his lessons.

"I'm sorry," he mumbled, ashamed. He'd almost jeopardized their mission—*and* had been reprimanded for it by Caean.

"It's okay," Caean assured him. *"Your feelings are completely valid, and I understand. I don't like it either. Can you try ignoring this part of humans for now? Please? We'll talk about it later, I promise."*

Zanoah just nodded once, almost invisibly but apparently enough that Ferox saw it and frowned.

"You okay?" Ferox carefully asked him, coaxing his gaze toward his worried white eyes.

"I will be," Zan said. "Sorry about that. We should keep going."

Despite how upset he was about this revelation, he still asked Ferox to explain the names and purposes of the other creatures they saw. No matter how macabre he thought this to be, he needed to know this information in order to blend in better.

By now, there were more houses, closer to each other and made of reddish bricks. Between them, the street was made of cobbles, not red like the houses but gray and rounder, like they'd been there for centuries already, slowly shaped by feet crossing over them every day. He had to admit, the city itself was pretty. Trees and bushes and flowers were planted in every possible corner, though they were losing their leaves. Ferox had explained the basics of seasons to him, and it was autumn in Srale, which meant it was cooler and the people would have to start relying on stored and imported goods soon.

Most houses were small, maybe two or three stories, judging by their windows, which was different than in Tadena. While apartments there had one sheet of glass as windows, in Srale, windows had some kind of grid in front of the glass. Or were the windows made of several smaller pieces of glass, fitted to the grid? He wasn't sure, and it wasn't important either.

Around them, people were strolling down the street, their clothes wide and flowing, mostly made from fabric in pastels or shades of beige, brown, or gray. Some dresses had flowers or other patterns on them, and they would catch his attention for a moment before his eye was drawn elsewhere. He could also see many kids running around, some playing in groups, some following their parents, while a baby was suckling on its mother's breast. She appeared relaxed, sitting on a bench underneath a tree. Srale was such a different place than Tadena, where people were always covered up in tight clothes and children were kept inside until they were deemed responsible enough to not get hit by the monorail, which was roughly at age ten. And you certainly never saw someone just exposing their private parts out in the street.

Zanoah decided not to think about it and instead followed Ferox toward something he was vaguely familiar with. He'd worked in a bar for and recognized a similar establishment when he saw one. This one had a different vibe, though, with lamps illuminating the whole room instead of creating a cozy atmosphere and men loudly laughing, big mugs in their hands that were surely filled with some kind of alcohol.

They sat down in a corner, and Zanoah realized Ferox hadn't really looked up the whole time, not since they'd entered the city. Neither did he now, looking outside instead.

"Will you order for us? Two beers. Here's the money." Ferox pulled some coins from his pocket, shoving them toward him.

Zanoah frowned, but he could only guess that Ferox was hiding so much because he was technically banished from this town, and his white eyes were quite obvious to spot. Zan had never seen another person with such eyes.

When the bartender finally came to their table, Zanoah ordered two beers, then silently looked around the room. Ferox had tilted his head toward a table on their left, where two men were arguing. While Zanoah couldn't understand what they were saying clearly, Ferox appeared to be listening to their conversation.

"What are they talking about?" Zan whispered, quiet enough so only Ferox could hear it.

Ferox frowned as he turned back to Zan. "They're saying this Bas dude is a good leader, that he made some sort of deal with their neighbors for cheaper imports. They're happy about it."

Zanoah wasn't sure what this meant. He had no experience in politics or trading, but maybe Ferox did? If so, he wasn't explaining, and Zan didn't ask him to.

When the bartender came back with their mugs, Zanoah actually looked at the man, taking in his appearance. He was tall, with muscular arms, a barrel chest, and a fat gut. He had a thick beard and dark hair, and his face was red where Zan could see it behind the massive beard.

"Got business here?" the man asked. "Think I've seen you around."

He pointed a finger at Ferox, who laughed dryly. Zanoah tensed up, unsure of what Ferox was about to do. Zan wasn't sure what to say, either. He didn't know Srale or how people talked here.

"Basilios and his followers went to the next town, the one Srale trades with most, and threatened them. If they don't lower their prices, they might get shot or tortured or similar." Ferox tilted his head, staring right at the bartender. "Am I right?"

Zanoah's body felt cold. Had he guessed? Or had he already known all the time?

"You're even weirder than your quiet buddy here," the bartender said. "Does it matter how he got 'em to lower prices? Nah, it's good for us, so shut your mouth, or I'll make you. Weird ass dude."

The bartender's face had gotten even redder, if that was even possible, and his voice was angrier, like he didn't like being reminded of all the things Basilios had done. Seems maybe he had a conscience and a little remorse as well. Though Zan could be reading him all wrong.

"Let's get out of here," Ferox said. "I think we're not welcome here."

He sighed and slipped by the big man, heading toward the door, barely waiting for Zanoah, who scrambled to follow him. One last gaze toward the bartender revealed almost all the men in the tavern were staring at them now. Shit. So much for quiet and unnoticed.

"Ferox, what the fuck was that?!" he demanded when they were a few streets away, hidden in an alley.

"It's okay," his companion assured him with a smile. "I heard some rumors that Basilios was starting to threaten other towns, and I wanted to confirm it. We now know he's wreaking havoc outside of Srale. Think that's enough for us to try and stop him. What do you say, Caean?"

A frown appeared on Zanoah's face, since he felt used now. He wasn't just a messenger but a person himself. Also, Ferox had made a big fuss, and they'd gotten a lot of attention, which could be a big problem for them. But he didn't say that. Instead, he swallowed down his own feelings and just relayed what Caean told him to say.

"According to Caean," he began, "if he's already started pushing outside of the city, there's no turning back for him. He'll only stop if he's stopped by force. We should regroup and think about finding allies. I doubt Tadena would help, since they don't have any reason to, but we could think about Khelron and Raco. And don't use Zan like this."

Zanoah's frown got a little bigger, since he'd only said what Caean wanted him to and was surprised to hear himself say not to use him. It was weird but also reassuring to know Caean actually cared about him.

"Sorry, Zan, didn't mean to," Ferox said. "Let's see if we can get a look at the church or temple or whatever it is, maybe find out what kind of weapons these people have. And how many there are. Then we'll get back to Caean."

Get even closer to Basilios and his people? What was going on in Ferox's head? Especially now, since some people already knew there were strangers in town who weren't happy with what Basilios was doing. Zanoah thought it was a shitty idea. They should just get the fuck out of this town.

But he didn't say so.

Instead, Zan sighed and hoped for the best. "Alright, you know which way it is?"

For a moment, Ferox looked around, before pointing down the street. "Think it's this way, I've seen some signs."

Of course, there were signs. Everyone had to find their way to the temple, right? Zan scoffed. What an egocentric guy this Basilios was. He sighed and started following Ferox once again. When they finally saw a sign saying, "Church of Bas, 300ft," they slowed down to find a spot they could spy from better.

They were carefully wandering through a small alley, trying to figure out how to spot the temple without getting caught, when a person blocked their way, a gun in their hands. Zan's heart pounded as he heard steps behind him, and before he could even turn around, he felt a thud on his head and everything went black.

CHAPTER 16

Loud voices around him were talking harshly, interrupted by laughter and someone touching his cheek. Zanoah felt a hand grabbing onto his chin and turning his head upward. Slowly, he opened his eyes. His head hurt, and the light made him squeeze his eyes shut again for a moment. Then he blinked and tried to figure out what was going on.

In front of him, a woman with amber skin and eyes similar to his stared at him—no, not at him but at the scar on his cheek. He'd almost forgotten about it these last few weeks. Caean and Ferox didn't care about his mark of exile, and they were the only people he was ever around.

"Look who's awake," the woman said. "Your buddy came around a bit faster. Bas will be so glad to see you two."

She grinned at him and got up, making him realize he was sitting on the ground, unable to move. His arms were chained behind him to something that pressed hard against his back. He had so many questions. Where was he? What happened? And where was Ferox?

Worried, he looked around only to find his companion chained to a pillar a few steps away, staring at the woman. Unlike Zanoah, he had a gag between his lips. Thankfully, he looked unharmed.

Despite the shackles lashing him to the pillar, Zanoah forced his body up so he could stand and be at a similar height to the mysterious woman, who was now heading toward an open doorway.

He had no idea where they were, but the architecture was similar to the other buildings in this city. The walls, pillars, and arches were made of that same red brick. A fireplace was crackling behind them, warming his side and arm. On one side of the room stood two big couches, covered in some kind of sleek and slightly shiny material, white furs draped over them. They looked similar to the sheep he'd seen outside in the fields, which Ferox had explained were shorn for clothes and sometimes decoration.

It was only now that Zanoah saw someone else standing near the doorway, a man with a distinct similarity to the strange woman. He bore the same complexion, but his hair, a shade darker than his skin, was cropped shorter than hers. He held something in his hands, which Zanoah slowly realized was a weapon. It looked different from the firearms he'd seen in Tadena—bigger and more deadly but also more crude.

At least Zan still had the crown and could hear Caean's voice inside his head. *"I'm so glad you're okay! I'll get you out of there. Just, give me some time."*

"No!" If Basilios was here, Caean shouldn't get close at all. It would only get worse if they did. *"Stay where you are, please. We'll be okay and figure something out. Let's just wait and hear what he wants first, okay?"* Zanoah suggested, hoping Caean would give him and Ferox some time to find a way and get out of here.

He felt the deity struggling with this idea, but finally, Caean agreed, keeping quiet for now. Despite their presence being only a shimmer in a corner of his mind, their anxiety was palpable through their connection, and Zan knew he had to keep calm for both of their sakes. No need to worry Caean even more.

His attention shifted toward the door, where he could hear voices again. One belonged to the woman, and the other... He immediately knew it was Basilios when he saw him. Not only had he seen him in Caean's memories, but his aura couldn't belong to anyone but a deity. While Caean's aura felt calm and refreshing, Basilios' seemed to devour Zan whole. It felt like it would pull him right in, covering his mind and soul in a black mist. If Zan looked at him for too long, he started to worry he'd never see the sun again.

Still, Basilios was a sight to behold. A single black metallic band framed white, combed-back hair and made Zanoah wonder if every deity had some kind of crown. His clothes were simple but elegant: black pants and a thick jacket lined with white fur that was almost darker than his snow-white skin. What made Zanoah most nervous were his eyes. They were staring right at him, black and without any soul behind them—or so it appeared.

"Well, hello there," Basilios said. "You finally found your way to me, my little fledglings. Wondered if I got them all." The deity came closer, turning toward Ferox now, towering over him. He was so tall, even taller than Zanoah. "I felt you around, once or twice. Wondered why you didn't come closer. I know you feel the pull. To come here, to join me, be a part of me."

Almost lovingly, Basilios petted Ferox's cheek, causing Zan's traveling companion to stiffen and stare, white eyes meeting black ones. Zan could practically feel the younger man's fear.

"Good thing you're here now," Basilios continued. "And you brought the other missing one with you."

Basilios turned toward Zanoah, then stood before him in two long strides. Zan could feel his piercing gaze on his cheek, then his head—and Caean's crown. A smug smile slid onto Basilios' thin lips.

"You've been exiled from your home city, haven't you? Been a naughty boy? What did you do, hm?"

Zanoah didn't dare say anything, afraid whatever he said would be wrong and only provoke the man. It earned him a slap on the cheek.

"Speak when you're asked!"

"I...I didn't do anything naughty, only what I was asked," he admitted, his gaze lowered again.

All his training, the obedience smacked into him by his parents and brother, crept back to the surface. Doing what he was asked, not thinking for himself, being a good little tool—that's what he did best.

"Oh, is that so?" Basilios raised an eyebrow. "Never killed anyone? Never hurt someone? Broke a heart or two?"

The deity's chuckle made Zan shiver, but he shook his head. No one had ever loved him, so how could he break a heart?

"You're about to be of some good use, *son*." Basilios' big hand grabbed his chin, stronger than the woman before, forcing him to look straight into those dark, cold eyes. "I see you, Caean, and I know you see me. You care about this one, don't you? Wouldn't have given him your crown otherwise. I know you're close. Come here, my love, and I won't hurt them. We can all be a big, happy family instead. You back by my side, and these two being good sons. They deserve to meet their siblings, don't they?"

It took a moment for Zanoah to realize what was going on. What Basilios had just said made Caean's anxiety worse, and for a moment, Zanoah caught a glimpse of them running through the forest.

Zanoah squeezed his eyes shut and tried escaping Basilios' influence for a moment. He had to stop Caean from coming here. *"Don't come here, please!"* he begged. *"If he gets you, he won't let you go again! Please, Caean, don't."*

His pleading was to no avail. The determination and resignation radiating from Caean made him realize, whatever he said, he couldn't change their mind. *"Don't give him the crown. I'm sorry,"* he heard them whisper before the wall between them went back up. No effort of pushing and kicking against this wall brought him closer to Caean's mind again.

Zanoah's eyes opened again, staring right back at Basilios, still so close to him. Ferox had told him he'd felt a pull toward this man, but for Zan, it was the opposite. He just wanted to get away from him, run until he couldn't feel this dreadful aura anymore.

"They won't come. They're not dumb." Zanoah tried to keep his voice strong, confident, but he knew it wavered.

"Oh, of course they'll come!" Basilios said. "They've always been too soft for this world, taking humans in their heart and caring for them. Don't worry, it's not like I want to kill them. No, I've actually missed them."

Maybe he even heard some sincerity there, but Zanoah wasn't sure. He couldn't believe Basilios was anything but a heartless man with no remorse.

"Until they're here, let me introduce you to a couple of your siblings. I think you've already met Sarab and her brother, Sohan. Most of the others will come back in the evening. Until then, you'll get some time for yourself. Sohan, keep an eye on them, will you?" Basilios patted Zan's cheek once again before glancing at Ferox. "Ah, and get rid of that thing in his mouth. Let them talk. That's no way to treat your brothers."

Immediately, Sohan took some steps toward Ferox and forcefully pulled the gag from his mouth before withdrawing again, following his sister and the deity toward the door. There, he stopped, right in the frame, leaning against the bricks. To keep an eye on them, Zanoah was sure of that.

"You okay?" he asked Ferox, still confused and worried about all the things Basilios had said. "Why does he call them our siblings?"

If they could figure out what was going on, maybe they could also figure out a way to get out of here. They needed to before Caean arrived and was bound to Basilios once again. He couldn't allow that to happen.

Ferox was still shivering a little, his light eyes wide open. "I...don't know. You don't feel his effect at all?"

"If you're talking about wanting to get as far away from him as possible, I feel that. But nothing else, no pull toward him."

Apparently, this wasn't what Ferox had expected, since he frowned. For a moment, he looked lost in thought, then he nodded. "That's good, really good. We can use that. I... Zan, I don't know if I can get away from him, not by myself." His voice had gotten quieter, quiet enough that hopefully Sohan wouldn't hear them talking. "You have to get out and stop Caean from coming here. I would only hold you back. I can distract them so you can get out, but we have to get rid of these cuffs."

Zanoah already knew that he couldn't just leave Ferox behind. He had to figure out a way to get him out of here, as well as keep Caean away. And it wouldn't be easy. He wasn't even sure if he'd be able to get *himself* free. Carefully, so as not to alarm their guard, he pulled against the cuffs. Maybe, if he used all his strength, he could break them. It was worth a try.

But then what? he wondered. First, they had to find an escape route. If they just ran, there was no way they would get out of here. Not alive. He knew firearms had a much longer range than they could outrun. As naturally as possible, Zanoah looked around the room, trying to find out if there was a different exit than the one Sohan was guarding. But the windows were bolted shut, with bars covering the glass. The door would be their only way out of here. Maybe, if they rushed their guard? It would be dangerous, but so was this whole situation.

Shaan had trained him in a lot of things but never what to do if he got captured. It was never about how to get out alive, only about how to gather information and be useful—even in death. Time and distance had already shown him just how fucked up his relationship with his brother was, but his current predicament made him even angrier about it. All those years spent training and for what? To die in some strange city at the hands of a deranged deity?

We have to get out of here.

"Can you break your cuffs?" he mumbled, his eyes on Sohan, who was way too relaxed to be their only guard. Had Basilios lied? If they could get his firearm, maybe they could shoot their way out of here...

"Nope," Ferox said, "but I can try picking them open. But it'll take some time."

Did they have time? Not really, but he wasn't about to leave Ferox here, and he didn't stand a chance alone, especially not against a powerful deity like Basilios. After all, deities got their power from prayer, and Basilios had a whole city praying to him.

"Try it," he finally agreed. If Ferox needed some time, he would make sure he got it. "Tell me when you have it."

Ferox gave him a small nod, one he almost missed. As Ferox started picking the locks, Zan turned his attention to keeping an eye on Sohan in case he or anyone else came closer. But no one did. The room and the hallway beyond were silent, and he couldn't even hear any footsteps or voices coming from further away. Instead, he heard a very soft click to his right.

"Zan, now," Ferox whispered.

Zanoah flexed his arms, putting all his strength into it until the metal broke. He stumbled forward but caught himself instantly. The cuffs were still around his wrists, but the small chain connecting them was broken. As fast as possible, he straightened up and ran toward Sohan. Ferox had already tackled him, using his momentary surprise to overwhelm him.

For a while, it looked like he and Ferox had the upper hand. Two against one was good odds, and they were using that to their advantage. But just as he grabbed the firearm from the guard's hands, he felt cool metal pressing against his temple, stopping him dead in his tracks.

"Let it go and get up, very slowly." It was Sarab.

Where had she been hiding? Why hadn't he heard her? Why hadn't Ferox heard her? He was the one with such good hearing, after all. But even Ferox was staring at her in disbelief.

For a moment, Zanoah contemplated just shooting her, but he'd never used a firearm, and it would be for nothing if he got killed immediately afterward. Instead, he slowly put down the gun and got up, still feeling the barrel at his temple.

"Good decision," Sarab said. "Now, hands on your head and move it. You, too. Bas wants to see you, anyway."

Her voice was cold, but there was some undertone to it that he couldn't quite read. Was she happy about something? Sad? It was hard to figure out. The gun was taken from his hands, and Sohan jumped to his feet again, pointing his gun at them as soon as he had it back. There was no choice but to do as she said and slowly walk in front of the siblings, turning down a hallway toward the entrance to this house.

"Ah, so you are rebellious, after all." Basilios stood in the entrance, the double doors wide open, overlooking the streets in front of them. He barely glanced at the two prisoners, saying, "And you're strong. Good genes, huh? You've been trained well. I'll make sure to take that into account next time."

Instead of saying anything, Zanoah kept his mouth shut. It wouldn't make a difference anyway since Basilios was already distracted again. He was staring at something—no, someone—walking toward the mansion.

It took Zanoah a moment to make out the details, but when he realized who it was, his body froze. How had they gotten here so fast? Basilios' aura was almost drowning out all of Caean, a thick black mist covering the green-golden shine of the deity of nature. That's why he hadn't immediately understood who was approaching.

"There you are, my love," Basilios said. "I've waited for you for so long."

He smiled broadly and hugged Caean close, pressing his lips against theirs, while Zanoah could do nothing but watch helplessly.

Zan barely registered what was happening. They'd all been brought back to the same room as before, and he and Ferox were restrained again, this time with more than just cuffs; there were solid chains holding them in place.

Basilios was watching them, one arm around Caean's shoulder, pressing them against his body. Standing next to him, Caean looked even smaller and more timid than they normally did. One thing was clear; Basilios had been right that Caean was too good and soft for this world. They should have left Ferox and Zan here, should have run far away as fast as they could.

Anger and helplessness were brewing inside Zanoah, and he was scared to hear what Basilios had in store for him now that he had Caean back.

"Give me the crown." Basilios held his hand outstretched. "Caean's mine, and I won't have you think you're special."

Zan couldn't do that. He *wouldn't*. Caean had specifically asked him not to give their crown to anyone, and he wouldn't ignore their wish. He could only imagine what Basilios would do once he got the crown and strengthened his connection to Caean. It could be catastrophic.

"I won't," Zan said. "And you can't make me."

The smile on Basilios' lips vanished, and a sharp pain seared across his cheek as the deity of power struck him. He didn't care. He would do whatever he could to protect Caean. In his current predicament, he couldn't do much, but he could at least deny this asshole their crown. Caean had explained that they had control over their crown, over who could wear it, and that no one could take it by force, neither from them nor from Zanoah.

"Gag them both and bring them downstairs," Basilios ordered. "Tell the others to prepare for devotion tomorrow evening."

Sohan nodded in acknowledgment, pulling Ferox's gag back up, while Sarab pushed a piece of cloth between Zan's lips, binding it tight.

In the corner of his eye, Zanoah saw another person approaching. It was a woman of a similar age as Sarab and Sohan but shorter, and her skin was a little darker. He didn't care who she was, only what she was holding. He would recognize those chains anywhere. They were made of Luskite, similar to the ones Kelcie had used to keep Caean imprisoned. These were a little different, two bangles and a thicker ring, all connected by chains.

The woman put the bangles around Caean's wrists and the bigger ring one around their neck, like a collar. Caean winced, and Zan remembered how they'd told him the chains not only burned their skin but also suppressed any of their abilities.

"Thank you, Nanaki."

Basilios nodded at her in acknowledgment but didn't give her any more attention. Neither did he look at Ferox and Zan. Instead, they were pulled away—away from Caean, who looked so defeated. Zanoah could only imagine what they were going through, being right back at where their journey had started, only with a worse handler.

Zan and Ferox were taken down a flight of stairs into a basement, then through a thick metal door, where their chains were attached to sturdy rings in the floor. Their gags were pulled from their mouths again, but it didn't really matter. Zan didn't feel much like talking. He just sat there, despondently looking around him, though there wasn't much to see. There were two blankets on the hard stone floor, but that was it, and there were no windows, nor any other way out besides the metal door.

For a long time, they kept silent, sitting against the wall, staring into the dark. Zanoah didn't know what to say. He only wanted to speak to Caean, to apologize to them and be there for them. But he only hit a wall, over and over again. No matter how hard he tried, he couldn't even get a glimpse beyond it.

"I'm sorry, Zan," Ferox said, drawing him out of his head. "If we hadn't gotten caught, none of this would've happened."

Zan looked over at his "brother," as Basilios had called him. He still didn't understand what exactly that meant. This was his fault. If Ferox hadn't raised a stink at that bar, or if they'd just left the city after he had, they wouldn't have been caught, and Caean wouldn't be in Basilios' hands now. But Zan would never say so out loud. He should've told Ferox to stop, to get out when they had had the chance, but he hadn't.

Maybe he should've let Ferox distract the guards after all, left him here on his own. But that wasn't who Zanoah was. Once he cared for a person, he took care of them and didn't just leave them behind.

"We fucked up," Zan said, taking part of the blame. "And now Caean's paying the price for it."

Being chained down here was the nicer option, honestly. At least these chains didn't hurt them. But Caean's chains were agony for them, and it killed Zan to think about what they were going through.

"What do you think he'll do tomorrow?" Ferox asked. "What's this thing, devotion?"

Zanoah shrugged, not sure what exactly would happen either. But he had an idea. "Back in the cave, Kelcie and her people had a similar thing. They called it 'Protection Day' and held it every 50 days. They prayed to Caean and then took their force. I doubt Basilios will give up his power, though. Maybe it's similar, with all the praying, but it strengthens him instead?"

He could only guess, and he hoped it wouldn't be too bad for either of them. This whole city seemed to enjoy having Basilios as their leader, but he had a sinking feeling that neither he nor Ferox was going to have a good time.

He didn't know how much time had passed since they hadn't said anything to each other in a long while. There was nothing to talk about, only regret and guilt boiling inside his chest. It mixed with a burning hatred toward Basilios and worry for Caean. He couldn't feel either deity at all, and it was impossible to penetrate the wall between Caean's mind and his.

He was only pulled out of his own head when a young woman entered the room, carrying a tray of food and two cups. Zanoah's first thought was that she must be cold in her flimsy dress, especially down here, in the basement. The fabric barely covered her skin at all, and it didn't conceal her belly, either, which was round and very much pregnant.

When she came closer, he realized she was pale in an unhealthy way and had dark circles under her eyes. Immediately, he felt a flash of sympathy for her. Living in this house with Basilios must take its toll, although he didn't know why she was living here if it was that terrible.

"I've brought you food and water," she explained, setting down a cup and plate next to him.

Before he could even think, he'd grabbed her wrist, keeping her close. She was their only chance to get more information about what the fuck was going on upstairs. But there was only one thing on his mind, only one real concern.

"Is Caean alright?" he whispered, worried someone outside, a guard, might hear him.

She looked at him, and he could see she was deciding if trusting him was a good idea or not. Finally, she said, "They are...until tomorrow."

What did that mean? Zanoah frowned, trying to piece together what was going on here. Just what the fuck was this "devotion," and what did it entail?

"Why?" he asked.

"He...wants to make Caean his bride. The real deal this time and not just a replacement that's going to die. He wants them to succeed where so many others have failed. Human bodies can't deal with growing a half-deity baby—at least none before me could."

She smiled bitterly, her innocent, young face showing all the sorrow and sadness she must have endured so far. She was pregnant with Basilios' child, and he wanted to do the same to Caean, use them to breed. Zan remembered what Caean had told him, about Basilios wanting a child with them. So, he hadn't given up on that goal, then.

"This can't be," he gasped. "I have to get them out of here before this shit happens."

No matter what Caean had already gone through so far, Zanoah wouldn't allow for this to happen. He would take Caean far away from here, even if he had to kill Basilios himself. He didn't care. He wouldn't allow anyone to use them ever again.

"If you promise to take me with you," the woman whispered, "I can help you. I don't care where I go; I just want to get out of here."

With pleading eyes, she looked at him. Zanoah contemplated if this really was a good idea. A pregnant woman, especially one already weakened, would slow them down. But she'd offered help. He didn't know what kind, but she certainly knew the house better. And maybe had connections outside the mansion.

He looked over at Ferox, who'd already finished his food and water while they'd been talking.

Ferox nodded. "It's our best chance."

And Zanoah agreed with him.

"We can't go to any of the bordering cities," the woman said. "Basilios has an influence in all of them, and they'll just capture us and bring us back here again."

"Then back through the mountain," Ferox said, then turned to Zan. "Think your city would take us in?"

Zanoah sighed and shrugged. He wasn't sure if Tadena would allow him back in, but it was their only option, and they would be a strong ally if they agreed.

"We have to try," he said.

But he dreaded going back there. Zanoah didn't want to see Julyen or the High Chancellor again, didn't want to dredge up bad memories of his life there. But there wasn't much of a choice. They had to find allies, strong ones, to stand against Basilios. Without them, they would be lost, and he had no idea where else to go.

The woman tilted her head a little, contemplating. "I overheard Basilios talking the other day. He wants to stretch his influence to some mysterious city, Tadila or something, behind the mountains."

Tadila? Zan had never heard of a city by that name, but he'd also never heard about any other city before leaving Tadena. Were there other cities behind the mountain? Or was it just a mispronunciation of Tadena? He couldn't be sure.

"If it's the one you were talking about," she continued, "it might be in their best interest to get ready for a fight. Basilios will find a way over the mountain sooner or later."

Despite only knowing Basilios for a few hours, Zanoah had to agree with the woman. Basilios would find a way. He wasn't the kind to give up, no matter what.

"There's no Tadila anywhere, not that I know of," Ferox said. "The only city I've seen while strolling around was the one Zan's from. It's hidden behind a desert and a storm. What's the name again?"

"It's Tadena," Zan said. "It's possible he's been talking about Tadena, and the name got twisted. We'll go there. They're our best chance." Even if Zan dreaded seeing the people who'd exiled him and killed his brother again. "If we can get out of here."

The woman laughed. "Tadena? Surely, you're joking. That place is just a story, a legend people tell their children."

"I assure you, it's very real," Zan said.

He understood now, though, how Kelcie had known about the city. If Tadena was a legend here, she must've heard about it from Vance's mother or someone else from Srale. But, as with all legends, things get twisted, details get made up. Whatever she'd heard about the High Chancellor and the military, she'd further embellished when she'd lied to him about his parents' deaths. It was all a ploy to manipulate him, just like everyone else.

"What's your name?" he asked the woman.

"Zalika. We'll see each other tomorrow." She smiled at him and Ferox, then left them alone in their cell again.

Hope was such a naïve, fragile thing, and Zan had just gained some of it.

CHAPTER 17

Z alika came back the next day at noon. At least, that's what she told them, since they had no idea what time of day it was. She brought two cups of water and two slices of bread for each of them, just like last time.

"We can't get you out before devotion," she told them. "We'll have to do it afterward. I'm sorry, but your friend has to endure it somehow."

It took a moment for Zan to get what she was saying. If they couldn't escape before devotion, it meant Basilios would attempt to make Caean pregnant. He still didn't know exactly why he wanted to do that, but he understood that it would be bad.

"Basilios requires all his children to be present for devotion," Zalika said. "So you'll get out of the basement, and Caean will be there as well, of course. Lots of citizens will also gather and watch. After it's done, he'll take his children and go get drunk in a pub to celebrate. That's the time we'll use to get all of us out."

Zanoah frowned and put down his cup. Being dependent on a person he barely knew for such an important thing sucked, especially because he couldn't protect Caean at all. He couldn't even communicate with them, despite still having the crown. Caean hadn't lowered their wall at all—there was only silence.

"Is there really no way to get out beforehand? None at all?"

He was desperate, almost begging Zalika for another solution.

"Security is really tight," she explained. "He has not only his children here but also some other guards. Some will stay here after devotion, but we'll be able to handle them. My brother will help us. I wish I could do more, I really do, but I can't. I'm sorry."

Despite everything, Zanoah knew she was telling the truth. They were her only chance of escape, as far as he could tell. She'd be a fool to deceive them.

"I don't like it at all, but we don't have a choice," he agreed with a heavy heart, already dreading whatever was going to happen today.

Zalika gave them a thin smile before she got up and left the basement.

It didn't take long until Sarab and Sohan entered the room, both equipped with guns, which they pointed at Zan and Ferox. Another man was with them, looking at the prisoners almost nervously. He still came closer, gagging them once again and cuffing their arms before opening the chains connected to the ring bolted into the floor.

"You better be good boys and come without struggle. Else we'll just shoot you." Sarab sounded delighted by the prospect, and Zanoah knew better than to provoke her. They would have their chance, soon.

They followed Sohan upstairs and out of the building, Sarab right behind them. From what he could see, the mansion was huge, at least two stories tall and stretching wide. Right before the entrance, some sort of wheeled device was parked, two horses in front of it. He had no idea what this thing was called, but the man who'd changed their chains climbed on a bench in the front and grabbed hold of some straps, which were connected to the horses. The back half of it was open and included two benches as well, one back-to-back with the already occupied seat and the other one opposite of it. But since Sarab and Sohan stopped and told them to wait, it probably wasn't their ride.

Instead, he felt a person approaching behind them from inside the house. Zanoah instantly recognized the aura—Caean. With Basilios further away, he could feel them better, their golden shimmer not drowned by a black cloud anymore. Although it certainly looked like they were. Caean was naked except for the chains around their neck and wrists. Their hands were bound together this time, and their head was lowered, focused on the stone street in front of their feet.

Nanaki and another man he hadn't seen before escorted Caean toward what Ferox informed him was called a carriage, both of them holding guns. Zanoah couldn't help it. Despite knowing it was dumb, he still took a step toward Caean, trying to get to them, but a sharp pain in his hair pulled him back and made him wince.

"Don't you think about touching the goods," Sarab growled in his ear. "That's Bas' property."

His growing hatred for her was hot like the burning sun, but he had to control himself. It wouldn't help anything if he jeopardized their escape plan. He had to keep himself together, like Caean was. It looked like they had completely drawn back into themself, not thinking or feeling, only doing what they were told. Just like back in the cave.

Zanoah could see red marks everywhere the Luskite chains touched their bare skin, from their neck to their chest and down their stomach, as well as where their hands were chained together. He wanted to rip these chains apart and burn them so Caean would never feel this pain again, then take them into his arms and hold them forever, until all the pain was gone.

But he could do nothing. He had to endure, to wait and be patient. He had to watch them suffer right before his eyes.

His gaze followed Caean as they climbed into the carriage and sat down with their guards flanking them. Slowly the carriage started rolling, horses pulling it through the streets, the twins gestured for Zan and Ferox to follow on foot.

The streets were lined with people staring at them, mostly at Caean, apparently not giving a damn about how disgusting their behavior was. Some people even tried following the carriage to get a better look at the person sitting inside. He heard mumbling from all sides, all of it about Caean.

"This new bride looks way older and has no tits either," one person said.

"What the fuck is that thing and why is it bound?" another asked.

A woman sneered as the carriage rolled past, "Is that really the whore Basilios has been searching for?"

Her companion, an older man, said, "It's sort of pretty, and maybe now he'll stop stealing our daughters."

Another woman behind him gasped, "No, you can't say that! It's an honor to be his bride."

The man turned away, muttering, "They die from that honor."

Zanoah clenched his fists. *It?* Caean wasn't an *it*—they weren't some thing to be used and discarded. Caean was so much more than these people understood.

His chains felt too tight. The metal cut into his wrists, and the gag in his mouth made it hard to breath. But it was nothing compared to Caean's situation, so Zan pushed away those feelings. He had to concentrate on what was going on.

When the carriage stopped, he realized they'd arrived at their destination. Ferox had told him about temples, and this building surely looked as impressive as the ones he'd described. This temple was made of the same red brick as the other buildings in Srale, but it towered high above them. Black banners hung across the big building, in front of which more people were waiting.

Zanoah noticed it was mostly adult men who were assembled, their ages ranging from adolescent to elderly. They all watched Caean getting out of the carriage and walking into the building, their guards still right behind them. Zan and Ferox and were shoved inside as well, and pushed right to the front of the building. Several rows of benches sat in the hall, all facing some kind of table. No, something told him it wasn't a table but an altar.

He stared at the weird black wooden thing until Sarab pulled him onto the foremost bench to the left. Ferox was sat down next to him, then she chained them both tightly to the bench. Sarab sat down next to him and Sohan next to Ferox, but Zan barely noticed. He was too busy looking around the temple. Those who had been waiting out front now poured inside, filling the benches. Only the first row was kept empty, like an unspoken rule.

Soon he heard the heavy wooden doors behind them shutting closed, and it got silent inside. A moment later, Basilios appeared from behind a thick, black curtain next to the altar, stopping behind it. This time he was wearing a wide white shirt, loosely pulled together by strings in the front, and black pants.

His black eyes scanned the crowd, stopping on Zan and Ferox, and a satisfied smirk appeared on his lips. "My people, I am glad you could make it. I have wonderful news. We have found my missing children, and they're finally here, in my arms. Ferox and Zanoah." Basilios made a dramatic gesture toward them, and the sudden attention made Zanoah shudder, his skin feeling too tight. "And they brought me something even better. My beloved partner, my lover and bride, Caean. Come here now."

Everyone's attention immediately shifted toward Caean, who still had their head lowered. Their guard shoved them and forced them to start walking down the long aisle between the benches toward Basilios. When they reached the altar they stopped, not even looking up for a moment. Zanoah could almost feel Caean dissociating. He wanted to reach out to them, to soothe their fears, but he couldn't.

Basilios grabbed their shoulders and turned them around, one hand on their chin. He forced them to look up, like he was presenting a pretty gift to the audience. Zan noticed how Basilios skillfully evaded touching the chains with every movement, making sure not to get his own skin burned as well.

"Aren't they pretty?" he swooned, one cheek pressed against Caean's, pulling them into a harsh kiss.

Zanoah fists ached from how hard he was clenching them. He longed to get out of these chains and pull Basilios off of them, take him far away from Caean.

When Basilios guided Caean to lie down on the altar, the crowd started cheering. Zanoah's stomach churned, disgusted by this behavior. Why were people, mostly men, so primitive? If he hadn't known what this devotion was about, now he was certain.

"Pray for me, my people. Pray for power and strength."

Oh, mighty Basilios, deity of power and strength,

We humbly come before you to seek your divine blessings.

Basilios let his gaze wander around the people, grinning when they started mumbling their prayer. While the singsong got louder, he unzipped his pants and pushed Caean's legs apart. "Will you become my bride and bear my child?" he asked.

It was a whisper, barely loud enough to reach the first row, but Zan certainly heard it. And Caean did, too. Their head was tilted to the left, eyes empty and unfocused, almost clouded over.

"Don't worry, we'll get there," Basilios promised.

Zanoah's eyes were fixed on Caean's face, ignoring everything else. They winced as the crowd roared in prayer.

We offer our sincere gratitude and devotion to you,

And we ask for your continued blessings and support.

Of course, he understood what was happening, but he refused to watch any of this. He only kept his eyes on Caean's face, but he couldn't help but notice the thick black mist emanating from Basilios. This prayer was practically strong enough to touch. These people really meant it. They filled Basilios with so much power, he looked like he was overflowing already.

Carefully, Zan stretched his senses toward the mist and tried taking some of it in, like he'd done to gain some of Caean's force. It felt wrong. I wasn't warm and comforting like Caean's force had been; this was dark and sinister, a strength unlike any he'd ever experienced.

As soon as the mist touched him and got absorbed through his skin, it felt a little better. He could sense he was slowly getting the strength and courage to get rid of Basilios once he had the chance. And get rid of him, he would—for the things he'd done to Caean, for using them like this.

He glanced over at Sarab and Sohan, who both were in a trance, staring right at their leader. His gaze wandered toward Ferox, then gasped. His companion had the same look in his eyes as the twins. He was even mumbling the same words the others were. Basilios really had more control over people than Zan had feared. Ferox had given in to his pull.

Grant us the power to achieve our goals

And the determination to never give up on our dreams.

He didn't know how long this whole devotion lasted, but it felt like an eternity. Finally, he heard Basilios' groan, and the crowd cheered even louder. But he could only see the single tear running down Caean's cheek, dropping down onto the brick floor.

How he wanted to tear Basilios apart, rip him limb from limb and make him regret every single thing he'd done to Caean. Zan's chest tightened, and his breaths got shallower. He felt like he was going to black out, and maybe he did because the next thing he knew he was back in the cell in the basement.

It took him a few moments to realize that's where he was. And then a few more to remember that it was okay because that's what Zalika had planned. Their escape would only start now. And he would make sure to take anyone who stood in their way down. He would get to Caean, and he would get them out of here. Even if he had to kill to free them.

Zanoah didn't care anymore.

CHAPTER 18

Zanoah's muscles felt stiff, and his jaw was tightly clenched. He hadn't said a word toward Ferox, who was silent as well. They heard people walking around the house at first, but eventually, it got much quieter. The voices faded away, and the steps stilled.

"If you get in my way, I *will* leave you," he finally informed Ferox in a cool tone. He wanted his companion to know that he meant business.

Ferox narrowed his eyes in confusion. "What are you talking about? Of course I won't get in your way. I want to get out, too!"

Had Ferox even realized what'd happened? Zanoah looked at him and only saw honest perplexity in Ferox's eyes, though there was some annoyance in his words.

"You stared like a hungry animal while Basilios—" Zan cut himself off. He couldn't even put into words what he'd witnessed. "I know it's not your fault, but you're vulnerable to his power, his pull. I'll prioritize Caean, no matter what."

Glaring at him, Ferox asked, "I did *what*? You're just making this up now, aren't you? I know I'm more vulnerable to Basilios' pull, but I would never—"

"You did!" Zan insisted.

Ferox sounded quite pissed, but that didn't change how he'd behaved during the devotion. Yes, he was indeed vulnerable to Basilios and his force, just like all other men around here.

Ferox tried to protest, but Zanoah just shook his head. He had no interest in arguing with Ferox right now; he just wanted to get out of this shithole. And they wouldn't have much time to talk either, judging by the sounds he heard outside the door. Someone was fighting out in the hallway. He just hoped the people on his side were winning.

When the door opened, an unconscious guard rolled into the room, and Zalika stepped over his body, running over to Zan. She crouched down next to him, unlocking his chains, before helping Ferox with his.

"We have to be quick," she said. "They went out celebrating, but there are still some guards in the house."

A strange man dragged the guard into the room, grabbing his gun and pocketing it. Zan and Ferox edged away, watching the man warily.

"My brother, Helio," Zalika explained, seeing where they were looking.

Zan could see the resemblance now. They both had the same dark brown hair and dark skin. Even their noses were similar. Helio just looked even younger than Zalika, and was smaller, too.

"There's one guard still upstairs in front of the bedroom and two near the kitchen," Helio said. "Here, catch."

He threw a small metal key, and Zanoah could barely catch it fast enough.

"Go upstairs and get your deity," Zalika said. "They're in the bedroom. We'll take care of the guards downstairs and wait at the stairs for you. But hurry. It won't take long before someone reports what we're doing. These fucking people are way too devout."

Zanoah only nodded and followed Helio and Zalika upstairs, as quiet as possible.

"Here, take this."

Helio offered him a blade, a kitchen knife. Zan frowned at it before taking the knife. At least it was some kind of weapon.

"Here's the guard's gun, too," Helio said before motioning upstairs. "It might be helpful."

While Ferox followed Helio, listening to his whispered instructions, Zanoah crept up the stairs and carefully peeked around the corner. He could spot the guard, luckily with his back to him, looking out the window at the end of the hallway. Zanoah used the chance to sneak up on the guard and use the knife, cutting his throat. He had never killed before, but to protect Caean, he would do whatever was necessary. He could at least ensure the guard wouldn't be a problem anymore.

He grabbed the gun and slung it over his shoulder, then looked around for the bedroom. There were several rooms up here, and he had no idea which one Caean was in. He tried every door, getting more and more worried when he still couldn't find what he was looking for. But finally, he found a door that wouldn't open.

This had to be the one. He slid the key into the lock and turned it, hearing a satisfying *click*. Carefully, he opened the door, a little afraid of what he'd find behind it. Still, he had to get Caean, had to hold them and get them to safety.

The big bed filled almost the whole room and Caean looked so damn small lying on top of it. They were on their side, their back to the door, slightly curled up and staring at the wall. No one had cared to give them any clothes, but at least their hands weren't bound so tightly anymore.

"Caean? It's me, Zanoah. I'll get you out of here."

Slowly, he walked around the bed and crouched down in front of Caean, touching their cheek, but he got no reaction. Nothing, not even a blink. How thick were the walls Caean was hiding behind? There was no time to think about it now; he just needed to get Caean out of here.

Zanoah grabbed a thin blanket and wrapped Caean in it. Their lack of movement was worrying. It was almost like wrapping up a corpse. No, he shouldn't think of it like that. He lifted Caean up in his arms, gently cradling them against his chest, and left the bedroom to head downstairs. Hopefully, the others were ready to get the fuck out of here.

He was still careful, since Helio had mentioned two other guards, but since Ferox was already awaiting him at the stairway, he guessed they had been dealt with already. No words were exchanged between them. Ferox just looked at the wrapped bundle in his arms and nodded, heading toward the back of the house. Zanoah noticed he was holding a gun in his hands in addition to the two knives strapped to his belt.

Helio was waiting for them at a smaller door in the kitchen. "There are horses outside," he informed them. "We have to hurry and get out, fast."

Zanoah glimpsed a person lying motionless in one corner and assumed it was one of the other guards. "What's the plan?" he asked.

"You'll take one horse with the deity," Helio said. "I'll guide you out of here, but I don't know where to go exactly."

"I can lead us. I know the way to the tunnel," Ferox said quietly.

Zanoah had noticed he was more silent and reserved than normal. He was used to Ferox being bubbly and talkative, but now he was quiet and focused. Just for a moment, Zan wondered if Ferox had gone into combat mode or if their conversation earlier was still playing on his mind.

Helio just nodded and opened the door, checking left and right, before heading outside and guiding them toward four horses waiting hidden behind the next house. As soon as they started running, people would see them, and there wouldn't be any cover on these animals because they were just too big to go unnoticed. At least they were fast.

With Ferox's and Helio's help, Zan lifted Caean onto the horse, sitting down behind them, one arm firmly around their chest to hold them close, reigns in the other one. It felt weird to sit on a living, breathing animal, to use it as transportation, but he couldn't debate on the morality of it right now. Instead, he had to make sure not to slide down the broad back, so he grabbed the mane a little to keep the beast steady.

Before he was really ready, his horse started moving, following the other three, moving faster and faster. He couldn't even think about giving any directions and was glad his horse was keeping up with the others. As they raced through the streets, he clung to the mane with one hand. He had no idea what to do with the reigns, anyway.

It didn't take long until he heard shouts and saw people running toward the street and screaming at them, calling for Basilios. Zanoah tried to ignore it and kept his focus on getting out of here.

Houses rushed by, followed by fenced-in pastures. The forest was so close already that he could almost smell it. As they gained on it, he heard barks and several loud bangs behind them. Whatever was happening, he couldn't look back—shouldn't look back.

The horse's muscles underneath him were working harder, faster, to run away from all these loud noises, dashing into the forest and between trees. He had to duck closer to the horse's neck to make sure no low-hanging branch knocked them off the horse's back. As he did, Caean's light hair pressed against his neck and cheek, and Zan forced down a sob.

He barely registered the others hanging similarly low on their horses, still running and running. The further away they got, the quieter the barking and the bangs got, and soon, he could only hear hooves on moss, the horses' heavy breathing, and some birds chirping.

They didn't stop until they reached the mountain, right where the small gap between the rocks emerged, opening up into the narrow tunnel leading to the jungle. Ferox brought his horse to a harsh stop, and Zan's did the same, panting, fur wet with sweat by now.

It was already getting lighter again. Zanoah realized they had rode the whole evening and night to get here. Hopefully, it would make it harder for their pursuers to track them.

"Hurry up, we have to scare the horses away and hope they don't find the tunnel too fast," Ferox explained, already sliding down his horse.

Zanoah did the same, taking Caean into his arms again while Ferox pulled the halters from both their horses, explaining that it might be harder for their pursuers to identify the horses without them. A soft thump nearby reminded him of their new companions, and when he turned toward them, he saw Helio lying on the ground, his sister next to him.

"He's hurt," she said, tears in her eyes. "They shot him. Helio, come on, please. We have to keep going."

Zanoah could see a red spot spreading across his shoulder, blood soaking through the fabric fast. Zalika herself looked pale and in pain, but at least they were all still alive. Helio clenched his teeth and slowly pulled himself up, wincing in pain. When he started to slump down again, his sister gave him a hand, keeping him upright, despite struggling to stand herself.

"There's a lake behind the mountain," Ferox said. "We can wash up there and care for any wounds. If we stay here, we'll all be dead soon."

He'd pulled the last halter from the horses' heads and now slapped one's backside, sending them scurrying away. Hopefully, they would be alright. Zan noticed he was still holding the halters. Good, maybe they would be of some use later.

Ferox wrapped an arm around Helio so Zalika wouldn't have to strain under his weight. They were the first ones to squeeze into the tunnel, with Zanoah following behind, Caean in his arms. He knew it would be harder to cross this time; they had no light, some of them were wounded, and he had to carry Caean, but none of that was important.

They had to get through, no matter how long it took.

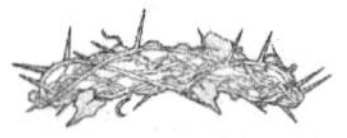

When he finally saw a dim light at the end of the tunnel, he was exhausted and couldn't even begin to guess how bad it had to be for the others. At least they were finally outside again and hopefully safe for now.

Ferox had an arm around Helio's waist, helping him toward the lake where they both sat down on big stones. Zalika stayed close, not leaving her brother's side. Zanoah followed them, very carefully lowering Caean to the ground.

Gently he brushed his fingertips over their cheek, sighing since there was still no reaction from them at all. Their eyes were closed, and that wall between the two of them was still up. As much as he wanted to care for the deity, he knew they had to take care of Helio's wound first.

"Ferox, you're bleeding too."

He heard Zalika's soft voice, and his gaze wandered toward the man he now saw as his brother. Ferox's shirt was red with blood, which seeped up his side. Zanoah grabbed one of the knives from Ferox's belt, then cut two long strips of fabric from the blanket he'd wrapped Caean in.

After Zanoah cleaned and bandaged Ferox's and Helio's wounds, all of them drank some fresh lake water. Then Zanoah carefully knelt down next to Caean, gently unwrapping their body. He still had the knife in his hand, and he wanted to get rid of these chains.

When he touched the Luskite, pain shot through his fingertips, burning his skin, but he didn't care right now. Instead, he pushed the knife point into the lock on the back of Caean's collar, wiggling it around and hoping it would unlock somehow. He had no idea how to do this.

"Here, let me help," Ferox offered, kneeling down next to him and grabbing the knife from his hands. It was easier this way, since Zanoah could hold Caean's head and their hair, giving Ferox more space to deal with the lock.

"Does it hurt you, too?" Zan asked. "The chains?" He'd been watching Ferox, waiting for some sort of reaction, but the man didn't recoil back when he touched the chains.

"Hurt?" Ferox furrowed his brow. "No, it tingles a little, like static. It hurts you?"

Zanoah only nodded, wondering if it had such an intense effect on him because he still had some of Caean's force inside him. Or was it the crown?

Finally, the collar was open and only the shackles on Caean's wrists were still attached. Gently, he laid Caean's head in his lap, holding their hand so Ferox could work on the shackle more easily.

All these burns, he thought sadly. It looked so similar to the wounds Caean had had after being imprisoned by Kelcie for so long. Their skin wasn't just red; right where the Luskite had touched their skin, blisters had formed as well.

"I'll take the chains, alright?" Ferox said. "We may need them again for Basilios."

Zanoah just nodded, carefully wrapping the blanket back around Caean's chest, holding them close. "Caean, can you hear me?" he whispered. "Please don't go too far away. I need you so much."

He pressed a gentle kiss to their forehead and took a slow, deep breath. He was worried he would never be able to reach Caean again, but at least they weren't chained anymore.

With a heavy heart, he turned to his other companions and said, "We should get moving. We have a long journey to Tadena."

Being back in the jungle was weird. With no birds chirping, it was almost eerily silent. The only things they could hear were their steps and the wind rustling the leaves. Sometimes, the small creek they were following got louder, whenever the water poured down rocks, but that was it. Even their conversations were few and far between.

The only things any of them cared about at the moment were walking and surviving.

Zanoah had no idea how far away Tadena actually was, since he'd been knocked out when the capsule dropped him off, and he wasn't sure how long it took him to get from there to the caves. It was also taking much longer to get through the lush, green plants because they weren't responding to Caean's presence. And while the flora wasn't attacking them, it wasn't helping them either. Ferox at least appeared to have a general idea of where they had to go and was leading them again.

Their nights were also much more uncomfortable now than they had been with Caean, since they couldn't just sleep in a bed of vines high up between trees. Zanoah briefly wondered if he could ask the jungle for help, but it felt wrong to use it now that it had calmed down and was offering them passage so graciously.

There still hadn't been any reaction from Caean, and every day, Zanoah got more worried. Not just about them, but also Helio, whose wound hadn't healed at all and who got weaker every day. His sister looked worse, as well. She was getting paler and paler and had had a low fever for the last two days.

The only one who appeared unfazed was Ferox, who was carrying the halters and chains, bundled together into a make-shift pack. He even had the energy to steady Helio, always staying close to the young man. His wound hadn't been very deep, more like a scratch than anything else, and he was keeping in high spirits despite their current predicament.

That night, like every night, they had laid down underneath a tree, Zalika and Helio close to each other. Ferox was already sleeping because he always took the second shift. While the other two weren't in any shape to help, Zanoah and Ferox split watch duty, making sure they both got enough rest but also kept their eyes and ears open. They needed to be on their guard if somehow Basilios and his people found a way to catch up.

Zan stared up at the two moons shining down through a gap in the canopy above, then back down at the deity, who was lying beside him. "Caean, I don't know if you can even hear me. I'm here, and I won't leave you." He sighed softly, leaning his head against Caean's, his eyes closed. "I know you're hurting. Please, let me take some of the pain and be there for you. I don't know what to do anymore."

His frown deepened, and his quiet desperation grew. He'd been so happy when Caean had trusted him before, when they'd opened up their mind and heart to him. Of course, he knew there was much pain and fear inside of them, but he could take it. He would be there for them.

Only when fingertips caressed his face did he realize he was crying, tears rolling down his chin and trickling onto Caean's blanket.

"Zan, I'm here."

Confused and shocked by the whisper, he opened his eyes wide, only to be met by Caean's stormy, teal gaze. Their hand was on his cheek, brushing his tears away.

"Are you sure you want to see behind this wall?" Caean asked him. *"I don't want to hurt you."*

He couldn't help but cry even more. How did they manage to still be so gentle and caring, despite everything happening to them? Although there was only a small crack in Caean's mental wall, just enough to allow their voice through, he could already feel pain seeping through. So much pain...

"Yes. I will be here for you," he promised. "No matter what. I want to help you deal with all this."

Caean nodded, then Zanoah felt the wall between them crumbling, being flushed away by a wave of emotions—not only pain but also guilt, shame, disgust, loneliness. There was so much. He could only hold Caean, both in the real world as well as inside of their souls, keeping them close while this ocean of emotions surrounded their little island, waves crashing into them, threatening to drown them.

"It will get better," he whispered, hugging Caean.

Their face was pressed right into the crook of his neck, like they were two pieces of a puzzle fitting together perfectly. All feeling of time and space was gone. Neither of them moved or spoke until the ocean around them slowly abated, and Caean relaxed. Almost.

When Zan opened his eyes in the real world, he saw them clinging tight to him, eyes closed and cuddled up to his chest, sound asleep. This was so much better, and despite experiencing all their pain and hurt, he couldn't help but smile.

"Sleep, Zan. I'll keep watch."

Ferox's voice startled him for a moment, but when he saw his brother watching him, he relaxed again and nodded. He was much more content now, and it didn't take long for him to fall asleep, feeling Caean close to him—not just their body but their mind as well.

The next morning he awoke worried and confused. He couldn't feel Caean close by like he normally could. Sitting up, he darted his eyes around, trying to find them. A relieved sigh left his lips when he saw the deity kneeling next to Zalika, giving her some plants, which she chewed slowly.

Caean wasn't wrapped in the blanket anymore. Instead vines and leaves covered their whole body, thicker than the moss they'd used before. On the ground nearby, he spotted the blanket, which had been converted into a backpack, using the straps of the halters.

His travel companions really had been busy already.

"You're up, good!" Ferox said. "Time to get going. According to Caean, it's about eight or nine days 'til we reach Tadena. Then we'll have to deal with getting in there."

Zan was already relieved to have Caean back, but he was even more glad of it now. They had a much better sense of direction, and Zan also wouldn't be slowed down by carrying someone anymore.

He was curious about one thing, though. "What are those plants you're giving her?" he asked, pointing at Zalika.

"To keep her fever down until we arrive," Caean explained. *"Nothing here can cure her, not with Basilios' babe in her, but it will keep her stronger."*

Despite what they were saying, Zan had to smile. It was so good to finally hear Caean's voice again, to know they were here, interacting with the world again.

Silently, they walked through the jungle, Caean in the lead with Ferox, giving him directions. Zalika and Helio followed behind in the middle, with Zanoah bringing up the rear. He wanted to keep everyone in sight, make sure no one got lost.

"You feel more like Basilios' force but...different. Purer. How did that happen?" Caean wanted to know around noon.

"When his people...prayed to him, some of his force seeped out. I just tried to gather some, like I did when you offered me yours, hoping it might help us in our escape. Didn't need it, though."

Caean tilted their head a little. *"I think it did help. You feel no exhaustion, barely any hunger, and need even less sleep than before. Even Ferox is tired by now—but not you. You both are parts of him, but you're still the stronger one."*

Zanoah frowned. What the fuck did that mean? How were they parts of Basilios?

"I only just learned about it while we were...there. When Basilios was freed about thirty years ago," Caean explained, *"some splinters of his soul chipped off and went into the world. It manifested in women getting pregnant. From what I've gathered, there are eight of you. He doesn't really know how it happened either, but for him, you're more like soldiers than actual children. That's what he's been trying to create with his brides. A human body can't handle the strain of growing a half-deity baby, though."*

Caean sighed, their gaze on Zalika's back. Even without them saying it, Zanoah understood that being made pregnant by a deity was a death sentence for the mother.

This was all a little hard to digest. He and Ferox only existed because splinters of Basilios' soul had found their way into their mothers. It felt so wrong, but at the same time, it explained so much. Why he hadn't been wanted. Why his parents had called him a monster. Why he'd been born with black eyes—Basilios' black eyes. Why he was stronger and faster than most humans. Why Ferox had such good hearing and sight.

He wondered if being a part of Basilios' soul was also the reason nature had never hurt him. Perhaps it had somehow recognized the splinter inside Zanoah and left him alone.

He wasn't human after all. It scared him more than he liked to admit. Zan had always wanted to be *normal*, to disappear into the crowd—and now he learned he was exactly the opposite: special, and almost one of a kind.

"Are you afraid of me now?" Zan asked. *"I killed someone."*

He worried Caean might see him differently. The realization that he'd actually taken someone's life had slowly begun to set in once his thoughts weren't stuck on worrying about Caean anymore. Zanoah hated himself for what he'd done. He'd never intended to kill anyone. He didn't even want to kill Basilios himself, despite what he'd done to Caean. Life was to be treasured, and he didn't want to be a murderer. And yet, he had become one, to save Caean. And deep down, he knew he would do it again if he had to.

Without hesitation, Caean shook their head and looked back at him with a smile. *"Of course not. You're still the same Zanoah I got to know. I don't care who your father is, and taking someone's life doesn't change you. You only did so to save me, and I'm grateful you did. But, Basilios being a part of you explains why you, and Ferox, feel so familiar."* But there was a thoughtful expression on their face. *"But there's still something else about you, too. Something I can't figure out yet."*

Zanoah briefly wondered what exactly that could be, but it didn't really matter. What mattered was that Caean wasn't afraid of him and still cared about him. They were also right. This did explain his immediate connections to Caean and Ferox and why he'd begun to see Ferox as a brother before he ever knew they actually were. Zanoah only hoped he would never become like his father, driven mad by his hunger for more power.

"How do you know all this?" he asked. *"Did he tell you?"*

There was a long silence, and he could feel another wave of pain and hurt radiating off of Caean. He regretted asking almost immediately.

But Caean said, *"No regrets. You* should *know. He forced a hole into my wall. I used the chance to snoop into his mind as well."*

If Basilios could manage penetrating Caean's mind, how strong was he really? It was hard to wrap his head around the sheer power Basilios possessed and used without a second thought to get what he wanted. It chilled Zan to the bone.

"He always wanted a child—his own child," Caean continued. *"And he wanted me to be the bearer of it. I always declined and always will. It's impossible to get another deity pregnant without their consent. And offspring between deities is forbidden. Not that he cares about any of that."*

More waves of shame and pain washed over to Zanoah. He grabbed Caean's hand, holding it. He wanted to reassure Caean that it wouldn't happen again. Whatever came next for them, he would protect them.

"There was a time when he really loved me, and I loved him." Caean shook their head sadly. *"Many, many centuries ago. At some point he forgot his place. Too many people hungry for power prayed to him, willing to give him their strength just to feel better about themselves."*

That was something Zanoah was all too familiar with. He'd been used as well so that other people felt better about themselves and got what they wanted without sacrificing any of their own comfort.

"And that's why he has no effect on you," they said. *"People naturally crave power—even Ferox does. But you...Zan, you* fear *it."*

For a moment, he closed his eyes, realization sinking in. Caean was right. They were so absolutely right, and he hadn't seen it all this time.

"I do. I fear, if I ever have power, I'll become like these people who used me. I don't want it, and it scares me," he admitted.

The only thing he wanted was to take care of the people he loved. Admitting that to himself meant that he had to admit something else as well. He had never loved anyone before finding Caean.

"It makes you strong," Caean said. *"Much stronger than Basilios."*

Caean smiled at him over their shoulder, and he couldn't help smile back. For the first time ever, he felt a warmer wave in his mind, one of affection. Caean cared about him—*truly* cared—something no one else had ever done before.

A soft and painful moan stopped him in his tracks days later. It was Zalika, who was hunched over with her hand on her belly, holding onto a tree.

"What's wrong?" Helio asked, staggering over to her. "Zalika?"

His shoulder had become infected, oozing puss despite them cleaning it regularly and using new strips of the blanket to bandage it every day. The siblings looked exhausted and beaten up, both feverish and slower these last days.

"I...it hurts," Zalika whined between her teeth, unable to stay on her feet. Instead, she sank down to her knees and wrapped her arms around herself, tears falling down her cheeks.

"How far 'til Tadena?" Ferox asked Caean, who signed, "about a day."

Zanoah debated what they should do. They couldn't leave Zalika here, but it would be hard to press on with her in this state. He wanted everyone to make it in one piece. Despite not knowing each other very long, he consider these people his friends. He didn't like seeing them in pain, and he certainly didn't want any of them to die.

"Her pain won't get better," Caean said, sounding fairly certain. *"Waiting won't help us."*

Zanoah kneeled down next to her, one hand on her back. "I can carry you. When we're in Tadena, they can help you. They have much better technology and health care than any other city. Can you stay strong for just a little longer?"

Zalika nodded, unable to speak, so Zanoah took her up in his arms, holding her firmly. He was already used to carrying someone like this, after all. She grabbed onto his shirt, clenching her teeth and trying not to show how much pain she was really in.

They five of them kept going as fast as possible. When night settled in, they didn't even stop. Sleeping wouldn't help, and they were almost there. Ferox kept his grip on Helio, helping him walk, while Caean guided them onward. When the jungle finally opened up early the next day, Zan could only see sand, as far as the eye could see. A desert stretched in front of them, and in the distance, a city could be spotted, clouded in a never-ending storm.

Tadena.

He was back where it all started.

CHAPTER 19

"How do we get there?" Ferox asked. "That storm looks vicious."

He was right; they couldn't just walk through the sandstorm. Zanoah hadn't thought about how they would make it across this nightmare to get into the city. He couldn't even remember how he and Shaan had done it in the first place.

"I might be able to forge us a way, but I'm not strong enough right now," Caean said.

Thankfully, this gave Zan an idea.

"Praying!" When the others looked at him, he explained, "We pray to Caean. If their force is more energized, they might be able to get the jungle to build a way."

It sounded odd saying it out loud like that, but it was their only hope to get into Tadena. And they were a deity, after all. After being quiet for a few moments, Caean nodded, although they looked embarrassed at the idea.

It surprised him to hear Helio's voice first, his voice strained and tired but nonetheless steady.

Caean, deity of nature,
You who breathe life into the earth,
Whose presence fills the land and jungle,
We come before you with humble hearts.

Soon, Zalika and Ferox fell into chorus with Helio, and Zanoah could already feel Caean's aura growing, becoming brighter and more vivid.

Bless us, Caean, with your wisdom and strength,

That we may learn from the cycles of nature,

That we may find peace and renewal in your presence,

And that we may always be mindful of our place in the web of life.

Their golden shimmer grew more and more radiant, and once again, Zanoah wondered if anyone else except him saw these auras. No one had noticed Basilios' black misty aura, and no one was paying any mind to Caean's now. Could they even feel it?

Quietly, he mumbled a prayer as well, putting his heart into it, all his affection and devotion for Caean.

We offer this prayer to you, Caean, with reverence and respect,

And we ask that you hear our plea and guide us on our journey.

"And I care more for you than words can describe," Zanoah finally whispered, watching Caean with fascination.

They glowed, and they looked so much healthier, bursting with life, the plants around their body lush and green. They didn't say or move at all except to turn toward the city. Vines shot into the desert, intertwining, and leaves and ivy started sprouting and growing, building a narrow tunnel.

"Let's go," Zanoah said.

This time, he was in the lead, with Caean in the middle trying to keep their little tunnel together. It felt almost endless, and he heard the storm raging around them, tearing holes into the thin wall of plants protecting them. Caean was pouring their force right into the plants, keeping them alive and sturdy enough to shield them. They still felt the wind and heat, and sand grains whipped at them, but it didn't burn them or send them tumbling away.

Finally, they reached the gates, which were much smaller than one might guess given how big the city was. They didn't open, though.

"My name's Zanoah Vargas, and I want to talk to High Chancellor Cato Antias!" he yelled, hoping someone heard him and would open the door.

Minutes ticked by. In the back of his head, he worried that someone remembered his name and would refuse to let him in. Maybe there was a list, people who were exiled that the guards were instructed to leave outside the city walls. He had no idea how long they stood there, Zalika moaning in his arms and Caean's aura getting dimmer by the minute, but finally, the door opened.

About fifteen guards, all with weapons drawn and aimed at them, stood in a half circle. By the pink stripes on their sleeves, Zan could tell they were Justicars and Executioners—three stripes for the former and four for the latter. He thought they would look angry, but when he stared at them, he realized their faces were full of...fear? Why were they afraid? Because they had found their way to the city? Because of their tunnel?

"Get in," a familiar voice said. "Your weapons will be confiscated for now. If you pull any tricks, I'll personally send you back out there."

Zan's immediately shot toward a man he knew all too well: High Chancellor Antias.

"Welcome back, Zanoah."

"We need two medics at the gate right now," Antias said into his wristband, giving orders.

Their weapons were taken from them, but Zanoah didn't even care. No matter what was going to happen, at least here, Zalika and Helio would get decent medical attention, and Basilios couldn't just barge in.

"What's in there?" Antias pointed toward the make-shift bag Ferox was still carrying.

Ferox looked quite unhappy after not only giving up his gun but also his knives. Zanoah tried giving him a reassuring smile, but it didn't really help.

"Chains we'll need later," Zan said. "I have a lot to explain."

For once, he had to be strong and not just follow orders; he had to stand up for himself and his friends, had to make sure the people he cared for were safe and Antias understood the danger that was approaching so he could prepare accordingly.

"Alright," Antias said reluctantly. "We'll keep them safe. These two will get medical attention as soon as possible, and you all will need a shower. Fresh clothes will be provided. Then, we can talk."

Zanoah just nodded. He wanted to take a really long shower and wash off all the bad feelings. Of course, he knew it didn't work like that, but at least he'd feel clean and fresh. What it wouldn't do was help calm the anxiety building up inside of him. This seemed too easy, being accepted right back into Tadena without a struggle. What was really going on here?

The High Chancellor had already turned toward his wristband again, talking into it to someone they couldn't see. "Get three rooms for our visitors ready."

"Sir, he has the mark," a guard sounded, pointing at Zan's scar.

"I know that. I put it there," Antias growled, making it clear that no one should doubt or distract him anymore.

It didn't take long before two medical flaicars arrived, and medics spilled out of them. They assessed the scene for a moment before bringing over a stretcher. Zanoah carefully laid Zalika down on it, smiling at her, but she just looked up at him silently, worry wrinkling her brow.

His other companions were staring at him, too, and he realized they'd all had become very quiet upon entering Tadena. It took him a moment, but it finally dawned on him that they'd never seen this level of technology, and they weren't used to being somewhere with no nature around them at all. Even Caean's leaves were slowly drying out. There weren't any plants to sustain them in here.

Antias, seeing that Caean was naked, ordered one of the guards to give them his long coat. Two of the guards hopped into the flaicars along with Zalika and Helio, and as he watched them being transported away, Zan hoped they would be alright.

Most of the guards had resumed their posts, but three of them remained with Antias, keeping watch on Zan, Caean, and Ferox. Not long after, another flaicar arrived, this time a bigger version with enough seats for all of them. As with every flying vehicle in Tadena, there was no driver; they all carried passengers around on autopilot. Ferox tried to ask about it as they were ushered into the flaicar, but Antias told him to keep quiet. They sat down inside—Caean next to him, their hand in his, and Ferox on his other side— and the Chancellor slid in opposite to them, guards flanking him.

Zanoah silently watched the city passing by as they headed who knows where. He saw the familiar gray buildings, many of them high-rises full of lots of tiny apartments. There were the colorful neon signs of business and the billboards advertising goods and services. What there wasn't was plants or trees, not even flowers. As much as Zan had hated the time he'd spent in Srale, he found that he missed seeing the natural world around him. Tadena was depressing and cold.

"You've matured," Antias finally said. He'd been watching Zan this whole time.

"I had to."

He'd been exiled, thrown out of the city to fend for himself in the jungle. There'd been no choice but to mature, not if he wanted to survive.

Antias was still watching him. "I know. It's a good thing. I hoped this would happen."

Zan's mood darkened, and his eyes narrowed, but he didn't respond. He was no longer angry about Antias killing his brother. Shaan had always treated him like shit, though it'd taken so long for him to see it. His brother had dug his own grave, and now he had to lie in it. Still, Zan remembered the classified information he'd dug up, all those secret experiments.

"Why are you allowing us to enter Tadena so easily?" he asked.

He wasn't sure if it was a good idea to be so direct with the High Chancellor, but he had to make sure they weren't just being led to the slaughter. It wasn't just about him anymore, but also about his friends.

Antias had a tiny smile on his lips, and he leaned forward, almost imperceptibly. "You have information, don't you? Otherwise, you wouldn't have come back here. You need help, and I'm curious about it. And who knows? I might need you as well."

Zan wasn't sure how he felt about that. What could Antias possibly need his help for? Whatever it was, Zan vowed that he wouldn't jeopardize his friends' safety, nor would he hurt any innocent people.

"We'll talk about everything later, in private, when you've freshened up," Antias said casually.

As they docked at one of the biggest high-rises, Antias exited the flaicar first. Zanoah slowly followed him, not letting go of Caean's hand for a moment.

"You will be shown your rooms now so you can clean up," the High Chancellor explained. "Then we'll talk, Zanoah. You have one hour. You will be picked up at your room."

Cato Antias nodded at him before leaving them with different guards, who had been waiting at the landing dock for them. There was one other person there, as well: Cato's assistant. Zan had seen her several times but never remembered her name for some reason.

"Follow me," she ordered. Her voice was strict, like she was used to people listening to her.

Right now, Zanoah didn't mind following her, and he hoped Ferox would comply and not do something stupid. He didn't know Tadena or how things worked around here, and he would only get into trouble if he tried running around on his own.

The prospect of speaking to Antias later made Zan anxious. A tiny voice in his mind wondered what exactly he wanted to talk about. For now, he tried to push it aside, concentrating on the task ahead. All that mattered right now was getting into that room and freshening up.

Despite living here for most of his life, Tadena had never felt like home at all. Instead, these walls were almost suffocating, too narrow and sterile to feel welcome. He knew deep in his heart that he hadn't come here to stay for good, just until the danger had passed. If they survived Basilios, they would find themselves a home, a real pretty one with lots of nature all around it. The thought made him smile, and he barely registered that they'd arrived at their rooms.

"These three are for you," the woman said. "There's clothes for you inside. Just leave anything that doesn't fit, and someone will come get them." When Ferox opened his mouth, she shook her head. "Keep your questions to yourself for now. I'll pick you up in an hour."

The last sentence was directed toward Zanoah who only nodded.

"You want your own room?" he asked Caean, wondering if they wanted their privacy right now.

They shook their head.

While Ferox tried pulling open his door, Zanoah watched him, then said, "You have to push it to the side."

He demonstrated for Ferox with the door to the room he and Caean would be sharing, sliding it into the wall. Everything was built very efficiently, since Tadena had such limited space. Ferox frowned, but he quickly figured it out, then glanced into the room before slowly entering it.

Before heading into his own room, Zanoah took one last look at the guards standing next to the doors. He was quite sure they would stay there and probably follow them if they decided to leave on their own. For now, he didn't mind. He had no ulterior motives or plans to make trouble. Instead, he let Caean into the room, then closed the door behind them, giving the two of them the privacy they hadn't really had since meeting Ferox.

Their room was quite small, barely big enough for a bed and a closet next to it. At least they also had a food and water dispenser.

"You want to shower first?" he asked.

"Will you come with me?" Caean suggested, almost shyly.

He had never heard their voice so insecure and confused. He could only guess at how big the difference was between their natural home and this city full of technology and science. Caean would need some time to get used it.

"I don't want to be alone," they admitted, smiling at him.

Zanoah couldn't help it; he had to take Caean into his arms, just holding them close and making sure they knew they weren't alone, never.

"Of course I'll come with you."

He was a little nervous, though he wasn't sure why. He and Caean had bathed together already, but that was different. Lakes and rivers weren't the same as a shower. They were more spacious, not as small and intimate. But he took a deep breath and, together, they entered the small bathroom. One half of the tiny room was a shower; the other one held the toilet and sink.

Slowly, he pushed the coat from Caean's shoulders, revealing more and more skin. Almost all the leaves had dried up and fallen from Caean's body by now, leaving them naked to the elements. Still, his gaze stopped at Caean's neck and their wrists, but the wounds were almost healed by now. Some of the plants had helped, but he suspected it was their prayer as well.

He hadn't expected to feel Caean's fingers pushing up his shirt, but he let them do so, just watching them. They were so perfect. How could anyone inflict pain on this perfect being? He just couldn't wrap his head around it.

Piece by piece, he lost his clothes—first his shirt, then his boots and pants—until he was completely naked as well. Instead of shame and vulnerability, like he'd always felt being naked in front of Julyen, he was happy—genuinely happy—to be here, safe, with Caean.

He felt their hand on his cheek, saw their wonderful smile and the spark in their eyes he had missed for so long. He could only follow Caean into the shower, being pulled with them, not thinking anymore, just feeling and following these feelings. He turned on the water, which was warm but still refreshing, and it engulfed them, washing away all the bad things they had endured.

Zan's hand found its way onto Caean's cheek as, gently caressing them. The two of them were so close, their chests touched, and he relished the warmth of their body so close to his. Their heartbeat mixed with his own, and he wasn't sure which was his and which was Caean's.

Caean's hand wandered a little higher to his neck. They pulled him closer, and before he realized what was happening, Zanoah felt soft lips on his own

Every single thought inside him ceased, and only feelings remained. His heart was exploding into little stars, mixing with Caean's golden shine, merging into one big beam of affection and trust. It shone over everything dark, illuminated the sky over their little island in their ocean of pain, which was now still and reflected every beam, every sparkle.

Lips so soft and without any urge for more than their innocent but perfect kiss still pressed against his, showed him for the first time in his life how love felt.

In the end, he couldn't recall how long they had stood there, kissing and enjoying each other's closeness without a care in the world. After all they had been through, they deserved this moment of undisturbed happiness and intimacy. It was all Zanoah had hoped for, longed for, his whole life, to be accepted and loved. Caean gave him exactly this.

At some point, Caean had pulled the crown from his head to wash his hair. Zanoah had explained the purposes of all the different small bottles standing in the shower. It was a luxury they hadn't had all this time, only living with river and lake water but no soap or shampoo. The two of them took advantage of the luxury, using every product available to them, cleaning every pore and strand of hair, until both of them were completely impeccable, all visible reminders of Srale and the jungle washed away.

He hadn't ever seen Caean this clean before, and it confused him a little. Still, he couldn't deny they were as beautiful as ever. Even their smile seemed stronger, more genuine. It beamed brighter than their aura. Zanoah could even shave his face here, although his beard wasn't really much to deal with. It still felt good to care for himself, to be more in control of his appearance.

"You'll be expected soon," Caean reminded him, standing close to the big window, their gaze wandering over the city.

Slowly, Zanoah came closer and stopped behind them, wrapping his arms around them, kissing their shoulder, before following their gaze outside. They were high up and had a nice overview of the city, but there was no green, no plants, only gray buildings and lots of neon signs, advertising all kinds of things.

"You want to come with me?" he asked, not caring if Antias would like it or not. They belonged together, and Caean had a big part in all this mess as well.

But they shook their head slightly, turning halfway toward him, giving him a soft smile. *"I'll try resting a little, and when you're back, I'll be right here,"* they promised, making Zanoah's heart beat faster for a moment. It was a promise to wait for him, to make this room their home, even if just for now. *"You better get dressed."*

Silently, he sighed but agreed. It only took him few steps to get to the closet, and he searched around a little, hoping to find something wasn't as skintight as Tadenan fashion usually was, until he found a basic white tank and black pants that were made of a sturdier fabric than the fashionable, fancy stuff he was used to. The bottom shelf even had several pairs of shoes to choose from, ranging from slippers to sandals and sneakers to boots, similar to the ones he'd been given after his banishment. Zan opted to go for these.

Then he peeked at himself in the mirror. He looked so different from the last time he'd been in the city. His dark, curly hair was shorter, but at least it was freshly washed and combed by now. Caean's crown was firmly held in place by its thorns. The wound on his cheek had healed and had only left a thin, light scar. Even his skin had darkened, tanned by the sun, no longer protected by the artificial dome shielding the city from aggressive UV-light.

"You look great. Confident and tidied up. Exactly what's expected of you for this talk." His gaze wandered toward Caean, who had sat down on the bed, watching him closely. *"I'll be with you all the time,"* they promised. Of course they would; they could see all he saw through the crown after all.

Zanoah knelt in front of them, leaning his head against their chest, his arms loosely around their waist. He felt their fingers in his hair immediately, sliding through the now soft curls, down to his neck.

"I'm still afraid," he admitted. *"I never had to stand up to anyone before and only followed orders. I never asked for something, and now, I'll have to ask for so much and hope the High Chancellor even believes me."*

His eyes were closed while he was slowly relaxing, enjoying the soft movements of Caean's fingers on his neck. Their presence alone had such a calming effect on him, soothing most of his thoughts and doubts.

"You are strong and have a good heart," Caean said. *"It's your time to demand and be a leader."*

This didn't really make it any easier. On the contrary, he was damn afraid of being anything but a good soldier, doing what was asked of him. It was already surprising to him that he could feel such affection for a person and not feel guilty about it. No one had ordered him to free Caean or to do so much to protect them, but he still had done it, out of his own free will, deciding for himself. It scared him.

"You will *be okay,"* Caean whispered, gently pushing his chin up and planting another kiss on his lips. Then they gave him a reassuring smile.

He had to believe them, had to believe in himself, no matter how often he had been told otherwise in all these years.

Before he could answer, he heard a knock at the door and the same strict voice that had greeted them before said, "Your hour is up. High Chancellor Antias is awaiting you."

It was Antias' assistant. He took another deep breath and another look toward Caean, still smiling at him, before he left the room. He had an important meeting to attend.

High Chancellor Antias' office still looked the same as it had several months before when he'd watched his brother die in here, when he'd gotten his scar and been banished. For a "fresh start," Antias had said. He hadn't been too wrong about that.

This time, Antias disregarded his almost throne-like office chair and led him toward a sitting area Zanoah had barely noticed before. Two comfortable-looking chairs covered in dark green fabric faced each other, and a small table sat between them.

"Thank you, Felicitas. This will be all for now." With a nod, Antias dismissed his assistant, who left the room immediately.

Zanoah noticed there were no guards in this room, despite one of them accompanying him all the way from his room to here. He also noticed that Cato Antias looked impeccable as always. He was once again wearing a white dress shirt and tight black pants. Shiny black boots covered his feet, and his black hair was straightened and combed back. A shiny green earring was dangling from his lobe, complementing his warm, brown skin. But, he looked tired. No, exhausted was a better word. There were dark circles underneath his eyes, and his face looked a little more lined. What had been going on these last months?

"Sit," Antias said. "We will be here for a long time."

He gestured toward one chair, sitting down on the other one. Silently, Zanoah took the other chair, leaning back just a little, still ready to jump and fight if needed. This room had a weird atmosphere, and he couldn't place if it was just because of his memories of it or if it had always been like this.

"So, will you tell me what happened to you these last months and what brought you back here?" Antias asked.

Zan's gaze wandered toward the High Chancellor, who was comfortably leaned back, his legs crossed, his blue eyes watching him intently. Though Antias was so relaxed, Zan was not. His heart pounded, and his hands were sweating. He pressed his palms against his knees and took a deep breath to keep himself as relaxed and focused as possible.

Zanoah hesitated, unsure where to even begin, but slowly words came pouring out: his long walk through the jungle to the cave, freeing Caean and heading toward Srale, finding out about Basilios, and what they had planned for their escape. He only left out little details, things that weren't important to the whole picture, like Basilios' devotion and his exact relation to Caean. Although he did mention how he and Ferox had come into existence, hoping desperately it wouldn't be a mistake to trust Antias.

When he was finished, he waited for a reaction, any reaction at all, but the High Chancellor just sat there, thinking, eyes fixated on a point behind him. The longer this silence went on, the more Zan's anxiety grew. His knee started bobbing up and down, and his breaths felt a little shallower. He couldn't help it. He'd never been a confident person.

"Deep breaths, you'll be okay," Caean's soft voice said.

He immediately relaxed a little. Following their guidance, he took deep breaths, which settled his heartbeat and his jiggling leg. He could almost see their smile before they retreated a little again, not wanting to distract him.

"That's a lot to unpack," Antias finally said. "If I hadn't seen the tunnel your companion built outside, I wouldn't believe you." He got up and started pacing. "So, you're suggesting this Basilios person wants to attack Tadena? How do you propose they'll do so? With what army?"

Zan frowned. He was glad Antias believed him, bu that wasn't how Basilios operated. "He doesn't need an army. The whole city of Srale will follow him if he says so, but he can get into people's minds, make them crave power. I don't know exactly how it works, but if he manages to get into your people's heads..."

He didn't finish that sentence, but it seemed he didn't have to. Antias understood, and he nodded and said, "If he manages that, we could face civil war. Everyone craving more power, not thinking straight or following chain of command. It could end in disaster. We'll have to prepare for this eventuality. Is there a way to kill a deity?"

Now, this was a question he didn't dare answer, even if he had one. After all, he still didn't trust any Tadenan completely, and he wouldn't risk Caean's life, not even if it meant Basilios lived.

"I don't know," he answered truthfully. "But he can be trapped. The chains, they can trap a deity, render them unable to use their abilities." He'd seen firsthand what they'd done to Caean, and he would very much like to see Basilios in these chains.

"You said your friend had been captured and held in a cave, that these people had such chains as well. Do you remember where the cave was?"

He hadn't expected this question, but it made sense, and he understood what Antias was hinting at. He wanted to go there and grab the other set of chains, just in case they needed more than one to cage up Basilios. But if they had two sets, they could also trap Caean, and Zan wouldn't let that happen.

"I can't remember," he said. "I just walked in one direction and got disoriented at some point."

It was the truth, but he was withholding the fact that both Ferox and Caean could probably find the cave easily. He wouldn't risk it.

He wasn't sure if Antias believed him or not, but the High Chancellor nodded, seeming satisfied with his answer, and stopped his pacing to turn to Zanoah. "You're free to go. I'll contact you if I have more questions. You'll be provided a new wristband and have full access to your account. Your brother's money will be transferred to you. As for your friends, they'll get a temporary bands, providing them with all necessities. They will be delivered to your rooms tomorrow morning. You can move freely in the city, but be aware that all of you will be tracked."

Zanoah had expected to be told to stay in their rooms, so this was a surprise. They were basically guests and would have all the luxuries and freedom they could want in a city—as long as they didn't leave. It was a gilded cage, but a cage nonetheless.

"How are Zalika and Helio?" he asked, worried about them, especially Zalika, who'd been in such a bad shape when they arrived.

"They're both being treated," Antias said. "Helio's wound will heal easily, but medics found another ailment. I think it's called cancer? From what they told me, he knew about it but thought it was fatal. Thankfully our medicine is much better, and he'll be fine soon. The woman, though..." He frowned. "They could stop her pain for now but aren't sure what's the best course of action yet. Her baby seems different, but after what you've told me, it makes sense. I'll relay the information, and they'll find a solution to help her. You can visit them tomorrow."

Antias' offer sounded almost compassionate. Zan had never heard such kind words from him. Was he being genuine or just playing to make him feel safe? Right now, Zanoah didn't care. He was just glad to hear his friends were alright...mostly.

"Thank you," Zan said. "There's just one thing. The information Shaan stole from you. What are these experiments about?"

He needed to know. If he was going to trust Antias, he had to figure out what was going on behind closed doors. Of course, he knew it was bold of him to ask, and in any other situation he wouldn't have, but this wasn't just about him anymore. His friends had been dragged into this mess as well, and Zanoah wanted to protect them.

The High Chancellor only gave him a tight-lipped smile that told Zan he wouldn't get any answers. "That's a talk for another time. I have to talk to High Chairwoman Nelius now, so if you'll excuse me, Felicitas will show you the way back to your room."

Antias opened the door, signaling for him to pretty much get the fuck out. Zan obliged, following Antias' assistant to his own room, deep in thought. He wondered what would come of this talk and could only hope Antias would take him seriously, prepare the city to stop Basilios. If not, they were royally fucked.

CHAPTER 20

After Felicitas escorted him back to his room, Zan thanked her and ducked inside. He was exhausted and just wanted to sleep, to stop thinking and feel safe for the night, holding Caean in his arms. What he hadn't expected was Ferox pacing up and down the room, while Caean sat on the bed, watching him.

Both of them had put on clothes, though Ferox had opted for his old shirt and pants. Caean had somehow managed to find a loose linen shirt, which they wore with some of the buttons undone. The black pants they wore were the right size, though, and they were barefoot.

Ferox's pacing made Zan nervous. Or, really, it made him *more* nervous. The two of them hadn't really talked at all since their escape. A lot had happened, and Zanoah had learned a lot about himself—about Ferox. Things his brother deserved to know.

"Finally!" Ferox exclaimed, throwing his arms up in the air. "The fuck you been? We gotta talk!"

Zanoah sighed and nodded. "What do you want to know?" he calmly asked.

"Well, first, how are Helio and Zalika? Have you seen them yet?"

Ferox really could be quite caring, thinking about their friends first. Zanoah couldn't help but smile, realizing how much he liked that part of Ferox.

"I haven't seen them yet," Zan said, sitting down on the bed next to Caean. "I'm visiting them tomorrow. You can come, too, if you want.

According to Antias, they're okay for now. Helio's shoulder is healing, and his cancer is being treated. They don't really know how to treat Zalika yet, but hopefully they'll find a way now that they know more about her baby."

Ferox's expression darkened. "What did you tell him about Zalika's baby? You didn't say it's half-deity, did you?" His voice was almost threatening, which took Zan aback.

"Yeah, I told him," he said, confused as to why that would be a problem. "They can't treat her if they don't know what's going on with her." He really was at a loss. What else was he supposed to do? Lie and risk Zalika's life?

"You do realize people like to experiment on things they don't understand, right?" Ferox said, glaring at him. "You told me yourself that they do experiments here! And that if they deem something to be too different or too dangerous, they kill it. Good job, Zanoah, really."

Zan was beyond irritated right now. Ferox didn't understand how things worked here. The doctors couldn't treat Zalika if they didn't know what was wrong with her. It was as simple as that. The part of him used to getting pushed around by people wanted to apologize, but there was another part of him—one that he'd only recently discovered—that wanted to defend his decision. Instead, he did neither, his anger winning out over both of those desires.

"Good thing I told him about us too, huh?" Zanoah shot back. "We're Basilios' spawn, fragments of his soul born to unsuspecting parents. We're not human, Ferox, not entirely."

Zanoah wasn't sure why he just threw that information in Ferox's face instead of explaining it gently, but he was just so exhausted. And getting judged for his decision didn't really help either. It made him feel small and unimportant again.

His brother stared at him, white eyes open wide in disbelief, his fists clenched tight. "You're joking. Fuck, Zan, this isn't the time for fucking jokes!"

Slowly, Zan shook his head, sighing. "No joke. It's true and you know—no, you, *feel*—that it's true. We were born with a fragment of his power, making us stronger than most humans. You learned to control it better, though. Your hearing and eyesight—that's also a part of it."

Before Zan could react, Ferox grabbed his shirt and yanked him up off the bed. Zanoah didn't even fight it. This was a lot for Ferox to deal with, and even if he didn't believe it right now, he would eventually come to see that it was the truth.

"If that's true," Ferox said, glaring at him, "you told Antias about all this? You fucking idiot! Do you have *any* idea what you've done?"

By now, Ferox was screaming at him, and Zanoah had no idea how to calm him down again. He hadn't seen Ferox so angry and agitated before, not even when they were chained up in Basilios' basement. Before he could carefully pull away from Ferox's grasp, his brother hauled back and punched him in the face. He tried to duck out of the way of the second fist flying at him, but Ferox was still holding him tight.

But somehow, the second hit never landed.

Zanoah blinked, confused and a little staggered from the hit. Looking out of the corner of his eye, he saw Caean's hand firmly gripping Ferox's wrist. It wasn't Caean's job to protect him, but he was grateful all the same. Zan could've fought back, and he probably would've won, given his training. But he didn't *want* to fight his brother.

Ferox tugged his arm out of Caean's grasp and scoffed. "*Really?* You get you're specimen number one, right? Don't tell me you're actually okay with him blabbing our secrets all over the city."

"I trust his decisions," Caean signed, smiling softly.

Letting go of Zan's shirt, Ferox stepped back. "We'll see."

He left without another word, and Zan stared after him, confused and anxious and half-convinced that he really was incapable of making good decisions on his own. But they needed to find allies, and in order to do that, he'd had to be honest with Antias. It was a huge risk, and he knew that, but so was doing nothing. And one of those options was a surefire way to end up losing to Basilios. As the door slid closed, Zan felt Caean's fingers gently touching his face, assessing the damage. He wasn't sure if the headache growing behind his eyes was because of the hit or because of all that had happened.

Right now, Ferox was reminding him too much of his dead brother. Shaan had had a similar temper and always thought about himself and his own safety first. It made Zan's heart ache. Was he really so unlucky to have two brothers who were so selfish and angry?

"He's scared and confused," Caean said. *"He's not used to being confined in a small room without nature around. Give him some time. Take him to see Zalika and Helio tomorrow. Maybe show him the city. Only then will we see how he really deals with the situation."*

If it was only that easy. He was good at being patient, at giving people the benefit of the doubt, of telling himself they just needed time. He'd been conditioned to do that his entire life, always putting other people's goals and needs before his own, until he was just a tool for them to use to achieve their dreams.

Warm hands framed his face, gently pulling him down a little. Caean placed a kiss on his lips, then his forehead, before hugging him close. Slowly, his arms wrapped around Caean, and he nuzzled into the crook of their neck, his nose pressed against the soft skin. Despite their shower, Caean still smelled like forest, wood, and earth.

"Don't think like that," Caean said. *"Let's visit Zalika and Helio tomorrow, yes? What do you want to do after that?"*

His mind went blank. No one had ever asked him that before. What *did* he want to do? He wasn't sure even. There was nothing in this city he cared for, nothing he wanted to see again. Still, there had to be *something* he wouldn't mind doing, right?

"Maybe...visit my old workplace."

It sounded more like a question than a statement, but it was an answer, wasn't it? That's what Caean expected of him?

"I don't expect anything of you," Caean assured him. *"Nor will I force you to do or be what you don't want to. I just want you to experience life on your own, without someone controlling your every movement."*

The only time he'd felt like this had been right after his banishment. He'd wandered the jungle alone, without anyone telling him what to do. There hadn't been any joy then, just the need for survival. But it could be different now.

"Will you come with me?" he asked shyly.

"If you want me to, of course."

Softly, he nodded against Caean's neck, exhaustion washing over him. They hadn't slept last night, too focused on getting through the jungle to the city. The meeting with Antias was draining enough, but his talk with Ferox had sapped him of any remaining energy.

Without words, Caean gently pushed him back onto the bed, smiling at him. He almost fell asleep with his clothes still on, but he managed to sit back up, taking off his boots, pants, and top. He kept his underwear on, though it was skintight and didn't really hide much. Caean, however, was wearing nothing under their pants. Either they weren't used to it, or they just didn't care. As they crawled under the blanket next to him, Zan realized he didn't mind. He trusted Caean.

This bed felt like a luxury. The last time he'd slept in one had been before his exile. He wouldn't really count the self-made bed in Ferox's cabin or the nooks in the cave as real beds since they hadn't had mattresses. He'd gotten used to sleeping on blankets or the forest floor, and now the mattress was almost too soft, too safe to relax on.

At least until Caean cuddled up against him, their face cradled in the crook of his neck, one leg pushed between his and one arm wrapped around his waist, clinging to him. Zanoah couldn't help but smile, and he pulled the blanket a little tighter around both of them, resting his cheek against the soft blonde hair, his arm holding the deity close.

He could feel Caean's heartbeat against his chest, slow and steady, their breath against the sensitive skin of his neck, slowing down a little. Caean had fallen asleep almost instantly, and cuddled up like this, it only took Zanoah a few moments before he fell asleep as well.

He couldn't breathe, couldn't move.

Desperately trying to gasp for air, Zanoah's eyes opened wide. He was engulfed in thick black smoke, and he was hanging from a high ceiling, his hands and legs bound by bronze chains. Through the smoke, he could barely make out gray stone right above his head and behind his back, forming a cave.

From far below, he heard sobbing. *Caean*. He'd recognize their voice anywhere. Desperately, he pulled on his chains, just wanting to be down there, next to Caean, who was seemingly impossible to reach. It was his job to protect them from whatever was going on, and he was failing. He wanted to scream, tell them he was there, not far away, but no sound escaped his mouth.

The smoke cleared just a little, enough to let him see Caean, who was kneeling on their lonely island, surrounded by the ocean of emotions. Right in front of them, Basilios held a collar, grinning deviously.

"You're mine," he said menacingly. "You can't run away from me."

Step by threatening step, Basilios came closer to Caean, who tried to crawl back toward the waves. Zanoah couldn't quite see what all was happening, but when they touched the water, a deep distress overwhelmed him, and he could hear Caean yelp. Then they drew their hand back and stared at the water.

Putting all his strength into it, Zanoah pulled on the chains, more desperate than ever to protect Caean. The urge to be strong, to finally be able to protect the one he loved, seared through his body, and the chains finally yielded, causing him to plummet to the floor.

Right as Basilios grabbed Caean's chin, the collar already touching their neck, Zanoah landed on top of him, pushing him away from the shivering deity of nature, before getting up to stand between the two of them.

"You will not get close to them ever again!" Zan shouted.

Determination flushed through him, filling every inch of his body. He grabbed Basilios' head and smash it right on the stones he was lying on, making sure he wouldn't stand up again. He even grabbed the collar from his hands and put it around Basilios' neck, before pulling him toward the waves. The deity's body was instantly devoured by the ocean, washed away out of sight, and the smoke cleared, leaving only fresh air.

As fast as he could, Zan knelt next to Caean, pulling them close and into his arms, holding them.

"It's okay," he said soothingly. "I'm here. He's gone. I won't ever allow him to hurt you again."

It was a promise he intended to keep, no matter what.

When he looked up, a small tree started sprouting in the middle of the island, only a tiny sapling.

Hope.

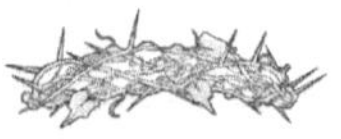

He jolted awake, sitting upright in their shared bed, trying to understand what had just happened. Had it been a nightmare? Or was it real? Had Basilios managed to break through Caean's wall against him? Not knowing bothered him, but he pushed that aside and wrapped Caean up in his arms, wiping away the tears rolling down their cheeks.

"I'm sorry I dragged you into this," they whispered.

Zanoah shook his head. *"I asked for it. I promised I'll be there for you, and I'll keep my promise. It was just a nightmare, right?"* When Caean nodded, he added, *"No matter what happens, we'll get through it together."*

Slowly, Caean relaxed again, sinking into him. Good. They needed some rest and some calm. He shifted a little so he was on his back, and Caean rested their head on his shoulder, their body pressed against his side, arm draped over his chest.

Eventually, Caean slid back into sleep. Careful not to startle them, Zanoah closed his eyes and ventured into their mind, wondering how it looked when they were sleeping. It was so open to him, no barriers or walls to stop him, and it reminded him how much Caean trusted him.

There they were, lying on their island, the dark water of the ocean calm now. Had it retreated a little? The island appeared bigger than before, and something else had changed. In the middle of the island, right underneath Caean, moss was growing, covering the gray stones. And the sapling wasn't a sapling anymore.

It had grown already, towering over them, not mature yet but already sporting an impressive crown of leaves, similar to the trees he'd gotten to know in the jungle. Silently, he sat down next to the tree, next to Caean, leaning his back against the strong trunk, and let his mind rest as well, diving back into sweet and refreshing sleep.

CHAPTER 21

There was no need to talk about what happened the night before. Both Caean and Zanoah, had seen the hope planted on this little island inside of Caean's soul, and it was enough for them.

In the morning, Felicitas woke them to bring them their wristbands. She reminded them they were free to go visit their friends or check out the city, then told them to be available if High Chancellor Antias needed to reach them. Zan nodded and closed the door, wandering back to Caean and sitting down on the bed next to them.

"It's weird having this thing back," he mumbled, staring at the wristband.

They didn't look like anything special, just a small gray band of barely visible polymer, but they were so much more than that. Every single wristband was adjusted to its wearer, containing all their information—not just their ID but also their bank account, messages, calls, keys, all the essentials one needed around Tadena.

"What happens if you lose this thing?" Caean wondered, turning theirs around in their hands, inspecting the gadget.

"It's connected to your DNA, so no one else can use or access it," Zan explained. *"Normally, people leave it on all the time, even while showering and sleeping. I'll show you how it works later when we see Ferox."*

That way he wouldn't have to explain all its functions twice. Hopefully, Ferox had calmed down a little, and they could talk normally today. Now that he'd had time to think about things, he understood why Ferox was so angry and worried, but he also wondered if he would've done things differently had he been in Zan's position. Maybe he would ask later.

First, they went into the bathroom to shower, this time using the sonic shower. Although Zan preferred regular water showers, water was scarce in Tadena, and he didn't want to waste too much of it. They'd already used a ton of it yesterday. It made him chuckle a little to see Caean's skepticism at the sonic technology, but in the end, they seemed satisfied, and both of them were clean and refreshed.

After getting dressed, he ordered some breakfast from the food dispenser, just two coffees and two bowls of cereal with oat milk. The coffee wasn't made of real coffee plants, but water mixed with a little aroma and artificially made caffeine, though Zanoah didn't mind. Tadenans were used to this kind of food, and so far, Caean hadn't complained either. It was easy to please them.

As the two of them ate, Zan stared into the bowl of oat milk, the memory of being reprimanded for his dislike of animals getting killed coming back to him. He never wanted to eat or use an animal. It'd been a lot to ride a horse already, but to raise an animal just to kill it? It made him shudder.

"I'm glad no animals are killed in Tadena," he said. *"If we ever get out of here, I don't want to eat meat."*

Caean smiled at him, and Zan relaxed a little. *"Me neither,"* they said. *"I never ate meat, and I only eat other animal products, like milk or eggs, if they're available in abundance, and it won't affect other living beings."*

Finally, they were ready to head out. The guard outside their door was gone; only the one next to Ferox's door remained. Zan hesitated for a moment before knocking at Ferox's door.

"Ferox? Want to come visit Zalika and Helio with us?" he asked.

There was no answer. Was Ferox still mad at him? He could make out a faint sound, but it took him a few seconds to understand what he was hearing. Was Ferox throwing up?

Debating whether or not he should enter without permission, he waited. But when he heard a cough, he decided to head inside. Ferox's room looked pretty much the same as his and Caean's. It had the same bed, closet, and food dispenser. As he glanced around, he saw the door to the bathroom was open. That's where the sounds were coming from.

"Hey, you okay?" he asked, peeking into the bathroom.

"This alcohol's fucking strong," Ferox whined before bending over the toilet again.

"Alcohol?"

His gaze darted over to the garbage can, where he saw empty bottles. Zanoah sighed and put two and two together. Ferox had apparently figured out the food dispenser and realized that it could also produce alcoholic beverages. Great.

Zan went over to the dispenser and searched for an option on the screen. Once he finally found it, he pressed the button, and the machine deposited a small, green pill in his hand.

"Here, take this. It'll ease the headache and nausea." At Ferox's skeptical gaze, he sighed again and added, "It's not like I've never had a hangover around here. It's fine."

He certainly wouldn't tell Ferox he'd only ever had one hangover and, after experiencing the effects of too much alcohol, had decided he didn't want to go through that again. Zan rarely drank at all now, though not just because of that experience; he'd seen how Shaan had acted when he was drunk, and he hated it. He didn't like the idea that any substance—be it alcohol or drugs—could take control over his body.

Ferox hesitated a moment long, then he snatched the pill out of Zan's hand and swallowed it.

"Drink some water and wait five minutes," Zan told him. "It should be better by then."

Zanoah got a glass of water for his brother, leaving him to it, then he headed back to Caean, who was watching the city from the window.

The view was pretty much the same as it was from their room: gray and boring, at least to him. But watching Caean wasn't boring at all, so he did that instead. They were absolutely beautiful, everything about them, but especially their smile.

"Ugh, stop swooning, or I'll puke again," Ferox mumbled behind him.

Zan turned to see him fall onto his bed and rub his hands over his eyes. He really looked like shit, with dark circles under his eyes and his hair completely tousled; even his clothes were looking worse than they were yesterday. Zanoah decided not to comment on his appearance since it was partly his fault.

"You should've told me much sooner what you knew," Ferox said. But he sounded tired, not angry. "It's been…a lot. I still don't trust these people, so being here was bad enough, but what you've told me—about us. Our heritage. How am I supposed to deal with that?"

He could understand where Ferox was coming from; he, too, had had to struggle with the knowledge that he contained a piece of Basilios. Though, for him, it had been kind of a relief to know where he'd come from and to finally be able to understand why he was so different.

"It doesn't change who we are," Zan said gently. He was glad Ferox was calmer today, that his brother wasn't fighting with him anymore. "All it really does is give us some clarity. You're still the same guy you were before you knew about this stuff."

"I know." Ferox sighed "It's still weird though. And I'm still mad you only told me about it now. I got to know about my own heritage after this Chancellor dude!"

Ferox shot him a dark look, but at least he didn't jump up and punch him again. They would be alright—or, at least, Zanoah hoped they would be.

"I'm sorry," Zan said. "In the jungle, I was worried about Zalika and Helio, and after we arrived here, there just wasn't any time to talk about this."

"Yeah yeah, whatever." Ferox sat up again. "Speaking of Zalika and Helio, you said we get to visit them today?"

"Yeah, but you should eat first. And put on your wristband."

Zanoah pointed at the small table, where he'd spotted the small bracelet. Ferox had either been too preoccupied with his hangover or too skeptical to put it on yet. Zan grabbed the wristband and a densely nutritional cereal bar from the food dispenser, then handed them both over to Ferox.

"What does this thing do, anyway?" Ferox asked, nibbling at the bar while turning the wristband around in his other hand.

"Put it on, and I'll demonstrate for you," Zan said. "Caean hasn't seen its functions yet, either."

Ferox darted his eyes between Zan's and Caean's wrists to see if they were really wearing the device, then put it around his wrist. Immediately it tightened, leaving no space between skin and polymer.

"Alright. So, you can use this as keys," Zan explained. "There's a control panel next to your door, and you can lock or unlock it with your wristband by just holding it against the panel. You can also decide who's allowed to enter your room with their key. Then there's messages. I've checked, and there should already be some contacts in there."

Zanoah held his left arm in front of him, showing his companions the names displayed over the inner side of his forearm in blue writing. All this had become so natural to him in his twenty years of living in this city, but he could see how confused the others were.

"It's a projection of light coming from the wristband," he told them. "It reacts upon your touch, see?"

To demonstrate, he touched Ferox's displayed name, and immediately his brother's wristband displayed the message *"Incoming Call – Zanoah."*

"You can decline or accept the call. There's two options: one for a private call, where only you can hear the person speaking." He pointed at a small symbol with one head next to the wristband. Then he showed them the other one, which had three silhouettes. "And this one's for a group call.

Then Caean would hear everything as well. Messages work similarly, but you use the displayed keyboard to type."

This was probably more important for Caean since calling would be a problem for them. Zanoah also demonstrated this option, typing a small message to Caean. It didn't take long until he got one back and saw Caean's proud smile. It made him smile as well, just glad to see his friends happy and to have a different option of communication for Caean.

"Alright, there's also your bank account on there," Zan said. "Antias told me you'd get some money so you can buy things in the city."

He displayed his own bank account and was stunned at his current balance. It was a *lot* of money, and he was sure he hadn't had even a quarter of that in his account when he was banished. Was this some sort of inheritance from Shaan? He hadn't expected him to have *any*, assuming that Shaan had spent all his money on alcohol and other dumb stuff.

"ZenithCoin is used throughout Tadena," Zan explained. "You can pay with it at any store. When you want to cash out, you hold your wrist against the display. I'll show you when we're out. It's a bit weird to explain." But Zan felt sort of proud in that moment. For once, he was the one teaching people things and not the other way around. It felt sort of like he was paying Ferox back for all the knowledge he'd given Zan about Srale and the forest.

"What if this thing gets stolen and my money used?" Ferox asked.

"It's linked to your DNA," Zan said. "No one else can use your information. You could even take my wristband and use it as yours; it would access all your data."

"Wonder where they got my DNA from," Ferox mumbled, barely audible.

Zan decided not to answer since, if he was truly honest, he didn't know either. There were some mysteries about this city he hadn't unraveled.

"I'm still not sure about this thing, but I'll give it a shot," Ferox decided after scrolling around his wristband for a few moments.

"You want to shower or change before we visit Zalika and Helio?" Zan asked.

Ten more minutes wouldn't make a difference, and Ferox would feel better after a nice shower, especially after his long night and exhausting hangover.

His brother nodded and headed into the bathroom, closing the door halfway. It wouldn't have surprised him if Ferox had just left it open. He never seemed to care much about who saw him naked and who didn't.

"You ready to venture into the city?" Zan asked Caean, who was still standing next to the window.

"Are you?" Caean countered.

Was he? Was he really ready to head back out into the city? It would be louder and fuller than in Srale and even more different from the quiet jungle. Although he should be used to it, Zanoah dreaded it a little, the sudden change from peaceful nature back to the buzzing life of this mega-city.

"'Cause as long as you're there," Caean continued, *"I'm ready for it."*

Zan and Caean smiled at each other, and Zan's shoulders relaxed. With them by his side, it wouldn't be so bad. They weren't Shaan, who made him do things he didn't want to and shoved him into situations that were hard to handle. This was Caean, who cared about him more than anyone else ever had.

"I'm ready for it, too," he said.

And he truly felt that.

After Ferox was ready to go, they had headed out. As they made their way to the monorail station, Zan noticed with some surprise that Ferox wasn't wearing his regular clothes. Instead, he had on a basic brown shirt and some blue jeans. Maybe his brother was getting used to being here after all.

Zan explained to his companions that most of the big towers in the city, like the one they were staying in, had a station either directly connecting it to the rail-network or one not too far away. "And public transportation is actually free, so everyone uses it," he added as they hopped on board, heading for the medical center.

That was one of the things he actually liked about Tadena. It didn't matter if you were rich or poor, at least everyone could use the mono-rail—although rich people used their private, automatically-driven flaicars most of the time.

While on the monorail, Zanoah pointed out some things in the city and explained what some of the buildings were, like the power plant. Although mostly under the surface, one big tower still stood out above ground, surrounded by smaller houses. No one lived too close, at least no one with a lot of money. Around the power plant were slums, a district Shaan had often visited but rarely took Zan with him.

The building they were headed to was a big tower as well, this one covered in blue and red neon signs; some were blinking, while others just displayed crosses and lettering. It was hard to miss the medical center.

It felt weird to take charge, but here in Tadena, it was Zanoah's job to introduce Ferox and Caean to new things until they figured it out for themselves. So, when they arrived at the medical center, it was also Zan who went up to the reception desk and asked for Zalika's and Helio's room numbers.

"Top floor, rooms 483 and 484," the person at the front desk informed them. "No one is allowed to enter the woman's room at the moment, but you can see her through a window."

Zan just nodded and headed toward the elevator. As the three of them rose to the uppermost floor, he said, "I've never been this high up. Only been in here twice—once when we arrived from outside and later when I got an infection. But we were always on much lower levels."

Like most things in Tadena, money and influence dictated how high you were, literally and socially. Zalika and Helio had only gotten such good rooms and care because Antias had personally ordered it, and for that, Zanoah was grateful.

When the elevator doors opened, they walked along the long hallway, searching for the correct room numbers, and finally found them. Both had windows looking in, but they were darkened so no one could see inside. Zanoah looked around for a nurse or doctor to tell them what was going on with Zalika and was lucky enough to see a nurse leaving her room.

"I'm sorry, we're here to see Zalika. Can you tell us if she's okay?" he asked, being as friendly as possible. Playing nice was often the best course of action in high society circles.

For a moment, the nurse looked him up and down, checking some notes on his own tablet before he nodded. Probably checking to see if Zan was allowed to even know about Zalika. The glass cleared up, and they were able to see into the room. Zalika was on a hospital bed, her eyes closed, and she appeared to be sleeping. Cables were attached to her arms and upper body, and she looked so damn small and fragile in there.

"The doctors took the baby out and put it in an incubator," the nurse explained. "It's safer for mother and child like this, especially considering the origin of this baby. They still don't know if she'll make it, but they're hopeful. For now, she's been put in a coma, so her body can heal from all the trauma she experienced from her pregnancy. Her cells were rapidly degrading while sustaining the child. So far it looks good. The degradation has stopped, but there's no way to be sure the process is reversible."

Slowly, Zanoah tried to understand everything they'd just been told. It was a lot all at once, and there was so much technical information he had to wrap his head around. Although he wasn't dumb, he'd never been interested in science.

"So, basically, you're saying you don't know if she'll ever wake up again or even survive?" Ferox put into words what they all had been thinking.

"I'm afraid so." The nurse frowned. "I would love to give you some more positive news, but I'm afraid there isn't much where she's concerned. Her brother, on the other hand, is doing quite well."

With a subtle movement of his hand, the glass darkened again, blocking their view into Zalika's room. The nurse ushered them toward the next room, and without a word, he opened the door and entered.

"Woah, hey, visitors!" Helio said.

He was sitting on his bed, grinning at them and looking much fitter than the day before. His skin wasn't so gray anymore, and the dark circles under his eyes had lifted a little. He was wearing a tight tank top and wide pants, both in the typical white of medical center clothing. It looked good on him, complementing his natural features, the dark skin and hair.

"I've been asked to give you this." The nurse grabbed a wristband from his pants pocket, handing it to Helio. "You're not allowed to leave the medical center yet, but at least you can reach your friends on this and learn more about the city."

Without a moment of hesitation, Helio put the wristband around his wrist and curiously checked its functions. Zanoah smiled. It was refreshing to see someone be so open and relaxed about their situation, despite all the shit they'd been through.

As the nurse fussed with him, he said, "I have to check your shoulder and take some samples, then give you your infusion. Do you want your visitors to stay, or should they wait outside?"

"Of course they can stay! It'll be nice to talk to someone who's not poking and prodding at me."

Helio smiled at them broadly and took off his top, then obeyed the nurse's urging for him to turn so he could check the wound on his shoulder. When the big plaster over top of it was lifted, Zan saw that it looked so much better already. There was no sign of the infection, and the wound was rapidly healing.

"How are you feeling?" Ferox asked, sitting down on a chair next to the bed and cautiously watching what the nurse was doing.

"Oh, much better!" Helio said enthusiastically. "I don't feel dizzy all the time, and my shoulder's not hurting anymore. I don't like the infusions, but they'll apparently help against my cancer."

Helio shrugged, resulting in a small, annoyed noise from his nurse, who was trying to put the new plaster on his shoulder.

"Sorry!" Helio looked at him over his shoulder, grinning at him with puppy eyes.

"Yeah, yeah." The nurse waved a hand at him. "Turn around, please."

Helio swung his legs over the bed, now sitting facing them. He looked so much younger now, although he was still very thin, almost emaciated.

"How old are you anyway?" Zanoah wondered. "And Zalika?" It was hard to guess, but he was quite sure both of them were younger than him and Ferox.

While stretching his arm toward the nurse and having a needle poked into the crook of his arm, Helio tilted his head a little. "Hmm, Zalika's twenty-one, and I'm eighteen. Well, maybe. Not sure what date it is. Could already be nineteen."

So, they really were some years younger, especially Helio. It made Zan angry again that Basilios had preyed on such a young girl, pretty much sentencing her to death. He couldn't even put his feelings into words, just watched Helio's blood filling two little tubes.

"You're still eighteen, but your birthday should be next week," the nurse informed him, still concentrating on drawing Helio's blood.

"You deserve a better life," Ferox said, finding the words Zanoah couldn't. "When you get out of here, we'll check out this city, alright? You seem like you want to have some fun."

Zanoah was glad to hear him say that. Ferox needed company, too, someone he could connect to and do things with. Zan knew he was pretty much glued to Caean, which meant he didn't have a lot of time for the others. Sure, he would also like for them to do things in a group, but it wasn't the same. Having someone to confide in was important.

"Ready for your infusion?" the nurse asked Helio, who sighed and nodded.

He'd put his tank top on again and was now lying on his bed and stretching out his other arm toward the nurse, revealing a small tube fixed in the crook of his arm.

"So, you've heard about Zalika, right?" Helio said. "You've seen her?" When Zan nodded, he admitted, "It sounds so mean, but I hope this baby doesn't survive. Nothing good can come of it." Helio twitched for a moment when a small bag of clear liquid was connected to the tube. It slowly dripped into Helio's body as he sighed and said, "Sure, every life has a right to live, but...I don't know. It's just wrong."

Zanoah wasn't even sure what to think about this. So far, he hadn't thought about the child as its own individual life, only as a danger to Zalika's health. Now, this became a whole different problem. Caean had told him a union between two deities was forbidden but how about a half-deity child? How powerful would it be?

"It's not in our hands," Ferox said. "If it dies, we won't have to worry 'bout it. If it survives, we'll deal with it then. First, we hope for Zalika to get healthy again."

Zanoah was grateful to have Ferox around. Right now, he was being quite helpful and reassuring toward Helio, and it helped Zanoah to not worry as much either.

That is, until he saw Helio grabbing a fistful of his blanket and panting silently.

"You really okay?" Zan asked, concerned. Helio was clearly in pain.

"Yeah, yeah, the infusion just burns inside. It's not really a nice feeling, but it should help." It took Helio a moment longer to relax and continue speaking. "I got cancer in my kidneys and it...what was the word?"

"He has what we call stage 4 cancer," the nurse explained, checking the infusion from time to time. "Means the cells spread and metastases formed throughout his body, from kidneys to colon and close to his heart. Some weeks later, and he would have been dead, if not because of the infection then because of the metastases in his heart. Right now, we're fighting back the mutated cells with a chemical. It attacks only cancerous cells, but it's still uncomfortable. Better than some old ways, though, like chemotherapy. And it has a much higher chance of recovery—about 95%, no matter which type of cancer."

Zanoah was a little overwhelmed again by all the information being thrown at him. Still, he understood one thing: Helio would have died if they hadn't come here at all.

"I helped Zalika escape because I knew I would die sooner than later," Helio said, his eyes half-closed. "I didn't care if I was killed getting her out. This is...it's like getting a second chance at life, and I want to use it."

Before Zanoah couldn't say anything, Ferox grabbed Helio's hand, squeezing it slightly. "You will. When you're better, we'll explore the city together, alright? And if that's not enough for us, we'll go out into the world and explore it all."

It was such a wonderful promise, and Zanoah really hoped for both of them that they would get to experience a life like that, full of wonder and new things. They deserved some happiness.

Helio just nodded, his eyes closed now, a small smile on his lips.

"The infusion is exhausting on his body," the nurse said. "He'll sleep for some hours. You can come back in the evening or tomorrow."

The nurse led them outside the room, but it was alright. They would visit Helio again, and they could also text and call him now.

"So, want to see more of the city?" Zanoah asked.

Caean and Ferox exchanged a glance, then the two of them nodded.

Inside Zan's head, Caean said, *"I look forward to seeing where you come from."*

Zan smiled, realizing that for once, he was actually excited about being in Tadena.

CHAPTER 22

Tadena was exactly how Zanoah remembered it: loud, hot, and exhausting. Ads on neon signs buzzed on every corner, illuminating the city even more brightly—as if the scorching sun outside the dome wasn't enough.

Zanoah regretted opting for clothes made of a thicker fabric that couldn't absorb his sweat easily. Clothes like that weren't designed to be worn on an everyday fashion. It wasn't a surprise that all three of them were soon sweating, their clothes sticking to their bodies.

They were wandering around the city, Ferox and Caean curiously looking at shops and buildings. And while he tried to enjoy his time with his friends, Zan had to deal with the overwhelming sense of being back in Tadena instead. The neon signs buzzed in his ears; voices and electronic music were everywhere; the light was much too bright for his eyes. Add all that to the sweat trickling down his face and neck, and Zan's senses were overloaded.

But his companions wanted to see the city, so Zanoah didn't comment on it, just followed behind them. This was their first time here, so they should get to decide where to go and what to check out. Besides, Zanoah had quickly realized that he didn't make a good guide. He'd never cared to get to know huge parts of this city.

Caean was particularly interested in a small shop that sold necklaces and other trinkets. Zanoah was delighted to hear that they wanted to go inside because he'd always enjoyed coming here. While he'd never actually bought anything from it, he used to wander around it, seeing what it had to offer.

Besides jewelry, this shop sold expensive handcrafted clothing. While Caean was checking out the clothes, Zanoah looked at all the jewelry, wondering if he should get a gift for Caean. He wanted to, but he wasn't sure what they would like. The items in here were made of polymer, like most things in Tadena, but they were painted in colors most Tadenans disliked—shades of brown, beige, copper, or brass. He'd never understood why because people in this city preferred flashy items in bright neon colors. But he was grateful for it because bright and flashy wasn't really Caean's style. These colors suited their earthy nature better.

Finally, he decided on a small, round, brass-colored pendant on a black strap. But as pretty as it was, he frowned at it. He hoped he would be able to get out of this city again one day, go find a real shop where he could get jewelry actually made of metal, not just some synthetic material painted to imitate something it wasn't.

When he went to pay for the necklace, the shop owner, a tiny old woman with graying shoulder-length hair, stared at him—or, rather, his head. "Where did you get this crown? It looks fascinating, almost real."

"It's real, and it's one of a kind," he said vaguely. There was no way he was going to tell her the truth.

He could see more questions coming from her, but he just grabbed the clothes out of Caean's hands and smiled at the old woman.

"I'd like to pay for these too, thank you."

The woman frowned but still told him the total, which Zanoah paid, holding his wristband against the small display next to her counter.

"Do you want your purchase delivered to your home?" she asked

For a moment, Zanoah almost said no. Caean had only picked out a couple shirts and some pants, which they could easily carry. But it was hot, and they wanted to walk around the city some more, and eventually they'd get sick of lugging it around.

"Yeah, that would be good," Zan said. "I'm not sure what address is on my account, though."

It should've been changed to his new room, but the address the woman relayed to him was his old home, the one he'd shared with Julyen. It made his throat feel a little tighter to hear, and his skin itched.

"Oh." It was all he could say for a few moments. Then he choked out, "C-could you use their address, then?"

He pointed at Caean, who had gone back to looking around the store but was nearing the register again, holding an item in their hand. Zanoah couldn't really make it out, but it was rather small.

"I'll pay," he told them, but before he could do anything, Caean put one hand on his arm, shaking their head softly.

"I want to try," they signed, making Zanoah smile.

By now, the storekeeper was staring at them, though. Zan had forgotten one very important thing: disabilities were non-existent in Tadena, or, at least, that's what they wanted people to believe. And Caean had just signed, not spoken, which was highly unusual.

"So it *is* true," the shopkeeper said. "You're not from the city. I've heard rumors, about outsiders and an exile coming back, but..." She stared at Zanoah now, seeing his scar, then gasped. "It really is you!"

Zanoah felt really uncomfortable being treated like some curiosity, and he shuffled from one foot to the other. Sure, he should've known people would talk, but it was different knowing about it and actually experiencing it. Especially since other people, like Felicitas and the nurse in the medical center, hadn't treated him like this. He still wondered what exactly the scar meant and how people knew about its meaning.

"Um, could we please just pay?" Zan asked, just wanting to get out of here as fast as possible. "High Chancellor Antias granted us refuge himself, so it's not like we're here illegally."

"No, no, my boy, you don't understand," she said. "I'm not doubting any of that, but you've been outside the city! You've seen other things than all the gray and neon in here. There's a different world out there!"

Her gray eyes sparkled, and she came closer, almost like she expected him to just pick her up and fly her out of the city. Even if he could, he wouldn't, not when Basilios was out there somewhere.

"I..." He trailed off.

His gaze wandered toward Ferox and Caean, searching for some help, but Ferox had left the shop already and was waiting outside, while Caean only shrugged. Not helpful at all.

"There's more outside, yes," he said. "But at the moment, it's dangerous. Maybe that will change someday, but it's safer in here for now."

When he saw how defeated she looked, he almost regretted saying it. He hadn't wanted to make her sad, but the wrinkles around her eyes were now even deeper and darker than before.

"Will you tell me more about the world? When you have time?" she asked, almost coyly, almost pleading.

"I'll try, but I can't promise," he agreed slowly, hoping that was sufficient. He didn't want to disappoint her by promising and not being able to deliver.

Her face lightened up a little once again, and she nodded, finally allowing Caean to pay for whatever they'd found.

"Have a nice day!" Zanoah said, smiling at her, before leaving the store behind Caean.

Outside, he sighed. He hadn't expected that people would actually be interested in the outside world, though maybe he should have. When he and Shaan arrived about twenty years ago, they'd been curiosities.

"I thought you were kidding about how weird this city is," Ferox said. "Did you see how that woman looked at Caean when they were signing?"

Zan shrugged, a little embarrassed about the mentality of the city he'd grown up in. "Like I said, we don't really have disabled people here. At least, not publicly. If people are different, they tend to hide it."

"I don't intend to hide, if that's alright for you?" Caean said, eyes nervously darting over Zan's face to try and read his reaction.

Zan just smiled and nodded. "I'd never ask you to hide who you are," he assured them.

Caean returned his smile and pushed something into his hand—the item they'd bought before. It took a moment for Zanoah to understand what he was holding, but when Caean turned around and pointed at their head, it dawned on him. It was a thin, dark beige strap to bind back their hair. Carefully, Zanoah wrapped it around Caean's dreads, letting a few strands of loose hair frame their face.

Since Caean was in the perfect position right now, he also pulled the necklace out of his pocket and hung it around Caean's neck. The deity curiously looked at it before turning around to smile at him, signing "thank you" before kissing his cheek.

Zanoah grinned, and he felt his cheeks getting a bit warmer. He wasn't used to giving someone he liked a gift, but he liked it a lot.

"Yo, lovebirds, it's getting dark. Where can we go now?" Ferox asked.

Zan had completely forgotten he was there. He'd been so lost in Caean that the whole world around them had disappeared.

"We could go to a bar," Zan suggested. Then he frowned. "I worked there for nine years, though, so it could get awkward."

"Can't get worse than that old lady," Ferox replied. "Let's go there."

"You sure about that? You just had a hangover," he reminded Ferox.

But his brother only shrugged. "Not much else to do it seems."

As Ferox walked off, Zan took a deep breath, steeling himself to visit a place that held a lot of painful history for him.

It didn't take them long to reach Galaxya, the bar Zanoah had spent a lot of hours of his life in, mostly working behind the counter, entertaining guests and mixing their drinks. He'd gotten good at it over the years, but it was still a job he'd taken for Shaan and not something that *he'd* wanted to do. He'd never really had the chance to figure out what sort of job he might enjoy, just got guests drunk enough to spill the beans about whatever Shaan needed to know at the moment.

Although they weren't properly dressed—the crowd here liked their clothes dark and formal—they entered the bar. It still looked exactly the same as the last time he worked here several months earlier. The walls were a dark blue, almost black, with white accents, and the room was illuminated by blueish light, barely enough to find one's way around. Plush beanbags and couches were placed next to small tables, which were occupied by people of all ages, though most were around their mid-twenties to early thirties.

"Let's go there."

He pointed toward an empty couch in the corner. As the three of them sat down, his gaze wandered around the bar, taking everything in. It really was still the same. Only the songs were a little different, probably some new ones that'd come out after he left, though the sound system was still loud enough to make conversation difficult.

The feeling of being overwhelmed by his surroundings set in almost immediately, like it had almost every day he worked here. The music and lighting, the people talking all around him—it was too much for Zanoah. But Shaan hadn't given him a choice, so he'd had to get used to it, had to numb himself to these sensations. It was only at home, when Julyen was at work, that he could finally get some silence and calm himself down.

Behind the bar, he spotted a younger guy with neon blue hair mixing cocktails. Zan didn't know him, so he must be new. Might even be his replacement.

"What can I get y—You!" a woman exclaimed.

Startled, Zanoah's gaze snapped toward the woman standing in front of the couch. Tanyth was smaller than him and wearing a black miniskirt and shiny tights. The royal blue blouse she was wearing was see-through, leaving almost nothing to the imagination. Though her green eyes were partly hidden behind her platinum blonde bob, he was sure they were full of fury. He remembered very well how angry she could get whenever Zan fucked up.

"Where've you been, shithead?" she demanded. "You ditched us, and the rest of us had to work overtime to cover for you!"

"Um..." It took him a moment to figure out how to explain everything. "My brother was killed, and I got thrown out the city. Sorry I didn't officially resign?"

Tanyth stared at him, completely bewildered. Finally, she shook her head and sighed. "You've always been such a weirdo, but *this*? You fell on your head, huh?" She waved her hand dismissively. "Whatever, can you at least pay?"

Without a comment, he displayed his account balance for a moment, so she knew he could very well pay for them, no matter what they bought.

Her eyes bulged, and she gave a low whistle before saying, "Whatever you're involved in, I don't even wanna know. Sounds illegal. What do you want?"

They hadn't really looked at the menu yet, but Caean went for something fresh, and Ferox ordered a drink with a ton of alcohol, while Zanoah decided to get a Magic Skillet. It was one of his favorites, with its fresh flavor and nice turquoise color. On the rare occasions that he let himself drink, it was his go-to.

"Seems she doesn't really like you," Ferox said after she left, an amused smirk on his face.

Zanoah sighed and leaned back in his seat. "Yeah, well. I've never really been social and only did what Shaan wanted me to do. Means I had no friends or connections. She's right; I've always been weird."

He shrugged and tried smiling, but it came out a little crooked. Hopefully, he could use this second chance at life to make something of himself without Shaan controlling every single aspect of who he was—where he worked, who he associated with...who he loved. Lost in thought, his gaze wandered toward his left ring finger and the tattoo wrapped around it.

When their drinks came, Ferox smirked and raised his glass in a toast. "To new friends and still being weird," he declared before taking a big sip from his drink.

Of course, Zanoah immediately recognized it: Palm Velour, the same drink Shaan had always loved.

Several drinks later, Ferox wanted to dance. He tried to get Zanoah and Caean to join him, but they hadn't drank nearly as much alcohol and were both a little nervous. Finally, Zanoah sighed and got up, leading Ferox to the dance floor.

Ferox made a beeline for the bar first. "I need one more drink!" he exclaimed, more stumbling than walking straight.

Zanoah sighed again. This wouldn't end well, and he didn't really like caring for drunk people either. He didn't know what Ferox was like when he was drunk, but he worried his brother would be cruel like Shaan. Zan pushed the thought away, telling himself that Ferox was nothing like his late brother. He would never treat him the way Shaan did.

Before he could think about it more, his wristband announced a new message. Frowning, he checked who had texted him and was surprised to see it was Antias.

> You will be picked up in 5 minutes outside Galaxya. Be alone. I need to speak with you about an important task.

That sounded ominous. And five minutes wasn't much time to get outside either, especially with Ferox here.

"It's fine," Caean said. *"I'll stay here and keep an eye on him, make sure he gets home safely. If something's up, I'm with you all the time."*

Caean smiled at him, and Zanoah relaxed immediately. Right, he wasn't alone anymore and didn't have to deal with things all by himself.

"Put the tab on my account, alright?" he told them. *"I've got enough money. I'll see you later."*

He hesitated before leaning down and placing a gentle kiss on Caean's lips. It would be weird being without them again, but they still had the crown and their connection. There was no way they would get separated, not connected like this.

Since he couldn't spot Ferox, he had to trust Caean to take care of his brother and instead headed downstairs, taking the elevator to the bottom floor, where a dark flaicar already waited. A guard opened the door for him, and Zanoah nodded at them before getting into the vehicle and sitting down. After the door was closed behind him, the flaicar started moving, and it was then that he realized he wasn't alone in here. Someone sat opposite him, looking at him calmly.

"Welcome back to Tadena, *darling*."

Julyen.

CHAPTER 23

Zan had expected pretty much anyone else—Felicitas or maybe Antias himself picking him up. But he certainly hadn't thought he would see Julyen again, not like this, not without warning. And to make matters worse, it was just the two of them, no guards, nothing stopping the awkward silence between them.

He could only stare at his husband, his response stuck in his throat. The last time he'd seen Julyen had been in High Chancellor Antias' office, watching his brother die. Back then, Julyen had been a Justicar but he'd obviously climbed the ranks by now. Zan spotted a different uniform, the four pink stripes on his shoulder indicating that he'd become an Executor, maybe even leading his own division.

The dark gray uniform covered his whole body, though his helmet was retracted, leaving his head bare. Even his hands were clad in gloves. A small gun was strapped to Julyen's belt and another bigger one, sat next to him on his seat.

Julyen was tired, judging by the dark circles under his green eyes, which had gained an edge he hadn't seen before. His red hair was still a little tousled, though, like always. Some things apparently never change.

"So silent, huh? How many drinks did you have?" Julyen leaned toward him, opening his hand to reveal a small pill—the same kind Zan had offered Ferox that very morning. "Take it. I need you clear-headed."

Without thinking twice, he followed Julyen's order. Despite his husband being two years younger than him, Zan had always let him take the lead in their relationship. It made it easier to stay on his good side and to dig for the intel Shaan needed from him.

Swallowing the pill, he closed his eyes and took a deep breath. This wasn't the old days, he reminded himself. Shaan wasn't here. Julyen knew the truth now. And Zan wasn't the same man who'd left Tadena all those months ago. There were so many unspoken things between them, but this wasn't the time or the place for that conversation. Not here, in a flaicar taking them... wherever.

"Where are we going?" he wondered instead, trying to focus on more important things.

"Vault. I'll tell you when we're there."

Julyen was on edge, eyes darting around the cabin, almost like he was checking for cameras or microphones. Minute after minute, Zan could feel the alcohol in his veins dissipating, leaving him completely sober and even more anxious and insecure than before. His palms were sweating, and his hands were a little shaky.

Their journey felt too long, though they didn't really go very far. When they finally stopped in front of their destination, Zan saw it was a tower close to the center of Tadena.

Julyen, who'd put his helmet as they got out of the flaicar, had his weapon in hand, leading Zan to the door. "We're here by order of High Chancellor Antias," he informed one of the guards at the gate. There were several of them, as well as a few more patrolling around the perimeter.

This tower—the vault, Julyen had called it—didn't look any different from all the others around them. But Zanoah had heard rumors of a library and some old data stores hidden underneath a heavily guarded tower. This had to be the place.

"No weapons, no helmet," the guard said.

Then he looked at Zanoah, taking in his scar and the crown, and frowned, checking the data on his pad again. The guy was probably wondering if they really should allow him entrance. Zanoah caught a glimpse of the monitor, where a new picture of him with the scar and crown was displayed Stamped over top of the photo in green was a message saying, "Entrance Approved."

"Nothing funny down there," the guard warned. "You have two hours. If you need more, the High Chancellor has to grant you more time."

Julyen nodded, putting his weapons in a locker next to the door and closing it with his wristband. Then headed toward the elevator, beckoning for Zan to follow. Though it took him a moment, Zan finally hurried after him, still confused about what was going on here. Why had Julyen come to pick him up? Why had he taken Zan here? And what did Antias need them to do?

He pondered all of these questions—and about a dozen more—as they rode down in the elevator. Finally, they arrived at the very bottom floor, where they stepped out of the elevator and walked through a scanner. It didn't beep, meaning they were clear to proceed, and yet another guard opened a door for them. Between all the guards and the scanner—which was only ever used in high-security buildings, Zan knew whatever he was about to see, it was something very few ever had.

Without hesitation, Julyen entered the room, not caring about Zan hurrying behind him to catch up. What Zan saw was absolutely astonishing: rows and rows of books shelved neatly next to each other and relics displayed under glass or clear polymer cubes, protecting them from dust and time.

Julyen headed deeper into the vault, with Zan on his heels, who looked around curiously. There was so much down here, so much that he never knew existed. It was amazing.

Turning around a corner he saw Julyen leaning against a wall between two bookshelves and saying, "We can talk here, in private. Your wristband won't function down here, though."

Zan couldn't help but check it, seeing that Julyen was right. The screen was black, and none of the buttons were working. He wasn't sure what was interfering with the device, but he suspected that any technology that came down here would fail. Whatever this place was, Antias wanted to keep it a secret.

"What are we doing here, Julyen?" Zan asked.

Julyen frowned and sighed deeply, rubbing over his eyes for a moment, before he turned toward the bookshelves. "Cato sent us here because he suspects that the storm outside the city was caused by a deity a long time ago. High Chairwoman Nelius apparently knows things about it, but she won't tell him. He thinks some of the information about it has to be stored in this vault, and since it's about a deity, he hopes it'll help us find a solution to beat our new enemy. High Chairwoman Nelius doesn't know we're here, and she *can't* know. She has her own agenda, and I wouldn't be surprised if she wanted to make a deal with this deity."

Zan had barely processed what he'd been told when Julyen started walking away. He snagged hold of the man's wrist, saying, "Wait, wait, who's High Chairwoman Nelius?"

Julyen turned back to him, his body almost deflating, like he was fed up with keeping it all inside. "Right. You don't know. *No one* knows." He didn't just look tired now; he looked like he'd been carrying around the weight of the world on his shoulders. "Cato Antias isn't the highest authority in Tadena. No High Chancellor has *ever* been. There's someone else behind him, the High Chairperson, and currently it's Nelius."

Zan's mouth gaped. "Are you serious?"

Julyen nodded solemnly. "As much as I'd like to tell you everything, that's not why we're here."

"What did you mean, she has her own agenda?"

"You should know. You've seen some of the data from the experiments she sanctioned. Controlling prisoners' emotions, making them into soldiers. If the experiments are successful, the military will be next. No more emotions for any guards or officers. They'd be basically soulless machines."

He shook his head. "Cato never agreed to her experiments, but he had no say in the matter."

What the fuck? Of course he'd known Shaan had found data about some experiments being done on people in Tadena, but he hadn't realized it was that bad. This sounded like a completely fucked up thing to do, dehumanizing people, robbing them of their emotions and basically turning them into puppets.

"Cato has to play by her rules, be her right hand, no matter what. That's why she hasn't allowed me to officially become his partner. In the public's eye, I'm just his fucktoy." A bitter smile crossed Julyen's face and for once Zanoah understood how fucked up this whole situation had to be, not just for Julyen but for Cato Antias as well. "It was also her who suggested, no, *ordered* Cato to direct me to hook up with you. To marry you. Not just to keep an eye on you and your brother but to keep Cato single as well."

For a long moment Julyen was silent, just staring at the books on the shelves, pain in his green eyes.

"Cato begged me to leave the military," he said finally, "so he wouldn't have to relay the order to me. I refused. If I'd left, I would've been the first one being experimented on. It's much easier to get rid of a regular citizen no one would miss. And my parents needed the money."

Shit, Zan hadn't known any of this—had never even expected it. Of course, he'd guessed that Julyen hadn't married him because he loved him but this... It was worse than what he could've imagined. Not just the order by itself but everything surrounding it.

"So...you knew I was lying to you from the moment we met?" Zan mumbled, unable to find other words. It was too much to process right now. All these years, Julyen had suffered as much as he had.

"Yeah, well, so was I. You think it was coincidence I was sitting alone at the bar you were working at on my twenty-first birthday? I had other plans, but...well. I did a lot because Cato asked me to, because he was ordered to relay orders to me. I didn't hate you, though; I never did. If you'd stayed in Tadena after your brother pulled that dumb stunt, it would've put you right in line for these experiments. Banishing you was the only way to keep you safe."

How could Julyen stay so calm while telling him all this? How didn't he resent him? Despite both of them using each other for years, listening to their superiors without doubting them for a moment, Julyen had still protected him. He'd known Zan would've preferred to die in the jungle than become part of such experiments, stripping him of his humanity.

"Thank you, Julyen. I..." He shook his head, unable to express what was going through his head. "I always knew you were going somewhere else after some of your shifts, meeting someone, but...I was happy about it." Because it meant he didn't have to put on a mask at home, to play nice and happy to be around Julyen all the time. Because it meant Julyen might have some happiness as well.

"Hmh, I enjoyed that time, too," Julyen admitted. "It wasn't all bad, though. Being married to you. But we do have to get officially divorced. Since you were banished, there was no way to get a divorce. Banishment isn't the same as death, according to some dumb ancient law, and it's supposed to be the last humiliation for a partner. I couldn't have married Cato, even if Nelius allowed us to."

Julyen shrugged, a bitter sadness on his face. Zan couldn't help it and closed the gap between them in a few steps, taking Julyen in his arms and just hugging him tightly for a moment. He felt how stiff his husband was, but slowly, Julyen relaxed and reciprocated the unexpected embrace.

Slowly, Zan loosened the hug and took a step back, glad to see Julyen relaxing a bit more. It was much nicer to see him like this, no matter how much resentment he'd felt toward him during their marriage. It wasn't Julyen's fault; it never had been.

"We'll get divorced as soon as possible," Zan said. "And I hope you can live happily and freely soon. You really love him, don't you?"

"For more than five years now," Julyen admitted.

That was such a long time, and Zan realized their relationship, or at least Julyen's interest in Antias, must have started when Julyen had still been a student at Open Mind, working as his assistant.

"Are you sure this High Chairwoman would want to align with Basilios?" Zan asked.

Another grim nod. "Unfortunately. From what Cato's told me about Basilios, Nelius is exactly the kind of person who would want to curry favor with him. She has power now, but she'll do anything she can to hold onto it." Then he gestured for Zan to follow him. "Let's look for anything related to deities or otherwise helpful, alright? We don't have much time, and if we can't find anything this time, it'll be hard for Cato to get us in here again."

Zanoah agreed, and they parted ways to search more efficiently. There would be time to talk later; now, they had to work their way through all these books, relics, and other curiosities, hoping to find a deity-shaped needle in a haystack. Having Caean in his head down here would really be helpful.

"Try looking for something dating back at least five centuries, possibly older," Caean said, causing him to smile. Of course, they knew what he was searching for.

"You heard what we were talking about?" Zan asked as he walked through the aisles, looking for the oldest-looking books.

"No, I've been occupied with getting Ferox back home. He definitely drank too much, and a girl tried to hook up with him. He didn't appear very interested, but he couldn't quite get the words out to tell her that. I took him home, and he's sleeping now. Wait, there, two rows back."

Immediately, Zan stopped and went back a few steps to look at the books Caean had seen. He carefully pulled one from its place on the shelf. It looked really old; its cover was made of leather, and something was printed on it in a language he couldn't read. So as not to damage the old book, Zanoah slowly flipped through the pages, waiting for Caean to say something else.

"It mentions the war and the fact deities were involved but nothing else," Caean said. *"Will this be enough to get you more time? It looks like this vault holds many mysteries."*

Zan just shrugged, not sure if it would be enough. Instead, he looked for Julyen and showed him the book and the passage about the deity-human war, hoping he knew better if this was the sort of thing that would merit a longer search.

Julyen smiled and sighed in relief. "Yes, with this, Cato can justify us being here. I may have to work some double shifts, though. High Chairwoman Nelius won't be happy if she finds out I've abandoned my post."

Zan was already happy they had enough evidence to keep their search down here going, but he still wondered...

"Where are you stationed?"

Julyen was an Executor now, which meant he probably had a more important post than guarding some entrance. But Julyen said, "In the slums, commanding a small unit of about ten people. It's always such fun to not know if the next person to cross you has a gun and wants to shoot you. Not."

"Let me guess, another specific order from the High Chairwoman?"

Julyen just shrugged and gave him a sad smile, which told Zan he was right. She really wanted to make Julyen's and Antias' lives as miserable as possible, and despite never having met her, Zanoah despised her.

"Let's go upstairs," Julyen suggested. "Our time's almost up."

Zan sighed in agreement and followed him to the elevator. They'd put the book in its place again, so no one could figure out what they'd been searching for.

In the elevator, he hesitated before asking, "You think Antias can also get Caean permission to go into the vault? They know much better what we're searching for."

"I can ask him, but no promises. It was already hard enough to get *us* down here."

Zanoah just nodded. If it wasn't possible, maybe Caean could at least help him through the crown, seeing what he saw, guiding him.

"I'll contact you tomorrow, after I know when we can go back down there," Julyen said as the elevator began rising. "And about a date for our divorce. Did you want any of your stuff? I stored most of it."

Yet another surprise. Zanoah had expected Julyen to get rid of all his things since storage space in Tadena was pretty expensive and there had been no reason at all to keep that stuff.

"Only my clothes, if you still have them. Don't care about the other stuff."

He'd never really had anything he cared about, no hobbies or heirlooms. No memories, either. He really had been such an idiot, giving his life fully into Shaan's hands. But what else could he have done? Shaan had been his only family.

"Sure, I'll send it tomorrow," Julyen said. "And I'll accompany you home. Gonna spend at least the night with Cato. Come on, let's get out of here."

Julyen smiled at him, grabbed his weapons from the locker, and headed toward the flaicar waiting for them. And for once, Zanoah felt comfortable following Julyen, even smiled as he did.

CHAPTER 24

Zanoah spent the next several days mostly underground, searching around the vault for any helpful hints about the involvement of deities around Tadena or some sort of leverage over High Chairwoman Nelius. Antias had managed to grant him full access whenever he wanted to come here, and Zanoah intended to use every moment. They didn't know if or when Basilios would arrive here, and he wanted to be as prepared as possible.

While Caean couldn't accompany him, they had asked to visit the greenhouse tower, assessing the situation there and maybe even helping the crops to grow a bit better. Ferox, on the other hand, was only interested in visiting Helio during the day and partying at night. He never even asked where Zan went every day, but Zanoah was honestly used to people not caring about him or what he did unless he did something wrong. It still hurt because he considered Ferox a friend, but more and more every day, he was coming to realize that Ferox wasn't much different from Shaan.

In the vault, he concentrated on searching through all the old books and scrolls, some of which were even older than the city, judging by the ancient, fragile pages. Every evening, Julyen joined him down in the vault, still in his uniform, silently looking through the books Zan hadn't touched yet. He was a comforting presence; Zan liked knowing he wasn't all alone in here, even if the two of them could go hours without seeing each other. Only when they found an interesting paragraph did they take the book and go show the other, talking about whether or not it would be helpful.

Without being forced to be around Julyen, to be intimate with him and play his happy husband, Zan started liking him. He'd never appreciated the humor his husband had despite their shitty situation or how full of life Julyen could be. It had always annoyed Zan while they were living together, irritated him because he wasn't used to having a positive presence around him.

"I've got a free day tomorrow, so I'll pick you up at 10 in the morning, and we can finally get rid of these." Julyen held his hand up, spreading his fingers a little to present the very visible tattoo around his ring finger. "Then we're free of each other. You want to introduce your friends to me someday?"

It was an interesting question, and Zan hadn't even thought about it yet. There had never been a time before when he'd had friends to introduce. The more he considered the idea, though, the more he smiled.

"Sure," he said. "Though Zalika and Helio are still in the medical center and Ferox...well, no idea what he's up to at the moment, actually."

Which left him only with Caean. Introducing the two of them could be awkward, considering how close he was with Caean and his past with Julyen. But he didn't want to hide Caean—ever. And Julyen might already know about them, since he surely had talked about him with Antias.

Thinking of Antias brought another question to mind. "Julyen, can I ask you something?"

Julyen looked at him curiously over his shoulder. "Hm? What is it?"

"Why the scar? Wouldn't it have been enough to just throw me out of the city? Why this mark? And why do people seem to know what it means?"

"Oh, that. It's a very ancient law. Cato found it in the vault, too. But it's also an urban legend in the city. That's why some people recognize the mark." Julyen glanced at the scar. "It's faded a lot already, though."

It had. The wound had healed up rather well, and the scar was a lot lighter than he'd expected it to be, which Zan was quite glad about it.

"I know you're probably still angry about what happened, Julyen said. "But Cato knew you'd survived getting into the city somehow, so he hoped you'd also survive getting thrown out. He wouldn't have exiled you otherwise."

Zan frowned, since he still couldn't remember how the fuck he had gotten into the city the first time. Antias hopes had proven correct, but it was still a big risk he'd taken with Zan's life.

"Were you the one who packed that bag for me?" Zan asked, remembering the backpack that had been inside the small capsule. It had helped him a lot to have food and a water purifier.

Julyen didn't answer him, only smiled, stretching a little before he got up.

It was already late, and they were heading toward the elevator, ready to call it a night. Zan's head was spinning a little, not being used to being under artificial light with his head in books all day. He was hungry, too, because no food or drinks were allowed inside the vault.

"Did you eat at all today?" Julyen asked. "Or drink enough water?"

Zan just shrugged, feeling dizzy. Time passed weirdly inside the vault because there were no windows to the outside world, and even the clock on his wristband wasn't perfectly reliable down here.

"Damn, Zan, you need to take care of yourself, alright?" Julyen gently scolded. "Doesn't help if you end up in some forgotten corner 'cause you forgot to drink some water."

He felt an arm around his hip, holding him upright, guiding him toward the flaicar waiting for them.

"Sorry, think I forgot to take a break today." He shot Julyen a crooked smile and swayed a little. "These books are interesting."

Julyen's worried green eyes and freckles swam a little in front of him as his soon-to-be-ex-husband leaned toward him to push him back into his seat.

"No reason to forget yourself," Julyen said. "I'll get you home and then you need to have a good meal, alright? Here, at least drink some water."

He got handed a bottle and grabbed it from Julyen, taking a bit gulp before sighing in relief. At least he hadn't been outside and under the sun the whole day, sweating away. The shield might hold back some of the UV-light but not the heat.

Normally, when they arrived at their high-rise, Julyen stayed in the elevator to ride up some more floors, but this time, he got off at the same floor as Zan, still steadying him and helping him walk until they arrived at Zan's room. The door slid open almost immediately, and he saw Caean waiting for them, one brow raised.

"We've not been formally introduced, but I'm Julyen. Take care of him, will you?"

Zan was handed from Julyen's arms into Caean's, and he leaned into the deity a little. He felt better already, but it was always nice to be so close to Caean.

"Remember, tomorrow, 10am," Julyen reminded him, making him sigh and nod.

Of course, he wouldn't forget their divorce date. He wanted to get this over with, too.

"Good. Have a good night and rest a little. No adventures the rest of the day," Julyen joked, grinning at him, then Caean. Before leaving them alone, he added with a wink, "And, uh, take good care of him, huh?"

The implication of that statement wasn't lost on Zan, and he blushed. He had no desire to sleep with Caean—not now, at least. Not really. It was weird to even think about, giving that they'd both had such bad experiences with sex. Maybe someday he'd be ready—*they'd* be ready—but not tonight. Maybe...maybe not for a very long time. Maybe not ever...

"You know I can see what you're thinking about?" Caean teased him a little, pushing him toward the bed and sitting him down there.

He felt his cheeks burning even more.

"It's all good, Zan, don't worry. When we're ready. And even if we're never ready, sex isn't that important in a relationship."

Zanoah was comforted by that. It was good to hear his…partner validating him, reassuring him that it was alright. To hear that he wasn't weird because of his lack of sexual drive.

"Here, eat. You forgot it all day."

Caean pushed a nutritional cereal bar into his hands, and although he would prefer something else, Zan just bit into it, glad to finally be able to eat. He even got a bottle of water as well, slowly feeling better as his head stopped spinning.

"Will you tell me about your day?" Zan asked. *"How was seeing the greenhouse?"*

Though he could've peeked into Caean's mind through their connection, he'd been fully engrossed in looking through the books and hadn't really seen what Caean had done today. It was quite nice hearing about it now, and because of their bond, he could even see Caean's memories of helping some plants to grow, consulting with some scientists and suggesting some other fertilizers and placements.

Zan smiled happily. It was great to see how Caean got so invested in their own passion and enjoyed helping. He also grasped how good Caean had felt in the greenhouse, closer to the little vegetation Tadena had to offer.

"Sorry I dragged you here to probably the only city without any nature," he mumbled.

They were both laying on the bed, Zan on his back, staring at the ceiling. He felt Caean pushing themself up on their elbows, so they could look at him better.

"We didn't really have a choice," they said. *"And it won't be forever, either."*

Caean smiled at him despite the threat still looming, the uncertainty if they would even survive when Basilios attacked. *If* he attacked. It was possible that they would just wait here for weeks, months, maybe even years, without seeing a trace of him.

"If it's, so be it. At least we're not alone."

These words made Zan tilt his head a little to look at Caean, smiling at them as well. Gently he pushed a strand of hair to the side to see their face even better. Yes, they were right. No matter what, they had each other, and this was already a big improvement from everything they had experienced beforehand.

A gentle kiss relayed these feelings without Zan saying a word. It was all they needed. Each other.

Why was he so nervous? It was absolutely silly, but still, Zan was pacing up and down their room while waiting for Julyen to pick him up. Today, he would finally get divorced, and it felt like a really big thing to him.

Caean only watched him, a little amused, sitting on the bed and checking some news. Zan had noticed they were interested in politics and local news, trying to stay up-to-date and figure out what was going on in the city.

When he heard the knock at their door, he almost jumped, then opened it immediately. Julyen was standing there in civilian clothes for the first time since Zan returned to the city. He had on a tight, light gray shirt, slightly shiny black pants, and black boots. He couldn't deny one thing—Julyen certainly was attractive.

Julyen grinned at him. "Ready to get divorced?"

Zan slowly relaxed. It would be fine. Yes, this was important, but that didn't mean it was bad. He had nothing to worry about. So he just nodded and put on his own boots.

"Want your friend to come, too?" Julyen asked. "I don't mind having an audience."

He hadn't even thought about this, but his gaze wandered toward Caean, a question in his eyes. He wouldn't mind either, but he'd leave the decision up to Caean.

"Talk about awkward," they joked, but they smiled at him and got up to leave with them.

It might be a little awkward, but it would also be kind of nice to have Caean with him. They certainly helped him relax. In the monorail on the way to their destination, he couldn't help but hold Caean's hand,. It was a short trip—only two high-rises further—but it felt right to touch Caean, to feel them beside him.

When the monorail stopped, Zan followed Julyen, who looked so relaxed today. It might be because he wasn't in uniform, but it was more likely that he was happy to take the next step toward his future with Antias. And as Zan and Caean walked hand-in-hand, he realized this was a big step for *him*, too. Whatever the future might bring, Zan had Caean by his side.

The divorce itself went by pretty fast. They only had to sign a form with their fingerprints and then their marriage was legally ended. Right after all the legal issues were settled—which didn't take long because Zan made no claim to Julyen's money nor he to Zan's—their tattoos were lasered off. It would still take some time before it was fully healed, but soon, nothing would remain of their marriage, neither legally nor visibly.

"Wasn't so bad, was it? Let's go get a drink. Or do you have other plans today?" Julyen smiled at him happily, already heading for the elevator to take them down to the street.

Zan was fine with that. His finger still hurt a little because of the laser, but otherwise he felt really good. Free. He wasn't bound to anyone anymore, in any way.

"Sounds good. I've got nothing planned." Then he turned to Caean, not wanting to make plans without them. "How about you?"

"I have an appointment at 2 in the greenhouse, but I'm free until then," they signed.

Zan nodded and translated for Julyen. Although they could communicate in a different way, they both had agreed it was quite weird for others if they only spoke in their heads.

Julyen's eyes lit up. "That's so cool! I really want to learn this...what's it called?"

Julyen was quite curious, and it made Zan chuckle a little. He hadn't expected people in Tadena would want to learn sign language, especially not military personnel, but Julyen was more open-minded, despite always following orders so well. Though, when he thought about it, he realized Julyen only really followed Antias' orders, which made sense.

"It's called sign language," Zan explained. "You use it to communicate with someone who's deaf or mute or both. I'm not really good at it yet. but Caean's teaching me. Ferox also taught me some basics."

And once again, he wondered what his brother was up to. Hopefully not getting into trouble. If he was, Antias would probably have already told him, so he didn't worry too much.

"Huh, that's interesting," Julyen said, sounding genuine. "Never needed that here, 'cause, y'know, no one's mute or deaf. But if you're still learning, how do you know what's right and swrong?"

"We're communicating differently most times," Zan replied. "When I'm wearing Caean's crown, we're mentally connected. Then there's no need for any sign language."

"Wow, Zan! You've really matured. Never thought you would let anyone so close. Especially not in your mind and heart." Julyen smiled at him.

"That's pretty cool, though. And it explains why you look so happy every time you look at them."

Zan could feel his cheeks getting hotter, and he sought help from Caean with a gaze but they only shrugged, smirking a little.

Julyen nudged him with his elbow, his smile growing wider. "And you're adorable like this. Really, I'm glad you're happy."

This made Zanoah proud and a little emotional. Julyen was being honest and genuine and really sweet. But it was more than that. Despite all the hardships he'd been through, Zan was glad he'd been banished, that he'd gotten to know and love Caean. Without his exile, he'd never be as happy as he was now.

"Drinks are on me today," Julyen said as they arrived at a coffee shop. "To celebrate our divorce, but also so we can get to know each other again—better this time. Get what you want."

It really wasn't much of a coffee shop since it didn't offer coffee, just differently flavored and colored drinks. Still, people loved going here, getting all the pink and purple and turquoise drinks, so Zan wanted to try one as well for once, choosing a pink one called Berry Breeze. Since he now knew how fresh berries tasted, this would probably be a little weird, but he wanted try it. Caean got themselves a Minty Marvel, which was a pretty turquoise, while Julyen went for a Caramel Crush.

"Ah, I love this one!" Julyen swooned while taking another sip from his drink through the straw. "Can't drink much of this 'cause it's so sweet, but once in a while it's nice."

For a moment, Zan hesitated before testing his drink as well, grimacing. Yeah, this really was...different.

"That's...really sweet," he said after trying and failing to find words for what this tasted like. He could see Caean reacting similarly, which amused him.

"Oh, you've never actually tried these?" Julyen marveled. "Zan! There's so much you missed in Tadena, so much you can still show your friend.

I only have, like, one free day a week, but I can take you around to some things you haven't done yet. No pressure this time around."

Zan was a little taken aback by the offer at first, but he had to concede that Julyen was right. Thanks to Shaan, he really hadn't experienced all that Tadena had to offer. In fact, he'd never really enjoyed life at all. But he'd been given a fresh start—and someone he wanted to spend his life with. Why not see what all he'd been missing out on?

"Sure. I probably only know like a third of Tadenan culture." Then he nodded at Caean's drink. "Can I try yours?"

They held their cup toward him so he could try a sip. It wasn't as sweet as his, but it tasted just artificial as well. He decided not to tell Julyen these same drinks would taste better if they weren't made in Tadena, where they had to pretend they knew what berries really tasted like.

They walked around for a while until their cups were all empty, though Julyen finished his much quicker. Zan and Caean were once again holding hands, their fingers entwined, just enjoying being so close, being able to casually walk around and explore the city. Julyen happily played their guide, pointing out things Zan never knew existed. With Caean by his side, he felt like he wanted to explore them all.

At some point, though, their walk had to come to an end, and Julyen said, "Zan, we should get to...you know. And your appointment's soon, too, isn't it, Caean?"

Caean nodded after taking a look at their wristband, and Zan sighed. Back to the vault for now, hoping to find some hidden information in one of these books. There had to be something, somewhere.

"See you in the evening," Caean whispered, placing a gentle kiss on his lips, before turning around and heading off.

"You're really in love, aren't you?" Julyen asked him softly, smiling at him.

Zan could feel how big and happy his own smile was. "I am. Never thought I could feel like this," he admitted. "Caean's...they're different from anyone else I've ever known. They like me for me. No, they *love* me for me. They don't judge me. They believe in me, support the decisions I make. They make me feel...good."

"Take good care of them and yourself," Julyen said. "True love is hard to find."

Zan couldn't agree more. From what he'd seen, most people were only interested in short relationships, only lasting for a few weeks—sometimes even just a night. Often it was about sex, not connection. Opening yourself up to someone was a whole different thing. It made people vulnerable, and people didn't like being vulnerable. At one point in his life, Zan would've been one of those people. Not the sex part, obviously, but the not wanting to feel vulnerable part. But it was different with Caean. Loving them made him stronger, more confident.

Before Zan could respond, he heard a low noise he couldn't quite place. It sounded a little like a thump or someone popping a can of soda open. Confused, he looked around, wanting to ask Julyen about it, but when he looked at him, he screamed and ran toward him.

Blood. There was so much blood pouring down Julyen's neck, soaking into his gray shirt, and Zan could barely catch him when he fell to the ground, unable to speak. Zan acted on instinct, pulling off Julyen's shirt to press it against the wound on his neck, trying to keep him awake.

"Please, no," he begged, crying. "Not like this. Not now. Julyen!"

CHAPTER 25

In hindsight, Zanoah could barely remember what happened after Julyen was shot. At some point, medics arrived, pulling Zan back so they could take care of Julyen. Some Supervisor questioned him about what happened, but Zan hadn't been very helpful. He hadn't seen who shot him, and he couldn't remember noticing anything suspicious prior to hearing the shot.

The High Chancellor checked on him personally but asked him to get back into the vault to distract himself, but Zan knew he was also selfishly concerned with finding something to help them in their fight against Basilios. Or...maybe not so selfishly. Despite shock still clouding his brain, Zan noticed Antias was worried—very much so. *And* pissed. He probably thought High Chairwoman Nelius was behind the attack on Julyen.

After that, Zan got some wipes to clean his hands of Julyen's blood. He'd somehow managed not to get any blood on his clothes, but it didn't really matter. Julyen was still in trouble—could already be dead for all he knew—and Zan had a job to do. He hoped whatever he found could help take down a deity—and whoever was behind what'd happened to his ex-husband.

Down in the vault, Zan's body slowly relaxed, though his hands were still a little shaky. The last few months had been so full of death and hate and people he cared for getting injured. He didn't know if Julyen would be alright since he'd lost a lot of blood. To make matters worse, down here, he couldn't even get updates on the situation. He would have to wait until he was back on the surface and his wristband reconnected to the wireless network.

While his thoughts still wandered off from time to time, Zan tried to focus on the section of books he'd found yesterday. They were interesting and old enough to document the founding of Tadena.

Slowly, a headache crept up, but he tried to ignore it, focusing on the text. It spoke of a patron to the city, some higher being protecting its people, and Zan could only guess it had to be a deity. The writing was partly obscured, faded with age, and he could only piece together what he could still read: *"- a storm of such magnitude - not a curse - shield - people of Tadena - protected from the war."* Although it wasn't much information, it helped Zan to understand a lot more. Tadena had been around during the war of deities and humans, and a deity had been in the city, one able to summon a storm raging for years and years on end.

He wondered if this deity was still around in Tadena. If so, why hadn't they been noticed? Caean had also told him that all the deities had retreated, fallen into a slumber, by their own decision.

As he contemplated all of this, his eyes fell on a door at the very back of the vault, one that was always closed and bolted. Neither Julyen nor him had been able to enter it yet, and he couldn't stop wondering what was behind this door. Would it offer more answers? He could only guess, or...he could try to open the door one more time.

As he got up, he had to hold onto the table so he wouldn't topple over immediately. He hadn't noticed that he was sweating and his shivering. His headache had spread throughout his body, and now all of his limbs ached. Still, he wanted to find out the truth, so he left the book right where it was and headed over to the closed door.

"Caean, have you ever heard of a deity able to summon storms?" he asked. *"From what I've read, they protected Tadena and made the storm, acting as a shield."*

With every step, his body felt heavier, and it was harder to focus on dragging his feet toward the door. What was going on with his body?

"That doesn't matter right now. What's wrong with you, Zan?"

He felt Caean's panic, but he would be alright, wouldn't he? It was just a little fever. The adrenaline was probably finally leaving him, and his body was going into a slight shock.

"Get out of there and I'll pick you up, now," Caean insisted.

Zan just shook his head, his eyes focused on the door. *"I'm so close to the truth. I can't stop now. It's just a fever."*

Finally, he reached the door, but when he twisted the knob and tried to pull it open, the door didn't budge. Of course not. What had he expected? Still, he rattled the door, ignoring Caean's worried voice in his head, telling him to get out of the vault for now, to rest.

The light went dim, and he barely felt his body colliding with the hard floor. He shivered, staring at his trembling hand, which was pale and clammy. He felt awful, and he just wanted to get out of there now, but he couldn't move anymore. Besides, he was so far from the elevator that there was no way he could get to it.

His muscles convulsed, and pain shot through every fiber of his being, making him scream and scream until he was unable to stay conscious. Instead, his mind drifted into Caean's, trying to escape the pain and utter helplessness.

It was weird. So far, he'd only been in Caean's mind when they were talking or dreaming, and he'd always still been himself. But now, he felt like a passenger, unable to act or speak, only watching what Caean did and said. He was momentarily amused at the idea that he was having an out of body experience, but then another thought occurred to him. Was this how Caean had seen through his eyes, like they'd done in the caves?

Caean was now running through the streets of Tadena, frantically typing into their wristband. Zan hadn't realized how good Caean had gotten in such a short time, but it made sense. Next to sign language, which only a few people understood, it was their best way to communicate freely.

> Either you get him out of there or I'll go in!

Zan read the message as Caean typed it, not knowing who the message was for or what were they talking about. He'd never seen Caean so direct with what they wanted, so demanding. But proud that they were pushing for their wants and needs.

It took him a moment to understand which building Caean was now entering. Wasn't this the one he was in? The one that had the vault in its basement? But what were they doing here?

> Felicitas will bring you the antidote and go downstairs with you.

The message popped up on Caean's wristband.

> Can't get there sooner. Ten minutes, max.

Whoever wrote that message, it made Caean even more furious, and Zan saw gray walls fly past as Caean sprinted toward the gate, not caring about the guards shouting at them. They just burst through the guards like they weren't even there. Zan knew this would get them in some big trouble. Why couldn't Caean wait just a little longer for Felicitas to accompany them?

His thoughts were so slow, swirling around like a thick syrup, unable to put one and one together. He could only watch Caean standing in the elevator, pacing up and down, knocking out the last guard before passing the vault-doors.

By now, he was used to this big hall with bookshelves on both sides and hidden nooks everywhere. It was so familiar, despite seeing it through

Caean's eyes. He heard a weird sound, and immediately Caean ran in the direction it was coming from. What *was* that?

Confused, Zan watched them following the sounds he slowly recognized as painful whines, until they turned around a corner and saw...*him*. Slowly, Zanoah pieced together what was going on here. Caean had been so worried about *him*, lying here in pain, slowly dying for some reason. They had pushed through several guards, without any regard for their own safety, to get to *him*.

It was unnerving being outside of his body, looking down at it as it writhed in agony. Zan didn't feel anything here inside Caean—not pain or fear or the shivers that wracked his curled-up form. All he could really sense was Caean's desperation, their anguish, their deep love for him.

"Please go back, Zan," they pleaded. *"I know it's so much easier to run from pain, but please. Don't be like me."* They whispered those last words.

Zan immediately understood what they meant. He was running away from pain, shutting off his brain completely and building walls to keep the world out. He hadn't even done it on purpose; it had been so easy.

For a moment, he watched Caean holding his body, their hand on his chest. They were sending waves of refreshing green force flowing into him, which gave him the strength to dive back into his own body. Immediately, pain flooded his senses, and he screamed, grabbing onto Caean's arm, tears forming in his eyes and flowing down his cheeks.

"You'll be okay, I'm here," Caean whispered, still holding him, their force slowly dulling the pain.

Despite their help, Zan was still sobbing, fearing this feeling would never stop, that this nightmare would never end. He had no idea for how long they sat there until he heard footsteps and another voice. He didn't care; he was more concerned with trying to stay awake, to not let the exhaustion and pain overwhelm him.

When he felt a different, sharper pain in his chest, he yelped and grabbed Caean even tighter. As his vision slowly cleared up, he carefully looked around. The pain was ebbing away finally, and he wanted to thank Caean for saving him. But he got distracted by something before he could.

Right in his chest, poked into his heart, was a big syringe. A vaguely familiar woman was injecting a blue liquid into his body. This must be the antidote someone talked about in Caean's messages. No matter how weird it felt, he could feel his body relaxing, and with every heartbeat, the pain got a little easier to deal with.

"You're back, hey, welcome," the woman said. He realized it was Felicitas. "Good thing you only had a small dose of poison in your blood. By accident, I guess." She pushed the sleeve of his now torn open top to the side, revealing a small cut. "Thought so. Julyen was the target, but you were in the way and got some poison, too."

"Wait, wait, what?" he asked slowly, his tongue feeling heavy in is mouth.

As Caean helped him sit up again, Felicitas explained, "Julyen was shot with poisoned ammunition. He's still in surgery. It was the same poison your brother used, so you probably know how it works. After Shaan's death, our scientists researched the poison and what it does to a human body. As soon as it reaches your heart, you get these symptoms, especially the excruciating pain. The antidote is only useful when administered directly into the heart. Sorry about that." She gave him a sheepish smile.

Zan's mind was reeling. *This* was what Shaan's final moments were like? Antias really had given Shaan the easy way out. He wouldn't wish the sensation of his body being cooked alive on anyone, not even Shaan.

"Sorry I didn't listen to you, Caean," he mumbled, his head down. If he'd only left the vault earlier, Caean wouldn't have had to come running down here to save his sorry ass.

"I'm just glad you'll be okay."

They gently made him look at them, and he gazed into their beautiful but worried ocean eyes. Caean's thumb carefully wiped away some more tears before they pulled him closer, placing a soft kiss on his lips. He really was thankful Caean had saved him, given him the strength to hold on until the antidote arrived.

Slowly, Caean got up and helped him to his feet, an arm around his hip to keep him steady since his body was completely exhausted by now.

"There's a deity behind this door," Caean said.

Surprised, but also a little confused, Zan looked at Caean. They didn't seem shocked; in fact, they'd said it very matter-of-factly. But Zan was thrumming with excitement and anticipation. This door held the answers they'd been seeking.

Caean tilted their head a little, like they were listening to a voice behind the door, one no one but a deity could hear. *"But she's very weak."*

It took them only three steps to reach the door, and the moment Caean's hand touched the knob, Zan heard a *click*. Caean opened the door, revealing a circular room made of stone with several torches hanging on the walls. As Caean and Zan stepped into the room, the torches lit by themselves, illuminating a figure in the middle of the room.

Curled into herself like an embryo, a once young woman was lying on the ground, clad in what looked to have once been a beautiful black dress. The fabric was now torn and ripped, eaten away by time. Her face was hollow, and her skin looked like it would crumble to dust if she was touched. Caean let go of him to get closer to her, then knelt down beside her.

When they touched her shoulder, the woman only turned her head a little, looking at Caean for a long time, her eyes a stormy gray. Despite being able to hear Caean's thoughts, Zan couldn't figure out how they were communicating. It was something different entirely. This was all happening so fast for him, and he was still recovering from his near-death experience. Just when he thought he was getting his bearings, something happened that threw him off again.

The deity grabbed onto Caean's hand and smiled before dissolving into a white powder, one he had only seen at the top of the mountains. He caught a glimpse of Caean's thoughts, confirming it was snow. A weird energy swirled around the room, and he thought maybe he was imagining it. Or maybe he still had a fever. But he'd seen and experienced so many impossible things lately; this was just one more thing to add to the list.

Caean grabbed a knife in a leather-sheath and said, *"Let's get out of here and then I'll explain what just happened."*

As Caean hugged him tight, Zan just nodded. He was in no mood to argue and wasn't strong enough yet to anyway. He was so out of it that he'd forgotten Felicitas was there. She was still staring into the middle of the room, blinking in disbelief. Zan couldn't worry about her now. He just wanted to get out of here and sleep.

Caean pushed the dagger into his pocket to hold onto and started helping him toward the elevator. The guard back on his feet, warily watching them from a distance. When he didn't move to stop them, Zan realized that either Felicitas or Antias had probably intervened, and he was grateful to have such powerful allies in the city.

Realization slowly sank in. Julyen was hurt. Caean had entered the vault by force. And Zan had seen a deity—the one who'd protected Tadena for so long—disappear.

He still didn't really understand everything that'd happened today, but one thing was for sure: things would never be the same.

CHAPTER 26

Despite his worries that they would get stopped while leaving the vault, there were no problems, and they headed toward the flaicar waiting for them. All of them were silent, although Zan wanted to ask Caean what exactly had happened down there. Was the other deity dead? Antias had asked him if it was possible to kill one, but he'd never gotten around to asking Caean about it. Was this even a good time to?

As the flaicar took off, he asked, "Where are we go—"

Before he could finish his sentence, Zan looked outside the flaicar and realized something was different. *Wildly* different. The city was still gray and busy like he remembered it, but the dome was *gone*. For the first time since he'd come to Tadena as a boy, he could see the sky and desert without the obstruction of the dome shielding the city from the raging storm outsi—No! No, there *was* no storm anymore.

"We're going to the medic center," Felicitas said. "Antias is waiting for us there."

He barely heard her, just kept staring outside. Although he knew the jungle was supposed to be right behind the desert, he couldn't see it. The ring of sand was still too vast for him to see past it, even without the sandstorm obstructing his view.

So many thoughts raced through his head. Now, without the dome and storm shielding Tadena from the rest of the world, Basilios would be able to get into the city much easier. They could only hope he was still far away, but there were other things to worry about, too. Were the people of Tadena even prepared to face such drastic changes? Once a way to cross the desert was found, they'd be able to leave the city, but they would have to deal with a harsher climate as well. The dome had protected them from more than just the storm.

His primary worry, though, was Julyen. As they arrived at the medical center, three guards met them and accompanied them to the elevator, heading to the top floor. While Zan was still a little wobbly on his feet, exhaustion flooding through every limb, Felicitas used this time to rapidly type a series of messages on her wristband.

Helio burst out of his room, not listening to the nurse behind him telling him to stay back. He looked much fitter, not so skinny and sickly anymore. "Zan! What's going on?" he asked. "I saw the sky change. Y'know what's up with that?"

"Not sure," Zan said, feeling bad that he hadn't been back here to visit Helio or Zalika since that first time. "You know where Ferox is?"

"Yeah, I'm here." Ferox had been standing behind Helio, but now he stepped forward and crossed his arms over his chest. "Like *you* should've been, too. What the fuck have you been doing that's kept you from seeing your friends?" Then his expression softened, though not by much. He still looked angry as he said, "You look like shit. What happened?"

Zan could only shrug, not sure what he should tell them, especially since he didn't quite understand what had happened, either. His brother was right about him being a bad friend, of course, but he really had thought Helio would be fine, and he'd been busy in the vault most of the time. Maybe that's why he never had friends. He was just too bad at keeping up any kind of relationship.

"Better get back to your room," he heard Felicitas say. "The situation might escalate very quickly. So far this floor's under Antias' control, but we think Nelius might take it by force. Be prepared."

All of them looked at her. She pulled her gun out of its holster, looking even more fierce than she normally did. Ferox's expression darkened, and his hand wandered toward his belt, where Zan spotted two smaller knives strapped to it. Ferox led Helio back to his room, and Zan was glad they had each other and would take care of each other.

Felicitas led Zan and Caean into another room on the same floor, and he immediately saw Antias standing next to a bed. He looked upset. No, he looked *pissed*. Glad that Antias was their ally for now, at least Zan carefully came closer and spotted red hair sticking out from under the blanket. Julyen.

"How is he?" he asked, genuinely concerned for his ex-husband. He'd seen the wound, how much blood Julyen had lost, but there was also the poison to worry about. At least it looked like Julyen was breathing, so he was still alive, wasn't he?

"He'll live, but he'll never be the same again." Antias pulled back the blanket, revealing not only a patch on Julyen's neck, where the bullet had hit him, but another big patch on his pale chest, right in the center, over his heart. "I wasn't fast enough. She had him drafted for her experiments. Soldiers without a human heart." He shook his head. "How does it change a person?"

The more Zan learned about these experiments, the more he wanted to forget about them again. It occurred to him that he could've known long before this if he'd just read the data Shaan stole. He wasn't sure if that would've helped the situation any, but now he would never know.

Antias pulled the blanket back up over Julyen, his eyes never leaving the man he so obviously loved. He bent down and placed a kiss on Julyen's forehead, then said, "According to medics loyal to me, he would have survived just with an antidote. Like you did. She used the situation to her advantage, knowing exactly how important he is to me."

"Wh-when..." Zan couldn't even get the question out.

"As soon as the antidote took effect. She has people here on staff. They got to him first. By the time I got here, it was too late." Taking a deep breath, Cato Antias turned to face Zan and Caean, his eyes sparkling and darker, more black than the usual blue, full of hate and pain. "She's mine. I'll be the one to kill her, and I won't hesitate."

"We won't get in your way," Zanoah immediately agreed.

At first, he was relieved. He never wanted to kill anyone, though he understood why Antias would. What had been done to Julyen was monstrous, and Antias wanted to make sure she couldn't hurt anyone ever again. But that relief turned to a troubled sort of acceptance when Zan realized that he would do the same for Caean. He wanted to rid the world of Basilios—now and forever.

Antias nodded, his gaze wandering toward the window and the phenomena outside. "Tell me what happened in the vault. Why is the storm gone?"

"I don't like using you like this, but will you be my translator?" Caean asked, helping Zan sit down. His body might be strong, especially with Caean's force helping it heal, but he still had just been poisoned and almost died.

"Of course," Zan told them. *"I want to know what's going on as well."*

Caean nodded and smiled at him before they started to explain to him what happened. Zan relayed what they were saying to Antias, who looked like he was having trouble processing all of it as much as Zan was.

The woman they'd seen was the deity of weather, according to Caean. She had protected Tadena centuries ago by conjuring a never-ending storm that engulfed the city to keep both other deities and humans away. With time, people had forgotten about her, trusting more in technology and all their little gadgets, making due with their limited space and resources inside the city. But forgetting about her also meant that she started to wither away until she was as close to death as she had been when Caean found her.

She'd locked herself in that vault, which could only be accessed by other deities, and she had her weapon, the dagger now hidden in Zan's pocket.

If Basilios or any other deity out to hurt her tried to enter the vault, she would stab them with the knife, which was made of Luskite.

While Caean said that, Zan pulled the knife from his pocket. The handle was made out of a dark, almost black wood. Carefully touching the blade with one finger, he immediately regretted it. Yes, this was indeed real Luskite, as it burned his fingertip.

But Caean had more to say. When the deity of weather saw Zan, Caean, and Felicitas enter her chamber, she realized how much time had passed, and decided to let go of this world because her people no longer needed her protection. Caean assured Zan and Antias that they hadn't suggested to her that she should pass on or give them the rest of her force. She had done so of her own free will. Though Caean had tried to coax her to hold on for a little longer, she'd had no intention of doing so, and Caean wouldn't dream of standing in the way of what someone else wanted to do with their own life.

"There's only two ways for a deity to end," Caean said. "You either pass on your energy to another deity, or you let your force spill into the world, without any control over how it'll affect whatever is around you."

So that explained what Zanoah felt in the vault. It hadn't been his imagination after all. But it also brought him to a terrifying conclusion. Basilios wasn't likely to give up his power if he died, which meant all of that force would spew out into the world, possibly causing more damage. Zan couldn't let that happen, so instead of killing Basilios, they had to find a way to put him back in chains and lock him up somewhere he couldn't hurt anyone.

Carefully, he slid the dagger back into its sheath and put it into his pocket. He may not be able to kill Basilios, but he could still hurt him with this.

"So, the dome collapsed when the storm stopped generating its energy," Antias said, staring out the window. Then he shook his head. "This is bad. With no dome protecting us, Basilios could just storm right into the city.

And given how power-hungry Nelius is, she'd jump at the chance to make a deal with him. It's a win-win for the two of them, and we'll all suffer because of it."

"So what do we do?" Zan asked.

"I don't know." He turned around, a look of dismay on his face. "You told me Basilios wants Caean for some reason. Nelius might offer them up to get a better deal out of him. I'll assign you more guards, and you'll get weapons as well. Have you ever used one before?"

Zan shook his head, though he wasn't really thinking about weapons. He was worried about Caean. He wouldn't allow Basilios to ever use them again. It wouldn't be like in Srale, where he'd waited until his perverse "ritual" was over. Even if it was dumb or risky, he would protect Caean from such cruelties before they happened.

"Felicitas will give you a crash course, then," Antias continued. "Your friends, too, if they want. You must be able to defend yourselves. No matter how much I dislike it, we also have to think about taking measures against Basilios' power. Both of you are immune, right?"

"Yes, but Ferox definitely isn't," Zan said. "And most other people aren't either."

Antias paced up and down the room, looking lost in thought, then said, "I might have an idea. Most soldiers already have a chip to control their hormones, but it's operated by High Chairwoman Nelius, so those won't be helpful at all. She can just leave them turned off and let Basilios have his influence. But there's a different way of administering the drug that chip releases, a pill. It's still experimental, but it might be our best shot."

Zanoah wasn't so sure about using some drug that wasn't tested yet, but the situation was dire, and they didn't have a lot of options. He'd seen exactly what Basilios could do, what an effect he had on people. Without some sort of help, there wouldn't be a way to defeat him.

"How many loyal soldiers do you have?" Zan asked, rubbing his temple as another headache crept up. This felt a little too close to what he'd been exiled for in the first place, trying to overthrow the leader of the city.

"Enough to counter Nelius," Antias replied, "but it will be a lot harder if we're facing Basilios' army, as well."

"At least we're better equipped in Tadena." Zan tried joking a little, but it came out sounding dead and wooden.

He was finding that he kind of missed their days in the jungle. Back then, there wasn't as much to think about, just staying alive and reaching their destination. He wanted those days back and hoped they could defeat Basilios and finally live in peace.

>I'm sorry for dragging you into this,< Caean wrote on their wristband, but it only made Antias sigh.

"If I'm assessing the situation correctly," he said, "Basilios would've come here sooner or later. Now it's sooner. And the trouble with our High Chairwoman isn't your fault." Antias gave both of them a small smile. "Get some rest. We'll all stay here at the medical center for now. Felicitas will show you a room and get you weapons, then tomorrow, you'll get some training."

Clumsily and only with Caean's help, Zan got up from his chair. Once again, their lives had been turned upside down. They couldn't even get back home—or, really, the little room that acted as their temporary home—but had to stay here, to be safe. At least they had each other, and when he looked at Caean, who was almost glowing and filled with more energy than he'd ever seen before, he realized that's all that mattered.

CHAPTER 27

"*We should get some rest,*" Caean suggested, standing at the door to their new room. It wasn't as comfortable as their room back in the high-rise, since it was an empty patient's room, but at least they were safe here and had a bed. It was more than they were used to, considering their time in the jungle.

"I have to bring Helio and Ferox up to date first. You can stay here, if you want."

If he didn't inform their friends what was going on, they would be pissed, and no matter how tired Zan was, he didn't want to let them down again.

Although Caean didn't answer him verbally, he felt their need to stay close, to not get separated again, to prevent anything bad from happening—again. A small smile crossed Zan's face, and he headed toward Helio's room, hoping Ferox would be there as well.

Even as he knocked at the door, he heard Helio's voice, begging and getting closer to the door.

"Please, not again, not today. You've been drinking so much these days."

Before Zan could open the door, it was ripped open from the inside. Ferox stood in the middle of the doorway, staring at him coldly. Something had really gone downhill between them, and he felt it must've started in Basilios' basement. Their friendship had cooled even more after Basilios' temple, and here, in Tadena, they hadn't had much time to talk at all. If they were to stand against their foe, together, they had to figure this out.

But first, he had to stop Ferox from leaving and instead make him listen to what had happened. Calmly, he returned Ferox's stare, not allowing him to leave the room.

"Helio is right," Zan said. "It's too dangerous to leave right now. May I explain what happened?"

Ferox didn't say anything for a moment, just stared at him. Then his gaze wandered over Zan's shoulder, spotting Caean behind him. Feeling his partner close-by gave Zan some reassurance and helped him relax more, knowing someone had his back. Finally, Ferox shrugged and turned around, leaning against the wall next to the big window and crossing his arms in front of his chest.

Helio looked from Zan to Ferox and back. His amber eyes were dark and tearful, but he gave Zan a grateful smile. "Thanks, I..." He took a deep breath. "Let's just...talk? I want to know what happened, too."

As Helio settled down on his bed, sitting cross-legged and watching him eagerly, Zan pulled a chair close and sat down. Caean, on the other hand, leaned against the wall next to the door, almost as if they were acting as a bodyguard.

"First of all, I'm sorry I didn't visit you again," Zan said. "It's not because I don't care about you. I've just been pretty busy these last days." There was so much to tell them, but finally he settled on, "High Chancellor Antias asked me to go into a vault underneath the city and find any information about a deity and their involvement with Tadena. It turns out Antias *isn't* the leader of this city. It's a woman named High Chairwoman Nelius, and she's bad news. He wanted me to see if I could figure out how to stop Basilios in case he came here and she tried to make a deal with him. I've been down there every day since we arrived. Today, I found proof a deity's actually responsible for the storm outside Tadena..."

For a moment his gaze—and not just his—wandered toward the window. It was still so strange not to see the storm surrounding Tadena, only vast desert and sand visible behind more high-rises.

"Caean found her, and she gave them her last energy, which caused the storm around the city to dissipate. I also got this." Zan stretched a little, to pull the dagger from his pocket and unveil it, so Helio and Ferox could see it. "It's made of Luskite and can hurt any deity. It may be helpful against Basilios."

Carefully, he put the dagger away again. He had no intention of touching the blade, since Luskite hurt him as well, and he'd been in pain enough today.

"What's all this about a High Chairwoman?" Helio asked. "Why would she make a deal with Basilios?"

"From what Antias told me, she's power-hungry and will stop at nothing to achieve what she wants. My brother stole data about experiments on humans that she sanctioned, and I've already seen what those experiments are aiming to do. It's...it's awful. Right now, Antias expects her to strike at any moment, to get rid of him—and us."

He told them about him being poisoned, about how Caean had saved him. Helio looked horrified and concerned, but Ferox just stared out the window, his back to them.

"What are these experiments?" Helio asked.

Zan swallowed hard, steeling himself to say this. "This afternoon, my ex-husband Julyen was shot and poisoned after our divorce. Nelius had his heart replaced with an artificial one. I...I don't know what he'll be like after this, but he won't be the man I knew."

Helio was staring at him, eyes wide open, clenching the fabric of his pants in his fists. Ferox was still staring outside, but slowly, he turned to look at Zan, his gaze cool.

"You never even told us you were married," he said accusingly. They were the first words he'd spoken this whole time.

Zan was shocked. That was hardly the most important issue at hand right now.

Before he could respond, Ferox said, "And you're responsible for destroying the storm. Our shield from Basilios is gone. I hope you have a plan to get rid of him, 'cause I sure don't want to get drawn into his entourage again. Like you said, I'm like a hungry animal once I'm under his spell."

Slowly, Zan's frustration changed into something else, something harder: a mixture of annoyance and doubt. Yet again, Ferox was questioning his decisions despite not having been there, despite not having to make the hard choices Zan had. And didn't he even care that Zan had almost died? That Nelius needed to be stopped before she created more of these...whatever Julyen had become?

Helio spoke up before Zan could. "Why are you being such an asshole? Zan literally almost just died! And you're mad he didn't tell you about his ex? The one who was just shot? I think that's more important here." He looked over at Zan. "I'm sure you did what you thought was best."

Helio's words appeared to have some impact on Ferox, since he looked at the young man still sitting on the bed, frowning for a moment. Then he said, "Maybe it's better if I go, then. No storm means I'll be able to leave this city." Ferox's gaze wandered toward Zanoah again, looking him up and down. "Everything with you goes wrong, anyway. It has from the moment we met."

Deep inside of him, these words tore open an old wound, one his parents and brother had fostered for so long. After all those years hearing that he wasn't worth a damn, that he was only as good as what he did for other people, he thought he was used to it. But Zan hadn't expected it to hurt so much, to hear such words from someone he thought to be his friend. No, his brother.

It stunned him so much that the he couldn't reply.

Helio's eyebrows shot up. "What? No! Ferox, don't go! Please!"

Zan didn't move from his chair, sitting there, deflated and defeated by Ferox's words, watching him leave the room in the corner of his eye.

Helio tried to follow him, but Caean's hand grabbed onto his wrist with remarkable strength.

"It's his decision. If he wants to go, let him," Zan whispered, unsure what to do now.

It felt like he'd just lost part of his family, a family he'd started to love and care for, and he didn't know how to deal with such a sudden loss. A dark part of him thought that maybe he wasn't supposed to be happy. Was it even worth it to open his heart? Why let people in only to get it torn apart again?

"Zan? I...I don't know what to say," Helio said. "I'm so sorry. I'm so bad with this stuff. Ferox didn't mean it. He's just scared. I'm scared, too. We all know we'll face Basilios again soon, and he's so strong and powerful. It's hard to resist him, and I think that scares Ferox."

Zan slowly looked up at Helio, who was crouched in front of him. His eyes were shimmering, like he was about to cry, and honestly, Zanoah felt the same. Every time he thought things were getting better, he was pushed down again.

"Maybe I should be the one leaving," Zan said glumly.

Now he felt Caean grabbing his chin and forcing him to look up. So far, Caean had never used their extra-human strength on him, but this time, there was no way to escape their grasp.

"If you even think about building a wall or leaving, I'll haunt your every dream," they promised. *"You're worth so much more than Ferox just said. Without you, I would still be chained up, being used by Kelcie in her cave. Always remember that. I need you, Zanoah."*

No matter how bad things were, Caean's words always had an effect on him. They reached some place inside him, buried underneath the scars and wounds of being used and neglected all his life—a vulnerable hidden core, so deep that he didn't know he had it. It broke the barrier and the tears he had held back for so long started flowing. He was unable to stop, crying and sobbing silently, so glad he wasn't alone but still so hurt and scared of yet another rejection.

"It's okay, I'm here," Caean said soothingly. *"I won't leave you."*

Warm arms wrapped around him, pressing him against Caean's stomach, as their hands stroked through his hair. He felt safe and loved, no matter what had just happened. Caean wouldn't leave him; he knew that.

Suddenly, he was back on their little island. It had grown bigger since the last time he was here, the ocean slowly retreating more and more every day. One single tree had become several, slowly filling the island and giving it a fresh, lively atmosphere.

Even here, Caean held him, not letting go for a single moment. There were no walls or borders between them. Even if everyone else left him, he still had Caean, still had this one anchor in his life, the person he could trust completely.

"Let's go to our room and rest, alright?" they suggested.

Zan could barely nod, even more exhausted now than before his little breakdown. Slowly, he looked up and saw Helio smiling at him.

"Sorry, you shouldn't have had to see this," Zan apologized, his voice a little raspy. How long had he been crying? He had no sense of time, but judging by the dark sky outside, it had been quite a while.

"Ah, don't apologize! It's fine," Helio assured him. "And I'm glad you have Caean at your side."

Caean smiled softly and brushed a strand of hair out of Zan's face. They appeared so strong, but Zan knew their other side, how broken and vulnerable they were as well. Still, they were strong for him, a bastion of calm.

The tears were slowly ceasing, and Zan used his torn top to dry his face at least a little. He could only imagine how he must look, his eyes red and his face puffy.

Taking a deep breath and letting it out slowly, he said, "Right. Antias said we'll get weapon training tomorrow. If you want to come, too, be ready." Wanting to distract himself from everything else, he asked, "How's your treatment going, anyway?"

"It's good!" Helio beamed. "I'm officially healthy now! Had my last treatment this morning. They just want to get some blood samples again tomorrow, but otherwise I'm good to go. I'd be happy to join you tomorrow."

Helio's smile brightened his own mood as well, at least a little. Zan hoped his friend would have a better chance at life now. If they survived Basilios, he would help Helio figure out what he wanted to do and where he wanted to go. It was the least he could do.

"Get some rest," Zan said. "You need it. I'll see you here tomorrow."

Helio smiled at them and opened the door, basically telling them to leave in a nice way. Caean gently pulled Zan out of the room, giving Helio a nod.

They headed to the room assigned to them and got ready for bed. The room was so sterile and small and unwelcoming, but hopefully it wouldn't be for long. Even their bed was small, made for only one person, but Caean pressed themself so close to his back, their arms wrapped tight around him, it wouldn't be a problem at all.

Slowly, with Caean kissing his shoulder, Zan fell asleep, hoping the next day would be a better one.

CHAPTER 28

Aiming a gun was much harder than Zan expected.

In the morning, Felicitas came to the medical center, gave him, Caean, and Helio uniforms that provided more protection than what they normally wore, and handed them their own firearms, including some extra ammunition. Then they headed into the basement of the medical center, which was connected to other official buildings by tunnels, and had found their way into a training room.

Wondering how they were able to use these tunnels so easily without meeting any of Nelius' troops, Zan asked Felicitas about it. She just shrugged and told him very few people knew about these tunnels at all. After learning about them a few years ago, Antias had ordered them sealed up, and now they could only be accessed if the High Chancellor himself granted someone access.

Their training that morning was odd. Because they were using a simulation, almost like a video game, Zan didn't feel like he was actually training at all. But it also felt like he was really killing people with his shots; their animated selves disappeared when they died in the simulation, and it gave him chills.

He'd only ever killed one person before, and it wasn't something he'd ever wanted to do again. Would he be ready to kill to protect Caean, to protect their freedom, to defeat Basilios? As much as he loved Caean, he still hoped there was a non-violent solution to all of this. Still, the more days they came here and trained, the more his aim got better, and the harder he tried to tamp down his anxiety over killing someone.

Dealing with all of this was way harder for Caean, however. They were a gentle soul and didn't like killing any living being. They pushed through the practice, but for the rest of the day, the were silent. There were moments when they were deeply lost in though that Zan could glimpse memories of them using vines to strangle people, and he felt their shame and disgust over what they had done in the past. Even though he understood that these were visions of the war, it still shocked him that Caean, who now honored every life, could've once killed people.

Deep down, though, he knew their anxiety over learning how to shoot was nothing compared to the fear they felt over seeing Basilios again someday. Zan really wished he knew how to help Caean relax, but all he could offer was empty promises. He couldn't guarantee that Basilios wouldn't come, that he wouldn't try to take them away again. And he couldn't promise that he'd be able to stop him from doing it. Of course, he would do everything in his power to protect them, but he just wasn't as strong as a deity.

One day, he silently sat next to Julyen's bed, watching him. All this time, he hadn't woken up once, just lay there, silent and pale, looking so small and fragile.

"The pills for our soldiers are ready," Antias informed him. "They'll be distributed today

But Zan didn't turn around, not yet. He knew Antias had worked a lot lately, figuring out a way to stop Basilios' power working on his people, pushing his scientists to mass-produce as many pills as they could.

"That's good," Zan said. "Helio will need one, too."

Antias sat down on Julyen's other side, brushing his fingertips against his freckled cheek, smiling sadly for a moment. Every time they were here, Zan could see the pain and rage burning inside the High Chancellor. Zan could tell he was ready to unleash that anger as soon as he saw the person responsible for Julyen's pain.

As much as Zan felt for him, there were still things he wanted to know—things he *needed* to know. Sighing, he said, "I...I know it's not an appropriate time or place, but...I don't remember how I got into Tadena twenty years ago. I only remember Shaan pulling me through the jungle and seeing the desert, but then it's blank. The next thing I remember is being in a room like this one. I've tried remembering, but I just can't."

And being in the medical center so much lately had brought back feelings of being alone and confused, memories of people taking his blood and talking about him like he wasn't even there.

"I hoped to remember, thought maybe whatever Shaan and I did to get here would help in some way. It sounds so dumb."

Zan was embarrassed the moment he said it out loud. It was selfish of him, and he knew he should be more worried about Julyen, about how to deal with Basilios, than he was with his past, and yet he couldn't shake his desire to know what had happened back then.

"I was just a teen back then myself," Antias said. "I've only read files and seen some footage of your arrival here. After I came to power, Nelius ordered me to monitor you and your brother closely. I know you had a different name, one your brother had to change. Back then, no scientist could figure out what made you so different. It was one of the reasons you were under surveillance so much. And now...well, now we know."

Back then, none of those scientists had any idea about deities, so even if they'd tested him for everything they knew, they wouldn't have found any answers. And it now made sense why he'd always felt watched, even more than Shaan had been. It hadn't been paranoia at all; they'd actually been keeping an eye on him because he was different.

All of that whirled through his mind, along with a million other questions. But what he really wanted to know was…

"What was my name?" Even as he asked it, he wondered if maybe he shouldn't have. There must've been a reason he'd forgotten all of this.

"Your name was Deuce," Antias said.

Deuce. Second choice. *Monster.*

Zan just shook his head and frowned, staring blankly at Julyen's hand, without actually focusing on it. His parents had named him after how they felt about him, from his birth.

And yet his forgotten name stirred something inside him, deep in a corner of his mind, especially when Antias said, "Try to remember how you got into this city. It might give us an advantage to defeat Basilios—or at least help us escape this city if we need to."

The room blurred and suddenly he was back in the jungle.

"How much longer? I can't walk anymore," Deuce whined, but his brother didn't care, only dragged him through the thick jungle, his hand firmly around his thin upper arm, leaving yet another bruise.

Every step got more exhausting, and by now Deuce was stumbling more than actually walking. They'd been on this journey for so long, and he still didn't have any idea where Shaan was actually heading. Did he even know where they were going?

After their parents had been killed, Shaan had packed only some essentials and food before shoving Deuce out the door. He hadn't even locked up. His brother had been so angry and so determined to go somewhere and "fuck this corpo up." Whatever he was talking about, Deuce had no idea.

"Please, Shaan," he begged, almost crying.

His feet and legs were hurting, and he had leaves and vines tangled in his hair. He just couldn't keep up with his big brother. His legs were so much shorter.

When Shaan stopped, he was relieved—but just for a moment. Then he saw the angry look on his brother's face and felt a harsh pain on his cheek. Instinctively, Deuce held his free hand against his hurting cheek, trying to numb the pain a little despite knowing it wouldn't work. It never did.

"If you don't stop complaining, I'll just leave you rotting here," Shaan growled, pulling him along once again.

Would that be so bad? To actually stay here in the jungle by himself? It sounded so...peaceful. He'd be able to escape his angry brother, who'd gotten harsher and more violent after their parents' death. But he couldn't say that out loud. He wouldn't be a bad boy, a burden.

Instead, he tried to force his small body to comply, to keep up with Shaan, no matter how much it hurt. Any sense of time he'd had was gone, and when they finally saw something besides lush, green jungle, he almost thought it wasn't real.

Why was there so much sand? And what was that big storm?

It looked dangerous, like it could just sweep them up and carry them far, far away. Still, Shaan dragged him onto the sand and toward the storm. The closer they came, the more panic built in his chest. But he knew better than to ask his brother to turn around or let him go. Shaan would only hit him again and keep dragging him into the storm.

Soon he felt the wind gushing around him, pulling on his clothes and hair, pressing into his chest. Every breath got harder and harder to take, and the sand flying everywhere stung his face and bare arms.

Suddenly, Deuce realized they couldn't survive such a storm. He would die here. He didn't want to die, not like this, torn apart by a freaky storm because his brother had lost his mind. His will to live seemed to expand around him, shield him from the storm. He could breathe more easily again, and while the sand was still hitting him, it didn't hurt as much as before.

Confused, he looked at Shaan, but he could only see him through a white veil. What was going on? His brother returned his stare and stopped dead in his tracks.

"What the fuck?" Shaan demanded. "You really are *a freak."*

Before Deuce could say anything, he was being lifted into Shaan's arms and pressed against his chest. He'd never liked being so close to his brother, but right now, he relaxed, glad his aching limbs could finally get some rest. He barely registered that he could see Shaan's face clearly again, the veil expanding around his brother as well, keeping them safe from the storm.

Despite being able to rest in Shaan's arms, he felt weaker and weaker by the minute, slipping in and out of consciousness as they continued trudging through the storm. Just when he thought he was going to pass out, slip into darkness one final time, he heard voices. Deuce lifted his head for a moment, trying to see what was going on, but it was all a big blur. He was just so tired...

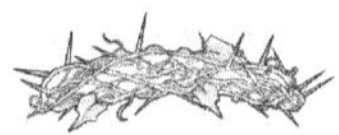

How had he forgotten all this? *He* had been the reason they'd survived the storm, and he could've helped Caean pave their way as well, shielded them from harm. But just remembering he could do something like that wasn't enough. Zan had no idea how to access it. It was hidden inside him and couldn't be found, even though he closed his eyes and searched.

"Zan? You're here," someone whispered, drawing him out of his head.

Slowly, he opened his eyes and saw Julyen's green eyes, only opened a slit, looking at him. He still looked so tired, but at least he was awake, which was a relief.

"Of course, I was worried about you! Your partner is..." Zan looked around the room, realizing Antias was strangely missing. When had he left? "Uh, he *was* here, too." He frowned, then pushed some stray strands of hair out of Julyen's face. "How are you feeling?"

"I...don't know. Tired. And...like I'm missing something? Are all my limbs still there?" As if to make sure, Julyen lifted his hands, looking at them for a moment, before his gaze wandered deeper, toward his legs.

"You legs are still where they're supposed to be, Julyen. But..."

How the fuck did he tell Julyen his heart was gone? It should be Antias who explained that to him. Why had he left? Where had he gone? And what was Zan supposed to say?

"Um...you were shot with poisoned ammo," he settled on. "The same poison Shaan tried to use."

Julyen's hand wandered to his chest, his fingers meeting the fabric of the plaster. So Julyen knew about the antidote and using an injection to the heart? Or was it more of an unconscious feeling to reach for it? Julyen had never been dumb, and Zan could see the realization in his eyes when he understood the patch was much bigger than needed for a simple injection.

"What happened to me? Zan, tell me!"

Julyen's voice was high and panicked, and there was no way to tell him gently.

"Your heart's gone," Zan admitted. "It was replaced with an artificial one, by order of High Chairwoman Nelius."

Julyen's eyes got wider, and he opened his mouth once, twice, seemingly trying to respond but unable to. Instead, he pushed himself up, sitting with his back against the headboard, then looked down at his chest and scratched at the plaster, pulling it off, before continuing to scratch the scar underneath.

"Stop it, please." Gently but firm, Zan grabbed his hands, holding them, to stop Julyen from scratching more. It wouldn't help. What was done was done. "It doesn't change who you are nor how much Cato loves you."

"No, no, no, you don't understand!" Julyen shouted. "She's got control over me now, and she'll use me to hurt Cato! Like she always did."

By now, Julyen was shivering and slipping into a panic attack. Zan had no idea how to deal with this. Thankfully, he didn't have to because he was pushed out of the way, and Antias took his place, pulling Julyen into his arms, holding him firmly against his own chest.

"I've got him," Antias said, his voice grim. "Go get your friends and get ready. Basilios and his people have just arrived."

In an instant, Zanoah's own mind blanked out, and his body went cold.

CHAPTER 29

About fifteen minutes later, Helio, Caean, and Zan were ready, dressed in their uniforms, their weapons ready. Zan had also strapped the Luskite dagger to his hip, hidden underneath his uniform. Although he didn't plan to kill Basilios, he still wanted to have a way to protect Caean and his allies if it came to it.

The door to Julyen's room opened, and Zan was surprised to see not just Cato but also Julyen leaving the room. Hadn't Julyen just woken up? Despite him looking strong and being on his feet, his eyes were still red from crying. Other for that, Julyen looked ready to fight, dressed in his own uniform and checking his weapon.

"Three for you as well," Antias said, handing Helio a bag.

The High Chancellor wasn't in uniform, just his dress shirt and black pants. Thinking about it now, Zan realized he'd never seen Antias wearing a uniform.

Pointing at the pills in the bag, Antias explained, "Each one has an effect for twenty-four hours. It's all we could make—enough pills for three days for soldiers under my command. Take one now; we're not sure how close to Basilios we'll get."

Helio hesitated, rolling one of the black pills between his fingers. Unlike Zan and Caean, he wasn't immune to Basilios' aura, so he needed to take it, but he looked uncertain, his eyes drifting toward Zan, who gave him an encouraging nod. Helio swallowed it, then stashed the other two in his pocket. Antias nodded and headed toward the elevator.

"What's the story with the High Chairwoman?" Zan asked, following after him.

"She called me to attend negotiations and demanded 'the deity and the exile' come as well," Antias explained. "It will be an ambush, I'm sure of that. Basilios' power-hungry troops will be there, but so will Nelius' own loyal brigade. They're elite soldiers without friends or family. They have nothing to lose, and they won't hesitate to follow her orders."

Caean shivered, and Zan wrapped an arm around them. "What do we do?"

"Jules will take you toward the slums, and you'll regroup with my troops there." Antias gave his partner a sad smile. "I'll stall them for as long as possible and try to find a peaceful way out of this."

Instantly, Zan's attention shifted to Julyen. He could imagine very well how much he hated the idea of letting Antias go by himself, but his face had become a mask, showing no emotion. Zanoah wondered if that was the result of no longer having a heart or if Julyen was just trying to keep Antias from feeling nervous.

They stopped at the elevator, and while Zan, Caean, and Helio went inside, Julyen turned to his partner. For just a moment, both of them were simply desperate lovers, worried about not seeing each other again and holding each other tightly. Although Zan could see them exchanging words, they were so quiet he couldn't understand them. He turned away to give them privacy. At least now he knew that Julyen *could* still feel, that cold demeanor of his simply for show.

When they parted, Julyen entered the elevator as well, by now maintaining a cool expression again. He was good at playing this game. "Put your helmets on. We'll meet some soldiers downstairs."

Immediately, they followed Julyen's orders, activating their helmets and covering their whole faces, making all of them look the same. Even Caean's dreads and the crown on Zan's head were hidden underneath the helmet. The more sophisticated electronics connected to the network had been disabled so that they couldn't be controlled by the enemy. Instead, they could only see through a slightly blue-tinted cover.

It took a while for Zan to get used to wearing all this stuff, especially walking in it, but eventually he got the hang of it. After what felt like hours, they emerged from the tunnels underneath the city, ending up in the slums. Zan recognized the architecture from visiting once or twice with his brother. Their group had accumulated more and more soldiers along the way, and there were even more waiting in the slums, split into several groups, just waiting for a signal. Which one, Antias hadn't specified.

Their group stayed together, and they stood at the side, Julyen's gaze toward the High Chairwoman's tower. It was the tallest building in all of Tadena, and until today, Zan thought it was just another government building. He wondered when the rest of the city would be told about Nelius, about the fact that what they thought to be true about their government was, in fact, a lie. For now, though, the more important thing was that the High Chairwoman's attempts at allying with Basilios be stopped.

It was quiet in the streets aside from some soldiers whispering to each other. Zan didn't listen to their gossip; his mind was on that tower and the man standing next to him.

"How did you get on your feet so quick?" he asked Julyen. "You were in a coma. Seems a little strange that you're here."

"Adrenaline shot and strong pain meds," Julyen replied, his gaze still fixed on the tower, as if he could change what was going on up there by keeping it in sight. "I wouldn't miss this for anything."

Before Zan could respond, a Supervisor, judging by the pink "V" on her uniform, approached them, and it took him a moment to recognize Felicitas. He hadn't known she held such a high rank. When he saw what was in her hands, his stomach dropped out, and rage boiled inside of him. Chains. The ones they'd brought with them. The ones Caean had worn.

"Oh no, you will not!" Immediately, he pulled Caean behind himself, protecting them with his own body. Helio stood next to him, creating a larger shield for the deity.

"They're not real," Felicitas said, shaking the chains. "It's just to fool Basilios and the High Chairwoman. You can touch them if you want to be sure."

He pulled the glove from his fingers and carefully touched the chain with his fingertips, testing several locations, before he nodded. It really was just a replica, made of a different material.

"Why did you make these?" Zan asked.

Felicitas frowned. "Because Caean will need to get close to Basilios, and we—"

"No!" Zan shouted. "You don't understand what he'll do to them!"

Caean laid a hand on his arm. *"It's okay, Zan,"* they assured him. *"I'll get close to him and find a way to get rid of him."*

He looked back at Caean, seeing the determination in their beautiful ocean eyes. There was fear there, too, but Zan could sense them pushing that down. They knew this could prevent a war, and they weren't going to waste a chance to rid the world of Basilios.

"Okay," Zan said after a moment. "What's the plan?"

"A small group will escort them to the tower. You two—" Felicitas pointed at Julyen and Zan. "—will act as their guard. Don't say anything, and do what I tell you, got it?"

Zanoah nodded and grabbed the chains from her, then turned to Caean, who disengaged their helmet. If this had to be done, it would be him who did it. He felt sick to his stomach as he slipped the collar around Caean's neck and the shackles around their wrists. It didn't matter that this was all a ruse. It was so wrong to put Caean through all this again, to stir the memories and trauma of being in Basilios' hands.

"It's okay," Caean said again. They leaned over and pressed a kiss to his helmet, then rested their head against the visor. *"It'll all be okay."*

Their walk through the city was almost as humiliating as the one through Srale, except this time he could feel Caean without any wall between their minds, and they were holding their head high. Felicitas led their little group, Caean right behind her, with Julyen on their right and Zan to the left. Five more soldiers trailed behind them. Helio hadn't been allowed to come but was ordered to stay behind as a backup.

Zan tried not to think about what they were doing, just concentrated on the way forward. Citizens stood on every street corner, wondering what was going on here. Although they were used to soldiers patrolling the city, they had never seen a person with such chains being paraded around. At least they didn't scream or throw things. Not like in Srale. No one hurled any obscenities either.

Finally, they reached the tower and were greeted by another group of soldiers. Their uniforms were slightly different with no rank markings, just a black strip where ranks were normally displayed. These guards denied them entry, surrounding Zanoah, Felicitas, Caean, and Julyen and making them give up their guns. Only after they'd been thoroughly searched were they were brought upstairs to a big conference room with a view of the whole city.

The first thing Zan noticed was Basilios' thick black aura. It reached him even before he saw the deity. Then he noticed the long glass table in the middle of the room. At the end of it sat a woman Zan had never seen before, so he guessed it had to be High Chairwoman Nelius. She wasn't at all like he'd expected her to be. She looked old, way past being alive even, and she was holding a small bundle in her arms. He frowned, wondering what it could be, then it dawned on him. Zalika's child. Basilios' real child.

It had survived—and here it was, sleeping in the High Chairwoman's arms.

To her right, Basilios sat, exactly as Zan remembered him: full of arrogance, legs crossed, leisurely leaning back. When Basilios saw Caean, a self-indulgent smile curled on his lips, and Zan wanted to slap it off. Antias was sitting on the Chairwoman's left, and despite his calm expression, Zan could see how tense he was. That wasn't surprising, given that the twins, Sarab and Sohan, stood behind him, weapons drawn, one pressed into his shoulder.

Besides a few other soldiers, there wasn't anyone else here. Zan had expected more people. Hadn't Basilios brought his army with him? Or were they hidden somewhere else, waiting to ambush the city?

Felicitas bowed slightly to the High Chairwoman before hurrying to the side so that everyone at the table had a good view of Caean in between Zan and Julyen. Basilios got up and slowly came closer, like he was approaching his prey. It was so hard for Zan to keep calm, to not to jump onto Basilios immediately and just throw him out the window or plunge the dagger deep into his heart. But he held back, shuddering as Basilios spoke.

"There you are," he said, almost purring. "Ah, how wonderful this city is! I should've come here sooner. They gave me everything I wanted. A high position, troops, even a child. A real child! Look at her, isn't she amazing?" Basilios grinned and pointed at the baby in High Chairwoman Nelius' thin arms, cradled into a blanket. "Of course, it's not exactly what I wanted, but...gotta make due with what I'm offered. They even saved the girl, so I can make more children! Exciting, isn't it?"

Worry and concern were radiating off of Caean, their eyes never leaving the baby. They had said that because it was always forbidden, it wasn't clear what a human-deity child would be like, nor did they know if one would be powerful or not.

Basilios came even closer to Caean and grabbed their hair, pulling at it so they had to look up to him. "I wonder what I'll do with you now," he said menacingly. "You've become worthless to me. Maybe I'll just let my soldiers have some fun with you. Sohan would enjoy you."

A shiver went through Caean's body, and though they appeared completely calm on the outside, Zan could feel their fear and disgust. It was mixed with grief over the lost love Caean once had for Basilios—and thought was reciprocated a long time ago. Their thoughts were a tangled mess, scared about what the soldiers would do to them and sad that their former lover was discarding them like a toy no longer worth playing with.

"Whatever." Basilios let go of them and shoved them back into Julyen. "First, we have a city to have fun with. Lucceia, turn off your little...what did you call them? Implants? Let your soldiers have some fun."

The High Chairwoman handed the baby to a soldier standing next to her, then tapped a button on her control panel while Basilios strode toward the window.

"Give me that," he ordered one of the soldiers and grabbed a gun from her, shooting the window. Apparently, it wasn't made to be bullet-proof and shattered completely, splinters of glass raining down, with Basilios standing at the edge.

It took Zan a moment to understand but then he saw black mist pouring out of Basilios and down into the city. It was the deity's force, his influence, spreading through Tadena, driving people mad, like he had done in Srale.

Caean was on the move before Zan even realized it, and when they jumped Basilios, it was too late for him to react. He could only watch both deities disappear as they fell out of the tower.

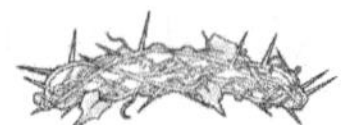

Caean and Basilios were gone, and Zan didn't know what to do now. Despite Felicitas' order not to move, to stand still and only listen to her commands, he wanted to run to the window and follow Caean, help them however possible, knowing full well he would die trying to follow them.

"Don't worry about me." He heard Caean's voice, just for a moment, and caught a glimpse of them still falling but clinging to Basilios, the fake-Luskite chain wrapped around the other deity's pale neck. He had to trust Caean knew what they were doing, though it hurt to see them in peril.

"You've got some bad guards," Zan said, forcing himself to look back at the High Chairwoman. "And here I thought your soldiers were well-trained."

High Chairwoman Nelius casually swiped around on her control panel, searching for something. Zan's gaze wandered toward Antias, but he didn't look like he knew what to do either. Zan held back a sigh. Had the High Chancellor brought them into this situation without a way out?

"Ah, here it is," Nelius said.

His attention shifted back to the woman in command, and as soon as her finger touched a slider on her panel, Julyen winced next to him.

"So, you *did* bring your fuckboy. Tsk tsk." She shook her head mockingly. "I told you to stay away from him. He's only a distraction, hindering your work. A *liability*."

Her finger slid higher, and Julyen started trembling more and more the higher the slider wandered, until he buckled, falling to his knees and holding onto his chest. How Zan wished to just use his weapon and kill the High Chairwoman, shoot her right in the head. But even if he still had his gun, her guards and Basilios' children were still in the room. It would be a suicide mission. He just wished he could help Julyen, take the pain from him.

The High Councilwoman smiled sickeningly. "Ah, there he is. He's mine now, Antias. You understand that? He always was, but you never understood the rules of property. You even tried using my own soldiers against me. They won't stop our new ally's troops, not with that little pill you gave them."

Antias didn't seem to hear her. He was looking desperately at Julyen, every muscle stiff, seemingly ready to jump to his aid. But Sohan pressed him into the chair, hand digging into his shoulder, reminding him of the weapons pointed at him.

"What do you want?" Antias demanded in a cool voice. But Zan could tell he was in distress, desperate for any solution to protect his lover and city.

"What *I* want?" Nelius scoffed. "I want to *live*, to be young again and see the world! I don't care about this city or what Basilios will do to it. He's given me the chance to do all I ever dreamed of."

Zan clenched his fists and resisted the urge to jump over the table and kill Nelius. How dare this woman's selfish desires put people in danger? How dare she give the city to someone as horrible as Basilios just because she didn't like being old?

"Then just go and leave this city alone," Antias offered. "Nothing's stopping you."

"Ah, but I've promised Basilios he could have some fun here first. I will witness this city falling into chaos and *then* I'll leave."

A big, satisfied smile appeared on her thin lips—and then they heard the first explosion.

Everything happened so fast. Nelius' soldiers cuffed Zan and Felicitas, then Julyen, who was still panting and clearly in pain, despite trying to hide it. Zan had no idea how his artificial heart worked, but he did understand there was some sort of control unit to send electric impulses there, and Nelius was using that to torture Julyen. The twins were still guarding

Antias, who was staring out the window in horror at the massive explosions taking down one tower after the other. In the streets, people were screaming, and shots echoed even over the chaos.

Sarab and Sohan were laughing, happily watching all this destruction. Zan couldn't believe they were in any way related, all of them having part of Basilios' soul inside of them. But he knew *he* was the weird one. He was supposed to be like them, to enjoy all this and be part of a bigger picture, but it just felt wrong. No one should use their power for such useless destruction and pain.

What worried him even more was Caean. Since their last message, Zan hadn't gotten an update from them, not even a glimpse. He didn't want to distract them, so he refrained from forcing his way into their consciousness. But that didn't stop him from being anxious that they were dead. He would feel that, right? Right?

From time to time, he could hear Julyen next to him whine and feel him twitch as another shock rocked his body. Nelius was just as horrible as the rest of this lot. He couldn't even put her title in front of her name anymore, not even in his thoughts. She was no High Chairwoman. She was a menace and a selfish, cruel person.

They watched a tower next to them fall, almost crashing against the facade, and the floor beneath them rumbled. It took Zan a moment to understand that the floor was crumbling and they were going to fall. He only had seconds to think when the floor started breaking, the table sliding toward a gaping hole in the middle. He heard confused shouts from Basilios soldiers, and even Sarab and Sohan stopped laughing.

Zan used the confusion to break his shackles and grab Julyen, pulling him over his shoulder and running toward the open window. It was more a stumble than a run, really, as he had to dodge several objects falling off the walls and sliding toward the hole. But he was still making it to his destination.

"Oh no, you don't!" someone shouted.

A moment later, his leg hurt, making him buckle to his knee. Fuck, Sarab had shot him. And despite the chaos, she had good aim, getting him right in the thigh.

"Fuck off!" Antias shouted, ramming his elbow in her face.

As she fell to the floor, knocked out, Zan though, *Good for her; she deserved it.*

Before he could get on his feet again, a shelf toppled over and blocked their way, shoving them toward the hole as it slid down the floor. Zan could only turn and press Julyen to his chest, trying to keep him safe. Antias rushed over to them, bleeding from somewhere.

"Any idea how we survive this?" Cato asked, his voice a little slurred, like he was close to passing out. There was no way Zan would be able to carry two people out of here, even if there was actually a way to walk out.

He didn't want to die here, not like this, and he wanted to protect these two. Praying to an entity unknown to him, maybe even to himself, he hoped he would be able to do what he intended to. It was their only chance.

"Hold onto me," Zan ordered. "I...hope we survive this."

He wasn't sure exactly what he was doing, but when they slid over the edge of the hole, he dove deep into his mind, searching for the part that had been able to protect him from the desert so many years ago.

Please, he begged. *I just need this once more.*

Hands grabbed his upper arm, and just a second before they hit a jagged piece of the collapsed floor several stories deeper, his sight became clouded. He still felt the impact, but it was like he'd hit a rubber mat instead of metal and hard plastic. But Zanoah couldn't relax. He grabbed tighter to Julyen and Cato, holding them close so his shield didn't have to expand too much, saving more energy.

Their fall felt almost endless, hitting the remains of different floors until there were no more floors, just a freefall right down to the street. Zan was glad he couldn't see too much and that what he saw was blurred, or else he'd be sure they couldn't survive this impact, even with his shield.

Everything hurt when he woke up again and realized he'd been knocked out. Slowly, to make sure nothing was broken, he sat up and tried to assess the situation. They were on the road, good. Julyen was lying next to him, turning to his side and definitely still alive but also still shackled. Then he noticed someone was missing. Where was Cato?

A bit wobbly, Zan got up to his legs, harshly reminded that he'd been shot when his leg buckled under his weight. He finally spotted Cato lying a few feet away from them. All the dust had hidden him well. Zan limped closer and kneeled down next to him, turning him around so he could see his face and check for a pulse. Thankfully, it was still there.

"Hey, wake up," he said, shaking Cato's shoulder. "We're not done yet."

The city was still in chaos, Basilios was still around, and they had a lot to do. A small moan came from Cato, and his eyes fluttered open, just a little, to meet his.

"Jules...where's Jules?" Cato asked.

His voice was coarse but so worried, and before he could answer, Julyen kneeled down on his other side, grabbing his hand.

"I'm right here," Julyen assured him. "Glad we've made it down. You okay?"

Cato nodded slowly and sat up, his normally perfectly styled black hair tousled, dust and blood smeared over his face and white shirt. It was the first time Zan had seen him all disheveled, and it made him like the man more. Right now, he didn't look like High Chancellor Antias but just like Cato Antias, a man who was worried about his lover and his city, a man who'd just survived the bombing of the tower he'd been inside.

It was Julyen who checked Cato for injuries, finding a scratch right over his ear. It looked like a bullet had grazed him, barely missing its intended target. He would be alright. Zan's own wound would be okay as well. The uniform had compressed a little tighter around it, stopping the bleeding.

Good thing they'd worn these uniforms or else this might have ended differently.

They still had a lot to deal with, but at least he doubted Nelius and Basilios' children had survived the fall. That was one less problem.

"We have to find Basil—"

He was interrupted by a high-pitched scream, full of pain and agony. It took him a moment to understand that it was Julyen, who collapsed to his knees, holding his chest, eyes wide open.

"Julyen! No, she can't—"

Cato was on his feet immediately and looked around, trying to find Nelius, who still had the controls for Julyen's heart. The young Executor was howling in pain, unable to stop. When Zan touched his chest, even he felt the electricity flowing through his body, radiating from his heart.

They had to find this damn control panel and turn it off.

"Over there!"

Zan pointed toward a corner, where he'd spotted a thin hand poking from between two fallen plates. Zan couldn't believe she had survived, but there was no other explanation. Cato ran in her direction, and Zan went to follow him when he heard another weird noise coming from above. When he looked up, he realized the tower hadn't collapsed completely yet, only tilted. It was only a question of how long they had until it would collapse on them.

"Cato, hurry!" he yelled. "We have to get out of here!"

"Turn if off! Now!" Cato pleaded, begging Nelius.

From his position, Zan couldn't see her reaction, but he doubted it was positive since Julyen's condition didn't change. Zan pulled him up into his arms, holding him close to his chest, despite feeling the constant flow of electricity. He could take it; Julyen had it way worse. They had to get out of here quick or'd get buried, and Julyen was in no condition to run on his own.

A low groan reminded him of the danger over their heads, and when he looked up again, he saw part of the tower sliding further, ready to fall any second—right down on where they stood.

"Cato, now!" he shouted, guessing they had about ten seconds to get out of here.

He started running, not wanting to get crushed. Ten seconds had been too generous of a guess. The moment he started running, he heard a loud rumble as the tower fell. He was already prepared to get squished, and he hoped he would be able to hold his shield up again, although he doubted it was strong enough to protect them.

But nothing happened.

When he opened his eyes again, he stood almost half a block away, Julyen still in his arms, Cato kneeling next to them, and before him stood...

Zalika.

CHAPTER 30

Zanoah had expected a lot of things, but seeing Zalika here hadn't been one of them. Today was just full of surprises.

He could only stare at his friend, looking so different but still like herself. Zalika was still wearing her white medical center clothes, which were now slightly gray from dust. Her feet were bare, and he wondered how she'd even gotten here. But when his gaze wandered up to her face, realization set in. He knew how and why she was here, alive and well, and why he could *feel* her. Not physically, but in a different sense—a deeper, more spiritual one.

Where amber eyes had been, blue-white sparks blistered, and a cable was wrapped around her head, almost like a...crown. Everything about her screamed deity, and having met a few by now, Zan was sure she had become one. Although he didn't know how it'd happened, he could feel her presence, tingling and pulsating, like electricity flowing around them. Now he could also see her aura, an electric blue, almost white, close to her body.

Only when Julyen, who was still on his arms, yelped and twitched again did Zan's attention shift back to him. He'd been so caught up in the moment, so distracted by Zalika, that he'd almost forgotten Julyen was still in pain.

"It's not working," Cato yelled desperately, and Zan saw him touch the control panel he must have grabbed from Nelius before the building had crashed down. Every time he touched the panel, Julyen's body jerked, like another shock was shooting through him.

"Stop, you're hurting him even more," Zan said. "It's reacting to your touch."

He didn't see Zalika coming closer until she was standing right in front of them, looking down at Julyen. She tilted her head a little, almost like she was analyzing him. When she reached for Julyen, small thunderbolts flew between her hand and Julyen's chest. As she pressed her hand against him, Julyen choked.

"What are you doing to him?" Zan demanded. He had no intention of making an enemy out of yet another deity, but he was worried about Julyen, and his sudden lack of movement was concerning.

"Figuring out how his heart is programmed," Zalika said, closing her eyes.

Cato rushed over, watching whatever was going on very carefully. "Can you help him?" he asked, voice choked with emotion.

Zalika didn't answer, but slowly, Julyen relaxed and took a deep breath. His eyes popped open, wandering from Zalika to Zan and, finally, to Cato. Tears formed in Julyen's green eyes, and as soon as Zalika let go of him, Cato carefully grabbed him and held him close.

"His heart had been connected to this panel. Only one person's touch could stop his pain; others increased it. The connection is disabled now." Zalika tilted her head again, but this time it was like she was listening to noises normal humans couldn't hear. "I have to go. Keep my city safe. And you should go find your partner, Zanoah. They're not in the city anymore."

Zalika didn't even give them a chance to respond before she shot up into the sky, glowing blue wings made of nothing but neon light searing out of her back. Was this a skill only she had? Or did all deities have wings? Once again, Zan realized he didn't know much at all about them.

He knew one thing though—he had to find Caean and help them with Basilios.

Julyen and Cato stayed in the city, hiding for now. Despite not being in pain anymore, Julyen was completely exhausted. Before Zan left, he broke Julyen's shackles so he could move more freely, then asked Cato to take good care of him. The High Chancellor nodded at him but said nothing.

Zan started running through the ruins of this once-modern city, following his instincts to where he guessed Caean was. If they wanted to have the advantage, they would've gotten Basilios out of the city, away from his people, and into the jungle.

For once, he was glad Shaan had put him through such rough training since running wasn't a problem for him, even with the wound in his leg. The uniform had done a good job compressing his thigh and stopping the blood flow for now while adrenaline helped with the pain.

Desperately, he searched for Caean's mind, catching glimpses of jungle and vines, of rage and satisfaction. Good, he had to follow that.

When he crossed the city gates, he didn't stop, just charged right into the desert. It was different without the storm, and so much easier to cross, although he deployed his helmet to protect him a little from the heat. The closer he got to the jungle, the windier it got, and he even saw some thunderbolts streaking down from the sky. This had to be Caean. They now had the deity of weather's force as well, and they must be using it now.

Zanoah headed straight in the direction of the lightning and finally saw Caean. The chains connecting their collar and shackles were broken, and their clothes were sporting some new tears. For some reason, they were staring at a tree trunk. It took him a moment to understand there was someone bound to the trunk with vines—so many of them that it looked like they were one with the bark. It was Basilios, whose power couldn't possibly match Caean's here.

"Are you okay?" Zan asked Caean, keeping Basilios in his sights. He didn't fully trust that those vines would keep him held forever.

"Yes. I need your help, though. Can you put those on him?"

Caean nodded at the ground next to them, where Zan spotted the chains. They had to be the real ones, the ones Basileios had used before. Where had Caean gotten them? Realizing that wasn't really important right now, Zanoah grabbed them and immediately felt the slight pain they always induced. Thankfully he was still wearing his gloves, so they only burned his hands a little.

"Oh no, you will not!" Basilios shouted. "You little worm! I should have killed you when I had the chance!"

Basilios' black eyes stared at him, full of hate, and his smug smile had completely vanished. Instead, scratches covered his pale face, and his hair was tousled. This had obviously been a wild fight, and Basilios had lost. Yet, that still didn't make Zanoah feel any better. Even bound by Luskite, Basilios could still find a way to break free and wreak havoc again.

Right now, he had to trust Caean to keep Basilios at bay while Zanoah put the collar around his neck. Basilios screamed and cursed at him even more. It was clear he didn't want to go back to being imprisoned, but that's exactly where he would be going again. And this time, it would be some place no one would ever find him.

After Basilios was completely shackled, Zan grabbed the chains in one hand, ignoring the slight tingling sensation, and his dagger in the other. "Don't try to do something stupid," he warned. "You'll go back into the hole you came from, and this time, you'll stay there."

Even if Basilios' cursing had been annoying, it had also been a lot more reassuring than the silence he got now. The deity's hateful gaze wandered from his face toward the dagger and back, and he saw a sly grin forming on his lips.

Basilios leaned closer, his lips almost against his ear, so Caean couldn't hear what they said without their mental connection. "You think so? Life has become boring anyway. It's always the same—settle down, see people go mad because of you, use their madness to destroy things. There's no surprises. I've achieved my goal of having a child—an *heir*. You think you'd be better than me, that you'd have a better chance of dealing with this power inside of you? That you could handle it growing every day, every time someone prays to you? Think it's time we found out."

Basilios' gripped his hand, the one holding the dagger, and pushed it right into his chest. Zanoah struggled to pull his hand away, but Basilios held onto it, impaling himself deeper and deeper.

"You think Caean will still love you when you become the monster?" he asked, laughing.

Zan could only stare at him, stunned by what was happening. There was a reason he hadn't wanted to kill Basilios. He wanted to protect Caean—had vowed to, in fact—but not like this.

The feeling of power pouring into his body was similar to when Caean had granted him some of their force back in the cave. But this time it was more, so much more, amplified by a million. It came at him like a hurricane, drowning out his every thought and feeling, and he barely realized he'd fallen to the ground and was staring up at the thick treetops.

Any sense of time or place vanished, and the only thing he perceived was black mist filling every inch of his body, choking him. It overpowered him, and he found that it wasn't enough. He wanted more of it—more and more and more until nothing could stop him. Finally, he could understand Basilios why he was the way he was. The urge for power was strong, and so was his desire to do whatever he wanted to. It was such a temptation.

His sight clouded, and the world looked so much darker now, but then a hand grabbed his. Caean. His eyes searched for them, and when they finally found them, their face was shrouded in black mist, and he couldn't see them clearly.

No, he didn't want this. He didn't want power and greed clouding his life, his judgment. He'd seen what it could do to other people. He wanted to stay himself, to keep loving Caean just the way he did, and he didn't want them to fear him.

So, he fought.

He pushed the black mist down, fought against the urge to grab more power, and instead accepted this change. This power could be used for good. With it, he could protect the people he loved and help them. He could make the world a better place.

In the end, he didn't know how long he lay there, staring into the treetops. Slowly, the flood of black mist ebbed until just one last wave hit him. Then there was silence. Everything stilled.

Sluggishly, he turned his head toward Caean and lifted one hand, gently touching their cheek. They were even more beautiful than he remembered, radiating a golden-green aura around them. Their skin looked so soft, and everything about them was just perfect.

He was a little confused when Caean helped him sit up, then pulled their thorny crown from his head. It was weird to be without it. He felt naked, and he missed the connection to Caean immediately.

Instead of the thorn-crown he was offered something else, something he knew as well. Caean held Basilios' black crown in their hands, offering it to him. Slowly, Zanoah stretched his hands toward it, carefully taking it and placing it on his head. This was a whole different thing than wearing Caean's crown. It didn't connect him with anyone else, but it made him feel...complete.

"What happened?" he wondered, his voice raspy, as if he had been screaming for a long time. His body was sore, and his head ached..

Searching for Basilios, he only found the chains on the ground. Underneath them was a small pile of what looked like ash.

Instead of an answer, Caean offered him their crown again and tapped the black one on his own head. He understood what that meant and exchanged crowns with Caean. It was an uncommon sight, Caean with this bla—no, white band around their head. Hadn't this crown been black just a moment before when he accepted it from Caean?

"Basilios killed himself and gave you all his force. You've become a deity. I never guessed he would ever do something that dramatic."

Caean smiled at him, taking his hand, and slowly it all came back to him. Right, Basilios had told him he would go mad dealing with all this power, and he remembered the temptation to just go crazy and snatch up more power. But that was gone, replaced by a deep desire for love and justice.

"You're different from him," Caean said. *"You fought the urge and won. You're much purer than Basilios ever was, and even if you will be tempted again, I'm here to help you. Look."*

He didn't know what Caean was talking about at first. But then he saw the mist around them—no longer black but completely white, like fog.

"You did this. And also this."

Now Caean tapped the crown on their head with one finger. It wasn't a simple black band anymore, but a white circlet made of two singular metal stripes entwined, so much gentler and softer than the black crown had been. It looked like it had been made for Caean and suited them perfectly.

He had changed all this from black to white? But how? Despite being a deity now, Zanoah was still confused and overwhelmed by what he was capable of.

"It's normal in the beginning," Caean assured him. *"You'll get better. And you won't be alone."*

A thankful smile lifted Zanoah's lips, and he knew he would manage. He had Caean, and they would both be okay. Basilios was no more, and they could live peacefully now. There was just one more thing they needed to do.

"We have to get back to the city," Zan said. *"Zalika might need our help."*

They hurried back to Tadena as fast as they could. Before they left, Zanoah put the dagger back into its sheath, hiding it in his uniform again, but he hadn't been able to stand the touch of the chains longer than a few seconds. It was much worse now that he was an actual deity and not just a splinter of one. Caean had hidden the chains in a ball of vines and leaves without touching them, leaving them where they could find them again later.

As they made their way to the city, Zan marveled at what'd just happened. He'd become a deity. It was still too much to wrap his head around, too bizarre. But it was true. He wasn't sure what all he could do, but he'd noticed that his thigh had almost completely healed. It surprised him at first until he remembered how quickly Caean's wounds had healed, even the ones made by the Luskite. The only scars on their body were the ones around their lips.

Soon, he would sit down and figure out what his new powers were. Right now, though, helping Zalika, Helio, and the city was more important. He didn't know how yet, but at least Basilios wouldn't be able to influence people anymore.

What they arrived to was chaos. Most of Tadena's highest towers had fallen, burying everything in their path—other buildings, people, it didn't matter. For a split second, he wondered how Basilios had managed to get so many explosives in here, but maybe he hadn't been the one to bring them. Maybe Nelius had put those in place before he arrived, but had she really been *that* mad?

"This way."

Caean pointed in one direction, and Zan could feel it, too: the presence of another deity. It had to be Zalika. There was a *lot* of noise coming from that direction, too, so they had no idea what they were in for, but they headed there anyway.

Upon arrival, Zan realized where they were—close to the power plant. People were pushing through the fence, weapons in hand, trying to break through. Others were gathering in front of it, almost like they were trying to defend it. Some of them were wearing clothing from Srale, while some were obviously from Tadena. There were also people in military uniforms, trying to keep the peace or stirring up the crowd, depending on which side of this conflict they fell on.

Zalika was flying over all of them, small flashes springing from her hands every other second, aimed at people's necks. And as soon as they hit, those people looked around, confused, but they were still pushed forward, unable to escape the stampede. Whatever Zalika was doing, it was working, but there were just too many people for her.

Zan could feel it, Basilios' influence still controlling them, the black mist clouding their minds. He wasn't sure how it was still persisting even after the deity's death, but he knew if he could get rid of it, that would help calm the situation. But could he really do this? Zanoah had never had such an important task, had never had to trust in himself so much.

"You can do it," Caean said. *"You're strong enough for this."*

They squeezed his hand and smiled at him, so reassuring and soft and caring. Their trust in him calmed Zanoah and boosted his own trust in himself. Yes, he could do this. He had done so much lately. He just had to believe in himself.

Taking a deep breath, he closed his eyes and concentrated on the task ahead. He couldn't pull Basilios' influence out of these people, but he could purify it, like he had done with the crown, with the force surging through his own body.

The power inside him grew, waiting to be released, but he held it in for now. Instead, his feet left the ground, and he opened his eyes, realizing he was hovering, big white wings made of mist keeping him in the air. Apparently Zalika wasn't the only one who could fly.

He steered himself right over the crowd, finally releasing the energy he had accumulated in his body, almost like an explosion of clouds, covering not only the crowd underneath him but almost the whole city. Just for a moment, he saw himself through Caean's eyes, a leader with misty white wings and clouded-over white eyes hovering above the people. Was this really him? He could barely recognize himself.

When the mist settled onto the people, touching them, the crowd calmed down. People were confused, and they looked around for a reason why they were here, unsure why they'd wanted to storm the power plant in the first place. Then they looked up at him in awe.

Zanoah tried to keep up what he was doing as long as possible, tried to make sure the mist reached as many people as he could, but at some point, he was exhausted. He barely had time to realize his wings had dissipated before he was plummeting to the ground.

CHAPTER 31

When Zanoah woke up again, it took him a moment to understand where he was. Wasn't this the home he shared with Julyen? That couldn't be. Had he just dreamed everything that happened? His banishment, Shaan's death. *Caean*.

He shot up, sitting on the bed and looking around him. The apartment still looked the same as before. There were Julyen's academic achievements displayed on the walls and Julyen's tablet on the desk. They'd never had Zanoah's things on display, though a lot of that was because he never really *had* things to show to begin with.

Slowly, he got out of bed, a bit wobbly on his feet and his muscles sore—had he overdone training with Shaan yesterday?—and headed toward the bathroom. When his eyes met his reflection in the mirror, he stopped. Carefully, almost as if he didn't want to destroy it, he touched the scar on his cheek, leading from right under his left eye to his jawbone. It was definitely there. Leaning a little closer, he also realized his left eye wasn't brown anymore but black. How had this happened? He didn't remember. But that meant he hadn't dreamed any of this. It was all real.

And it meant...Caean was real, too.

He heard steps behind him and turned on his heel, a little too fast. He was dizzy now, but it had totally been worth it. Standing in the door frame was Caean, watching him and smiling at him lovingly.

"Of course I'm real," they said in his head, and relief rushed over him. It had all been real. No matter how painful it had been, he would have hated being without Caean again.

A bit wobbly, he took two steps toward Caean and just hugged them, pressing them close to himself. Their arms wrapped around him, squeezing him tight. He only let go a tiny bit to be able to kiss them, again and again. He was so glad they were alright, glad they were *both* alright and alive. No matter what else happened, he needed Caean, and he never wanted to be without them ever again.

Caean brought him up to date while he got ready for his day. After he'd collapsed several days ago, Cato had taken control of the situation, becoming the new acting High Chairman for now. It meant that the citizenry learned the truth about how the government here really worked, but given what Cato and Julyen told them about what'd been happening behind the scenes, the people of Tadena were willing to let Antias continue leading the city.

Zalika was helping Tadena's engineers find efficient ways to use their technology to rebuild the city, while Julyen was part of the troop responsible for rescuing and sheltering citizens. Helio had volunteered to help him with that project. Since Julyen had decided to stay at Cato's place for now—and given how hard it was to find housing for people because of how many towers had collapsed—he had offered for Caean and Zan to stay in their old apartment. It felt a little awkward, but Zanoah was just glad they had a space to sleep and be safe.

While the bodies of Nelius and Felicitas had been found during the clean-up effort, Basilios' children were nowhere to be found among the wounded or dead. It made Zan a little nervous to know they were still out there, but he hoped he'd seen the last of them. Maybe they would find something to do with their lives besides wreaking havoc.

As for Zalika, after Zan's initial surprise that she'd become a deity, he'd thought about it more and realized it made sense. After the deity of weather disappeared, the city felt a vacuum, and it had called out to her, flooding her with its energy. Tadena's ever-growing technology had longed for a deity of its own—and finally had gotten one.

Zan wasn't sure how well she was settling into her role as a deity, but he knew she was quite happy she'd been able to save her baby girl and bring her to Helio, who'd kept her safe during the final conflict. From what Zan had seen, she was a good mother and really loved her daughter, despite the circumstances surrounding who her father was.

All in all, Zan had to admit that things could've been a lot worse. He wondered how Ferox was doing, whether he'd gotten out of the city before everything went down, but otherwise, his family was intact, and the city would bounce back, and maybe—just maybe—they could begin new lives.

Rebuilding the city would take more time, but the few last weeks had already been a big step. Every day, the towers got closer to completion, and there was even talk about expanding the city more into the desert. Plans for trading routes to Srale and other cities were also being discussed, mostly with Zalika and Helio, who had the best connections to other cities.

Caean helped as well, guiding a team of scientists into the jungle to show them some ways to harvest and grow fruits sustainably. While they were there, they'd also checked on the chains, but they were gone. They could only guess who had taken them, but it was a good bet that it was Ferox, though why he needed them, they weren't sure. He was the one who'd given Caean the chains before disappearing again, and Zan wondered if maybe there was something about them that called to him, if maybe Ferox could sense where they were for some reason..

Today was Election Day, and citizens across the city came out to vote for a new High Chairperson. It was no surprise to see Cato Antias winning with an overwhelming number of votes. He had protected Tadena and stood against the old High Chairwoman, then given his everything to keep the people of Tadena safe and rebuild the city.

To celebrate his win, they were all invited to a party at Cato's private residence, which had miraculously survived the explosions. Zan looked around the room, seeing the people he loved happy and carefree.

Zalika had changed already, adapting to the city. One side of her hair was trimmed short, and she wore a white crop top and tight black pants. She was chatting with a woman Zan didn't know, and she looked like she was already feeling at home in the city.

Helio had also settled in, becoming fast friends with Julyen, and Zanoah saw them now, sitting next to each other on the sofa, laughing. It made him smile. With the control panel for his heart destroyed, Julyen should be safe, and it was wonderful to see him this happy. Even Cato looked content, leaned back in his armchair, sipping on his drink.

"Oh, we have to tell you something!" Julyen exclaimed, grinning broadly and heading toward Cato to sit on his lap. "We got married yesterday evening!"

Proudly, he presented their hands and matching tattoos, which they'd hidden the whole day behind a ring in Cato's case and gloves in Julyen's. Helio immediately squealed and congratulated them, excited for them.

Zan smiled and said, "I'm very happy you can finally be together, openly and without hiding. You both deserve it." And he meant it completely.

"Thanks! I...I still can't believe it's real."

Julyen smiled a little sheepishly, and this made Zan even more sure he absolutely deserved all the happiness in this world.

"Will you all come to the inauguration ceremony tomorrow?" Julyen asked, leaning on Cato completely now, his husband's arm around his waist.

"Caean and I will," Zan said, "but we're leaving Tadena the day after tomorrow. It's not our home, and we want to see more of this world. And I want to find Ferox."

Although Zan had to tell his friends at some point, he felt sorry for dropping the news like this, pulling the mood down. But Tadena had never felt like home to him, and now, being a deity, he was still struggling with his force and keeping it together. Every time a citizen prayed for more power, it strengthened his own force inside him, and Zanoah was still overwhelmed by the pure energy pulsating underneath his skin. He didn't want to be around too many people because people always prayed for more power, in one way or another. He understood what Basilios had been talking about by now, how it could drive you mad.

Caean had told him they would be okay with living here, if that was what Zan wanted, but they also preferred to be away from big cities, where they had their privacy. They would be happier with a small house and big garden or maybe a cottage right in the middle of a forest.

Julyen got up and hugged him, almost clinging to him. He'd definitely had too much alcohol already. "We'll miss you! Promise you'll visit?"

Smiling, Zan returned the hug, glad they had become good friends. Julyen had never been a bad person; they had just been forced into a bad situation together.

"Of course we'll visit," Zan promised. "And who knows, maybe you'll be able to visit us sooner than you think."

Considering Tadena's plans to start trading with other cities, who knew what the future held for them. All Zan really knew was that Caean would be by his side, and that was what was important.

EPILOGUE

5 Years Later

It had been almost five years since he'd left Tadena. Many things had changed during this time—both in the city as well as in his life.

He was on a mission, a mission given by *her*, and he would do whatever he could to fulfill it. Sohan and Sarab were already in the streets, scouting, and the buzz in his earpiece reminded him of their presence.

"Five streets south of you. She's with her." Sarab's voice cut through his thoughts, and he took a deep breath.

He flicked the cigarette aside, not caring that it was still smoldering, and set his eyes on the intersection his target would have to cross soon.

Security in this city was shit, and they'd gotten in without anyone stopping them. The new High Chairman had become lax, allowing people to pass through the city freely. A good thing for him, and very helpful now.

"Two blocks," Sarab updated him, and he grabbed his pistol.

With practiced movements, he checked his gun to make sure it was loaded and working. Nothing would be worse than his weapon fucking up the mission now.

"Grab the kid when she's down," he ordered the young man beside him.

The man's disfigured face was emotionless, one blank and one dark brown eye staring back at him. They all had become accustomed to their deadly missions, some more than others, like the twins, who'd killed in the name of their father before and still continued to do so.

A motivation he could easily use for his own goals.

"Three...two..." Sarab reminded him of his mission once again, and he turned toward the intersection, his pistol readied.

There, their target emerged between high towers, a small child at her hand. It had been almost five years since he'd seen Zalika, and a sudden rush of guilt flushed through his mind.

He hesitated, just for a moment, watching her and her daughter. Zalika looked so healthy, so happy—she reminded him so much of her sibling—but he couldn't stop now. Her hair was shaved short on one side, the rest of it dyed a neon pink. A crop top revealed her stomach, and tight, black pants complimented her quite well. Even from this distance, he could spot some colorful tattoos on her arms and face, fingernails painted the same shade as her hair.

"We shouldn't wait too long," he was reminded by his companion.

Right.

Carefully, he aimed and shot without hesitation. The pistol was silenced, and only a low *pop* could be heard. The bullet hit her right where he had aimed for—deep in her chest, where her heart beat. A second shot hit her head, straight between the eyes.

She slumped down, and as she hit the ground, the power around them went out. A buzz went through the buildings, the neon signs, all the electricity around them, surging toward her.

He didn't care, just pushed the pistol back into its holster underneath his jacket.

"Let's go."

While he ran toward their target, he heard his companion's footsteps behind him, scuffling and slower than him. When he reached Zalika, he grabbed the dagger from his belt and kneeled over her, the blade pressed against her throat.

"Grab the kid and go," he ordered his companion, his eyes fixed on Zalika's now sparkling blue eyes.

The girl's scream was silenced, and boots met the ground rapidly as his companion ran away with her.

Zalika's body was twitching, electricity coursing through her, but she couldn't use her abilities. No, he had made sure of that. Would be quite a problem if she could, in a city full of technology. He stared down at her, without any sign of emotions on his face.

"Luskite bullets," he explained. "I'm sorry. I really am. But no one should have such power. Your daughter will be of use when we quash every single deity and cleanse this world of them."

Her lips opened, but no sound came out, and she looked more like a fish on dry land, gasping, bleeding from her chest and head. With a quick move, he slit her throat with his dagger.

"We have to go." Sarab said.

They really should hurry. Guards would be here soon, and he had no intention of fighting.

"Where's Sohan?" he asked while he got up and cleaned the blade on his black pants.

"He's with the kid."

He nodded, and after a last glance toward Zalika, he joined Sarab. They had to leave Tadena, had to run and bring the girl back to *her*. Had to flee the consequences of his actions, from the hate Zalika's sibling would surely drown him in.

One more target eliminated.

And soon he would have to meet his brother, to eliminate him as well.

ACKNOWLEDGEMENTS

Thank you, Cara, for helping me with all the editing, improvements, and formatting. You helped to shape this book into what it is now.

Thank you, Doom and Juniper, for introducing me into this wonderful circle of indie authors, for always keeping me motivated, and for guiding me through the whole process of publishing on my own.

A special thanks to Juniper for the beautiful interior graphics as well.

Thank you, Reikon, for being a big and amazing inspiration for Caean and for supporting this story.

Thank you, bro, for being there for me from the very beginning (literally). You've always been my biggest supporter, and I love you endlessly. You'll always be the best big brother I could wish for.

Thank you, Sara, for working on the cover art and for your patience with me. It turned out so incredibly beautiful and makes this book gorgeous.

Also, a big thank you to Bei (Ante Kun) for the beautiful chibis you made for the characters of this book.

Thank you, Gabe, for your help editing the last draft and for polishing my words.

And last but not least, a big thank you to all the ARC readers and anyone reading FIRST SNOW. You're awesome!

If you're looking forward to more of Zanoah, Caean, and Helio—keep an eye out for the sequel and short stories including them.

Also by Jake Vanguard

Deity Chronicles

FIRST SNOW (MAY 2024)

FIRST ROSE (MAY 2025)

Angelverse

Higanbana (AUGUST 2024)

ABOUT THE AUTHOR

Jake Vanguard (he/him) is a queer and trans author from Germany. He writes mostly dark fantasy including erotica, with the goal of making his characters suffer (sorry about that).

When not writing, he loves reading, gaming, and cuddling his kitties.

instagram.com/jake.vanguard/

www.ingramcontent.com/pod-product-compliance
Lightning Source LLC
LaVergne TN
LVHW020313200726
843507LV00012B/2088